100 DAYS IN DEADLAND

Part One of the Deadland Saga

A journey through Dante's Inferno

with a shambling twist

RACHEL AUKES

100 DAYS IN DEADLAND
Part 1 of the DEADLAND SAGA

Surprisingly Adequate Publishing
Edited by Stephanie Riva – RivaReading.com
Cover image © shockfactor – Fotolia.com
Warpaint font © Chepi Devosi – ChepiDev.com

ISBN-10: 0989901831
ISBN-13: 978-0989901833

For the Half Fast crew.
Because if anyone can turn the zombie
apocalypse into a good time, it'd be you.

CONTENTS

Foreword v
Map of Deadland vi

LIMBO: The First Circle of Hell 1

LUST: The Second Circle of Hell 77

HUNGER: The Third Circle of Hell 113

GREED: The Fourth Circle of Hell 155

WRATH: The Fifth Circle of Hell 199

ARROGANCE: The Sixth Circle of Hell 229

VIOLENCE: The Seventh Circle of Hell 257

MALICE: The Eighth Circle of Hell 315

BETRAYAL: The Ninth Circle of Hell 407

Afterword 437
CDC Case Definition: Zombiism 440
Acknowledgments 442
About the Author 443

FOREWORD

100 Days in Deadland is set in near-future Midwest America decimated by a zombie plague. In this truly unique story, our heroine—Cash, an office worker and weekend pilot—is forced on a journey through hell that echoes the one Dante took in the "Inferno," the world-renowned first poem in Dante Alighieri's epic medieval tale, **The Divine Comedy**. In both tales, there are nine circles of hell that must be survived, and the thirty-four cantos of the "Inferno" are reflected in the thirty-four chapters of **100 Days in Deadland**...reimagined zombie apocalypse style.

As Cash moves through each circle of hell, she witnesses the same sins that Dante had many centuries ago. However, where Dante often stood on the sidelines, Cash is thrown deep into the action. Like Dante's "Inferno," **100 Days in Deadland** is a story of the human condition. You will find violence, heartbreak, and tragedy. However, you will also find perseverance, compassion, and hope.

That said, this story is, above all, for your entertainment, so…

Enjoy, and watch out for zombies!

MAP OF DEADLAND

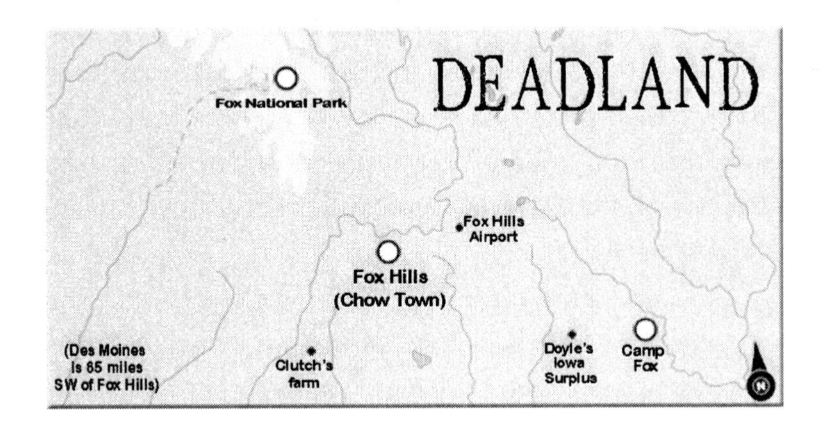

LIMBO

THE FIRST CIRCLE OF HELL

CHAPTER I

I paused on the way to my two o'clock meeting, and watched the woman standing outside the restroom with her forehead against the wall, clawing at the paint. After a long moment, I hesitantly reached out. "Excuse me, are you all right?"

At the sound of my voice, Melanie from Accounting turned her head. Her skin had a sickly jaundiced pallor to it, her eyes glazed over. She stared, swaying from side to side in a stilted trance-like manner.

I winced. "Christ, you look like shit."

She groaned, the jerky motion causing the line of drool hanging from her mouth to swing from side to side. She cocked her head as though trying to figure me out.

I took a cautious step back, not wanting to catch whatever bug was taking my coworkers and half of the

Midwest by storm today. Ever since lunch, people had started complaining of indigestion. The cafeteria's daily special had been known to bring on afternoon bouts of heartburn, but this was crazy. "You had the taco salad, too, huh?"

The door to the women's restroom swung open and a blur ran past us, startling me and knocking Melanie out of her stupor. Her lips curled in a snarl. Then she lunged at me, her jaws snapping.

"Shit!" Lucky for me, she moved slowly and I sidestepped to the left, leaving her to stumble clumsily onto her stomach. My papers fluttered to the floor while she floundered around. I threw out my hands. "What the fuck, Mel!"

She glared up at me, this time vocalizing a guttural growl that sent shivers up my neck. She jerkily dragged herself up. Fear crept into my nerves. I edged around her, careful to keep my distance, and pulled the bathroom door open and jumped inside.

I put all my weight into pushing the door closed, but Melanie was over twice my size. She heaved the door open, tumbled inside, and took me down. The air whooshed from my lungs. She pressed against me, her jaws snapping like she wanted to swear-to-God *eat* me.

Holy hell, I'd been scared in my life before, but this went beyond terror. When folks talk about fight or flight instincts, it's really fight *and* flight instincts. Everything I'd learned from self-defense classes was forgotten as I held my forearm against her neck while kicking and pushing with everything I had to get out from under her.

My arm shook under the weight. With a surge, I rolled her off me and shoved away. She grabbed at me, her fingers snagging my shirt and taking most of a sleeve with her with a loud rip. With nothing left to pull, the back of her head collided into the wall with a solid smack.

The bathroom door opened, and a high-pitched shriek pierced the air.

"Help!" I yelled while kicking away from Melanie, my Doc Martens squeaking across the floor, but whoever had opened the door had already disappeared.

A staccato pounding erupted from one of the bathroom stalls, matching the beating of my heart.

Knocking her head against the wall didn't slow down Melanie in the least. If anything, she was more pissed off than ever, now crawling at me like a clumsy, rabid dog. Out of the corner of my eye, I caught the yellow "caution: wet floor" sign propped in the corner. I grabbed it and swung just as she closed the distance, nailing her across the cheek.

Snarling, she charged and I swung again, this time breaking her nose. Thick brown blood sprayed out with every snort and hiss. She came back at me like I hadn't even hit her. With no time to swing, I shoved the hinged end of the plastic sign forward as hard as I could, karate-chopping her in the throat. The force knocked her back just enough for me to get solidly onto my feet.

Having her windpipe crushed put an end to the animal sounds and stopped her from spraying any more blood. Yet, even though she clearly couldn't breathe, she came at me again like she didn't even need air.

Terror froze my muscles.

My instructor had said a throat chop would take down an assailant in mere seconds. Yet, it had done nothing to stop a desk jockey from Accounting.

With the pounding and growling escalating from the bathroom stall a few feet away, I started swinging the sign relentlessly at Melanie's head. My heart pounded and my breaths came in gulps, yet Melanie kept on coming at me.

When she moved to pounce, I slammed the sign into her temple, causing her to misjudge her attack, and she head butted the wall instead. She turned around. Her forehead was a bloody mess, and she still didn't seem fazed.

"What the hell?" I asked breathlessly and swung again. The now-bloody sign's corner nailed her in the eye, knocking an eyeball out of its socket. Another hit made her eyeball swing until it finally flew free and bounced off the wall. I swung again and again and again, my blows echoed by whoever was pounding on the stall door.

Bones crunched, and Melanie collapsed face-forward onto the floor.

More of that gelatinous coffee-colored blood trickled from her head and pooled on the floor. I hit her with the sign one more time to make sure she wasn't playing possum, and I was about to kick her when the stall door swung open and Julie, the new girl, tumbled onto the floor. She looked up at me with that same sickly, *ravenous* look.

"Agh!" I smacked her in the face with the sign, and ran out of the bathroom, throwing the sign at her before I yanked the door open.

And I found myself in utter chaos.

I flattened against the wall in the corner where I'd come across Melanie earlier. Copies of my meeting agenda still littered the floor. Cubicle city was generally a quiet place except for the white noise piped in, but now people were running, shouting, and screaming. The pounding of work shoes across hollow floors echoed around me. Over a nearby cubicle wall, I watched as one man tackled another to the ground, his mouth clamping onto his victim's throat. The other man screamed. Red dots splattered the beige fabric walls.

I'd like to think that it was because I was in shock that I didn't run to help. But to be honest, I was scared shitless. Still watching the wall where the men went down, I ducked and crabbed down the hall, trying to ignore the anguished screams, focused only on avoiding the crazies. When the man's screams abruptly stopped, something in my brain kicked me into gear, and I took off running toward my cubicle.

A hand reached out for me, and I twisted away. The work alarms blared. Phones were ringing everywhere.

There were more screams and shouts in every direction. Some were begging for help, others were crying.

"Calm down! It will be okay!" a woman yelled from her desk. The next second, bloodied hands grabbed her and yanked her down as she let out an earsplitting scream.

Someone ran into me and I jumped back to find Alan from my team. He looked behind him before looking at me, his eyes wide. "This shit's fucked up. I'm outta here," he said under his breath as he headed past me.

Biting my lip, I glanced down the direction of my cube a dozen long feet away, where my bag and car keys waited in a drawer, and then turned back to Alan. "Wait up," I called out. "I'm coming, too."

He kept moving, and I sprinted to catch up. He slowed down, looking to the right, and I tugged him to the left. "This way."

We ran in the opposite direction of the mass exodus heading toward the main elevators. Alan hit the down button at the rarely used back bay of elevators. While we waited, a terrifying image shot through my mind of Melanie jumping out from the small six-by-six compartment.

Just as the elevator dinged, I grabbed Alan's elbow and tugged. "Stairs."

"Why?" he asked but followed me around the corner to the back stairs.

There were several others already heading down the steps. Alan pushed ahead of me, and I stayed at his back as he shoved past others, followed by a chorus of "hey" and "watch it."

We were only on floor eight, so we made it down the stairs fairly quickly. I paused at the third floor landing when I saw two men tackle a third man. One bit a chunk out of the guy's face while the other went for the screamer's throat. My adrenaline had already taken over, and my feet kept moving despite my shock. A gunshot rang out somewhere on the first floor. It was kind of like watching disasters on TV. It's so horrendously surreal that it doesn't fully register in the brain as reality. The whole Prima Insurance building had turned into the set of a slasher film, and unwillingness to face reality was the only reason I hadn't frozen.

Alan flung open the large glass doors. I rushed outside, shading my eyes against the afternoon sun, and scanned the parking lot. Some spaces were empty, some cars were tearing out of the lot, but most were still peacefully parked, waiting for their owners.

Gunfire erupted somewhere in the distance.

"Where's your car?" I asked breathlessly.

He turned around and looked at me like he'd forgotten I was still there. "Uh." He looked around. "There." He pointed to Lot C and took off toward it.

We were panting, but we sprinted all the way to his car, making wide arcs around other people running to their cars. It was a warm spring day, and my clothes clung to my sweaty skin.

Alan was an early-morning person, so his small Mitsubishi was parked only a few cars down the second row. He fumbled with before holding out a fob. The lights flashed, and I yanked open the passenger door.

I swept the papers and CDs off the seat with a brisk move and fell onto the hot black leather. I had my door locked before Alan had the key in the ignition. The engine roared to life, and he squealed the tires in reverse, throwing me against the dash.

I hastily fastened my seatbelt and held on.

"What the hell is going on around here?" he muttered, throwing the car into gear and squealing the tires again.

I swallowed. "No idea."

For the past two weeks, there'd been talk about a fast-spreading epidemic in South America that had been quickly moving northward, though I hadn't worried. The Midwest was a long distance from South America, and we'd closed our borders to Mexico over a week ago. And most of the military stood between us and them to make sure the borders stayed closed.

Strange. The epidemic in South America was said to cause violent symptoms, exactly like what I'd seen today.

Maybe I should've worried.

Today had started as a typical Thursday. I'd listened to the radio on the commute to work. There'd been more talk on the growing epidemic, but local news overshadowed talks of the epidemic. At Prima, gossip ran wild all morning about last night's attacks on joggers and walkers in nearly every southern state west of the Mississippi. Several paranoid employees had called in sick today.

Then, two cooks in the cafeteria got into some kind a brawl just before lunch. One left in an ambulance, and the other had been taken away in handcuffs. The news was reporting similar attacks across the Midwest and Western United States. With all that, would Prima close for the day? Hell, no.

Several worried employees had already left for home to pick up their kids from school. And now, not even three hours after lunch, half of the office was going ape-shit crazy on each other. Whatever was going on, it felt like I was caught in the middle of Ground Zero for some seriously screwed up shit.

I focused on breathing in and out and reached for the radio and fumbled with the knob. I wrung my shaking hands, wiped them on my black pants, but they kept shaking.

Alan cranked up the volume, and I noticed his hands were shaking even worse.

"Reports are coming in from Kansas City, Des Moines, and Minneapolis of a fast-spreading pandemic. Seek shelter immediately and avoid contact with anyone infected. The infected will display violent tendencies and attack without provocation. They do not respond to reason," an unfamiliar even-toned woman reported. *"If you or a loved one is infected, you should quarantine yourself immediately so as*

not to spread the virus. Do not go to the hospitals as they are at full capacity. Stay tuned for more information."

"That's it?" Alan asked. "That's all those idiots have to say about this thing? Nothing like how it's transmitted, or what we can do to protect ourselves?"

"Give it time," I said. The news last night had shown footage of random people attacking others without provocation, but I'd assumed the attacks were the result of some new illegal drug gone bad. The idea of a pandemic made my jaw clench.

My dad was a doctor. My mom was a nurse.

My parents, early-retiree snowbirds, lived in a southern suburb of Des Moines. With me as their only child, they kept their house in town for the warmer months while moving to Arizona every winter. I prayed that they were safe at home, that they didn't think to go help out at the hospital. I had to believe they saw the news this morning and knew better than to get caught in the middle of some off-the-charts violent pandemic.

I wanted to call them to make sure they were all right, but my phone was tucked into my bag, which was still sitting in a drawer at my cubicle. I looked over at Alan. "Can I use your phone?"

He felt his pockets and then frantically swerved around a fender bender before shooting through a red light. Sirens blared as a police car sped past us.

"I think it's still on my desk," Alan replied in between panting breaths.

"This is crazy," I said. "Everyone's gone crazy."

"It's got to be a terrorist attack," he said. "Chemical warfare or something that's making people go nuts. It's like they're jacked up on serious shit like bath salts or something. Damn it!" He swerved again. "This traffic is insane." He turned to me, his glasses slipping down his sweaty nose. "You live on the north side, right?"

I nodded. "Yeah, why?"

"I'm way out on the east side. Mind if we hit your place until the roads open up?" His voice cracked and he wiped his face.

"Sure." I scrutinized him. "Are you okay?"

He grabbed the wheel with both hands. "No, I'm not okay! What about today would make you think that I'm okay? That anything's okay? It's World War III out there. No, it's worse than that. It's like the end of the world out there!"

I got it, I really did. The proverbial shit had hit the fan, and the rational part of my mind had decided to curl up in the fetal position. "We got out early," I said with as much confidence as I could muster. "Hopefully we can beat the worst of the traffic."

As though on cue, a car veered in front of us and rammed into the concrete separating the lanes. "Watch out!" I shouted as Alan cranked the wheel, nearly sideswiping the vehicle. I could've sworn the driver looked in the same bad way that Melanie had. The SUV behind us wasn't so lucky because it rammed into the jackknifed car and started a domino-effect pile-up behind us.

Alan and I stared at each other, and he stepped on the gas.

In the background, the radio station had switched to interviewing people outside one of the hospitals.

"I thought the kid was lost. I bent down to help, and the little bugger bit me! Can you believe that? The kid damn near took my thumb clean off! He went nuts, like he had rabies or something. And now they won't let me into the hospital. They've got barricades in front of the doors, and cops are in full riot gear, just standing around everywhere. I'm stuck outside bleeding, and no one is telling us what's going on. We have a right to know!"

"You think you got it bad?" another male voice chimed in. *"You should've been downtown. This old bum attacked a woman. I saw it all. He was stumbling around all drunk-like, and then he just attacked. He went straight for that poor gal's throat like he thought he was a vampire or something. A couple guys tried to pull him off her, but he wouldn't let go. I jumped in to help, and he tore a chunk out of my arm. He wouldn't stop. Some guy had to shoot him. Can you believe it? It was insane, man. What's the world coming to?"*

My heart felt like it was going to jump out of my chest, and I found myself on the verge of hyperventilating. I punched in another radio station, only to find the same barrage of stories. No one had any useful information, just more of those horrific tales. I leaned back, tried to tune out the radio, and focused on the traffic outside. With every mile, the number of vehicles on the side of the road increased. Some cars were in pileups, others looked like they had stopped haphazardly, as though their drivers had decided to simply stop driving.

I sucked in a deep breath. "I think I killed Melanie," I said quietly.

"Melanie Carlson?"

"What?" I glanced at Alan. "Oh. No. The other Melanie."

"Oh." He frowned. "Did she try to hurt you?"

"Of course she tried to hurt me. She tried to *eat* me."

Alan was quiet for a time. "I bet she could eat a lot."

I belted out a laugh. Not because it was funny but because my adrenaline high was coming down, and with it, my shock. Alan laughed, too, though the stress was getting to him. He wiped his sweaty forehead with his arm and kept driving.

I'd killed someone today. The truth really hit me just then, and I let my head fall against the headrest. I hadn't even thought about the repercussions. Would I go to jail, even though it was an open-and-shut case of self-defense? I closed my eyes and rubbed my temples. I'd lose my job. That was a given. How the hell would I pay the bills?

And then there was Melanie. That poor woman's final minutes were in a bathroom of all places.

"No, no, no, *no*," Alan chanted.

Startled, I glanced up to find a massive pileup of cars dead ahead. Vehicles were mashed together, filling up every inch of open space in the four lanes in front of us.

An ambulance and two police cars were on scene but no tow trucks yet. Concrete prevented us from getting into the lanes of oncoming traffic, and a deep ditch prevented escape off to the right.

"Can you turn around? Take the last exit?" I asked.

He was staring in the rear-view mirror. "I don't think so. It's getting pretty crowded back there. Maybe we can find a way around this mess."

Doubtful, I scanned the wreck as we drew closer. People were running away, but not everyone. One cop was handcuffing a man who kept twisting his neck, trying to bite him. Several others were standing by cars, helping free the drivers and passengers. I narrowed my eyes.

Hell. They weren't helping free the people still in cars. "Oh, God," I whispered.

"What is it?" Alan asked.

"We have to get out of here," I said, staring at the crazies attacking the people in cars. It was like the entire world decided to go cannibal at the same time.

He frowned, pointing ahead. "Exactly how do you think we are going to get past this mess?"

"I mean *now*, Alan."

A man jumped out of his car and started firing his pistol into the mob. The sound must've finally registered what was underway because Alan's eyes widened, and he yanked the car around. Something slammed into our car and an explosive force threw me against the seat. Dazed, I blinked to see that we were now facing another direction.

Powder from the airbags sent dust flurries in the air. I shoved at the deflating white bag. The driver of the car that had t-boned us was still hidden behind his airbags. I glanced back at the horde of crazies to find them looking in our direction.

I unlatched my seatbelt and tugged on Alan's arm. "C'mon. We need to get out of here."

He muttered something, and shook his head as though to clear it.

"Stupid idiot!"

I looked outside to see the other driver climb groggily out of his car, shaking his fist. He stepped up to Alan's door, and pounded on the window. "Moron! What were you thinking turning around in the middle of the road like that?" he yelled.

"Back off!" Alan growled right back.

Alan was not a large man. He was my height and had maybe thirty pounds on me. To see him yelling at a pissed off guy only added fire to a tinderbox. Then I saw them coming our way. "Uh, Alan?"

"What!"

I pointed at several crazies with pallid skin stumbling toward us, their jaundiced sights homed in on the man standing outside our car. Their faces and chests were blood-soaked, and a few sported violent injuries of their own. One hobbled along with a broken leg. Another was missing an arm. Still another looked like half her throat had been ripped out. They moved slowly and jerkily but were relentlessly closing the distance. Alan looked and gasped.

The man outside continued to yell until he realized Alan was no longer paying any attention to him. He followed Alan's gaze. He cried out and took off running back to his car but was too late. All of the crazies attacked him at once. The driver screamed. It was an awful, bloodcurdling scream, but I couldn't see what was happening under the pile of writhing flesh and gushing blood. Not that I wanted to.

I glanced at Alan, and then opened the door and ran.

CHAPTER II

Tires squealed as cars rammed into the bottleneck. Gunshots rang though the air. With Alan at my back, we sprinted away from the crazies and into the oncoming traffic.

I headed straight for the midnight blue eighteen-wheeler just rolling in, with an American flag painted on its trailer, dwarfing the vehicles around it. Even though the truck was still moving, I jumped up on the driver's side step, pulled on the locked door handle, and pounded on the window. "Please let me in!"

The driver scowled. His eyes were covered by aviator-style sunglasses, and I couldn't see if he was watching me, the crazies, or something else. His lower lip bulged with chew, and with a wave of his hand he motioned me away.

I tried the handle again. No luck. I risked a quick

glance behind me to see that, sure enough, the group of crazies that had been huddled around a small truck was now headed this way. I swung back to the truck driver. "Please!"

After a long second, the window opened, and the barrel of a shotgun pressed against my chest.

I didn't fall back. I didn't jump to the side. Instead, I stood there as though waiting for him to shoot me. "I've got nowhere else to go," I said weakly.

He scowled even more, causing lines in his five o'clock shadow. He kept the shotgun level at my chest. "You bit?"

I gave my head a fervent shake. "No." Then I frowned, confused. "Why?"

He seemed satisfied with my answer, though he also didn't seem in the mood to elaborate. He cranked his head around mine and nodded toward Alan, who was hanging on right behind me. "How about you? You don't look so good."

I glanced back to find a sweaty, pale Alan.

"I'm f-fine," Alan replied with a stutter. When the trucker didn't respond, Alan threw up his hands. "I was just in a freaking car accident, man!"

The crazies were less than thirty feet away and quickly closing in. I snapped my gaze back to the trucker, pleading. "Mister, *please*!"

He moved his head slightly to check out the crazies closing in. He spit off to my right and pulled in his gun. "If you want to live, you'd better climb in."

I heard the *pop* of the door unlocking, and I stepped to the side to open it. "Thank you, thank you, thank you," I murmured as I crawled over him, knocking his cap askew, on my way to the passenger seat. Once there, I fastened the seatbelt as fast as I could in case the trucker changed his mind and tried to shove me out. Alan came in right behind me, only he collapsed in the cab behind us. The driver slammed the door shut, set the gun between him and the door, and grabbed the long shifter. Air shot from the brakes.

A crazy rammed the door and clawed at the now-closed window. The truck lurched forward, and the man in a bloodied business suit tumbled off the truck.

"Damn zeds," the driver muttered, his hat still crooked.

"Zeds?" I frowned, recognizing the term. "You don't mean..."

He pointed outside where several crazies stood literally dead ahead of us. "You know damn well what they are."

What the trucker had said made perfect sense, but it shouldn't be possible. Yet, not only did one of the infected try to eat me less than an hour ago, they moved like zeds—zombies—clumsily and relentlessly. No different from the crazies in front of us now. With no regard to their well-being, they kept shambling toward the truck barreling down the road on its way to meet them.

"I guess you're right," I said softly as the realization

of fiction becoming reality hammered at the tension headache already pounding behind my forehead.

The driver stepped on the gas, and I sucked in a breath. The heavy rig rammed through the group of crazies like a bowling ball, only these pins left behind goo and flecks of skin.

"Holy shit," I muttered as the trucker ran over zeds like they were nothing more than small speed bumps. The windshield wipers smeared brown streaks across the glass. He kept picking up speed, setting us up for a bull's-eye approach to the roadblock. I braced my legs against the dash the instant before he rammed into a small car jackknifed between an SUV and a minivan. Something heavy slammed against the back of my seat, followed by a muffled moan.

I looked back to find Alan crumpled on the floor. "You okay?"

"Nnnh, yeah."

The truck shoved the car to the side with metal-on-metal screeching. As we carved our way through the wreckage, the rig knocked around the sedan the zeds had swarmed earlier. The driver, still strapped inside, reached out to us with his only remaining arm. Even though he no longer had a face, the man watched us with unblinking eyes while his mouth opened and closed.

I shivered and turned away.

Once we broke through the bottleneck and put distance between us and the zeds, the road opened up.

In the distance, a few cars entered from the next ramp, but most of the traffic was headed in the opposite direction.

I grinned. "Hot damn! We got through!"

In response, the trucker glared. "I'd be surprised if I didn't bust something," he growled out. "She's not made for this sort of abuse."

I glanced in the side mirror to see a line of vehicles following us, though the zeds were closing in on the cars on both sides. The woman in a convertible never stood a chance. I snapped my gaze straight ahead to the open highway. After a moment, I found my voice again. "What you did back there…thanks. I mean it. You saved our lives."

He grumbled something under his breath.

The open road looked like freedom, and for the first time since getting mauled by Melanie I let myself relax. I felt halfway in control again even though I knew it was a false feeling. Too much had changed since this morning. I loved routines. I hated chaos.

Five days a week I sat in a small mushroom-colored cubicle in a sea of mushroom-colored cubicles, at the same desk I'd sat at for over five years since college. I was an actuary, which my parents thought was a pretty big deal, but really it just meant I ran a lot of reports and analyzed spreadsheets.

Two years ago, I'd saved up enough money to make a decent down payment on a fixer-upper in the Gussdale district, and most of my free time went to renovating the old bungalow. Well, to that, and flying. My Piper Cub was the one splurge I'd allowed myself after college. Dad had been a pilot, and I got my pilot's license the same week I got my driver's license. I rubbed my bare arm where the Cub logo tattoo—a fuzzy teddy bear—looked up at me.

After today, I'd probably never get the chance to log another hour in the Cub. The entire world had fallen apart before my eyes. After running a finger wistfully over the teddy bear, I looked out the window.

Startled, I pointed to the sign. "My exit is the next one coming up."

A small nod was the only acknowledgement I got before the trucker picked up a soda can from a cup holder and spit in it.

Another grunt from the back seat reminded me that I wasn't the only passenger. I turned around. Alan was lying on the floor, his face covered by his arm. "How are you holding up back there?"

No response. I frowned. He hadn't hit the back of my seat *that* hard. "Alan?"

Still nothing.

"Alan," I said louder.

Alan looked at me then. His tongue was hanging out as though he was panting. His eyes had yellowed, and his features morphed from confused to dull. Then he moaned.

"Oh, shit." I unlatched my seatbelt. The trucker was watching me, and he caught on fast.

"You've got to be kidding me," he said, taking his foot off the gas and reaching for his shotgun.

My intent was to grab Alan and toss him out of the truck before he went crazy. It seemed like there was a short window when Melanie had been out of it before going into raging attack mode. But I didn't get the chance.

I was halfway to Alan when the shotgun went off.

The next split-second was a blur. The shot blasted my eardrums. Alan's face literally split in half. Brownish blood and brain matter sprayed the cabin and me, and Alan's body slammed against the back wall. I may have yelled, but I couldn't hear it if I had. The only sound in my world at that moment was a loud, throbbing, constant ringing.

Even though I thought I'd just recovered from shock, it was amazing how quickly I was thrown right back into it. I stared at Alan's crumpled body in a daze. Dark liquid spread out from his head. I felt the truck come to a stop.

The trucker leveled the gun on me and said something.

"What?" I asked, his words nowhere near as loud as the ringing in my ears.

"I said…one good reason…blow your brains out."

It took a moment for his words to make sense in my head. Then I watched him, numbly, for a moment. "I can't."

A flash of genuine surprise crossed his face, but the

expression was lost all too quickly to anger. "I asked if you were bit, goddammit."

"I'm *not* bit," I said, before shaking my head.

He motioned to Alan. "And him?"

"I thought Alan was just freaked out from everything."

The driver sat there and scrutinized me for what seemed like an eternity. "Are you cut? Did you get any blood in your mouth or eyes?"

I looked down at my clothes damp with Alan's blood. With my black clothes, the dark blood blended in but the flecks of skin and brain dotted my shirt. "I'm okay."

"You sure?"

"Pretty sure."

"You better be more than 'pretty sure,' Cash. Because this thing spreads through contact. Blood-to-blood, saliva-to-blood. If you got it, you're going to be like your boyfriend before long."

I didn't answer.

He motioned over my shoulder. "Get out."

I looked out the window. I was still at least three miles from home. I thought of my tiny bungalow in a neighborhood full of tiny houses. How many neighbors were already sick? With my car still back at the office, where could I go?

Outside was already turning into a war zone…

A man boarding up windows on his house just off the interstate.

Two people running down a street.

The occasional pops of gunfire becoming constant echoes of *rat-tat-tat*.

A shape stumbling around a tree.

How many zeds stood between me and home?

The only thing I knew was that I would never even make it to my front door, let alone to my parents' house on the other side of town. It was both a miracle and luck that I'd already made it this far. Out there, on foot, I didn't stand a chance.

Operating on autopilot, I opened the door but couldn't make my legs obey. I lowered my head, and the tears came. It wasn't an act. I didn't want to cry, I *never* cried, but the tears just kept coming. My shoulders shook from exhaustion as much as from adrenaline and hopelessness.

Silence filled the cab for what seemed like an eternity, before I heard a heavy sigh. "I know I'm going to regret this. If you start looking sick, I swear to God I won't hesitate to fill your brain with buckshot. If you're not sick, I'll give you one day." He held up a finger. "One day. Then you're on your own. Got it?"

Sniffling, I nodded vigorously. "You won't regret it, I swear."

"I already do," he grumbled.

I went to pull the door shut; he nudged me with the barrel. "Nuh, uh," he said. "Get rid of your boyfriend first. And be quick about it. He's stinking up my cabin."

I looked back and winced. "He's not my boyfriend," I

said weakly before my gag reflex kicked in. I twisted and reached out the door just in time to throw up the pepperoni pizza I'd had for lunch. After several heaves, I was able to sit up again. Taking a deep breath, I glanced at the trucker. He was watching me carefully, but at least he didn't mistake my retching for getting "sick" and shoot me.

I wiped my chin and headed to the back of the cab. Fortunately, Alan was slouched over, his face hidden in his lap, which made it a bit easier to pretend that this wasn't someone I'd worked alongside every weekday. Dark, brownish blood and brain bits were splattered *everywhere*. Dazedly, I noticed the blood around Alan seemed darker and more congealed than it should have been, but I was no expert. My parents would know that kind of detail. I nudged him with my toe to make sure he was really dead, as though a shotgun blast to the head hadn't been convincing enough. *No response*. Some of the tension in my spine released.

Once I could breathe without gagging, I glanced around. A stack of folded bedding sat neatly in the corner, and I grabbed the top sheet already speckled with dark spots. Breathing through my mouth, I knelt by Alan and none-too-gracefully rolled him into the sheet. Frowning, I noticed his pants had been ripped, and I nudged the material aside to see a jagged wound in the shape of a human mouth.

"He was bit," I said, taking a long breath to keep from throwing up. "In the calf."

"Figured something like that was the case," the trucker replied.

I continued wrapping Alan in the sheet, trying to distance myself by imagining this was anything but a human body, but my subconscious kept reminding me. Once he was fully wrapped, I tugged and dragged him to the door and had meant to lower him gently to the ground, but he was heavier than me and the position was awkward. The sheet-wrapped body slipped right out of my hands and landed on the concrete shoulder of the interstate with a solid thud.

I stared at the body. While Alan deserved better than to be left at the side of the road to rot, I really, *really* didn't want to leave the safety of the truck and risk being left behind. Biting my lip, I turned back to the trucker.

He shifted the truck back into gear. "You're cleaning up the rest of this mess when we get to my place."

I collapsed onto the seat and slammed the door shut just as the truck moved forward. I let out a breath and stared outside, focusing on nothing in particular as the trucker drove and weaved around cars. As we left the city behind, traffic shrunk to nil. Other than a couple small military convoys and state troopers, few vehicles were heading into town, and those vehicles were speeding down the interstate, as though they were in a hurry to get to Des Moines.

No doubt they were trying to get to their families.

While I'm abandoning mine.

I sat in a numb trance, my head resting on the headrest. *Stay safe, mom and dad. I'm coming back. I promise.*

The radio was on, but the CB radio was louder, with truckers constantly reporting in status of the interstates. All the talk was of zeds and blocked roads. Every couple minutes I found the trucker eying me.

"I still feel okay," I said each time I caught him looking at me.

Seemingly assured that I wasn't going to go zed on him, he put on a Bluetooth and reported in on the CB. "This is Clutch dead-heading at yard stick 153 on I-80 reporting in. Avoid I-80 eastbound near Des Moines. Just passed through a bad 10-50 with zeds rubber necking the area. Over."

"10-4, Clutch. This is Dog Man. Heading west from The Windy. How's the big road westbound outside city limits? Over."

"Hammer lane for now, Dog Man. But I wouldn't count on it staying that way. Two Rivers has been overrun. Zed city. Over."

Zed city. I thought of my parents, and the rock in my gut grew into a boulder, and I hugged myself. They'd be so worried right now, unable to get a hold of me.

They were okay, safe at home. They *had* to be okay.

"Same with The Windy," the other driver said. *"Also heard The Circle and The Gateway are zed city, too. Whatever this thing is, it's spreading hard and fast. I saw a guy get nearly decapitated and he was back on his feet in two minutes*

joining up with the other nut jobs. Have three beavers on board, and hoping to make the Big Miss by dark. Over."

"Picked up a seat cover myself. Watch your six, Dog Man. Clutch over and out."

Clutch removed his Bluetooth, clicked off the CB, and turned the radio back up.

He shot me a look, then returned his focus to the road. I noticed he wasn't as old as I'd first assumed—mid-forties, maybe. And he was big and tough and scary. He'd straightened his cap, hiding more of his brown crew cut. He wore nothing fancy, just old jeans and a T-shirt, with tattoos covering his arms. His clothes were clean, whereas I looked like I'd just escaped a war zone.

Which was too damn near the truth.

Clutch nodded toward the red cooler at my feet. "Grab me a beer, Cash." Then he tacked on, "Grab something for yourself if you're thirsty."

I didn't care that his last sentence came out more like a gripe than an offer. I reached in and pulled out a beer and a bottle of water from the ice. "My name's Mia. You go by Clutch?" I asked. "Or, at least that's your CB handle, right?"

He didn't reply.

I handed him the can and opened the plastic bottle. The water was cold and oh so good. After throwing up, my throat was raw and my mouth tasted awful. The water soothed and I swooshed it around my teeth. I drank the entire bottle before opening my eyes. "So," I said, drawing out the word. "Where are we headed?"

"My place."

Three long tones beeped on the radio.

"About time," he said as he cranked up the volume.

"This is the Emergency Broadcast System. This is not a test. Repeat, this is not a test."

Three more tones sounded before a man's voice came on. *"This is Doctor Jon Meriden, managing director of the Center for the Disease Control. A state of emergency has been declared for the continental United States. An epidemic is now affecting the Midwest and quickly spreading. Houston and Kansas City are considered the worst locations and should be avoided. Cases of the virus have been reported in all major cities in the United States, southern Canada, and all of South and Central America. Any borders that remained opened as of this morning have now been closed. Cases are also being reported at Hong Kong International Airport.*

The virus has been confirmed to be a member of the Marburgvirus *family. Scientists are working hard to identify the new virus, and it is believed to have originated in South America. However, due to its symptoms and the mannerisms of the infected, we've assigned the layman term* zombiism *to the superbug.*

Symptoms include slow and awkward movement, jaundice, and severe violent propensities. We strongly urge you to distance yourself from anyone displaying these symptoms. If you come into contact with someone displaying any of these symptoms, the CDC recommends quarantining yourself. If you are infected, symptoms will begin to appear anywhere from minutes up to an hour, depending on severity of initial infection. The more severe the initial infection, the quicker you will succumb to the virus. Treatment is not available at this time.

We have traced the entry of the virus into the United States to several dozen contaminated shipments of produce from Mexico. At this time, we recommend you do not eat any fresh produce imported within the past three days.

The superbug is transmitted through contact with bodily fluid of an infected person. The slang term 'zed' is trending across the Internet and radio. Should you hear this term, it simply refers to an infected person or persons.

Due to the ease of the virus' transmission, all public transportation and air travel have been suspended until further notice. Travel is not advisable and is considered unsafe. If you must leave your current location, expect delays and likely increases in lawlessness. Emergency responders may be overwhelmed. Please be patient and remain where you are. Gather emergency supplies should you need to evacuate to a temporary location. Do not panic.

All military units have been assigned to contain the spread. All inactive and retired military personnel have been reactivated and should immediately report to the nearest base for assignment. Martial law is now in effect. Stay inside, stay safe, and help will be on the way.

We will report on all channels every thirty minutes. For more information, go to www.emergency.cdc.gov online."

Three tones sounded once more, and the radio resumed to what sounded like a national talk show sharing more information about the "zombie outbreak" and how to protect against zeds.

"How are you feeling?"

I glanced over at the man next to me. His hands were tight on the wheel as he watched me.

"Fine." I realized he was asking about symptoms rather than my emotional well-being. "Really, I'm still okay." Terror had long since given way to hopelessness. "The world's seriously fucked, isn't it," I stated quietly.

"Yeah." He spit into the soda can. "We're all fucked."

CHAPTER III

When we pulled into Clutch's driveway, I wouldn't have been surprised to see a sign that read: *Abandon all hope, all ye who enter here.*

Not that the farm wasn't lovely. Fields and woodlands went on for miles and miles. Just above a valley, a long gravel lane led us through several acres of woods, with flowers blooming along both sides. The lane opened up to a classic farm setup: a two-story white farmhouse standing boldly alone with three sheds as backdrop. A tabby cat lounged under a tree, watching me.

Clutch pulled up along the largest shed and cut the engine. The whole scene was idyllic...and very, very isolated. I was alone with a stranger who'd killed Alan and run down several zeds like they were nothing.

Sure, I'd killed Melanie, so I guess I wasn't any

different. But, what if he changed his mind about letting me stay for the night and killed me? Almost as bad, what if he wanted "favors" in exchange for shelter? I'd been terrified of being alone in this mess, but I suddenly wondered if being alone wasn't the safer option.

"What's up, Cash? You're looking at me like I'm about to dismember you."

Startled, I realized Clutch had taken off his sunglasses and was now watching me. His piercing hazel eyes seemed to see too far into me.

I blinked a few times. "Just feeling like a fish out of water. That's all," I replied in a rush, opening the door and jumping outside. In the fresh air, I stretched my tight muscles as I stood before the sun dipping low in the sky. The weather was beautiful, a spring evening with a gentle breeze.

Clutch walked toward the house, and I followed. "I wouldn't have guessed you for living on a farm," I said.

"Why?"

"With you being a truck driver—"

"I'm from a fourth-generation farming family on this land. I just drive truck in the off season for extra income."

He unlocked the porch door, but instead of opening it, he turned around and studied me for several long moments.

Any confidence I'd built bled away under his scrutiny.

"Stay here," he ordered. He didn't wait for an answer

before disappearing inside, leaving me to wait. The peaceful chirping of crickets was the only sound besides the ringing in my ears, and I realized that the same isolation I feared about this place was the key quality that made it all the safer. The farm was in the middle of nowhere, far from any city. The yard was big enough to see zeds coming from the woods on any side, and the trees concealed us from the roads.

Clutch returned with an armful of rags, some rubber gloves, a garbage bag, and a couple spray bottles. "There better not be a spot left in the cab when I check it out."

I nodded dutifully, taking the supplies.

"There's a light in the cab. Just be sure to turn it off when you're finished. I want to keep everything fully charged in this cluster fuck."

"Light off when I'm done," I replied with a robot-like tone.

He grunted before turning back into the house.

With a sigh, I headed back to the truck and started scrubbing away every last drop and bit of Alan.

Four hours later, I peeled off the yellow gloves covered in brown goo and chemicals. With a sigh, I dropped them into the garbage bag and tied it shut. Even with the industrial-strength stain remover, Alan's blood had been a bitch to scrub away, and I wouldn't know if I got everything until daylight. I'd been desperately motivated to do a good job. I only hoped it was good enough that Clutch wouldn't make me leave before the National Guard got the whole zed thing under control and I could return home.

I sprayed every surface in the cab with one more round of disinfectant before turning off the light and stepping outside and groaned. I was flat-out exhausted. My arms were numb. My lower back hurt. My thigh muscles ached. Every inch of my body throbbed.

Despite the stench, I'd kept the truck doors closed while I cleaned in case any zeds showed up. After taking several deep breaths of fresh night air, I sprayed my grimy body with disinfectant, knowing it probably didn't do any good, but figured it also couldn't hurt.

The half-moon was fully overhead now, sharing just enough of its light for me to hurry to the house without tripping over anything. I was half surprised to find the porch door unlocked. Looking down at my Doc Martens, I suspected the black leather was as grimy as I felt. But, there was no way in hell I could scrub them until tomorrow when—hopefully—I could feel my fingertips again. Stepping inside, I took off my boots and left them on the unlit porch.

A savory, meaty smell wafted forth, and my stomach growled. It was late, and I'd lost whatever had been left of my lunch after Alan died. I hustled forward, only to be blocked at the mudroom by a towering Clutch. He was wearing different clothes, and his hair was still wet. Gray peppered his stubble. Lines marked skin that had seen a lot of the outdoors.

He was handsome in a hard way. Maybe it was his eyes. There was an intensity in his gaze. Even without his tattoos, he would've had an aura of power.

Or, maybe it was because he had a pistol leveled on me.

My eyes widened as I met his gaze.

He grimaced. "Relax. If I was going to kill you, I would've done it outside where you wouldn't make a mess."

I chortled. Like that made me feel any better.

It was then I noticed that he was also holding a rag and a small bottle of gun oil. "You were cleaning your gun."

He looked me up and down before narrowing his eyes. "Take off your clothes."

I pulled together the collar of my utterly destroyed shirt. "What?"

"I don't mean it that way. Jesus." He ran the back of his hand over his face. He laid his weapon on the washer, reached behind him, and pulled out a garbage bag. "You're covered in zed sludge, and I don't know how contagious that shit is. Everything's got to go. I'll burn it tomorrow."

He held open the garbage bag. I shot him a hard glare while I unbuttoned what was left of my shirt.

He sighed. "Don't worry. I won't look. You're not my

type, anyway. Too scrawny."

"Scrawny?" I asked but received no response.

Clutch kept his word, looking over my head while I stripped out of my disgusting clothes. I stopped at my bra and underwear. "Nothing soaked through."

He glanced down and grimaced, like he wasn't enjoying himself. I scowled. I wasn't that hard on the eyes, and I was petite, most certainly *not* scrawny.

"Turn around," he ordered. "I have to check."

I gingerly spun and felt his eyes on my back. I shivered, more self-conscious than I'd ever been in my life. If I'd known how this day was going to turn out, I wouldn't have worn a thong. Then again, I would've done many things differently.

"I think they're savable," Clutch drawled out in a rough voice. "Throw both in the wash when you're done with your shower."

Turning back to face him, I covered my chest as best I could with my arms, though thankfully Clutch was busy looking anywhere but at me.

"The shower's upstairs. Second door on your left. I set out something you can wear for tonight. Dinner will be ready by the time you're done."

"Got it," I said and hustled past him.

"Oh, and Cash..."

I paused.

"Be sure to scrub good and hard," he called out behind me. "You've got bits of your boyfriend's brain in your hair."

Bile rose in my throat, and I bolted up the stairs, taking them two at a time. Once in the bathroom, I took deep breaths, refusing to look in the mirror. When I had control of myself again, I pulled off my remaining clothes in a rush, cranked on the shower, and hopped in before it was warm.

The cold water that ran down the drain was brown at first, with little flecks of things I didn't want to think about. I set the water as hot as I could stand, grabbed the washcloth, and started scrubbing. Clutch clearly wasn't married, because the shower/tub combo only had a bar of soap and a bottle of generic shampoo.

I washed my hair three times before I felt relatively confident that it was clean. And, I scrubbed at my skin until it was red, standing under the spray until it was lukewarm.

Stepping out, I grabbed the towel left out on top of a thin stack of clothes, and dried myself off. I caught my breath when I looked into the mirror. Dark circles underlined my bloodshot eyes. Fresh bruises marred my chest courtesy of Melanie. I looked like shit, plain and simple.

Picking up the clothes he'd left, I found a pair of white long john bottoms and a gray T-shirt with ARMY across the front. Both were huge on me. The shirt nearly went to my knees, and the bottoms slid down every time I moved. Sifting through the well-stocked medicine cabinet, I found a couple large safety pins and tightened the long johns around my waist.

I couldn't find a brush, so it took ten painful minutes to finger-comb through my snarled, unconditioned mess. Finally, my strands began to resemble hair again, with its bold red streaks interlaced with the black. Reaching for the dental floss, I pulled out a long strand and used it to tie my hair back before it snarled all over again.

Glancing down at the discarded pile of underwear, I grimaced. I really didn't want to touch anything that I'd worn today. I probably should've tossed it, but I went ahead and wrapped the towel around the tiny pile of undergarments and carried everything down to the washer in the mudroom.

I walked past the kitchen on my way to the mudroom, and saw Clutch pulling plates from a cabinet. His back was to me, though I had no doubt he knew I was there. His back was broad, like he worked out every day. He was well over twice my size. Part of me felt safer, part of me worried how easily he could overpower me.

My stomach growled loudly, and I hustled to the mudroom. After stuffing my dirty clothes in the washer along with Clutch's clothes that were already in the tub, I went double-duty with the detergent, and started it up.

When I returned to the kitchen, he handed me a cold beer, silverware, and a plate covered with a huge steak, a baked potato, and steak sauce poured over the entire thing. He motioned to the living room. "I eat in there."

He grabbed his own beer and dinner, and I followed him, taking the couch when he claimed the recliner.

I dug in before opening the beer. I was thirsty, but I was even hungrier. With the plate on my lap, I sawed at the T-bone, cutting off the next piece while chewing on a piece twice the size I should've cut. "This is really good."

My words were muffled as I chewed loudly, but Clutch seemed to make them out. "It sucks wasting a good T-bone on the stove, but I don't know how long the grid will stay up. Figured I may as well clean out the freezer now."

I swallowed, the steak going down painfully hard in my suddenly constricted throat. I cracked opened the beer and took a long swig. I hadn't even thought about losing electricity. What else would give out? Water? Phone lines?

Stores would be closed, which meant no fresh food. My sudden reality made me set my fork down. "How long do you think it will be until the military makes it safe again?"

His left brow rose. "I think it's already too late. The outbreak spread too fast and too hard. If we didn't get out when we did today, I doubt we'd be talking tonight. You better start getting used to this way of life."

"But the military—"

"Doesn't stand a chance against millions of zeds," he interrupted. "It's a numbers game. The zeds are spreading too fast. There's no way our guys can keep them in check. Not without nuking every populated area. And that would also take out any survivors."

The next bite tasted like cardboard. And the one after that. If nearly everyone turned into a zed, there wouldn't be anyone left to fight them. Even soldiers weren't impervious to a zed's bite if they were caught unaware or without ammo.

If I hadn't hitched a ride with Clutch, I'd still be in Des Moines, surrounded by zeds right now. Out here, miles from any town, I was relatively safe. More important, I wasn't in this alone. I looked up. "I have skills." *Not really.* "I can help." *I have no idea how.* "Give me one more day, and I'll prove it."

He shook his head and held up a finger. "The deal's for one day."

"An extra pair of eyes and an extra pair of hands can't hurt. I can help," I added.

"Do you know how to fire a gun? String a snare?"

"I can learn."

"It would take you months to become proficient, even if you had the aptitude for it." He leaned back. "You'll only slow me down and eat my food."

"Then I'll go out and get us more food."

"First time I take you with me, you'll get bit, and then I'll have to put you down."

"I'll be careful." I jutted out my chin. "Besides, I killed a zed today."

"Really?" The corners of his mouth curled upward. "And exactly how did you manage that?"

I thought for a moment. *With sheer luck and a miracle.* "With a 'wet floor' sign."

He looked confused at first, then smirked, but shook it off. "You'll be a drain. You'll use up more resources than you could possibly bring in."

"I'll go get us whatever we need. If something happens to me, then you'll be on your own again. It's a no-lose situation for you."

He rubbed his eyes. "Not good enough. I'm not set up here to take in strays." He looked up, his gaze hard with resolve. "The deal was for one day. Come tomorrow, you're on your own. I'll get you to a car, but then we're done."

I wanted to argue. God, I wanted to beg him to change his mind. Instead, I looked down at my plate and gave a tight nod.

Clutch turned on the TV, and flipped through channels. It looked like nearly all the channels were offline. Only one news channel remained, and the reporter was giving updates on the major cities. With the TV as a backdrop, we finished the meal in silence.

When Clutch stood, I came to my feet. "Here," I said, reaching for his plate. "I'll clean up."

He probably thought I was trying to show him how I could help, and he'd be right. He eyed me for a moment before holding out his plate. "I'll secure outside. When you're done, there are a couple plastic jugs I set out. Fill them with water."

"But you're out in the country," I said. "Don't you

have well water?"

"I do," he said. "But the pumps still need electricity. I have a manual pump outside that will still work if the power goes out, but that's no reason to not be prepared in case it's too dangerous to leave the house."

"Oh." I headed toward the kitchen and paused. I debated for a moment before asking, "Do you have a phone? I'd like to call my parents. They're still in Des Moines."

A flash of sympathy flashed on his face, and he pulled out a cell phone and set it on the side table. "I tried to make a call earlier but couldn't get through. Phone lines are probably still choked." The look on my face must've bothered him, because he added on, "But go ahead and give it a shot."

"Thanks."

He left without another word, and I went about cleaning up. After filling the five-gallon jugs, I sat on the couch and watched the cell phone still resting on the side table. I'd been putting off the call, afraid of having my worst fears confirmed. After cracking my knuckles, I grabbed the phone and punched in my parents' number.

Call Failed.

Next, I tried to send a text message.

Message failed.

"Damn it," I muttered, tossing the phone on the cushion next to me and leaning back, covering my eyes.

"No luck?"

I jumped at Clutch's voice. "Service is still swamped. I'll try again in the morning."

He turned away.

"Need help with anything else?" I scanned the room, and my eyes fell on the windows. "I could help you board up the windows."

He followed my gaze. "I'll get to those tomorrow. I'm far enough out of town that as long as we keep dark and quiet, we should be okay for tonight. From what I've seen, zeds operate with minimal physical acuity. It won't take much to defend this place against a few who find their way near the house."

"I can help in the morning," I offered hopefully. "Many hands make light work, you know."

He watched me. "Get some sleep, Cash. You'll need your strength for tomorrow."

He turned and headed up the stairs. He didn't say I was staying. But he also didn't say I was leaving, and I clung onto that tiny splinter of hope.

"Why do you call me Cash?" I asked as I followed him upstairs.

"You were dressed like Johnny Cash when you jumped onto my truck."

"Oh." I thought for a moment "I guess I do wear black a lot." I glanced down at the oversized T-shirt and long johns. "But not always."

Clutch showed me to the guest bedroom containing only an old dresser and a full-sized bed. No pictures hung on the wall. The bedding was flannel and, though dated, looked enticingly comfortable.

I pulled back the comforter and found myself shoved onto my stomach. Clutch's weight bore down on me from behind. My face pressed against the mattress. I tried to fend him off, but he managed to pull my arms behind my back, and I heard the zip of a plastic cord as it tightened around my wrists.

"Asshole!" I yelled out, kicking, while he all too easily did the same to my ankles.

"You keep going on like that, Cash," he murmured from behind me. "We're going to have zeds from a twenty-mile radius upon us."

I quieted, kicking at him as he backed away. No matter what he had planned, I refused to go down without a fight. "*Asshole,*" I muttered.

Clutch pulled the comforter out from under me. I tried to roll off the bed, but he pulled me back and then, surprisingly, covered me with the blankets. He positioned the pillow under my head.

Frowning I looked up at him. "What are you doing?" My voice cracked.

"I don't want to wake up to find a zed loose in my house," he said before walking to the door, where he paused. "If you don't turn, I won't have to kill you in the morning."

Then he turned out the light and left me alone in the dark.

CHAPTER IV

I bolted awake at the sound of a thunderous gunshot. My wrists and ankles were free, the plastic ties lying in broken pieces beside me. I jumped to my feet, and every muscle in my body protested. With a wince, I made my way to the window. The sun had not yet peeked above the trees bordering the backyard, but in the glimmer of morning light I caught sight of Clutch dragging a body and disappearing around the side of a smaller shed.

A zed? Someone else?

I scanned for more signs but found nothing. The yard stood empty except for a large vegetable garden that had been tilled for spring planting and three, twenty-foot cylinders of propane sitting side-by-side. Beyond the yard stood acres and acres of woodland, making it impossible to see if there were more intruders out there.

The birds had started singing their morning songs again, which meant my hearing hadn't been permanently damaged by the shotgun blast yesterday. The birds chirped like the world was peaceful, but they lied. The world was deadly and vicious. And, instead of getting ready for work, I was about to head out and fight for my life.

I rubbed the pink scrapes that marred my wrists where I'd wriggled to pull free last night, but the plastic hadn't stretched. I wanted to crawl back into bed and pretend that it was Wednesday—not Friday—the day before the world I knew ended. But, I needed an early start if I was going to find a safe place before dark. After a quick stop at the bathroom, I headed downstairs to find Clutch sitting in his recliner, decked out in camos, eating eggs, and watching the news.

"Breakfast is in the kitchen," he said without taking his eyes off the TV.

I wanted to strangle him for what he'd done to me last night. But while I'd lain in bed, working at my restraints, I'd realized he was protecting himself. To be honest, I would have done the same if I'd been in his place had I thought of it. This whole time I'd been thinking of how bad *I* had it, never once thinking of how bad he had it. Clutch had allowed two strangers—one infected—into his truck and brought one of those strangers into his home. Before I'd fallen asleep, I'd made the vow to myself to let go any remaining anger.

I'd enough to deal with the way it was.

I stepped into the kitchen to find fried eggs, bacon, and toast already on a plate. After having a huge steak dinner, I was surprised that my stomach was already growling. Then again, running for your life burns a lot more calories than punching keys on a computer.

I took my seat on the couch and dug in while watching some national news channel. The reporter looked ragged, like he hadn't slept or been home since yesterday. A map of the United States was behind him with red Xs over every major city. The map then expanded to the world, showing parts of Europe and much of Asia in red.

"The infected are considered dead by all medical definitions, but yet they continue to move…and feed," the reporter said. *"For lack of a better term, they are undead. Their bodily functions, such as heart rate and blood pressure are nonexistent. Their blood has congealed and they will not bleed out, which the CDC believes accounts for their stiff gaits.*

If you must come into contact with the infected, use extreme caution. Destroying the brain stem is the only known method of killing an infected. Due to lack of blood flow, the brain seems to be their only critical organ. A bullet directly through any other normally vital organ, such as the heart, has proven ineffective. However, they can be incapacitated by decapitation or removal of limbs, but they will continue to pose some risk even incapacitated.

The high fever that sets in before the virus takes over seems to destroy most brain activity, which means they can be outsmarted if you do not panic. The infected are violent and hungry and do not seem to require rest. The CDC believes that their insatiable hunger is caused by the superbug altering the hypothalamus in a way to promote transmission of the virus. While a bite is the fastest way to transmit the virus, any direct contact with infected saliva or blood may lead to infection. Even a small open wound, such as a scratch or blister, carries risk of infection. The CDC does not believe the infection can be transmitted by mosquitoes or through contact with animals bitten by the infected, but that doesn't rule out the possibility of infection through those means.

We have reason to believe the virus originated from a new biologically engineered pesticide where the cells were coated with silica. When the pesticide was combined with a specific cleaning agent, the cells were shown to mutate.

There is no cure. Infection rate is believed to be at or near one hundred percent. Once infected, the virus will take control of your body, and you will either die or turn violent. This was all the information we received before we lost contact with the CDC."

Clutch tossed me his cell phone. "Phone service seems to be unclogged," he said while the reporter started reading off a paper he'd just been handed.

I stared at the phone's screen and already knew why the phone lines were no longer clogged. There weren't enough people left to make calls. No one left to go to work or school. Ah, but the schools would be closed today, anyway. "Today's Good Friday."

"So?"

I shrugged. "No reason, I guess." I swallowed and

redialed the number I called nearly every day of my adult life. I tried not to think about how my parents could've been calling my phone over and over and not getting an answer. And if they hadn't been trying to call…I tried not to think about that at all.

After the fourth ring, the call went to voicemail. My heart panged.

Hi. You've reached the Ryans. We can't come to the phone right now, but if you leave a message, we'll return your call as soon as possible.

I took a deep breath and tried to sound cheerful. "Hey, Mom and Dad. I hope you're okay. I wanted to let you know that I'm out of town and safe. And I'll see you soon." I went to hang up, then added, "I love you."

I also sent a text message to them before I opened my email though the phone's web browser. Nothing but the usual spam. I sent off a quick email, filling my parents in on where I was and assuring them I was safe. I left out the parts about Melanie and Alan and sleeping tied up the night before.

With that done, I handed the phone back to Clutch. "Thanks."

He gave me an almost gentle look before he reached behind him and plugged the phone back into its charger.

I thought back to the gunshot this morning. "Any zeds pass through the area yet?"

He paused. "Just one."

Something in the way he spoke made me look up.

"You knew him, didn't you?"

After a moment, he gave a tight nod.

"Sorry," I said, not knowing what else to say.

After that, the news reporter's voice was the only sound as I finished my breakfast. The military had set up roadblocks and bombed bridges, but I suspected Clutch was right. They were facing a losing battle at containing the zeds.

The reporter ran through a list of every major city considered no longer viable, which was government-speak for saying the military had pulled out and the city had been overrun by zeds. He could've saved ten minutes by saying nowhere was safe, because there didn't seem a city left unaffected in the States. Contact had even been lost with Hawaii and was spotty with Europe and Asia. The northern parts of Canada and Alaska seemed to be the only places still keeping ahead of the outbreak, and I imagined masses of survivors were heading north already.

Clutch got to his feet, and I moved into action, taking his plate and heading into the kitchen to clean up. He disappeared down the hall, reemerging once I'd finished, with knives and guns strapped to his chest, waist, and thighs. Yesterday, I would've been terrified. Today, I felt protected. He may be dumping me off, but at least I'd be safe as long as I was still with him.

Which wouldn't be for much longer.

A sense of doom weighed me down as I laced up my stained Docs, tucking the long johns into the boots. I tied the oversized shirt at my waist so it wouldn't get in the way in case I had to run.

Coming to full height at over a half-foot above me, Clutch nodded, and I followed him silently out of the house and toward the big rig. Every step I took dripped dread onto my veins. When we reached the truck, he opened the passenger door and climbed up and inside. I waited under the sunshine, leaning against the tin building, while he spent the next several minutes examining the cab. Done, he hopped out and looked me up and down.

My muscles tensed, and I held my breath. Clutch would send me off on my own soon. While I wanted to make sure my parents were safe, I couldn't imagine how I'd possibly get to them without getting myself killed. I'd barely gotten out of town yesterday. To head back to the city after a day of those things infecting others…I shivered.

"We need to get you gloves if you're going to help hang boards over the windows. Those hands of yours will get all sliced up otherwise."

It took me a long moment before his words sank in, and my clenched jaw inched open. Without thinking, I squealed and hugged him. "Thank you!"

I let go about the time he pushed me away.

I held out my hands. "I won't let you down. I swear it."

"It's just for another two days," he said, holding up two fingers. "As I told you before, I don't have the supplies to take in an orphan. Then you'll be on your own. Got it?"

I nodded, hoping, praying that I'd be able to convince him otherwise within two days. "Deal."

"Okay, Cash," he drawled. "Let's get this place secure."

Three days later…

Clutch and I got along just fine. His clothes were huge on me, but it was nothing that an extra hole in one of his tactical belts couldn't fix. He liked things quiet. When he did talk, he barked out military jargon and acronyms I didn't know. I felt the nervous need to fill the silence. Even with a bad shoulder, he was a hell of a lot stronger than me. Without caffeine, headaches shortened my temper. When Clutch ran out of chewing tobacco two days ago, he got cranky.

But I never complained. Not once, even though more than once I had to walk away to cool down.

After all, Clutch was the only thing that stood between me and a world full of zeds.

"When the power goes out, we can't count on the generator. It's damn fussy and works only some of the time, and when it works it's noisy as all hell," Clutch said while we worked on setting up an early warning system around the perimeter. "As soon as we use up the perishables in the freezer, we're going to have to ration."

I strung another tin can on the wire. "I'll start inventorying food and supplies tonight, and I can start planting in the garden in a couple weeks. My mom and I had just picked up supplies for expanding her herb garden last weekend."

I swallowed a lump, remembering that had been the last time I'd been with my mother. Focusing on surviving kept me busy enough to not dwell on Mom and Dad, but I still thought about them. Often.

"We'll have to make a run into town for seeds."

"Oh. Okay." Until the outbreak, I'd never realized how dependent I'd been on stores for everything. While we could set up the farm for long-term survival, there were some bare essentials, such as seeds, that we needed from town to get us started. Once we had a garden, we could prep our own seeds for next year, though I had a lot to learn.

Not that I could even think of everything I'd yet to learn without stressing. Surviving each day was enough of a struggle. "How about all those bags of seed in your shed? Can we use those?"

"The seed corn and soybeans?"

"Yeah."

"We can, but we won't want to depend on them. Seed corn is bland. It doesn't taste anything like sweet corn, but it would provide some basic nutrition at least.

Soybeans are a solid option. But no matter what we plant, we're going to have to go old school and plant by hand. The tractors and combine make too much noise."

I nodded in acceptance. Funny thing, before all this, I'd always been the leader with both coworkers and with friends. Now, I found that I could follow just as easily. Strange how quickly people can change.

Clutch's life before the outbreak had been completely different from mine. He knew his stuff. He'd served two tours in Afghanistan and became a doomsday prepper when the economy turned to shit a few years back. I had complete trust in him, even though I'd known him for only a few days. To be honest, I trusted him more than I had anyone in my life, maybe even more than my parents.

I still couldn't reach them, though I continued to send them an email every day. The email became my journal, proof that I still existed. I'd never gotten a reply, so I could only hope that they were hunkered down somewhere safe without access to the Internet. I knew it was a weak hope, but I held onto it nonetheless.

The last news channel had gone offline yesterday, leaving nothing on the TV. We'd scanned radio stations every few hours. Nothing was left on FM, and only random updates were sent through AM, and most of those came from folks holed up like us. No one reported anything on Des Moines, and I had to assume that whatever was left of the military had pulled out. Each night, I prayed for my parents' safety, even though in the pit of my stomach I suspected I'd never see them again.

"That should cover everything for now." Clutch came to his feet after tying the last wire. "I'm heading out."

Taken aback, I stood. "What for?"

"The chaos should have settled down enough by now. I need to scout the area to see what we're up against. And I need to start stocking up our supplies before looters clear out the town."

"I'll go with you," I said right away.

"No."

"I can stay in the truck and watch for zeds. It can't hurt to have an extra pair of eyes."

His lips thinned before he released a drawn-out sigh. "Let's get you some gear."

Feeling a surge of anxious excitement, I headed back to the house with Clutch.

"Come on," he said, and I followed him into the room he'd disappeared to every day. A metal desk sat in the center and a bookcase filled with books, magazines, and boxes covered much of one wall in the small room.

It looked like Clutch had an extensive library of manuals covering the spectrum from survival and first aid to gardening and canning. There was an entire section on organic farming. "Nice library," I said.

"I like to be prepared." He pulled out a book and then twisted on something. A loud click sounded, and he pulled the *entire* bookcase out. Behind it was an even smaller room, lined with metal cabinets and a rack of least a dozen guns, knives, and other weapons.

My jaw dropped. "Holy shit, Clutch. You've got a hidden room."

"Gramps had this room put in way back during the Depression. He'd always said a person needed to be prepared for the worst." He motioned me to come closer. "Give me your belt."

I pulled it off, and held up my pants—an old pair of Clutch's cargos—while he slid a sheath and holster onto the canvas strap.

He handed it back to me. I was still fastening the belt when he held out a knife. "This tanto is yours to keep. It's a good blade, so take care of it. This should be your go-to weapon in close quarters, especially in dealing with zeds."

I slid it into a black plastic sheath, which he then snapped shut.

"Have you ever fired a gun?"

"Sure. I had a BB gun when I was a kid."

He gave me the same exasperated look I'd seen many times over the past few days. "I'll take that as a 'no'." He held up a gun and stepped through the basics of loading the cartridge and firing it. He dumped bullets into my left hand and handed me the pistol in the other.

I looked at the gun in my hand, the gun rack, then at the gun in his holster. "Why's mine so much smaller than yours?"

"That's because mine's a Glock and yours is a .22.

Yours is a great starter pistol because it doesn't have much recoil. Show me you can use it well, and I'll let you try my 9mm."

Dropping the extra ammo into a cargo pocket, I repeated everything he'd shown me to make sure I understood.

"We can't afford to attract attention, so only go for your pistol as a last resort. And whatever you do, don't fire unless your target is less than eight feet away. Save your bullets. The .22 is a baby and will just piss them off from any distance greater than that."

"Thanks." I holstered the gun.

"Be careful. If you're bit, you'll turn. There are no second chances out there. Got it?"

"Yes."

"Good. Let's go."

He locked up, grabbed a small backpack of extra gear, and we headed to the shed where his black 4x4 super cab pickup truck waited. He topped off the gas tank at one of two large cylindrical fuel tanks set up behind the shed. We were strapped in and heading down the lane in no time.

Clutch drove slowly down the gravel road, turning left, then left again. He continued until he'd made a full square loop around the house. The next time, he went one road farther out, and repeated the process. He slowed down near each of the three farmhouses we passed but never stopped. I saw no signs of zeds, but I also saw no people. Cattle still grazed in the fields.

Everything looked deceptively normal, completely different than how busy Des Moines had been a few days earlier.

"We'll check each one out later," he said, moving on. We continued the scouting mission, me watching for zeds and Clutch watching for I-don't-know-what until we pulled onto a paved road, and he came to stop.

"What if there are people still living there?" I asked.

"Then we leave them be. I'm not taking in any more strays."

I had thought about that, too. And, though I knew it was selfish, I didn't want to have another mouth to feed. We had a good thing going, and another person would only throw a wrench into that dynamic. I also felt guilty thinking that way, knowing we were equipped to help others. "At least we'll know who's in the area. We only clear out the places that have been abandoned. Mark the others as off-limits." I thought for a moment. "What now?"

He turned right. "Let's check out town."

I swallowed. It had been over three days, but it felt like an hour ago now that we were back on the road. "Are you sure it's not too dangerous?"

"We have to know what we're dealing with. Today will be a quick recon. Just to the edge of town. I need to hit two stores before they're looted…if we're not too late already."

We drove for several miles without seeing a single car or zed. Only one house, with its windows boarded, showed signs of survivors. As Clutch didn't know them, he quickly laid down the law that we'd avoid that particular farm for now.

My anxiety climbed when we passed a sign that read: *Fox Hills, 3 miles.*

I focused on breathing normally while scanning for zeds.

He stopped the truck at a roadblock. Cars and debris were piled across the road.

"Who do you think did that?" I asked.

"National Guard," he replied. "I heard it on the CB during the outbreak. When they saw that zeds prefer to stick to flat surfaces, they blocked all the roads to contain the spread as much as they could."

Clutch pulled the truck into the steep ditch, and I held on, waiting for the truck to tip over. It sure felt close, but once past the roadblock, he climbed back onto the road, nearly getting stuck in the mud at the bottom.

Just on the other side of the roadblock was a sign indicating that we'd just entered Fox Hills' city limits. It wasn't a huge town. According to the sign, 5,613 souls lived here. But the idea of 5,613 zeds lumbering around was downright petrifying.

We came to the Wal-Mart first, a new monolith standing alone on the outskirts of town. A couple dozen cars sat in the parking lot like the store was still open, and I wondered where the drivers to those cars were. "I need some things if we're stopping."

His brows furrowed. "What do you need?"

"Some clothes that fit would be good. A sports bra." The lacey bra I'd been wearing was pretty but worthless for the work I'd been doing the last few days. "And…" I bit my lip. "I'm going to need some, uh, feminine products within a couple weeks."

"I'll see what we can find," he said, wrinkling his nose. "You definitely need gear. My clothes are too loose on you. Too easy for a zed to grab. Same with your hair."

"My hair?" I twirled a handful of the long, silky strands.

"A zed could grab it and pull you down."

"Oh," I said quietly, and disappointment flared. "I suppose I could cut it."

I heard another engine and jerked my head to find the source. A red SUV came tearing around the corner of the Wal-Mart, and one of the cardboard boxes stacked on top tumbled off. As it approached and slowed, I gripped the arm rest. Inside, I could see three occupants. A male driver, a woman in the passenger seat, and a teenage boy leaning forward between the two front seats. Clutch stopped, and they pulled up alongside. The man was favoring his bloody arm, while the woman, who I assumed to be his wife, cried in the seat next to him. She was pale and bleeding profusely from her cheek and neck. *Bitten.*

"They're neighbors," Clutch said before rolling down the window. "Good people. They live a few miles west of me."

The man leaned against his steering wheel as he rolled down his window.

"Frank," Clutch said with a slight tilt of his head.

"Clutch," the man replied, and I cocked my head. Everyone called him Clutch?

Clutch nodded toward the Wal-Mart. "How's the pickings?"

"I bet there's plenty in there," Frank said. "But we just grabbed what we could off the back of a truck behind the building. There are zeds everywhere. Even in the unloading area."

Clutch nodded. "You bit?"

The other man grimaced, and then looked at his wife and son. "Afraid so. We both are. We needed food and underestimated the bastards. They just never *stop*."

My jaw tightened. Clutch and I were about to do the same thing, maybe even to the same store, and I wondered how many zeds were where we were headed.

"Sorry to hear that," Clutch said before nodding toward the backseat. "And your boy?"

"Jasen's too fast," the man replied with a proud smile in his son's direction. "The zeds can't get close to him."

I looked from the teenager to his parents and back again. Wet streaks lined his cheeks, and his eyes were red. Oh, the poor kid knew exactly what was in store for his parents.

"He's not safe with you, you know," Clutch said in a low voice.

Frank lowered his head. "I know." He gave a long

look at his wife. "We're just going to get these supplies home for Jasen before..."

Silence filled the air.

Frank's wife leaned forward. "Please, Clutch," she said, sobbing and oblivious to her injury. "Please look after our son. He's just a boy."

"I'm not a boy, Mom," the teenager replied. "I can take care of myself. I'll be all right."

Clutch didn't speak for the longest time. When he did, his words sounded like they were weighted down. "Jase, how about you come on over and climb in my truck."

Jase's mother gasped. "Oh, thank you! Jasen's a good boy. He's strong and smart and you won't be sorry. God bless you, Clutch."

Frank's face instantly lifted. "You're a good man. I wish I could—"

"Don't worry about it," Clutch interrupted.

"I'm not leaving you guys," Jasen broke in from the backseat.

"Jasen," his father said, sounding exhausted. "You've got to go."

"Not until you get sick. The guy on the radio said that he heard that not everyone got sick," he replied.

"That's just a rumor, Jase," his father said.

"Besides, Betsy's still at home," Jasen said. "I'm not leaving her locked in the house to starve to death."

"Betsy?" I asked.

"The dog," Frank replied with a sigh.

"Your parents are going to get sick, Jase," Clutch replied. "Soon."

"I know," he replied, the words barely above a whisper. "I can't abandon them now. They need me."

"Go with Clutch, Jasen," his mother pleaded to her son. "You'll be safe."

"I'm not leaving you like this, Mom."

Clutch sighed. "We're burning daylight. The offer stands, Jase. You know where I live. Come on by anytime. I'll be home in a few hours. Just be careful to not attract any attention."

Jasen nodded before sinking back into the shadowed seat.

"No, Jasen," his mother said. "You go with Clutch."

Clutch rolled up the window and pulled away, and we could hear Jasen's mother piteous cries for us to stop.

"He's going to die, staying with them like that," I said.

"Probably," Clutch replied. "But it's his choice. If he left with us, that regret of abandoning his parents would fester and eat him up inside. If he makes it through the day, maybe we'll see him again."

"Maybe," I mused, wondering what it would be like to have to take in a kid. Clutch already complained about the amount of food I ate. A teenage boy could easily eat twice my share. If Clutch suspected there wasn't enough to go around, would someone have to leave? The thought sat like a rock in my stomach, because I suspected if Clutch had to choose, he'd choose the son of a friend over an unskilled girl he didn't even know four days ago.

"So everyone calls you Clutch?" I asked, forcing myself to change the subject. "I thought that was just your CB handle."

"It came from a tractor incident back in grade school," he replied.

My brows rose. "What happened?"

"Don't ask."

I smacked the leather and smirked. "You're killing me here."

"Well," he drawled out. "When I was just learning how to drive the tractor, I hit the gas instead of the brakes, and drove *into* my dad's shed."

I burst out laughing. "I bet your dad wasn't happy."

"No. No, he wasn't."

I caught a movement that had been nearly hidden by a minivan, and I sobered. "Look," I said, pointing at the blonde woman coming around the minivan.

Dark stains marred the front of her shirt and her mouth. Her arms, what was left of them, swung limply with each step. Then I saw the boy hobbling behind her, dragging his left leg. He couldn't have been more than three or four. He was also covered in blood. He followed her like she was his mother, though according to the news, zeds retained minimal cognitive functions, let alone memories.

I shivered at the thought of a kid getting attacked.

What kind of monster would go for a kid?

"You can't think of them as people anymore," Clutch said, and I found him watching me. "That kid would kill you the first chance he got. Any of them out there would. They're the enemy. Out here, you either have to kill them or be killed."

"I know," I said as Clutch drove past a row of new houses. A garbage can sat at the end of each driveway waiting for a pickup that would never come, a stark reminder that civilization had just *stopped*. "But knowing it is easier than seeing it."

"You'd better come to terms with it quick because we're stopping up here."

I looked out the window to see Clutch pull up to a row of old brick buildings. He stopped in front of a pharmacy, wedged between a barber shop and a clothing store. The sign overhead read Gedden's Drug. The store was small and easy to miss. The glass window next to the door was intact. Through it, I could see decently lit aisles, and everything looked quiet and nothing appeared out of place. A Closed sign hung on the glass door, and I hoped they'd locked up before any zeds got inside.

"No telling how many are wandering around outside so we'll have to be careful," Clutch said, and I followed his gaze to the end of the block, where another zed limped across the street. Tires squealed, and a truck lurched around the corner, barreling right over the zed. Someone let out a whoop, and the truck tore past us.

Clutch gripped his gun. Neither of us moved until they'd turned another corner.

"Trouble?" I asked.

"Don't know." He drove us around the store and down an alley alongside the building to the lower-level back entrance off the street. It only had one door, and it was closed. The small parking lot backed up to the river.

I grimaced. Two cars sat in spaces marked Employee Parking. At least the door to the pharmacy was still intact. "Looks like we may have a couple helpful smiles in the aisles," I said, nodding toward the cars. "At least it doesn't look like anyone else has been here yet."

"Looters think short-term. The idiots will go for things like cash, booze, and electronics. The smarter ones will go for food, drugs, and ammo first. I'm surprised no addicts have hit this store yet for pain killers, so we need to treat this run as our only shot. The more drugs we can load up on now could save our lives when winter hits."

That's what I respected about Clutch. He was always thinking ahead. Not just a day ahead, but months and years ahead. Being a prepper, he already had a full year's supply of food tucked away in his basement. Well, six to eight month's supply now that he had me hanging around. The basement was lined with shelves, and every shelf was filled with food, water, and supplies.

His need to be prepared started with something he'd seen in the military, but I was thankful for his worst-case-scenario mindset now. "So what's the plan?"

"I go in and check it out. You keep watch out here. Keep the doors locked and stay low. If that truck comes around again, lay on the horn, and we'll cut our losses. If everything's good, when I give you the all-clear, follow me in. Once inside, get to the pharmacy and load up on every antibiotic and any other drug you can find for sickness and injuries. When in doubt, throw it in the cart. What we can't use ourselves, we can barter with. We won't be coming back. I'll hit the aisles for painkillers, Imodium, and other supplies. If anything happens, you run straight to the truck and lock yourself inside. I got a key and can unlock it from the outside. Got it?"

I nodded, though the entire time my mind was locked on the potential for caffeine. Clutch had to be the only trucker in the world who didn't drink coffee. My life had done a one-eighty, and while I'd fallen into a new routine more easily than I'd expected, my brain hadn't. It still craved its daily fix, and reminded me with a headache every morning.

Clutch checked the door, and it didn't open. With the butt of his rifle, he broke the glass, unlocked the door, and disappeared inside.

Silence put every single one of my nerves on edge. I scanned the open lot, watched the door, and then repeated the process. After a couple minutes, my leg started to shake with nervous adrenaline. No zeds showed up in the alley or from another building. After five minutes, I was convinced we'd arrived without being noticed. After five and half minutes, I opened the door and stepped onto the pavement.

Come on, Clutch. Where are you?

I had taken four steps closer to the building, still looking out for zeds or looters, when the back door opened, and Clutch held up his hand. *All-clear.*

I closed the distance in a heartbeat. "Any problems?"

"Nothing I couldn't handle."

I followed him into the building and up the stairs. He hopped over a bundle, and I stopped cold. A body wearing a white lab coat lay crumpled on the steps. The dark gore around its head looked fresh. Even though it had only been days since the zeds came out, I was surprised how quickly I was becoming desensitized to the sight of dead bodies.

I glanced up at Clutch. "Your doing?"

He looked over his shoulder and shot me a quick nod before continuing on. With my teeth clenched tight, I took a cautious step over the body, part of me afraid that it would twist around and bite me in the ankle, just like Alan had been. As soon as I cleared the body, I rushed up the remaining steps to meet up with Clutch at the top.

"I took out two zeds, so the place should be cleared, but be careful. They're slow, which makes them quiet." He motioned to the left. "Pharmacy's that way."

I nodded and watched Clutch head off in the opposite direction. I nervously edged toward the counter with PHARMACY written in all caps above it. Clutch was counting on me. This was my first chance to show him I could help him in the field. When I approached the pharmacy, another fear hit me as I stared at the rows and rows of drugs. How the hell would I know what to take?

I grabbed two red shopping baskets and jumped over the counter. Nearest to the counter, I recognized a few of the names, such as *Prednisone* and *Amoxicillin,* so I assumed that this was where the most common stuff was kept and used my arm to slide everything into the cart. From there, everything looked to be arranged alphabetically, so I just grabbed anything that sounded or looked remotely useful, leaving little behind for the next looters.

When two baskets were overfilled, I climbed back over the counter to track down Clutch. I heard him rustle off to my side. I smiled, turned, and lifted my baskets. "Look what—"

A zed tumbled from the top shelf of the aisle and landed in a heap in front of me. It clumsily climbed to its feet. It still wore a smock with the name LAURA on a pin. A chunk was missing from its neck, but it looked otherwise uninjured. Except for the jaundice and hungry stare fixed on me.

"Clutch!" I dropped the baskets. The zed staggered toward me, and I reached for the knife, but it didn't budge. I realized it was still snapped into its sheath, and I fidgeted with getting the tanto free. The zed was almost upon me. I instinctively shoved it back. Its mouth snapped at me. I finally pulled the blade free. The tip of another blade suddenly protruded from its mouth, and I stumbled back.

The blade disappeared. The zed collapsed, revealing the man behind it glaring at me.

"You bit?" Clutch asked.

I shook my head.

He picked up at least a dozen shopping bags, sliding them up his arms and shoulders, watching me. "Let's go."

Still holding onto the knife, I grabbed the baskets and hustled around the zed.

Clutch moved fast. He was back to the stairs and down the steps by the time I reached him. I'd expected him to head straight to the truck and half expected him to leave me behind. But he stood at the door, waiting for me.

Outside, he checked around and under the truck. He didn't speak, just opened my door and then climbed in on his side. I dropped the baskets in the backseat and was in the front seat by the time he revved the engine. He tore out of the parking lot and turned in the direction of the farm.

The tension was palpable in the cab.

"She dropped down from the top shelf. She must've hidden up there to get away when she was attacked, and stayed until I walked by—"

The steering wheel creaked under Clutch's grip. I

didn't speak another word the rest of the way back to the farm. Unease roiled through me as he pulled up to the house and slammed on the brakes. I grabbed the baskets, tossing in bottles and boxes that had spilled out on the rough ride back. Once outside, I closed the door and stood for a moment. When I turned and looked at Clutch, he was looking straight ahead, both hands on the wheel.

I knocked on the window.

He moved, and the window rolled down.

"I messed up," I said. "You told me to be careful and I wasn't. You told me to run, and I didn't. I should've been ready."

"No, Cash," Clutch graveled out. "I was the one who messed up. I knew you weren't ready, but I let you come along. You're not ready, and you'll never be ready."

And then he drove off, leaving me standing under quiet, gray clouds.

LUST

THE SECOND CIRCLE OF HELL

CHAPTER V

Clutch didn't return to the farm.

I paced the yard for over an hour, checking traps and alarms, waiting for him. At first, I'd been afraid that he'd send me packing and I'd be on my own. But then my fear morphed into something much more useful.

Anger.

I wasn't mad at Clutch.

He'd been right all along.

I was mad at myself for not being stronger, for not being prepared. Even if he let me stay, I had to be able to depend on myself to get out of trouble, and right now I couldn't.

I headed straight back to the house, grabbed the kitchen shears, and walked upstairs. I put the garbage can in the bathroom sink. I stared in the mirror for a long second. Then I sucked in a deep breath, lifted the shears, and chopped off a twenty-four-inch chunk of hair.

Then, I cut a second chunk.

I cut until there was nothing left to cut.

It had taken me years to grow my hair to the length it'd been. I'd always considered it my best feature. Yet, now, without all that hair, my head felt light and free. *Empowering*. After running a hand through the dark stubble, I nodded to myself and headed back outside.

I marched to the smallest tin shed for supplies before picking out a solid tree in the middle of the open backyard and sprayed the outline of a zed on its trunk. Then I hammered the sandbag I'd stuffed with rags about where a head would go.

I took out my knife and put everything I had in my swing, completely missing the bag and impaling the tree instead.

"Damn it," I muttered, examining the tanto blade to make sure I hadn't damaged it. Taking a deep breath, I focused on the bag and swung very slowly, this time hitting the bag nearly dead center.

I'd never had any kind of training with weapons except for pepper spray, so it was improv based on what I'd seen on TV and what I knew about zeds. Slashing would be a waste of energy since to kill a zed its brain had to be destroyed. I knew better than to throw the knife because, if I threw my knife, I'd no longer have it to take down the next zed lurking around the corner. I had neither the strength nor the weapon to decapitate. And so I focused on stabbing.

I spent the next five hours trying to figure out how to kill a zed using nothing but my knife. I grunted as I thrust and stabbed at the bag, the entire time Clutch's words *you're not ready* echoed in my ears. But he was wrong about one thing.

"I *will* be ready." I said out loud before every strike.

The poor tree suffered. I missed the bag as often as I hit it. I almost sliced myself wide open once. After that, I became more conscious of every movement. With short breaks to rehydrate, another two hours of stabbing, with sweat drenching my skin, I finally discovered my rhythm. Stabbing became a semi-natural extension of my body, though I knew I'd be foolish to assume I was an expert yet. The tree didn't move or bite.

Zeds were a different story.

An engine rumbled in the distance. I sheathed my blade, grabbed the canteen, and took a long drink of water before setting off toward the house to meet Clutch at the driveway. As the engine noise grew louder, I slowed. Whatever was coming down the drive wasn't nearly as hearty sounding as Clutch's throaty truck.

Setting down the canteen, I pulled out my pistol and moved cautiously toward the drive. A familiar red SUV emerged from the tree line. Several boxes were still on top, and it looked like the back was piled full of clothes and bags. The SUV stopped abruptly in front of the house, and two boxes tumbled onto the ground. I warily holstered the .22 when I saw the driver.

He didn't look so good.

Frank's teenage son sat, shoulders slumped, with both hands gripping the wheel. The kid stared at the house. He was covered in blood, though most of it was crimson, not thick and brown like that of zeds. The painful realization hit me that, with Clutch gone, the responsibility fell on me to prevent the kid from turning.

I waited. After a moment, he wiped his eyes and then opened the door and stepped out. He was a tall kid for his age, about the same height as Clutch. But, where Clutch was filled out with muscle, Frank's lanky son was still very much a boy.

"You're Jase, right?" I asked. "Call me…." I'd first thought to give him my real name but realized that Mia Ryan no longer existed. Who I'd been died four days ago during the outbreak. "Call me Cash."

He held out his bloodied hand, noticed it, and pulled it back. He simply nodded instead. "Where's Clutch?" he asked.

"He'll be back later." I took in a deep breath before speaking my next words. "I hate to ask this, but I have to." I paused. "Are you bit?"

He looked down and shook his head. "No," he croaked, and he cleared his throat. "I'm not bit."

"That's a lot of blood for not being bit," I countered.

He shook his head harder this time. "It's Betsy's." His voice cracked again, and he glanced back in the truck, running a filthy hand through already mussed sandy blond hair.

The poor kid looked like he was about to break. I wanted to make Jase take off his shirt to prove he hadn't been bitten, but instead I kept one hand near my pistol and put the other hand on his shoulder. "Well, let's get you cleaned up then."

He wiped his nose and then nodded, taking a few steps with me toward the house. Then he stopped and pulled away. "Wait. I can't leave Betsy…"

Frowning, I watched as he went around to the other side of the SUV. He returned, carrying what looked to be a small collie. Much of the fur on her back was matted with blood, and her eyes were glazed over. Whenever Jase moved, she whimpered.

I grimaced. Betsy looked in bad shape. With the amount of blood on her fur and covering Jase's shirt, I doubted even a vet could help.

When we reached the house, I didn't open the door. "Listen, Jase. You know how contagious zed blood is. You and Betsy can come into the mudroom, but you can't come inside, not until you're both cleaned up and in the clear. Got it?"

Jase nodded and sniffled again.

"All right." I opened the door and he stepped inside, cradling the dog to his chest.

Inside the mudroom, I rummaged through the cabinets until I found where Clutch kept his rags and cleaning towels. I grabbed the thickest one in the pile and made a nest on the floor. Jase carefully set Betsy down on the towel, but she still yelped at the movement, her back legs kicking out. He collapsed next to her, keeping a hand on her, and making small cooing sounds.

I left them, locking the door behind me. It took some time, but I found a disposable plastic bowl that would work. I returned to Jase a few minutes later to find him petting Betsy. The motions seemed as soothing to him as it was for the dog. I set down the plastic bowl full of water near Betsy, but I doubted she'd drink. Her eyes had closed, her breathing labored.

I put a glass of water on a shelf near Jase before taking a seat across from them. The news had said that dogs didn't turn, that bites were simply fatal, but I kept a close watch on both the collie and the teen, anyway. I'd left the .22 in its holster but had it ready.

"Mom turned first," Jase said softly. "Dad told me to leave the room, but I stayed and watched. He shot her. Right in the head. He had to shoot her twice before she quit moving. God, the blood…" He sucked in a breath. "Then Dad, he turned the rifle on himself, but he just couldn't do it." He rested his head on the wall behind him. "We're Catholic, ya know. He couldn't do it. He shot Mom because it wasn't murder since zeds don't have souls. But he had to be able to get back to Mom."

I stayed silent. I didn't voice my thought that Frank had been selfish. No boy should be asked to kill his own father.

As Jase spoke, his voice became stronger. "So he

handed the rifle to me. He hated himself for it. I could tell. But I didn't mind. He was my dad, ya know? He raised me good." His voice cracked and it took him a couple breaths to continue. "It was my turn to take care of him. But, then he started to turn…and then I…"

He looked at me then. "I couldn't do it. When he looked at me, I thought that he was still in there, somewhere, but then he came at me. I stumbled back and tripped. Dad—no, he wasn't Dad anymore—when he *growled* at me, I knew he was gone."

Jase's gaze went to the collie, her breaths had become weak and shallow. "Betsy was yapping, and then she jumped at him. Can you imagine a twenty-three pound fur ball flying through the air?" He chuckled, and then put his head in his lap. "He picked her up, just like he did every day to let her kiss him. Except this time, he bit into her. God," he cried out. "He just kept biting and biting. Betsy was crying so loud. I raised the rifle and started shooting. I shot at him until the mag was empty, but he didn't even slow down. So I ran at him. I used the butt of the rifle to nail him in the head. I don't know how many times I hit him before he finally let her go."

Jase sighed. When he spoke again, the words were just a whisper. "At least Dad's with Mom now."

I found his lip trembling. "I'm sorry about your parents."

"It's my fault. If I'd shot him when I should have, Betsy wouldn't have been bitten. She'd be fine now. She jumped in to save me. *It's my fault.*"

"No," I scolded. "We all make our own choices. You waited because you loved him. Betsy attacked because she loved you. Don't drown out her bravery with your regret. Honor her by holding memories of her bravery."

He sniffled and scratched behind the dog's ears. "You're a good girl, aren't you, Betsy Baby."

The dog showed no reaction, and Jase leaned forward and hugged onto her.

My vision blurred, and I looked away, while the boy said good-bye to his dog.

After several minutes, when I was confident that Betsy wasn't coming back, I climbed to my feet and stepped outside to give the kid space. From inside, I could hear Jase sobbing.

I walked out to the small shed, grabbed a shovel, and picked out a patch of grass under a shade tree. It took me over forty minutes to dig a hole that would hold a twenty-three pound bundle.

By the time I returned, I was pleasantly surprised to discover a boy, not a zed. Jase's face was blotchy, but he'd stopped crying. His hand rested on Betsy. His eyes held a faraway look that I'd seen in Clutch's gaze every now and then. It was a look of someone who'd been to hell and didn't quite make it out.

Something tugged Jase back, because his eyes slowly focused on me. He opened his mouth to speak but closed it.

"I have a nice spot picked out back," I said, breaking the silence.

With thin lips, he carefully wrapped the collie into the towel and followed me. He clutched his precious package against him and kissed her before setting her down gently in the center of the hole. I intentionally moved slowly and dropped the first shovel of dirt carefully onto the bloodied towel. Jase clasped his hands together and his lips moved as he recited prayers.

"I didn't bury them," he said aloud. "Mom and Dad. I-I couldn't do it."

I paused. "I'll see that they get a proper burial."

He swallowed visibly, and then nodded.

I went back to shoveling. The hole filled in quickly, until a small mound of black soil was all that remained of Betsy. Leaning on the shovel, I looked at Jase. He was clearly exhausted. The poor kid should be at school, hanging with his friends, not burying his family. We had about an hour before the sunset. "I'm going to get started on dinner," I said. "Take all the time you need."

With that, I left Jase to mourn. If he hadn't turned yet, I figured the odds were low that he would. I returned the shovel to the shed, and headed back inside, locking the front door behind me, just to play it safe. Jase knocked just a few minutes later. I grabbed a garbage bag and went out to meet him. He'd already kicked off his tennis shoes. I held open the bag. "Anything with blood on it goes. Leave the shoes outside for tonight." Though I had my doubts, I added, "We'll see if we can scrub them clean tomorrow."

"I packed clothes. They're outside," he said in a daze.

"You can grab them in the morning," I said, still holding out the bag.

In went his T-shirt, then his jeans and socks, and I looked him over for bites. Other than some bruises and a few scratches, he looked unharmed. But the scratches worried me.

When he went to pull his boxers off, I stopped him. "If there's no blood on them, toss them into the washer in the mudroom on your way in. The shower is on the second floor. I'll grab some clothes for you, and set them outside the bathroom door for you."

"Thanks, Cash," he said and I moved to let him in.

"And be sure to scrub good and hard." After a moment, it hit me that I'd just echoed words Clutch had told me the first night.

While Jase showered, I set three steaks under the broiler, skipping the sides. I was simply too hungry and too tired to go to the effort. I jogged upstairs and stopped outside Clutch's bedroom door. I reached for the handle but paused. I'd never been in there, and it felt almost like I'd breach some unspoken rule by stepping inside.

Instead, I turned and headed into my room and grabbed a pair of long johns and a T-shirt from my pile. They'd fit Jase better than they fit me and would get him through the night. Dropping the clothes at the bathroom door, I hustled back downstairs and finished cooking the steaks.

I wrapped Clutch's steak in tinfoil and set it in the

refrigerator. Each of the remaining steaks went on a plate. Just like Clutch had done, I drizzled steak sauce over each steak and grabbed a bag of potato chips.

Jase came down the stairs. "I'm not very hungry tonight."

I dumped some chips on both plates, and handed him a plate. "Eat. You need to keep your energy up."

He followed me like a lost puppy into the living room, much like I'd felt four days earlier. I took an edge of the couch and motioned for Jase to sit. I wolfed my steak down while he pecked at his. After cleaning off my plate, I grabbed a beer. I'd almost grabbed two but changed my mind and poured a glass of water instead for Jase. After a quick stop in Clutch's office for something I'd need later, I scanned through the TV and radio stations but came across nothing but static.

Clutch had left his phone at home, and I sent an email to my parents. Even though I suspected no one was left to read them, I kept writing them. I needed to send the email as much as I hoped my parents read them. By the time I sent the email, Jase had finished his dinner. He looked out of place, and I wondered if I'd looked that insecure when Clutch took me in. "Let's get you to bed," I said, coming to my feet.

That it wasn't yet nine and Jase didn't object was a clear sign the kid was beat. He followed me up to my room. Instead of turning on the light, I said, "Now that the sun has set, don't use lights upstairs. We don't have the windows upstairs boarded, and the light is too easy to see from a distance."

"Okay," Jase said as he felt out the dark room.

Even though he didn't act sick, I knew what I needed to do. I pulled out the zip ties I'd picked up in the office. "Listen, Jase..."

He turned around, noticed the plastic. His eyes widened and he took a step back.

I sighed. "I wish I didn't have to do this, but it's a necessary precaution until we have this whole zed virus figured out. If you turn, and I'm asleep, well, you see what I'm saying. We both know you're bigger and probably stronger than me. If you fight, I won't be able to get these on you. So I'm asking you...please let me tie your ankles and wrists. It's only for tonight and it's just a minor discomfort. Come morning, if you're healthy, the ties will come off. Will you do that for me, Jase?"

After a moment, he nodded and then took small steps toward me. He gave me his back, and I strung the restraint around his wrists, careful to not make them too tight but making sure they would do the trick. I went to the bed and pulled back the blankets. Jase laid down in an almost robotic manner, and I pulled the strap around his ankles.

Stepping back, I tried to smile. "I know it's not comfortable, but it's only for one night. Try not to think about it."

"It's okay," he said, rolling to his side. "I get it."

I patted his back. "You're a good kid, Jase."

"I'm not a kid," he muttered.

Sadness pricked at my heart. "No, you're not." *Not after today.*

I locked his door, and headed downstairs. I cleaned the mudroom and headed back inside, leaving the SUV and everything inside for tomorrow. At eleven, after a hot shower, I locked the door, figuring I'd hear Clutch drive in. I curled up on the sofa and passed out within seconds.

I was dreaming of cans rattling when something niggled at my subconscious, a warning percolating to the surface.

Cans rattling…

I shot awake.

The sound of tin banging against tin continued. I jumped up from the sofa and grabbed my belt with the .22 and knife strapped on and was ready to go. That the cans still rattled was an ominous sign that a shitload of zeds was passing through.

Once I pinpointed the direction the sound was coming from, I opened the window. From the outside, the window was completely covered by wood two-by-sixes, except for small sniper holes covered by plywood sliders.

With a clear night sky and a full moon, the yard was brighter than the living room, and I sighed in relief. Only one adult zed. It was hard to make out any more details in the dark at this distance. Sure enough, the dumb bastard had snagged the tripwire and was now dragging a line of cans as it lumbered across the yard.

I don't know if zeds retained some hint of humanity and they sought out houses or if it was a predatory instinct. Whatever it was had the zed heading straight toward the house as it sniffed at the air. I scanned the yard for more, but saw no others.

I glanced at the .22 in my hand. My heart hammered a warning: *don't go out there.*

I headed into Clutch's gun room and used only a flashlight to not screw with my night vision. I shone the light over the guns, settling on a cluster of hunting-style rifles and shotguns that looked less complicated than the black military-style rifles. I grabbed the rifle in the middle that looked the most straightforward but also big enough to get the job done.

Holding the flashlight in my mouth, I checked the weapon, burning precious time since I really had no idea what I was doing. Once I verified that its magazine was loaded, I turned off the light and headed back to the window.

Careful to be silent, I slid the barrel through the sniper hole and took aim. The zed was less than a hundred feet away and lumbering through an open area, spotlighted by the moon.

I pulled the trigger.

Nothing. Not even a click.

Mentally cursing, I pulled the rifle back and looked at it. *Stupid safety.* I slid the black switch and aimed again. My first shot clipped the zed's neck and nearly knocked it down, but it kept coming. The recoil kicked my collarbone, sending white pain shooting through my shoulder. It took me a moment to fix my aim.

"Cash?" Jase called out from upstairs.

"Just a zed passing through," I said. "Go back to sleep, Jase."

I took a deep breath. The second shot took out the zed.

Silence filled the night.

My collarbone pulsed from the recoil.

I knelt against the window, watching, waiting for more zeds to show up at the sound of the shots.

After my knees hurt and my tired eyes could no longer focus, I closed the sniper hole, switched the safety back on, and collapsed on the sofa.

My grip on the rifle never relaxed as I faded off to sleep.

I awoke the next morning to find Clutch watching me. He was in his recliner, eating steak sandwiched between two biscuits. He was wearing the same clothes from yesterday, and he looked utterly exhausted.

"You cut your hair," he said, rubbing his shoulder.

I sat up and ruffled my hair, and found that it was sticking up *everywhere*. After a couple attempts at trying to tamp it down, I gave up. "Your warning system works," I said. "A zed snagged on it last night."

Clutch nodded like he'd already seen the corpse. "You okay?"

"Yeah." I reached for the rifle but realized it was gone. I glanced around, but it was nowhere in sight. I paused and remembered the most important thing. "Jase is staying with us now."

"I know," he replied with his mouth full. "I saw the SUV outside."

I came to my feet. "I should go check on him."

Clutch swallowed. "Already did. He's not sick, so I cut him loose, and he's out cold."

I let out a deep breath and closed my eyes. "Thank God."

"You did good."

I swallowed and faced Clutch. "About yesterday, I'm sorry. I—"

"Do we have any eggs left?" he cut in, coming to his feet. He stretched his back, and his joints cracked and popped.

I frowned. "Yeah, I think so. Why?"

"I'm hungry. If you wouldn't mind cooking up a couple for me, that'd be great."

I thought about pressing Clutch to talk more, but then I simply replied with a "sure" and headed for the kitchen to fry up several of our last dozen eggs. I stood there, thinking about Clutch. He was the sort to shove things deep down. If he didn't want to talk about something, it was impressive how quickly he could change the subject. I imagined he'd done that his whole life. I already knew about the bad dreams—I heard the muffled sounds and curses he let out in his sleep. Twice I'd stopped outside his closed bedroom door. Once I touched the handle. But I hadn't entered. Not yet, anyway.

I slid eggs on each plate, and I paused by the mudroom. Inside the door was a pile of military and hunting gear. Lots of OD—olive drab—with tags still attached.

I headed back to the living room and handed a plate to Clutch. He glanced up with his bloodshot eyes.

"Where'd you find all the military stuff?" I asked, taking my seat.

"There's a surplus store in town, and it hadn't been hit yet."

I raised a brow. "I figured that would be a hot place for looters."

"Me, too. Surprisingly, it wasn't even locked. Most of its gear was still there."

"Any zeds?" I asked.

He shrugged. "Nothing I couldn't handle."

The room was quiet, except for the clanging of forks on plates.

"You were right yesterday," I said quietly.

Clutch paused for a second before taking another bite.

"You're right," I said louder. "I'm not ready yet. But I will be. I swear it. The way I see it, there's two types of people left in this world: survivors and victims. And I sure as hell plan on being a survivor. All I ask is that you give me a chance."

He gave a hint of a smile, but the dark circles under his eyes overshadowed any other expression.

"Why don't you get some sleep," I offered. "I can work on whatever you need today. Once Jase is up, I can start getting him up to speed."

We sat in silence for a moment, before he nodded. "Move everything from the back of the truck to the office and sort it. I grabbed whatever shit I could, but there's got to be a lot more to grab at the surplus warehouse out of town."

"You bet," I answered, popping to my feet.

He nodded, rubbed his stubble, and then stood and moved slowly and stiffly up the stairs. He paused. "Be careful out there, Cash. Zeds will start drifting through these parts in bigger numbers soon. I saw three on this road yesterday."

"I'll keep on the look-out."

Ten minutes later, I had rubber gloves on and checked out the SUV, while keeping a constant watch for zeds. Fortunately, the vehicle had leather seats, making it easier to clean. Jase had put Betsy on the passenger floor mat, so I threw it out. After scrubbing down everything with bleach and disinfectant, I grabbed a wheelbarrow and went to the backyard to where I'd killed the zed last night.

With most of his head gone, it was impossible to tell its age, but by the filthy coveralls and flannel shirt, I'd guessed it had been a nearby farmer. Spring winds buffeted me today, but at least the zed was downwind so I didn't have to smell its rankness. After dumping the body into the fire pit and tossing the rubber gloves on top, I poured some gasoline over the corpse and felt pride when I tossed the lit match. I hadn't freaked out. I'd protected the house. For the first time since this mess started, I felt like I had a shot at surviving in this new world.

I ran a hand through my short hair. Already I was glad I'd cut it, for more reasons than to eliminate the risk of zeds grabbing at it. The winds would've turned it into a snarled mess by now, and I no longer had to deal with the hassle of hair in my eyes.

After the fire charred the zed, I cleaned out the SUV, dumping everything into the mudroom. From there, I headed to the truck. When Clutch said he'd loaded up everything he could, he wasn't exaggerating. Both the bed and backseat were piled full of tan, green, and black gear.

It bothered me that he had put himself in danger. He had gone on a looting run, with no lookout, no backup, because he couldn't count on me. *Never again.*

On my tenth or so trip, Jase joined me. He was still wearing the long johns and T-shirt from last night. He was moving slowly, looking around like a lost lamb. He'd pulled out a pair of jeans and a T-shirt from a bag I'd carried in from his SUV.

"Hold up," I called out and closed the distance and

handed him the armful of duffels and other things. "Take this to the office. It's past the kitchen and to your right. Then, once you change into your clothes, help me unload the rest of the truck."

"My shoes—"

"Are now melted rubber," I said. "Go through the gear in the office. There might be some boots to fit you. Otherwise, we'll grab shoes from your house."

At the mention of his house, his face fell. Jase was quite a bit taller than me, but in his face, he was still a boy, a boy who'd seen far too much. I hadn't really thought about how bad he'd had it since yesterday. I grabbed the armful back from him and set it on top of a box. "Let me see your wrists."

He held them out. There were some faint pink lines, but it was obvious he hadn't struggled.

"I'm sorry about having to do that. You know that, right?"

He nodded. "Yeah, I know."

"Did you have breakfast yet?"

He shrugged.

I cocked my head. "What did you have?"

He jutted out his chin. "I had some chips."

I rolled my eyes. "C'mon. I'll make you something. You're going to need your energy. I plan to keep you busy."

He muttered something but obeyed. I washed up and cooked up the rest of the eggs and toast. It was already ten in the morning. I figured it would get him through until lunch at least. "Clutch was out all night and is sleeping in, so keep it down. Once you change clothes, you can help me finish unloading."

He slid the eggs between the slices of toast and squeezed the sandwich together. "Sure thing, Cash."

I ruffled his hair, and he wrinkled his nose.

I smiled. "I think we'll get along all right."

Several dozen trips later, Jase and I had filled the small space of the office with surplus gear and had sorted out the groceries, toilet paper, and other odds and ends from the SUV.

We spent the next two hours quietly sorting all the gear into piles. Clothing by size, bags by type, cots, and everything else in piles of similar items. I even made a pile of my own stuff. Cargo pants with large pockets, button-down camo shirts made of not-so-soft hearty canvas, black sports bras, olive drab tank tops, a heavy-duty rain jacket, a thick winter coat, a tactical belt, and two pair of boots. My old Doc Martens had held up great so far, but the abuse was already starting to show.

I changed in the mudroom. It felt good to wear something in my size. The knife and gun sat more comfortably against my waist on the smaller belt. For the first time in a long time, I felt a genuine smile.

I went back to find Jase, and he started chuckling. "You look like G. I. Jane."

"Looks who's talking. You look pretty badass yourself. OD looks good on you." He'd already changed out of his clothes and into fatigues, changing his look from high schooler to soldier in the blink of an eye. He still had a youthful face, but the clothes infused him with confidence that I hadn't seen this morning.

"Dad always thought I'd join the ROTC," he said, and the smile dropped from his face. His next words were barely a whisper. "I-I don't think I can go back there."

I sobered. "Clutch and I will take care of it. Let me know anything else you want from your house, and I'll see that we pick it up."

After a stalled silence, he mumbled, "Thanks."

I motioned him up. "Let's grab some fresh air."

Jase followed me outside. It wasn't yet time for lunch, so we walked the perimeter, checking Clutch's simple yet effective early-warning systems.

"You're lucky you found Clutch," Jase said as we walked.

"It wasn't just luck," I replied.

"What do you mean?"

I kneeled, checking a tripwire. When I stood, I faced Jase. "My mom always hated that I didn't go to church." I smiled, remembering how she scolded me. Then I sobered. "I was never what you call a true believer so once I moved into my own place, I quit going through the motions. I don't know why I'm still here when so many good people aren't, but I think there had to be something more at play than just luck when Clutch pulled up and took me in when I needed help the most."

"You're saying it's a miracle or destiny or something like that why Clutch saved you?"

"Is that any different than luck?" I scanned the yard one more time and then headed over to my tree.

I pulled out my blade and began practicing. Jase sat off to the side, watching me but more often watching the mound of dirt a couple trees down. There was nothing I could say. He needed time, and I hoped that with time, he'd heal.

"Can I get weapons, too?" he asked while I stabbed.

"Ask Clutch," I replied. I'd give him weapons if I could, but it wasn't my place. Every weapon here belonged to Clutch, except for the two he'd given me. If and how he distributed his weapons was up to him. "Now, keep an eye out for zeds."

The rhythm came easier today, like my body remembered the motions from last night. Muscles in my biceps and thighs reminded me that I needed to get in better shape. And I worked at doing exactly that.

After about an hour into my workout, I had to tape up the sandbag because it'd been thoroughly shredded. With the bag wrapped in silver, I went back at it.

"Put your left leg forward a bit more. You'll be less likely to be knocked off balance."

I jumped to find Clutch behind me. He'd shaved and had changed clothes, though he wore as many guns and knives as usual.

I turned back to the tree and spread out my feet. After a few awkward stabs, the wider stance put more strength into each thrust.

Jase clapped. "Looking good, Cash."

"Now come at me," Clutch said.

My eyes widened, and I held up the tanto. "With a knife?"

He chuckled. "I've been watching you. I'm not worried."

My attack was hesitant, and he scowled. "Damn it, Cash. You can do better than that."

My next attack wasn't much better, but as I got more and more aggressive, Clutch had to work at avoiding me.

"Better," he said. "But you need to remember that evasion should always be your first choice. If you're forced into an attack, defensive maneuvers are more important than taking the offensive. Zeds will come at you with their teeth and hands. Looters and common criminals will be worse because they can think and use weapons."

The next time I attacked, Clutch swung out, and I barely jumped out of the way in time. I was thrown off balance, and he knocked me down with a kick from behind.

"You're relying too much on your weapon. Put it away, and focus on your body. You need to be able to protect yourself using just your hands and whatever is readily available."

I sheathed the blade and spent the next hour alternating between getting my ass handed to me and watching Jase get his ass handed to him by a seasoned military vet. I was on the ground more than I was on my feet. Clutch was relentless. Once, I nearly got the upper hand with a self-defense kick to his knee, but he jumped back before my foot connected. In return, I got a well-placed hit to my solar plexus.

I collapsed to the ground next to Jase and sucked in air.

Clutch took a seat on the grass next to us and rubbed his shoulder. "Tomorrow we'll head a few miles out and practice shooting."

"I can shoot," Jase quickly offered up.

"What's your weapon?" Clutch countered.

"I'm a decent shot with a rifle. I've hunted both deer and ducks before."

"Well then, we'll see what you can do," Clutch said.

I laid back on the soft grass, staring up at the clouds. Lying there, I realized that even though Clutch was no longer on active duty, he'd never really left the military. He was a Ranger—he had to be one of the best in my mind—and I think that was how he defined himself. Though I suspected his nightmares came from the tours he'd served. Driving the truck, farming, those were just jobs. Clutch was a soldier. He worked out every day as though he were still in the military. And now he expected the same from Jase and me.

Every part of me felt bruised, while Clutch wasn't even breathing heavily, though I knew his joints ached at the end of each long day. Cracking my neck, I glanced at Clutch who was cleaning his nails with his knife. I noticed his nose had a bump from where it had been broken.

Under his gruff exterior, I could tell he was fiercely protective of me and now Jase. Clutch would've made a great father, that was, if he could've tamed his militant ways. Then I realized, for all I knew, he was a father. "You have any kids? A wife? Girlfriend, maybe?"

The knife paused, and he looked at me. "Why?"

I shrugged. "Just curious."

"Clutch had a hottie around for a while," Jase chimed in. "I saw you two in town a few times. She was blonde, curvy, and..." he whistled.

After a minute, Clutch sighed. "I never found someone I wanted to settle down with."

A wide grin spread over my face. "See? Sharing isn't so hard now, is it?"

He smirked before looking up to the sky. "Looks like a storm will be rolling in later." He pulled himself up, held out a hand, and helped me to my feet. "Not too many folks know about the warehouse for Doyle's military surplus store, but someone will come across it soon enough. It's too close to Camp Fox for it to be missed. I want to get a truckload or two while we still can." He glanced at Jase and me for a moment. "I could use a lookout."

My brows rose with hope. "I'm in."

He turned to Jase. "Think you can hold down the fort?"

Jase jumped to his feet. "You can count on me, sir."

"I'd better show you what to do in case anyone or thing shows up." They started to head off, and Clutch paused, turning to me. "Meet at the truck in fifteen."

"Wilco," I replied with a grin and a salute. Knowing this was my second chance, I took off at a jog to get ready.

Fifteen minutes later, I leaned against Clutch's truck, holding on to a two-foot-long bolt cutter. When Clutch appeared with weapons and the backpack he always carried, I nodded toward the house. "Do you think he'll be okay?"

"Kids are resilient. Give it time. He'll get there."

We climbed in and headed down a different gravel road than we'd driven down the day before. Fields of black, waiting to be planted, went on for miles and miles.

"Where's this surplus warehouse?"

"It's southeast of town. At an old farmers' co-op," he replied.

We drove along for a while, past several farmhouses. I saw only one zed wandering in the fields, but I think I saw another one standing at the window inside one of the houses we passed.

The winds had started to pick up, almost whistling through the truck. Then I saw something. "*Wait,*" I said.

Clutch slowed. "What is it?"

I pointed to the big galvanized corn bins. "I thought I saw someone."

"Zed?"

I shook my head. "A woman, I think. She was running too fast, but she must be running from something."

Neither of us missed the two men sprinting toward the bins next, also far too fast to be lumbering zeds.

Clutch's jaw clenched. "Sonofabitch."

A woman's scream pierced the air, and I gasped, cranking my neck to try to see anything.

"Damn it." He yanked the truck into the driveway, throwing me against the door. He reached for the shotgun. "Stay here and stay low. Whatever you hear, do *not* let yourself be seen."

"Okay," I said, frowning.

"Is the safety off the .22?"

I pulled out the pistol and checked. "Yes." I also unsnapped my knife's sheath.

"Stay out of sight." He gave me one last look and then jumped out of the truck and flattened against the side of the bin.

I moved the seat back as far as it could go and crouched on the floor, holding the gun in one hand, and the bolt cutter in the other. The driver's window faced the bin, but from my low vantage point, all I could see was metal and sky.

Shouts and gunfire erupted, and I tried to make myself invisible. Then…silence.

A minute later, Clutch opened the door and I jumped up. "What happened?"

"I took down both tangos, and I'm going to check out the other buildings in case they weren't alone. Stay put."

"And the woman?"

He grimaced, and then slammed the door.

I retook my position on the floor and waited. Was she dead? Whatever it was couldn't have been good because Clutch had looked enraged. I wanted to go check on the woman, to see if I could help, but I didn't want to break my word to Clutch even more.

After three minutes ticked by, my muscles began to cramp. The door snapped open behind me, and before I could turn, an arm wrapped around my neck and yanked me from the truck. I tried to yell out but couldn't breathe. I struggled but was only pulled harder against my assailant.

"Well, well, well. What do we have here," an unfamiliar male voice whispered in my ear. His breath reeked of booze and his body stank of sweat.

I swung the bolt cutter behind me, and he cursed. His grip relaxed enough so I could suck in air. I twisted around and swung again. But, this time he was ready. He caught the bolt cutter and wrenched it from my hand. I went to punch him, but he grabbed my wrist and jerked me tight against him as though we were slow dancing. He chuckled. Shivers covered my skin. The winds howled around us.

I looked up into the face of a man with a half-grown beard and greasy hair. He pulled me even tighter against him while he licked my cheek, and I winced.

"Oh, we're going to have fun, you and me."

He threw me to the ground and fell on top of me. My face was shoved into the dirt. Panic blurred my vision. He was too busy grabbing at my pants to notice that I still had the pistol. I couldn't get onto my back, but when he yanked on my cargos, I was able to aim it under my armpit. I fired, and he cursed, jumping back. "Wha?!"

I spun onto my back and fired three more shots. The first shot had only startled him. My next three hit him solidly in the chest and stomach. It was different than in the movies. There was no blood spray, only three red dots growing on his shirt. He looked down and frowned as though he hadn't felt any pain.

He looked up and his face turned red. "Bitch!" he yelled, spittle flying from his mouth. He tackled me, punching me in the face, and—blinded by white and black stars—I pummeled his head with the gun handle. I kept pounding his temple until he fell lax. With a grunt, I kicked him off me.

I pulled myself up into a sitting position, gasping and spitting blood, unable to see through the stars. Every inch of my face hurt. He'd very nearly knocked me out. As my tunnel vision slowly widened, I could see Clutch running toward me. When he got close, he looked at me and then at the guy who was already starting to come back to consciousness. I struggled to aim my gun, but Clutch was in the way. He kicked the man in the gut and then fired two shots at my attacker's head.

Clutch knelt by me. "You okay?"

I came to my knees, spit out some more blood, and ran my tongue over the nasty cut on my lip. "I need a bigger gun."

He belted out a single laugh, helped me to my feet, and held me up until the wooziness passed.

I rubbed my cheek. "Damn, that guy hit like a sledgehammer."

"He's had plenty of practice."

I looked up at him, but he was scanning the area.

"The woman..." I said.

"They hurt her. Bad."

Shivers crawled over my skin. There were too many victims of the zeds already. Adding more unnecessary victims poured acid onto my emotions. I looked over at the guy Clutch had put down. "I'm glad you killed him."

"Some folks need to die."

A flurry of movement caught my eye, and I turned to see another man run toward a truck in the distance. "Clutch!" I yelled, wincing at the sharp pain in my cut lip.

Clutch turned, a look of unadulterated fury washed over his face, and he bolted after the man.

The guy was a couple hundred feet away. My .22 was worthless at this distance, so I ran for the truck, jumped in the driver's seat, and gunned the engine, kicking up pebbles.

Clutch was closing the distance, but he was still too

far away. The man had already climbed into a dusty blue minivan. Clutch kept running even as the vehicle cranked around and sped directly toward him.

Clutch stopped, took aim, and fired at the windshield. Buckshot fractured the glass. The minivan was going to hit him head-on, but he fired again. I was on my way to T-bone the van, but I wasn't going to get there in time.

At the last second, Clutch dove to the side.

I floored it to intersect the van, but it sped away, spinning out on the gravel road before straightening and tearing away from us.

I stopped, got out, and ran toward Clutch.

He was already on his feet, checking the shotgun.

"Are you okay?"

"Fucker got away." He grimaced. "I didn't recognize him, but he knows that there's someone else out here now. We'll have to be on our guard."

"If we hurry, we might be able to chase him down."

He shook his head. "It'll draw too much attention. We'll find him again."

I nodded tightly, and then looked at the bin and started walking.

"Cash, you don't need to see that. I'll take care of it."

I kept walking. The girl wasn't far away, just out of the line of sight from the truck. She was covered in dried blood and bruises, making it impossible to tell her age, but she looked young. Probably hadn't even graduated from high school yet. Could've been one of

Jase's classmates, even. Her nose was broken and one arm was bent at an unnatural angle. All the skin had been scraped from her knees.

She was nearly naked, her skin sallow. The wind flapped the tatters of clothing left on her. Her poor body looked like she'd been abused and broken since the virus outbreak started. She belonged in a hospital. Now, without doctors and medical technology, there was nothing that could be done. She lay there, one eye swollen shut, staring into nothingness. It was a blank stare. I thought she'd already died, but then she blinked.

I realized that it was only her spirit that had already died.

A tear trickled down her cheek. I came down on a knee and wiped the tear away with my thumb. I found it hard to breathe, like a fist had wrapped around my heart.

She tried to speak. Her pale, broken lips moved but no sound came out.

I pointed the pistol at her temple. "I'm sorry." They were the only words I could manage to get out without choking.

She closed her eye and gave a weak smile.

I held the .22 as close as I could get it without touching and pulled the trigger. The blast made me jump, and I let out a sob.

I came back to my feet, staring at the girl, her destroyed features now relaxed.

Finally, she'd found peace.

Tears streamed down my cheeks.

I knew Clutch stood at my back. I had a protector, something this girl had never had. The first raindrops landed on her, creating shiny trails through the blood and grime. I turned my face to the sky to let the cool rain wash away my tears. But the rain could wash away neither the sins nor the memories of what had taken place here today.

HUNGER

THE THIRD CIRCLE OF HELL

CHAPTER VI

"I agree," Clutch said as we shoveled mud into the hole where Jase's parents now rested. "Zed sludge is the foulest odor in the world."

I would've chuckled except I was still too focused on breathing through my mouth, my bandana doing little to block the stench. The mud stuck to our shovels, making the process tedious, but we both agreed that Jase needed to know that his parents had received a proper burial.

"I'll finish up here. You want to finish loading the truck?" Clutch asked.

"Gladly," I said and jogged away before Clutch could change his mind. I sucked in fresh air, though hints of decay still saturated the air.

Jase had made one hell of a mess in the living room. Frank's wife hadn't been too nasty, just a zed corpse with a headshot in the earliest stages of bloating. But Frank could've been an extra in a horror film. His head had been nothing but pulp, and from his chest up, he'd been covered in dried blood and sticky brown goo. The blood, if I had to guess, was canine.

Propped outside the front door sat bags and boxes filled with everything we'd found useful in the house. I grabbed the other two rifles Jase had told Clutch about and slid them behind the front seat before loading the remaining food from the cabinets and supplies into the back of Clutch's black pickup truck.

This morning, Jase had also asked for us to grab his Xbox, and Clutch snorted out a "hell, no" before going off about how we were about to find ourselves in the dark ages. I grabbed the Xbox, anyway.

By the time I'd loaded the last bag, Clutch was headed my way.

He tugged down his bandana and didn't look happy. "Ready to hit the next stop?"

I swallowed and gave a tight nod.

Neither one of us spoke on the drive to the corn bin where we buried the girl. We strung the bodies of her assailants together with a tie strap and propped them against the corn bin.

Finished, I pulled out a can of red spray paint I'd found at Jase's house and painted large letters on the bin above the men: *R-A-P-I-S-T-S.*

I stared at the letters for a couple minutes. With no law enforcement, it seemed fitting to somehow note these men's crimes. When I tossed the can on the ground, Clutch gave me a nod and headed back to the truck.

We drove around for an hour, scanning for the minivan, and only saw a zed here and there. The bastard was either long gone or had gone to ground, and neither option did us any good. I felt like our duty wouldn't be done be until we could find the fourth rapist. Only then would the poor girl finally be avenged.

All in all, taking care of corpses took us five hours. We sat in the truck and ate the sandwiches I'd made this morning.

"Check out the warehouse next?" I asked between bites. I had the bolt cutters along, and Clutch had been hankering to get his hands onto all the surplus gear.

He nodded while he chewed.

Not even a minute later, thunder rolled, and the damn rain picked up again. I watched heavy drops pelt the windshield. "It'll be tough watching for zeds in this."

"Agreed. We'll try again tomorrow," he grumbled as he wiped his hands on his pants.

"At least the storms should keep other looters away, too," I offered.

He grunted. "We can only hope." And he started the truck.

By the time we'd returned to the farm, the rain had become relentless. Jase stepped out from his cover under a nearby shrub. With the rain parka, he blended seamlessly into the foliage around him. He unlocked the heavy chain and pushed at the gate. Metal screeched as he shoved it open. Something clanged, and the gate broke free from its rollers and swung out at an odd angle.

"Damn it. I knew we were going to have problems with that piece of shit gate," Clutch muttered before gunning the engine through the open space. Once through, he jumped out of the truck and I followed.

It took all our strength to right the gate. The wind pushed against us and the hail pelted our heads. Once the gate was back in place, we tied it to the barbed wire fence we'd reinforced with chain link on each side. It wasn't pretty but it would at least hold the gate and slow down anyone—alive or otherwise—trying to get onto the farm.

A thunderous boom shook the ground. A crack echoed through the air, followed by a large branch off an old maple tree slamming into the ditch behind us.

"C'mon!" Clutch yelled out, his voice a whisper over the wind. "We need to get inside. Now!"

We ran to the truck. Even though there was a backseat, Jase and I both tumbled onto the front bucket seat.

The truck lurched forward, buffeted by the wind that seemed to come at us from every direction. "This one's going to be bad," Clutch muttered.

Going to be? Spring storms in the Midwest were known to get nasty. But, maybe because I'd lived in a city where buildings tempered the winds, I didn't remember a storm this bad in a long time.

Hail bombarded the truck, the noise deafening. When we reached the shed, both Jase and I tumbled out to slide open the large door. The hail hurt, and the wind had become vicious. The sky had turned an ominous green. We started pulling the door shut while Clutch drove the truck into the shed. Once in, he jumped out and helped slide the large door closed.

Hail sounded like an atrocious muddle of drums on the shed's metal roof.

Then the screaming winds mysteriously stilled and the hail stopped.

We all stood and looked up as if we could see through a metal roof. Chills crawled over my skin.

"This can't be good," Jase said.

"We should get to the cellar," I said. I headed to the side door to make a break for the house, but Clutch stopped me.

"No time. This way."

Jase and I hustled behind Clutch through the winding stacks of seed corn waiting to be planted and to the far corner of the shed. He moved aside a couple empty pallets to reveal an earthen-colored tarp. He lifted the tarp and opened a round steel hatch.

"Cool! A bomb shelter," Jase said from behind me.

"I wouldn't call it that," Clutch said, getting down on his knees and pulling out a lantern. He pressed a button, the light clicked on, and he handed it to me.

The winds picked up again, howling like banshees, touting impending doom.

Holding the lantern in one hand, I gingerly climbed down the ladder into the dark hole. The small light lit up the dismally small space below. It couldn't have been more than a five-by-five-foot hole, with the walls taken up by shelves of food, water, and a shotgun vacuum-sealed in plastic. A small square fan covered what I assumed to be the only air vent in the bunker.

Jase landed right behind me. "Cozy."

The walls were rough concrete, but it still smelled of dank earth. "What is this place, Clutch?" I asked.

"My TEOTWAWKI hole," he replied after locking the door above us. "Made it myself."

Sudden silence boomed in the small space.

"The end of the world as we know it," I clarified to Jase when he shot me a confused glance. Clutch had used the acronym the day I met him, back when I could still rely on the Internet to get my answers.

"I built it to support one person for fourteen days. But it's tornado-proof, so we'll be safe for tonight. There's no way anyone or anything is going to get in here without a blow torch and several hours of extra time." He tore open a bag and pulled out a metallic sheet. "I have only one blanket, so we'll have to share."

As I sat next to Jase and dried my pistol, I wondered what would await us in the shed when we went to open the hatch in the morning.

"We could set up a fenced-in pasture out back," I offered while we sat around a huge breakfast feast, cleaning out the last of the food from the freezer and refrigerator. Since the storm had blown the power out, the mood was somber. My final bite of steak marked the beginning of rationing. Clutch said we'd get used to being hungry. I wasn't so sure.

More so, it was an eerie feeling to know that there was no one left to bring the power grid back up. Even though Clutch had a generator, he'd made it clear that it was for winter use only. It was old and loud and would only attract attention. It also used diesel fuel, and he had only a couple hundred gallons left in the diesel tank out back that had been used for his farm equipment before the outbreak.

No more TV, radio, or ice. No more Internet. No more email to my parents.

"Livestock will attract zeds," Clutch countered, bringing my attention back. "Besides, that's too much meat for the three of us. It'll go bad too quick."

"Not if we find goats," I said.

"Have you seen any goats around?" Clutch said.

"What if we smoked the meat?" I asked.

"Mm, I love jerky," Jase added. "Can we try it, Clutch?"

He scowled. "That means we'd have to keep a watch

on the fire. If it puts out smoke that can be seen over the trees, then we can't use it. The smell of smoked meat may also pose a risk. It could attract attention."

"We'll make sure it's good and sealed," I said. "Any risk whatsoever and we won't use it."

He watched me for a moment. "And you know how to make a smokehouse?"

I shrugged, and then smirked. "No, but I bet you have something in your library."

He sighed. "See what you can find. But I check over anything you build before you start a fire in it."

"Deal," I said, and Jase gave me a high-five.

"Don't you first need to build that chicken coop you've been talking about?" Clutch added.

I'd planned a pen out of chicken wire and two-by-fours to be connected to the smaller shed so that zeds, wildlife, and raiders couldn't easily get to the chickens. It wouldn't be pretty, but it would do the job. "I saw chickens at a farm a couple miles that way." I pointed. "I'll pick them up today and put them in the shed until I'm done with the coop. They won't last long on their own."

"That's the Pierson's," Jase added. "They're nice. Moved in just a couple years ago."

"We'll stop on our way back from Home Depot if there's time," Clutch replied. "If we don't get that roof patched, we're going to have serious problems, no thanks to all these rains."

While we'd huddled together in our underground

tomb, a twister had blown through. We'd been fortunate. The machine shed and two smaller surrounding sheds were left untouched except for some dents and bent corners courtesy of wind damage. The storm had uprooted one tree and split another in the backyard, but we decided to leave them where they fell since they provided decent obstacles for zeds.

One of the wood covers had snapped off a ground-floor window—a quick repair. The only real damage was to the roof of the house. When we checked out the roof the next morning, all Clutch said was, "I've been meaning to get that roof redone one of these years."

"And the surplus," I added. If Clutch thought there was some badass stuff tucked away in the warehouse, it was going to be Christmas for us. I was keeping my fingers crossed for a Jeep.

"It's going to be a busy day," Clutch said.

"I'll stay back and guard the house," Jase offered.

"Negative. You're both coming. Home Depot is big. If I knew where I could get shingles anywhere else, I would, believe me. I need extra eyes and ears there."

"But who's going to protect the farm when we're gone?" he asked.

"We'll lock the gate up good and tight before we go. That should cover us for a few hours," Clutch replied. "And you can carry in today's water before you gear up."

Jase slumped.

I gave him a reassuring pat. With the power out, we

had to get our water from the manual pump outside.

A thump against the outside wall sent us all to our feet. "I'll check it out from the living room," I whispered, pulling out my pistol. Clutch had upgraded my .22 to a Glock 9mm after the run-in with the rapists, and the weight felt good in my grip.

"I'll take upstairs," Jase whispered before taking the stairs three steps at a time.

Clutch nodded and reached for his rifle.

I headed toward the source of the sound and paused, waiting for the next thump. When it came, I took the window on my left and slid open the peephole. The yard looked clear under the overcast sky, though with the peephole, I couldn't see anything against the walls.

I turned to Clutch who was now behind me and shrugged. When I turned around to look outside again, I found a jaundiced face staring back at me. I jumped. "Shit!"

"*Ahhnn.*" The zed pounded on the wood and began to chant the meaningless sound over and over as though it was saying, "Let me in." The window frame vibrated under the pressure.

"Cash?" Clutch asked.

I lifted my pistol, held it just inside the sniper hole, and fired. The pounding stopped and daylight shone through the hole once again.

Jase came running down the stairs a moment later. "The yard's clear. That was the only one I could see."

"It never should've gotten this close to the house. We

need to take shorter breaks with the three of us together," Clutch said. "No more than fifteen minutes without anyone on guard every three hours."

"That gives us less time to plan and report status," I said.

"We should use treadmills," Jase said.

"What?" Clutch and I asked at the same time.

Jase gave us a wide grin. "Treadmills. We should surround the house with them. Any zed who comes up to the house will step onto a treadmill and will just keep walking and walking. Then we don't have to stand guard at all."

"Exactly how are you going to power a hundred treadmills?" Clutch asked.

Jase shrugged. "Solar power, maybe."

"Oh, solar power. Of course. I'll pick some up on my next grocery trip," I said drily.

Jase flipped me the bird. "Jeez, can't you guys take a joke?"

I smiled, though Jase had a point. It was too hard to find humor in a world that had given up.

Clutch sighed. "C'mon. Let's hit the road."

Jase's smile dropped. "I'll grab my stuff."

As we headed out to repair the gate, the weather reflected Jase's mood. The sun refused to shine, giving reign to a gray mist instead. I felt sorry for the kid. Going into Fox Hills would bring back a lifetime of memories for him. Where he went to school, where his mom picked up groceries—everything we'd drive by would be a stark reminder of what he'd lost.

With the gate back in place and operational, Jase sulked in the backseat while Clutch drove down the gravel road. Jase feigned nonchalance, but in the side mirror I noticed that he stiffened as we drove by the empty ranch house he grew up in. It looked deceptively welcoming, the scene of death hidden within its red brick walls. My overactive imagination feared that Jase's parents somehow had come back again and dug out of their graves. Fortunately, the house disappeared behind us with no sign of zeds, those related to Jase or otherwise.

Another mile down the road, Jase and I got out to move a small tree that had fallen across the gravel. Broken branches littered the gravel, and one low part over a culvert showed signs that the road had been underwater a few hours earlier.

A bloated zed lay floundering under the shallow rapids of a rushing creek beyond the culvert. Trapped under a log, its arms flapped clumsily at the water.

"I don't get it," Jase said from the backseat. "That thing's probably been underwater all night. How can it still be alive?"

"They're not alive, they're just...echoes of life," I answered honestly. It's what I told myself every day so that I no longer thought of them as people. When the time came to kill—not in self-defense like when Melanie had attacked me—if I believed that they still felt or thought, I wasn't quite sure I could go through with it.

When we reached Fox Hills, we had to lay down plywood in the muddy ditch to get around the roadblock. From there, Clutch drove down Main Street, straight through the center of town. The store we needed was on the opposite side of town, and rather than burn precious gas, he'd made the call to risk driving through the more populated areas of town. It also gave us a chance to see how many zeds we'd have to deal with if we were to start looting houses.

Last night's storm had wreaked havoc on Fox Hills. Plastic trash bins that had lined driveways the day of the outbreak were now strewn about. Garbage was scattered *everywhere*. Diapers, magazines, and milk cartons littered every open space, looking like the aftermath of a wild party. Every now and then we saw a zed with its head shoved in a garbage bag, going after an easy meal.

"They'll eat *anything,*" Jase said.

"Yeah," I replied, though we all already knew their favorite meal.

Clutch drove around trees that had been ripped from the ground, and their branches crunched under the truck's tires along with garbage. A tree had smashed a convertible. A Honda and a Chevy were slammed together like bumper cars. Every now and then, we saw a zed lying motionless on the ground, which meant they must've taken serious blows to the head during the storm. But the storm hadn't taken out nearly enough. More zeds than I'd seen last time wandered aimlessly outside, open doors and broken windows the only hints as to where they'd come from, though I suspected most of the zeds still lumbered around inside their homes.

I held the pistol on my lap. I had the tanto, but it was still in its sheath. My real confidence builder was the crowbar I'd found in one of Clutch's sheds. Whenever we left the farm, I carried the crowbar since the knife was short and required me to get awfully close and personal to do any damage. The crowbar, on the other hand, was a power driver of cold iron.

At the sound of the truck's engine, zeds turned and lumbered in our direction, sniffing at the air, but as we put distance between us and them, they soon lost focus and returned back to their eerie shuffling.

"Hey, you!" Jase yelled, opening his window. "Over here!"

Several zeds emerged from the shadows, coming at us. At the way their expressions changed when they homed in on us, I could imagine their mouths watering at the sight of three healthy people.

"Hell, kid. Are you calling every zed to us?" Clutch spat out, stepping on the gas.

"What are you doing, Jase?" I asked.

He kept waving, not answering our questions, but after a moment, he slumped back in his seat. "I saw someone. A lady. But she darted around the corner of that house over there."

"We ain't a search-and-rescue, kid," Clutch said, then added more softly, "Roll up the window."

"But we have to help others if we can," Jase countered.

"She didn't want our help," I said. I'd seen her, too. She looked in her late fifties or early sixties, and she'd been carrying a baseball bat. We'd made eye contact just before she ran. Was it bad that I was glad that she'd run away rather than toward us? Any orphan we took in was another mouth to feed.

I was pretty sure I saw another couple—a man and a woman—watching us through shuttered windows from a small starter home. I didn't mention them to Jase. I figured if they needed help bad enough, they'd run to us.

It wasn't our job to play hero.

Selfish? Hell, yeah.

But honest. And necessary to survive. After all, I was only human.

Besides, after seeing what had happened to the girl at the corn bin, I realized that laws and scruples were no longer viable in this new world. Now, people scared me as badly as zeds.

What I saw next made me burst out laughing.

The guys turned to me, and I pointed. "Look. A zed kabob." Off to my right, a zed had somehow gotten itself skewered onto a still-upright parking meter, with the thick round top of the meter embedded in its ribcage. Its arms and legs flailed uselessly like it was trying to air-swim. The guys didn't find it funny, and we continued on.

A stoplight was down in one intersection, and we had to turn around and find a detour. Two more detours past smashed cars and fallen power lines, and we were back on Main Street. I carefully noted every obstruction on a small notepad.

It took us twenty-three minutes to drive six miles through town and to our destination. Home Depot was a new massive store on the outskirts, sidled up against an old elementary school of all things. A wood privacy fence went out from behind the school to enclose what I assumed to be the playground.

A sense of bad omen settled into my stomach. I turned in my seat to face Jase. "When the outbreak hit, when did they let out the schools?"

He shrugged. "I don't think they officially closed, but I know some parents picked up their kids, anyway. It all happened so fast. At the high school, some of the teachers let us out early, and I drove my bike home. But those who rode buses…I-I don't know how they got home."

I grimaced. "I'm guessing school is still in session."

"You have a bike?" Clutch asked.

Jase nodded. "Mom and Dad got me a kickass Suzuki for my birthday. I've been practicing up for motocross. I'm going—I mean, I was going to race at the county fair this summer."

I could hear the enthusiasm in Jase's voice bleed out as he spoke.

"The bike's at your house now?" Clutch asked.

"Yeah, why?"

"Because a bike is the perfect vehicle for us to scout the farm and surrounding area. We'll pick it up on our way back. Don't worry. You'll get plenty of motocross practice in." He sighed as he turned into the large parking lot. "Add the bike to our ever-growing to-do list."

Jase gave a low whistle. "That's a lot of cars."

"Are you sure there's nowhere else that might have roofing supplies?" I asked.

Clutch grimaced. "'Fraid not."

He pulled into an open area toward the back of the parking lot. If zeds came at us, the one thing we had on them was speed. Having the truck at a distance from the store could be a lifesaver when it came to putting space between us and hungry zeds.

We checked our gear and weapons. We left the Kevlar vests at home since they were heavy and zeds tended to go for the face or extremities. With the black Kevlar helmets and gloves, we looked like Special Forces, but I felt nothing like an experienced soldier.

Clutch looked at both of us. "All right, we've got to be smart about this. No fuck-ups. We get what we need, then we're out of there. The other supplies in there aren't worth the risk, not until we know the place is cleared out. We go in silent and we stick together. We know zeds hunt off their senses, so we move slow and silent. Always keep a direct line to the exit. If either of you screw up, I might decide to leave your ass behind.

Got it?"

Both Jase and I nodded.

Clutch left the keys in the ignition in case we needed to make a quick getaway, or, worse, in case he didn't leave the store with us. "Let's do this. Exactly as I taught you. Follow my lead. Silence from here on out," he said and opened the door.

I gripped the crowbar. We moved as a trio of dark-colored shapes slowly through the parking lot. I'd expected that we'd have to take out a couple zeds in the parking lot, but nothing emerged from around the cars. Not a good sign. Because the owners of those cars had to be somewhere.

We flattened against the wall on either side of the wide glass entrance, and Clutch bent around to scan the area. He frowned and led us down the sidewalk to the exit door. He scanned the interior longer this time before finally nodding. Forcing myself to breathe, I stepped next to Clutch, holding the crowbar up. The sliding door didn't automatically open. Just as we'd expected, the power grid for the entire area was down. Clutch pulled at the door while I stood ready to knock back any zed that may attack. Jase stood at our backs, a rifle slung on his back and a long wood-handled axe in his hands.

Clutch pried the door open just enough for us to squeeze through one at a time. Clutch went in first. Once through, he crouched and flattened himself against one of the checkout counters. He held his machete out while he checked the area behind him.

When he gave us the *all-clear,* I went in next, moving exactly as Clutch had done. When Jase reached me, he tapped my left shoulder. *Ready.* I did the same to Clutch's shoulder, just like how he'd made us practice.

Clutch moved to the edge of the counter and looked left and right. After making a quick hand motion, he crossed the aisle, keeping slow and low, until he flattened against the other side. I moved but abruptly pulled back when I saw a zed in the aisle, sniffing at the air. Taking a breath, I waited until it faced the other direction, and I crossed the aisle. Jase followed.

We continued this process, avoiding zeds and following Clutch, as we moved deep into the belly of the store. For the number of cars outside, there were surprisingly few zeds meandering around, which made me wonder exactly where all the drivers to those cars had gone.

Clutch clearly frequented this store because he led us to the aisle we needed without any wrong turns or detours except to bypass zeds. I opened the duffel, and he slid in several heavy stacks of shingles. Jase stayed at my back and scanned the entire time.

"Uh, guys?" Jase whispered.

I glanced up to see a zed come around the corner and into our aisle. It'd been badly gnawed. One of its arms was nothing but white bone and stringy sinew. We didn't move, hoping it wouldn't see us.

We weren't that lucky.

It only took a couple seconds for the zed to sniff the air and home in on us. It moaned and stumbled toward us. *It's like a freaking bloodhound,* I thought to myself. Clutch stood, walked right up to it, and swung, his machete taking off the top of the zed's head with a single powerful slice. The zed collapsed, and he caught the body just before it hit the floor and laid it down quietly.

He returned and grabbed the duffel as though nothing happened. On our way out, we nearly walked into a small group of zeds and were forced to backtrack. As we neared another aisle, Jase nudged me. "Look," he whispered and pointed at a glass display case.

My mouth opened, and I tugged Clutch and then pointed.

He saw the display case, looked around, and then headed toward it. On proud display behind the glass was a little piece of heaven. Small camping axes, knives of all sizes, and the Cadillac—black machetes. While Clutch's arsenal of rifles and pistols was impressive, he had few blades, with the exception of a machete and a wood axe, his blades were knives.

He felt around the back of the display case, then around the edges. When the glass didn't slide open, he grabbed Jase's axe.

"It's locked. Get ready to move fast," Clutch whispered. "Know what you want, and grab it. Don't try for everything. We head straight to the truck two seconds after this breaks."

He stood, laid an empty duffel against the glass, and then brought down the heavy end of the axe. Even with the fabric, the sound of breaking glass echoed through the store.

Clutch grabbed a couple small axes in one swoop, and then got out of the way. Jase and I were smaller and could reach in at the same time. We both went for the machetes, and then I grabbed an axe, sliding both into my belt.

"Let's go," Clutch said aloud, and we headed down the aisle.

We made it two rows over before we hit a roadblock of a half dozen zeds. We turned to the left and ran. Jase pulled ahead, though Clutch was quick. I struggled to keep up, my shorter legs a clear detriment in outrunning zeds.

The guys came to a screeching halt in front of me. The zeds had discovered the opened door, and had flocked toward it, moaning as they pressed through. That was, until they saw us, and their moans grew in volume as they changed direction en masse toward us.

A quick glance at the entrance door proved no better option.

Clutch looked around. "There's a door to the lumberyard on the side." He took off at a run. We followed, weaving around stray zeds. Clutch kicked the door open, and we burst outside.

I sucked in a breath.

At least fifty zeds turned our way. They must've fled

outside when the outbreak happened, only to be corralled in the lumberyard. The herd moaned and came at us. We ran toward the front gate, only to find it locked with a big ass padlock.

"Oh, shit," Jase said. "We're so dead."

We couldn't go back inside because we'd already drawn the attention of every indoor zed. The herd closed in. Some were wearing orange vests with nametags, others in casual jeans and T-shirts.

"We need to get to higher ground. Stay with me," Clutch called out and led the charge.

He ran toward the herd, and then cut to the left to dodge outstretched arms. Jase was insanely fast and moved ahead of Clutch in no time. By the time I reached the corner, the herd had blocked off the aisle the guys had taken, and I cut to the right, jumping over a stack of hoses. A zed stood in my way, and I swung the crowbar, smashing its head and knocking him to the side. I kept running, dodging zeds, swinging only when I had to, until I found the guys again.

Jase was climbing the lumber stacks on long shelves lining the back wall. Clutch had climbed into a forklift and was headed straight toward me. I ran to the side as Clutch skewered the closest zed. He jumped off the still-moving forklift and quickly caught up to me. "Get your ass in gear, Cash!"

With one final surge, I flung the crowbar onto the second shelf before leaping for a stack of two-by-fours. I'd been working out, but one week of strength-building didn't cut it. I awkwardly held on to the end of a two-by-four and prayed it wouldn't give. When it didn't move, I swung, trying to get my leg over the edge. A zed grabbed onto my foot, and I kicked out. Its grip relaxed, and I used its head to step off, pushing myself onto the shelf.

Clutch had also leapt onto the shelf, though he made it look easy.

Gasping for air, I got back on my feet, and followed Clutch. I grabbed on to a metal shelf post, and pulled myself up to the next level. A gloved hand reached out from above, and I grabbed on, letting Clutch pull me up to the stack he and Jase were on. I hugged on to him as soon as I felt the solid surface under my knees.

Still on a knee, Clutch pulled back and looked me over. "You all right?"

I nodded. "Yeah, thanks."

"Come and get us, you stinky zed bastards!" Jase yelled out, flipping the zed the bird. Jase was on his knees, panting, looking over the edge.

"Jesus," I said. "You're a freaking mutant, Jase. I've never seen anyone run that fast."

He grinned. "State 100-meter and 400-meter relays. Twice. Not to mention Fox Hills' varsity football team's best tight end."

I couldn't help but smile. Until I looked over the side. The zeds gathered below, looking up, reaching and groaning, as though begging us to come back down. Some tried to climb, but they fell back after the first step.

We'd use up all our ammo to clear out the herd below. And who knew how many more the noise would draw out. Already, the zeds from inside the store were filtering outside to join the soggy herd surrounding us. Why were there so many here? It had taken Alan nearly an hour to turn. That should've given most of these folks time to get home and turn there. Though, I remember the news had said that the worse the injury, the faster they turned. Many of the zeds below had serious bites.

And they looked ravenous.

I glanced at Clutch, who seemed to be thinking the same thing.

"C'mon," he said. "Let's get to the top."

I poked my head out and looked up. There were three more shelves to climb. The fact that I was scared of heights did nothing to help my nerves. Jase took the lead. He climbed like a monkey, amped up on pure adrenaline. Clutch went next. Even with the heavy duffel and being laden with weapons, he climbed like he carried little extra weight. I double-checked my weapons to make sure they were secure, and I started to pull myself up the side. It was like climbing a rope on a jungle gym, except the bars were unforgiving, and if I fell, I'd get eaten.

At each level, Clutch helped pull me up, and we took a few minutes to rest, although I think it was mostly for my benefit. If not for the gloves, my hands would've been raw. Even with gloves, I felt blisters forming.

Once we reached the top, I lay down on the stack of thick plywood and panted. Clutch scanned the area, and I pulled myself up to gauge the situation. Large shelves holding stacks of wood, blocks, and boxes lined the three walls. We had plenty of horizontal movement up here, but getting to the ground without becoming zed-food would be a challenge.

Clutch set down the duffel. "You two stay here. I'm going to check things out."

I pulled myself up as Clutch leapt onto the next shelf over. He moved slowly but with a gracefulness that belied his size as he leapt from one shelf to the next. I looked out over the wall to see open countryside. A zed shambled along here and there, but otherwise, it was wide-open. The problem was we were a good twenty feet up, without any ladder or rope to get down the wall.

"We're so dead," Jase said at my side. "We're going to die, aren't we?"

I punched him in the arm. "I don't ever want to hear you say those words again. Clutch will figure out something."

"Yes, ma'am," he replied quietly.

We sat in silence after that. When Clutch finally returned, Jase didn't complain, not once.

"Find anything promising?" I asked.

Clutch pulled off his helmet and ran a hand through his hair. "It's a hell of a jump, but the roof of the elementary school looks like our only shot. Our other option is to wait it out and hope these guys move on."

"You think they'll move on?" I asked.

"No chance in hell," Clutch quickly replied.

I slid my gloves back on. "I guess we'd better get going then."

The shelf we needed was four over from the one we were on, and I moved more cautiously than Clutch. Once I reached the shelf, I looked over at the school. "For once, I wish you were exaggerating," I grumbled. When he'd said it was going to be a big jump, he should've said it was going to be an Olympian feat. Not only was the roof nearly a good five feet lower, there was what looked like an eight-foot gap between the shelf and the roof. If I didn't make the roof, the fall would likely kill me.

To make matters worse, a lone zed was stuck in the alley, blocked on one side by the playground fence and the other by a car. It was on the ground, its legs mangled as though it had been caught between the car and the fence at some point, and it had dragged itself around in circles, if the brown trail was any indication.

"Oh, Jesus—"

My glare cut off Jase's words and he clamped his mouth shut.

"If I go first," Clutch said. "One of you will have to throw me the duffel."

I almost chuckled at the absurdity. There was no way I could throw a fifty-pound bag two feet, let alone fifteen. "I'll go first," I said. "I'll catch." What I meant was, *I'll use my body to block the bag's momentum and hopefully not die upon impact.*

He nodded, and I backed up to the edge of the shelf overlooking the lumberyard. If I thought about it, I knew I'd freak, so I didn't wait. I took three big breaths before sprinting forward. At the other edge, I kicked off into a scary-as-shit long-jump. Just when I thought I'd never reach the edge of the roof, I landed on the flat surface, falling forward instantly. The air whooshed from my lungs, and my teeth snapped shut painfully when I hit my chin. I slid down a couple feet before coming to a stop on the abrasive shingles.

I rolled over and coughed and wheezed.

"You okay?" Clutch called out, and I held up my thumb.

Once I could breathe again, I pulled myself up and inched my way back up to the peak. "Throw me the bag."

Clutch held up the bag, and I held out my arms and swallowed. Jase stood off to the side, watching with wide eyes. Clutch swung the duffel in a wide arc and released it with a grunt. I stood there and waited for the smack-down, and Clutch's aim was dead-on. The duffel hit me square in the stomach, and I fell backward, holding it to me. I slid several feet down the roof, but the duffel's canvas helped slow my descent. By the time I sat up, I found Clutch on the roof with me.

"Nice catch."

I coughed and handed him the duffel. "I don't think I

have tits anymore."

He gave that deep rumble of a chuckle, heaved the bag onto his back, and winced.

"Your shoulder?"

He rubbed it. "Yeah. Twisted it when I threw the duffel."

He reached out with his other hand and helped me to my feet. We looked over at Jase. He stood there, frozen. The zed in the alley was groaning, reaching up.

I motioned him over with one hand while still holding my bruised ribs with my other. "You can do it, monkey boy."

He looked down once more and then slowly backed up. With a half-crouch, he rocked back and forth before kicking off. He easily closed the distance and landed solidly on the roof. But his footing gave way, and he kicked out and went tumbling down the side. He grabbed at the roof but kept sliding until he disappeared over the edge.

"Jase!"

Clutch and I moved cautiously down the angled roof to the edge. Jase was on the ground, holding onto his ankle. Instead of the parking lot side, Jase had fallen into the playground. *Shit.* I scanned the enclosed area but saw no movement.

Jase winced. "My ankle. I think it's broken."

"Can you stand?" Clutch asked.

Jase grunted, was able to get to his feet, but he favored his right leg.

"Good. Now, do you see a door in the fence? Or, is there anything around you can use to climb back up here?"

As Jase looked around, I scanned the privacy fence, but found only a gate at one end, and it had a large, shiny padlock on it.

"There's nothing down here," Jase said, holding up his hands in defeat.

"Jase, do you see any zeds around?" I asked.

"Not out here. I see some inside, though. Oh, God. They see me."

"Bloody hell," I muttered. "I'll handle this."

Clutch eyed me. "Cash…"

"He's injured. I'm not. You can pull me up once we get Jase to safety." Before I had a chance to think about how dumb the idea was, I shimmied down, holding onto the edge until I had to let go. The drop sent shockwaves up my shins, but I landed without twisting anything.

"Godammit, Cash," Clutch said from above.

I also heard a small pounding behind me. I turned to see children watching us through a classroom window. They were young, one of the earlier grades, and they were no longer alive. They watched us hungrily, smacking their small hands against the glass.

I hooked my fingers together to make a step. "Climb up, and be quick about it."

Jase didn't argue. With a grunt, he stepped into my cupped hands with his good leg. I lifted his weight as high as I could, using my legs. Clutch reached down from the roof. It wasn't quite enough. Jase stepped onto my shoulder, and then his weight vanished. I looked up to see his legs disappear onto the roof.

Clutch reappeared an instant later. "Now get your ass up here, Cash."

I jogged around the playground, looking for a jump rope but finding only rubber balls and jungle gyms. I fidgeted with the padlock at the gate, but I had nothing to pick the lock with, not that I even knew how to pick a lock. I tried to jump up to grab the top of the privacy fence, but it was too high. With a sigh, I looked at the windows, each filled with hungry, hollow little faces.

"Is there any rope in the truck?" I asked.

Clutch thought for a moment. "I've got tie straps." He moved. "I'll come down, and you can go grab them."

I held up my hand. "No. Then you'll be stuck down here. Go for the truck."

Glass shattered, and I jerked around to find a teacher stepping through the now-broken window. I pulled out my new machete. "Get Jase to the truck. I'll catch up."

"We're not leaving," Clutch yelled back.

I swung the machete, nearly decapitating a teacher with its hands and forearms covered with little bites. "Go. Hurry!" I wasn't used to the blade, so my aim was off. The second swing killed it. Small zeds tumbled out of the window. A gunshot rang out. A boy in jeans and a sports jersey dropped. Another shot. A girl with pigtails dropped. Several more shots and the rest of the zed kids dropped. The ones still held inside were pounding harder on the glass now, in a frenzy to get out.

I looked up at Clutch to find him reloading. "The shots will draw more zeds to the school," I yelled up. "Take Jase and get to the truck before the parking lot fills up."

"No," Clutch replied.

I watched him. More glass behind me shattered. "I won't let you die for me." After a quick glance at the newcomers, I went for the only door that I knew would be unlocked.

"Cash!"

I pushed open the glass door with my left hand, and swung the machete at the first zed with my right. The kid went right down. The hallway was not nearly as congested as the classrooms, which I noticed nearly all had their doors closed.

I jogged down the hallway, shoving zed kids out of my way, thankful for the thick gloves and jacket I'd worn. A zed could bite through it eventually, but at least it'd have to work at it.

I turned the corner into the main hallway and froze. A couple dozen three- and four-foot tall zeds with three adult zeds turned to face me. One growled, and the groans began. They lurched forward.

I spun around to backtrack, but the hall had filled in behind me as well, with a zed wearing a tag reading

HALL MONITOR leading the group. I lunged for the double door to my left and jumped inside. After making sure the door was shut tight, I spun on my heel.

"Fuck me."

I'd found the school cafeteria. Food trays were scattered across the floors. The buffet line had been ravaged. Several bodies, with most of their skin and muscle gone, were sprawled on the floor, covered in writhing maggots. And now, the large room was full of food-stained, bloodied zeds, and every single one of the bastards were focused on me.

They staggered toward me with outreached arms, and I jumped up onto a table, then onto the next table, sliding through spaghetti sauce that I knew wasn't really spaghetti sauce.

I slid the machete in my belt and leapt, grabbing the fluorescent light hanging from the ceiling. Surprisingly, it held. Miraculously, my adrenaline helped me pull myself up, safely out of reach of the small arms. But larger arms connected to zeds in lunch lady uniforms reached perilously close.

"I'm not going to die," I muttered and punched up at the ceiling. The white panel moved, and I realized this was one of those drop-down ceilings that allowed space for wiring and cables.

Gripping the metal frame, I swung and kicked up, knocking out another white panel, catching my foot on the frame. Using the strength of my legs, I was able to pull myself up and above the frame.

A sea of jaundiced dead faces looked up at me, growling, reaching, and chomping. I moved carefully and slowly onto the next frame, careful to distribute my weight over two rows of metal framing. I had no idea how much weight these ceilings were meant to hold, but they sure as hell couldn't have been built for human travel.

I crawled over one panel to the next, pausing every few panels to catch my breath. My directions were jumbled in the darkness. I had no idea if I was heading toward the parking lot, back to the playground, or if I was going in circles. I lifted the edge of the panel to find that I was still in the cafeteria. Zeds stood under the opening I'd made in the ceiling in the opposite side of the room, still looking up, sniffing the air, reaching, mouths opening and closing like baby birds.

A crack of light filtered in through the corner I'd lifted and lit up the wall of concrete blocks in front of me. *Shit.* The ceiling ended where the wall separated the cafeteria from the hallway. My arms and legs were already shaking. I had to figure out something or else I'd fall right down into the cafeteria again. Except this time, I'd never have the strength to get back up here.

But there was nothing up here except space, wiring, and…air ducts. My attention shot to the large duct leading straight through the center of the cafeteria and through the concrete wall. Many smaller ducts ran off it like a spider's legs. Ducts looked so much bigger in the movies, but I prayed that this one would be big enough.

It *had* to be.

I made my way toward the metal duct. Sweat burned my eyes and tickled my neck as rivulets ran down to soak my shirt. By the time I reached the duct, I was exhausted and clumsy, nearly tumbling off the ceiling grid twice. I moved alongside the duct until I found where one section ended and another began. Both were held together by screws. I pulled out my tanto and used the tip to unscrew the first screw, and then the next. It was a painfully slow process to take out the six screws on the sides I could reach.

I pushed against the duct but it didn't budge. Trading my knife for the axe, I pulled back a few measly inches and swung. The metal clanged and dented, echoed by moaning and shuffling below. A couple dozen hits later, the duct broke open. I slid the axe inside and shoved myself through. Sharp metal from the axe's damage dug into me, but I continued to squeeze into the tiny boxed-in darkness until I filled up the area of the duct.

I sneezed in the dust-laden air, causing the zeds below to echo with moans. Using my elbows, I pulled myself forward. I could see nothing except light filtered in from vents every eight feet or so.

At each vent, I paused and looked down. The hallway was filled with shoulder-to-shoulder zeds sniffing the air. When the duct split into three pathways, I decided to head left over the hallway, hoping it would bring me to the front doors. I followed the duct, through several more intersections.

I sobbed out in exhausted frustration. My cramped muscles burned. My helmet clanged against the metal, but there was no space to take it off and leave it behind. When I finally reached a vent where I could see the front doors, I rested my head against the vent and nearly cried.

The glass doors were blocked by zeds.

Biting back a whimper, I backed up about ten feet until I came to an intersection and I took the first right. This duct led to a room with a couple office-style desks. It wasn't a classroom, which gave me some hope.

Seeing no movement below, I fidgeted with the vent until I figured out how to remove it, and it dropped, landing on the floor with an echoing clang. Something moaned, and a shadow moved. A female, wearing khakis and a blue blouse with dark stains, stepped on the vent and looked around.

"Can't I get a break?" I muttered.

Moving slowly, I reached out of the duct with the axe. The zed must've heard something because it looked up right as I swung. The axe caught it in the forehead, and it tumbled back, taking the axe with it.

I grabbed my machete and waited for another one, but none came. I breathed in and out and waited. Dropping down feet first into a room with possible zeds was not my idea of a good time.

Careful to not bang my helmet on the metal, I lowered my head out of the vent to scan the room. It was an office with two desks and glass walls. The principal's office was just on the other side of the glass wall to the right, and it was still occupied by a zed in a tailored skirt suit. She rocked on her feet, looking out the window.

The other glass walls faced two angles of the hallway, giving full views of the zed near the front doors. At least both doors were closed, but I had no idea if they were locked or would hold back the weight of zeds pushing against them.

I'd be in a fishbowl the moment I dropped.

Like the principal's office, the fourth wall had a nice wide window overlooking the school parking lot. I could make out only one zed, and it was trapped inside a car. Maybe the zeds who'd escaped the Home Depot had followed Clutch's truck when he left with Jase.

God, I hated maybes.

Unless the window was heavily tinted, the sun had nearly set, which meant I'd been crawling around this place for at least eight hours. I wasn't the least bit surprised, not with how exhausted and thirsty I was. I even wondered if I'd be able to stand once I got out of this duct. My stomach had quit growling hours ago. My throat was parched, and my clothes were soaked.

I pulled my head back in, and shimmied forward over the opening so that I could back up and drop feet first into the room. I would've preferred to go head first to see around, but the opening was too tight, and there would be nothing to grab onto to keep me from breaking my neck from the drop.

After sliding the machete back into my belt, I squeezed through as quietly and motionlessly as I could to not draw attention. About halfway through, I heard a pounding on the glass. I shoved myself through the rest of the way, and I finally popped through, dropping onto the floor.

The moment I landed, every zed, including the principal, clambered to get to me. Putting a foot on the dead zed's chest, I grabbed the axe handle and yanked it free. I ran to the window, swung the axe, and the glass shattered apart. The hallway door behind me cracked. I saw a handbag under the desk. I grabbed it and jumped on the desk and through the window.

I had no time to barricade the window, and I started running through the parking lot. Clutch's truck was long gone, which I'd expected. They would've been idiots to wait around to get overtaken by zeds for the slightest chance that I'd survived.

Three zeds came out from around a minivan in front of me. I stopped, dropped the purse, and pulled out my Glock. Three shots. Three went down.

Slinging the bag over my shoulder, I ran to the car where I'd seen the zeds and ducked behind the trunk. I dumped out the contents of the large purple purse, and sifted through the pile of crap that had tumbled out until I found the one thing I needed. Coming up on a knee, I held up the car key, and hit the unlock button. Lights flashed and chirped on a car parked near the front door.

Five zeds had already emerged through the broken glass window. It wouldn't take long for the parking lot to be flooded. With the Glock in one hand, the key ring dangling off my pinky, and the axe in another, I ran toward the car.

The zeds staggered toward me, but I was faster. With a cursory look through the car's windows, I yanked open the car door and climbed inside.

Dropping the axe on the passenger seat and the gun on my lap, I slid the key into the ignition. The engine started with pop music blaring from the speakers, and I shoved the gear into reverse. The car barreled over the zeds coming around behind and struggled as it dragged itself over the bodies.

I needed a tank. I got a fucking Prius.

Zeds stumbled at the car, and I swung the car around, shifted gears, and peeled out. I took off my helmet and threw it onto the seat next to me and turned off the CD player before picking up speed. I barreled right down Main Street, taking out another four zeds on my way through. The Prius was no truck and one of the zeds clung onto the hood for several blocks before I finally managed to throw him off.

The compact car wasn't made for demolition, but I was counting on its gas mileage. It showed a near-empty tank of gas (who the hell drives on an empty tank?), but being a Prius, the computer indicated it had plenty to get me back to the farm. I sped straight back through town the way we'd come this morning, and nearly ran into a Humvee at the second detour. It was full of people, including the couple I'd seen this morning.

The blond guy manning the .30 cal machine gun on top waved me down. He might've been a soldier, or he might've been friends with the bastard raiders from earlier. I stepped on the gas, and the tires actually squealed as I sped away.

The Humvee followed for several blocks before slowing and breaking away. I checked the rearview mirror all the way back to the farm to make sure I wasn't followed. When I reached the lane, I found the gate closed but unlocked, and I frowned.

This wasn't like Clutch. He never made mistakes like this.

I didn't have the strength, but somehow I managed to slide the gate open and then closed and locked it. As I drove down the lane, I scanned the trees for raiders and zeds, but my eyes could barely focus. My body was way past its limits. I prayed that the farm was still safe because I wasn't sure I could defend it.

When I pulled into view of the house, I cried out with relief. Clutch stood at the truck, holding two rifles and a shitload of ammo. He set everything down. "Cash!" he yelled, jogging toward me.

I stumbled out of the Prius, and fell to my knees. Adrenaline had abandoned me, leaving me without strength. But then Clutch was there, picking me up.

"You're safe now," he murmured as he carried me into the house.

Sighing, I rested my head against his chest and listened to his steady breathing. I laid my hand over his pounding heart. It felt good to feel something alive again. I'd killed children today. Even though they were zeds, they still wore the guise of innocence. And still, I found killing was easy.

It's the living with yourself afterward that's tough.

GREED

THE FOURTH CIRCLE OF HELL

CHAPTER VII

Exhaustion claimed me, and I sank deeper into Clutch's safe arms.

Saying nothing, he carried me into the house and rather than bringing me to the sofa where I'd slept since Jase came to live here, he carried me upstairs.

"Cash! We were so freaking worried!" Jase yelled out through the open door of his bedroom.

Without pausing at Jase's room, Clutch carried me straight into his bedroom. I barely stayed awake while he helped me out of my sweat- and dust-drenched layers, leaving me in only my sports bra and underwear.

He left, returning moments later with wet washcloths. He ran the cloths gently over my skin, likely checking me for bites and injuries more than cleaning me, but I didn't care. His touch felt good.

Finished, he helped me crawl under the blankets of

his king-sized bed, and tucked them around me. I groaned at the protective comfort of the blankets and pulled them tighter to me. "So good to be home."

Clutch grunted before disappearing again, and the next thing I knew he was nudging me awake. I grumbled as he lifted my head up and held a glass of water to my lips. My hands wrapped around his fingers on the glass while I clumsily slurped at the contents. The cool water drenched the dust and debris lodged in my raw throat and I coughed. Once I could breathe again, I gulped down the rest. He wiped water from my chin before he lowered my head back to the pillow and stepped away.

At the door he paused. "I never should've left you behind," he said, his voice a rough whisper.

I shook my head. "I made you go."

"No. You didn't." Then he walked away, closing the door behind him, leaving behind only silence.

"Clutch," I called out with a cough, but he never returned. At first I fought to stay awake so I could talk some sense into him, but all too quickly I surrendered to a dreamless sleep.

I slept through most of the next day, though I remember Clutch checking on me several times. Each time, his calloused hand brushed across my forehead and he made me drink water before letting me doze off again. One time, he wouldn't leave until I'd eaten a protein bar. I grumbled, he grumbled, and I ate it. Then I fell back asleep.

Nightmares of children that were no longer children yanked me back to consciousness. Luckily, instead of the moans of zeds, I came awake to the sound of stacking plates and the smell of warm food.

Every muscle in my body griped when I climbed out of bed. After a full-body stretch, I forced myself through fifty sit-ups and fifty push-ups to get my blood pumping. My body hated me for it, but I pushed through it. Finished, I headed across the hall to the bedroom I'd given up to Jase when he moved in, and grabbed fresh clothes from a drawer I'd kept in the dresser.

Without power, we had no water pressure for a shower the three of us shared. I sighed in relief when I found four buckets of clean water waiting next to the tub. I poured them into the tub, stripped, and settled into the biting cold water, trying to scrub away the memories from yesterday, with little success.

Not having warm water tended to speed up the cleaning process. Shivering, I jogged down the steps to find Clutch cooking dinner on the tabletop propane grill we'd moved into the kitchen after the power went out. He gave me a small nod before turning his attention back to the food. I grabbed a spoon and reached into the pot, but he grabbed my wrist. "Nuh-uh. You have to wait like the rest of us."

I pouted and then smirked. "Hurry up. I'm starving," I ordered and headed into the living room, the only light from a small lantern.

"Hey, Cash," Jase called from the sofa.

I nodded toward his left foot propped up on a chair, a thick wrapping around his ankle. "How's the leg?"

He rubbed his ankle. "It's just a sprain. Clutch says the swelling will be down enough in another day or two that I can start putting some weight on it again." He looked up. "Wow, you slept for like twenty-four hours straight."

"She needed it," Clutch said before handing Jase and me each a bowl.

I grabbed a seat next to Jase and dug into tonight's specialty—a steaming mix of mystery meat, beans, and rice.

Clutch returned with his own bowl and a warm beer.

"So tell me about the school. Were there more zeds inside?" Jase asked.

I paused before taking a bite. "Yeah."

"What was it like? I bet it was scary," he continued.

I kept chewing. The memories were bad enough for me. No one else needed to have them haunting their conscience.

Clutch gave me a knowing look but said nothing. He finished his dinner and beer before I was even halfway through mine. He came to his feet. "I should get back outside."

I looked up. "Have you been covering both Jase's and my shifts?"

He didn't reply, but the dark circles under his eyes told me enough. He looked beat, and I'd bet he hadn't slept once in the past two days.

"I'll cover all of tonight," I said. "You're on bed rest, effective immediately."

He raised a brow. "You're ordering me around now?"

I smiled. Then nodded.

A smirk tugged at his lips before he relented. "Wake me when you need a break. Don't overdo it because, at sunrise, we need to start hitting the farms around here hard and fast. A vehicle drove by slow yesterday, which I'd bet are looters scanning this area."

"Shit," I muttered. While I'd expected looters to sniff around this area sometime, I'd also hoped that they'd take their own sweet time before doing so. There were literally hundreds of miles of roads in the area. Why couldn't they leave our four-mile stretch alone?

"We need everything we can get and fast," Clutch added. "And, I'm out of beer and almost out of whiskey."

I grimaced. "I can't believe you'd drink warm beer."

"Warm beer is better than no beer."

"Point taken." I shooed him away. "Now go. Hit the sack. You're even grumpier when you're tired."

He grunted and cracked his neck. "Be careful out there. I saw a group of zeds pass through the field yesterday. We've been lucky they've mostly avoided the woods so far."

"I wonder why they haven't hit the woods," I said. After all, if I was a predator, they'd be a prime spot.

"I'm thinking they prefer taking easier routes since they can't get around as easily as us," Clutch replied before disappearing up the stairs.

So far, most zeds we'd seen had stuck to open flatlands like roads, yards, and fields. But a few had stumbled through the woods already, so they certainly didn't have an allergy to shrubbery.

I would've eaten faster, but my stomach was cramping from going nearly two days on only a protein bar, and I had to pace myself. At least I was wide awake. A near-coma was exactly what my body had needed. My muscles were amped. I wished it was morning already so that we could get started on looting the nearby farms. We'd been forced to put it off while we fortified the farm against looters. But we *needed* food and supplies. Even though winter was at least eight months away, we needed to hoard anything we could to prepare.

Running into zeds or looters was a chance we had to take.

"You were lucky you got back to the farm when you did," Jase mumbled with a mouth full of food. "Clutch was packing up to head back into town for you. I wanted to come, but he said I had to stay back and hold down the fort."

"He was an idiot," I said. When I'd seen Clutch loading weapons into the truck, I'd already figured he wasn't heading out for another solo looting run. Going anywhere after dark was a suicide run, especially to a particular elementary school. Clutch could've gotten himself killed for the infinitesimal chance that I was still alive. It was a miracle I'd gotten back to the house when I did. If he'd gone into town to look for me…if he hadn't returned…

With a shiver, I came to my feet and headed into the kitchen to clean up, all the time praying that those thoughts would never become reality.

After I had my weapons strapped on, I stopped by the living room. "You need help getting upstairs?" I asked.

Jase looked up from the book he'd been reading and shook his head. "Nah. I'll hang down here for a bit. I'm tired of being in bed." He thumped the book down. "I hate being cooped up like this."

"You'll be back on your feet before you know it." I gave him a quick wave and then headed outside. The sun had set, and I walked the perimeter around the house first. I'd always hated night-watch. Now, I had a whole new perspective. Even in the dark where zeds could lurk, I found the open space and fresh air a vast improvement over the school's cramped air ducts.

The walk down the long lane, with trees lining both sides, seemed easier tonight. Sure, a zed could shuffle out from the darkness at any moment, but the idea didn't terrify me as much as it had less than two days ago.

There was hardly a breeze, with every sound lingering in the air. My natural warning system of crickets chirping and frogs croaking was in full effect tonight. Insects and animals tended to go silent when zeds were around.

At the end of the lane, the gate stood solidly fastened to the barbed wire and chain link fence doubled up on both sides. I double-checked the locks. It was the only opening in the fence lining Clutch's property along the roadside. We'd reinforced the old fence with reams of chain link we'd taken from Jase's farm, but we needed much more to make it strong enough to hold back zeds and to build a secondary fence around the house.

A single human could climb easily over the fence or come through the woods, but with the deep ditches for Iowa winters, vehicles could enter the farm only through the gate. And, except for a couple trails, the woods surrounding the house served as a barrier against vehicles on three sides.

But the woods wouldn't hold back zeds, not for long. Clutch owned a few hundred acres and with a fence only along the roadside, the other three sides were wide-open fields. If the zeds passed through in large groups, we'd have some serious problems on our hands.

I leaned on the metal gate, staring out at the star-studded sky. The stars were so much brighter here than in Des Moines…or at least when too many city lights clouded the nights. I guess the stars would shine just as brightly everywhere now.

A clear night and smooth air: it would've been a perfect night for a flight. God, I missed watching the sun set from the air.

Even more, I missed my parents. They lived in a residential area not far from downtown. Mom had diabetes and needed daily insulin shots. If they were still in town, they'd be surrounded by hundreds of thousands of zeds by now. The first week, I mentioned the idea of heading into Des Moines for them, but Clutch had said it was too dangerous. After seeing Fox Hills, a town point five percent the size of the Des Moines area filled with zeds, I couldn't argue his logic.

My only regret was that I'd never even gotten the chance to say good-bye.

A rhythmic scraping sound off to my left drew my attention. Careful to avoid Clutch's booby traps, I made my way down the fence line until the zed came into sight. A green John Deere hat hung crookedly on its head. It had been an older man, with short white hair peeking out from under the hat. Its facial features were impossible to make out since decay had already started to set in. It dragged one leg, its boot grating the gravel with each step in a monotonous rhythm.

Step.

Scrape.

Step.

Scrape.

The signature sound of a zed.

Once I made sure it didn't have any friends, I stepped up to the fence. "Hey, fucktard."

The zed lifted its head, and sniffed in my direction.

Even with yellowish pupils, it seemed to see fine because it moaned and shuffled its way straight toward me, stumbling while walking down the ditch. When it finally regained its footing and dragged itself up to the fence, I pulled out my machete.

When it reached for me, I swung. Its head lobbed off and bounced on the ground. Its fingers had tangled in the fence, and I kicked the body, sending it backward into the ditch. Its hat had fallen off and landed near the head.

I leaned over the fence and watched the head for a good ten minutes. The thing just kept watching me, moving its mouth. I narrowed my eyes but couldn't see any kind of humanity left in its gaze. Its eyes were truly devoid of *anything*.

After scanning the area one more time, I climbed over the fence, looked at the head, and then brought the heel of my foot down. Its front teeth shattered. I stomped again and again until the skull crushed inward and the mouth finally stilled.

I picked up the hat and tossed it onto the body. The smell would be worse tomorrow, when I could safely move the zed's body farther away and cover it with dirt since we'd decided to quit burning the zeds we took down. It was too much work and the smoke could be seen and smelled from too far away.

The crickets resumed their chirping. The stars still shone brightly, happy in their places so far away from a world consumed by death. And so I climbed back over the fence and continued my patrol.

I rehydrated every hour. At four a.m., I headed into the house to check on the guys. Jase was sleeping soundly on the couch, a paperback copy of the *SAS Survival Handbook* sprawled open across his chest. I gently tugged it from under his hand, dog-eared the page, and set it on the floor. I tiptoed up the stairs and paused outside Clutch's room. Muffled grunts came from the other side. Every night was the same. A couple hours after he fell asleep, the nightmares would come.

Every other night, I listened, waiting for him to wake or fall back into a restful sleep.

Tonight, I turned the knob and entered.

Clutch lay in the middle of the bed, the sheets tossed around him. His skin gleamed with sweat. He grunted and jerked, lost within his dream.

Careful to not disturb him, I sat down on the edge of the mattress. I reached out and laid my palm on his chest. His blade swung out.

I sucked in a breath.

He stopped just before slicing my throat ear to ear. Blinking, his eyes grew wide. "Jesus." He fell back onto the mattress, pulling the knife away. "Damn, Cash. I could've killed you."

I let out the breath I'd been holding. "You were having a bad dream." Again.

He rolled onto his side, facing away from me. "It was nothing."

I slid up on the bed, sitting with my back against the

headboard. "Tell me about it."

"Everything all right outside?" he asked instead.

I sighed, disappointed. "Just one. No problems."

"What time is it?" he asked, sounding all too tired himself.

"Four."

He sat up. "I can take over the patrol now."

"No," I replied, not moving. "I'm wide awake."

He lay for a moment before sighing. "What are you doing?"

"I'm staying until you fall asleep."

After several long seconds, he gave me his back. "Have it your way."

I rested my head against the headboard and sat there in silence, waiting. I remembered when I'd had bad dreams as a kid, my dad would stay with me until I fell asleep. His presence chased away the imaginary monsters. I had no idea if it would help Clutch. His monsters were bigger and badder, but I couldn't let him go on every night facing them alone.

After Clutch's breathing became deep and regular, I crept from his room, grabbed another protein bar, and headed back outside. I had time to make another pass around the farm before the sky morphed from black to purple to orange. The world, for once, was at peace, and I savored watching the sun rise over the horizon.

Clutch emerged from the house looking refreshed, and we were ready to hit the road before the sun was fully over the horizon, with dew still creating sparkles on the grass. Jase limped outside to see us off, leaning on a tall stick for support, and armed to the teeth.

"I swear it, guys," Jase said. "It doesn't hurt bad. Take your time. I'll cover the place today."

Clutch nodded at Jase's stick. "Then why are you still using your crutch?"

Jase pursed his lips.

Clutch narrowed his eyes. "The only way you're staying behind is if you can shimmy up on the roof. That way, you can scan while you start replacing the busted shingles."

Jase grinned. "Heck, yeah, I can do that."

"Be sure to bring plenty of ammo with you. Watching for looters and zeds is more important than patching the roof," Clutch added. He started to turn, then paused. "Oh, and use a mallet. I don't want you drawing every zed in a ten-mile radius."

Jase gave an enthusiastic nod. "You bet!" He grabbed his stick and hopped back into the house.

I smirked. "You were planning on letting him stay behind all along."

He shrugged. "Ready?"

I held out my hand. "After you."

With a fleeting smile, he headed toward the truck, and I followed.

On our drive, we came across a group of zeds feasting on a cow while the rest of the herd huddled together in the far corner of the pasture. I gripped my rifle tighter.

"We need to conserve our ammo," Clutch said as though reading my thoughts. "They're still a ways from the farm. Maybe they'll keep moving on."

"We should at least cut the fence," I said. "Give the rest of the cattle a chance."

He sighed before slowing to a stop. "We won't be able to save all the livestock. The zeds will get to all of it eventually."

"I know, but at least we can help these few."

He jumped out and opened the back door and pulled out a bolt cutter. I got out and held my rifle at the ready. The fence was a simple barbed-wire, taking Clutch no more than four quick snips to open up a section for the cattle to escape should they find the gap. We were back on the road seconds later.

We saw a couple dozen more zeds, mostly alone or in pairs, walking aimlessly on roads and through fields. As we entered an older residential part of Fox Hills—what Jase named Chow Town after the Home Depot experience—the area was eerily quiet. With no people or cars, nothing moved except for the occasional zed.

"Where is everyone?" I asked softly.

Clutch didn't reply, just kept on driving.

When he pulled in between two zeds meandering on the pavement and into the parking lot, I let out a sigh of relief. Mabel's Garden Center was nothing near the size of Home Depot, meaning that there shouldn't have been nearly as many people there when the outbreak hit.

Hopefully.

Still, my stomach was in knots.

I kept my fingers crossed that the remaining zeds in the area had already moved on to find food elsewhere. Clutch backed the truck up to the front doors, so we could load and then get away quickly. We moved silently from the truck, knowing that even though the area seemed relatively clear, zeds lurked everywhere.

He looked at me. "You can stay outside and stand guard if you want. I can cover the greenhouse."

I pulled out the small axe and shook my head. "No. Let's stick to the plan."

We opened our doors at the same time. I scalped the first zed with a quick strike to its temple, and it fell lifelessly to the ground. I turned to see Clutch standing over a dead zed.

We walked up to the front glass doors and looked inside. A cashier still hovered at his cash register. With an axe in one hand and the machete in another, Clutch rapped on the glass, and the zed turned around. Its empty gaze leveled hungrily on us, and it stumbled forward. Another one emerged from an aisle. It had been an older woman, still wearing gardening gloves, and she'd been badly chewed upon. A third, another employee, headed toward the doors.

We waited until all three were at the doors, before counting down...*three, two, one.* I yanked the door open and jumped back. Clutch swung the axe and then swung the machete. One of the zeds refused to go down after a glancing blow, but my axe to its forehead finished the job.

We dragged the bodies out of our way, and scanned the rest of the place, finding only one more zed trapped under a collapsed shelf.

We wasted no time in grabbing all the heirloom seeds, fertilizer, and fencing we could find. If we could plant enough crops, we could get through the winter and have plenty of seeds for next year. We might even be able to take in another survivor or two, which we desperately needed. Defending an entire farm with only three people was exhausting work.

We were heading back to the front doors to close up the greenhouse when we saw them. All four men wore military fatigues—much like ours—and had automatic rifles slung over their shoulders. With shaved heads, the men looked all the same: white, dirty, and mean.

And they were currently in the back of Clutch's truck, stealing our loot.

Clutch threw me a quick glance, then whispered, "Stay inside, and be ready to run in case this goes to shit."

"Be careful." I pulled the rifle off my shoulder and leaned against the door, aiming at the men busy moving things from our truck to theirs.

Clutch fired a shot into the air, and they froze like skittish deer, one of them dropping his stolen cargo. They scrambled to raise their rifles as Clutch took a couple steps forward, keeping his Glock leveled on them.

The cleanest looking of the men relaxed and grinned. "Clutch! It's good to see a familiar face."

Clutch narrowed his eyes. "What are you doing here, Sean?"

One of the other men stepped forward. "You're taking things that don't belong to you."

"And it belongs to you?" Clutch countered. "I knew Mabel, and she's lying dead inside."

"It doesn't matter, Clutch. It's the rules," Sean said. "All supplies must go through the Fox Hills militia for reallocation. We divvy them out to citizens based on need."

Clutch chuckled, though there was no humor in the sound. "Based on *whose* need? Yours or theirs?"

"You'll turn over the truck, the supplies, and that girl with you," another man called out, pointing at me.

"Good luck with that," Clutch said before turning back to Sean. "Where's the government order establishing a militia?"

"There's no government anymore," Sean replied.

"Camp Fox has fallen?"

Sean stammered. "We—we're working in collaboration with the National Guard. We're helping them out."

"And who's in charge of this little militia?" Clutch asked.

"Doyle," one of the men said. "And he'll kick your ass for getting in our way."

"Let me see the government order from Camp Fox

instating Doyle as head of the militia," Clutch said. "Until then, you're all just bandits. And, I'll shoot any man who tries to take *anything* of mine."

The men kept their fully automatic rifles raised.

"But Clutch…" Sean pleaded

"You going to shoot me, boy?" Clutch guffawed at the man who looked about my age. "You might get in a lucky shot or two, but I guaran-fucking-tee that I'm taking every last one of your sorry asses with me. And I don't give a flying fuck that you've sold seed corn to me before, Sean."

"Let's just kill this asshole and be done with it," one of the men said, and I leveled the rifle to aim dead center in the middle of his forehead.

"Dibs on the girl," the third man added.

"Screw you," I called out, keeping my aim steady.

"Soon, girly," the man with the toothy grin said.

Sean patted the air. "There's going to be no shooting today. We're leaving." The men around him raised an uproar. Sean snapped around to his compatriots. "We're leaving! This place is going to be crawling with zeds soon enough the way it is." Sean turned to Clutch, looking exasperated. "You can keep this stuff from today, just because we have a history. But the militia is in charge around here. You'd be best to join up or get out of our way. And your little girl over there needs to be moved in with the other civilians at our camp for protection. The rules have changed. I'd watch your back if I were you."

With that final warning, they climbed into their truck. One of the men in the truck bed fired several shots into the sky. They whooped and one flipped us off as they sped away, kicking up rocks.

"Assholes," I muttered, coming around to stand by Clutch.

"Sean was right." He looked at me. "We're going to have to watch our backs. They've seen us. Sean knows where I live. And they know I won't play along with their games. That makes me an enemy. As for you..." He looked me up and down.

I shivered, even though the sun shone brightly in the sky. "Then we'd best avoid them."

He locked the lift gate and headed to the driver's side. "These guys are nothing but Doyle's dogs, using the façade of a militia to take what they want."

"Who's this Doyle guy?" I asked. "Someone to worry about?"

"He's a cocky asshole who's owned the surplus store for decades. He's also one hell of a survivalist. Armageddon would've been a wet dream for him."

We spent the next two weeks converting the farmhouse into a fortress and planting gardens, all the while killing any zeds that made the mistake of stumbling too close to the farm. We set up a sniper's nest not far from the gate to watch for Doyle's Dogs—what we'd nicknamed the self-proclaimed militia.

Jase turned out to be a great asset. Even though he slept until ten every morning, once awake, he was boundless energy, and his ankle healed quickly. Between the two of us, we could lift nearly as much as Clutch could.

We covered the first floor windows with chain link fence to hold back zeds and fastened strips of fencing up to the second floor windows, giving us a way to get inside in case the front door was blocked. We even boarded up the front door, leaving the only entrance in and out through the cellar door, which could be better secured from the inside. We reinforced the gate at the end of the drive so that intruders with anything less than a tank or heavy bolt cutters would have a tough time cutting the chains to get through.

Using the fertilizer we'd picked up at the greenhouse, Clutch introduced Jase and me to the art of setting explosive booby traps, multiplying the reliability of our existing perimeter protection tenfold.

But the three of us worked together only when absolutely necessary. Most of the time, we rotated shifts to have one person on guard duty. No more zeds passed through the yard, but more and more were showing up on the roads and in the fields. Only Clutch scouted the woods. Jase and I were neither gutsy enough nor good enough yet to go deep into the acres of tangled trees alone, though Clutch regularly reminded me that I needed to get familiar with those woods sometime. If the Dogs came at us, hiding in the woods could make the difference between life and death.

We figured that, at the speed zeds shambled along, it would take only a few months before they started spreading outward from Des Moines in a mass exodus. The four or five thousand zeds in Fox Hills were another story. We had to be ready for them *now*.

One thing that bothered me was that we hadn't seen signs of any more uninfected humans. Clutch had said that they'd hide out as long as they could, but it had been three weeks since the outbreak. Most would've run out of food by now and would be forced to loot. Not hearing any other traffic made me wonder exactly how few of us remained.

The hours not spent on fortifying the farm were spent training for self-defense and killing. My strength and skills improved quickly, though I had a long ways to go. I could now do fifty diamond pushups without stopping. And, my caffeine headaches had finally gone away. Jase was already in good shape from playing in sports. Even with his still-healing ankle, he could run up to windows, check out a house, and be on his way back to the truck before zeds had a clue he was there.

Where Jase was our designated runner, I learned I had a natural affinity for being a sniper. Clutch, of course, was our diplomat should any Dogs show up. He excelled at hand-to-hand combat and could handle any weapon. He was also our strategist. Building on our areas of specialty, Clutch began to lay out plans—for both offense and defense. We were transforming from three individuals into a team.

Hoo-fucking-rah.

Clutch gave both Jase and me our own rifles. They were matching M24s with all the accessories. I hadn't even heard of an M24 before the outbreak. Now, I spent hours practicing dry shooting, disassembling, and cleaning until I could use it in complete blackness. I could load the cartridges blindfolded.

Only when I'd perfected dry shooting—aligning my body position, sight picture, breathing, and trigger squeeze—did Clutch let me fire a real round. Rather than setting up a shooting range, Clutch had taken me several miles out until we'd come across zeds. At each outing, I was only allowed to use one cartridge to conserve ammo, which meant that I had to make every shot count.

The only differences between dry and real shooting were the noise and the recoil, both of which I'd been expecting and was ready for. It was during that first time, when I took out three zeds back-to-back at a hundred yards, that I saw the rare glimpse of pride in Clutch's eyes.

Back at the farm, I'd studied the art of learning my surroundings. I trained myself to look and listen while remaining focused on something else.

I could stab the sandbag head every time, better than Jase, and I'd even dodged a couple of Clutch's moves.

But I was nowhere near Clutch's class. He could still take me down any time he wanted. I gained a worship-like appreciation for Army Rangers after seeing what he was capable of.

"Every corner poses a risk," he said after knocking me on my butt. Again.

"Silence is my friend," I replied, coming to my feet.

"What is your best weapon?" He lashed out.

I dove to the side. "I am."

"What is your second best weapon?"

"Anything I can use to shoot, stab, blow up, strike, or throw."

Clutch moved, and I found myself in a choke-hold.

"OODA?" he asked, loosening his hold somewhat.

"Observe. Orient. Decide…" I pushed back into him, but he anticipated my move and pushed forward, and I elbowed him in the stomach. He relaxed his grip, and I twisted away. "Act."

He stepped back a safe distance and crossed his arms over his chest. "And your mantra?"

I smiled. He'd given me an assignment the night before to come up with one rule, which I could meditate on to prep for any mission, to keep from getting too nervous. His was *Hit 'em hard and hit 'em often.* I wanted something that spoke more to my own internal muse. "Get 'em where I want 'em."

"Meaning?"

"To never be stupid. Never let them get me where they can overpower me or take me down. Turn my opponent's actions to my advantage."

Clutch nodded. "That'll do." He looked around the yard. "That's enough for today."

I tugged off my leather gloves. Clutch was adamant that we wore gloves any time we worked or trained so that they became like a second skin. They made me clumsy at first, but I preferred them now, even with the rifle. If they could keep me from getting a cut that could get infected, or worse, a zed bite, they were priceless.

Walking back to the house, I scanned the yard. Jase would be at the end of the lane right now, checking the gate. He ran six laps a day down the long lane to scout for zeds and raiders. He'd turned into a regular grunt. Even though we all were decked out in military gear, Jase took the style to heart. He practiced running, crawling, and combat like he was at boot camp. I'd even found him trying out different types of mud to camouflage his face the other day.

But I also knew what he did at the end of the lane. He'd pause at the gate, and stare wistfully down the road, in the direction of his old home. It was a hard reminder of what he'd lost.

Keeping busy helped me to not think about my parents.

I kept very, very busy.

We remained vigilant, day and night, watching for intruders, especially for Doyle's Dogs. At night, we took three-hour rotations, to give each of us a solid six-hour sleeping break. With the physical labor, I could fall asleep the second my head hit the pillow on the sofa. I'd gotten into a routine and was pulling my own weight next to the guys. We needed more people, but the simple fact was, aside from Doyle's Dogs and possibly Camp Fox, we'd come across no one else in some time. Even the house with boarded windows now appeared abandoned, with its front door broken wide open.

As for our house, even if zeds could get inside, which I doubted, Clutch had jerry-rigged the stairs with C4 that he could blow at a moment's notice. I never knew C4 was even legal, so I had no idea how he had come to own it. Fifty foot of paracord was placed next to each upstairs window in case the house was overrun. In the cellar, we'd built a fake wall in front of the shelves to hide our food just in case looters managed to break in.

In the gardens, Jase stood watch while I planted, and then we rotated every hour. We'd planted nearly all the seeds we'd taken from the greenhouse. We'd even planted a few herbs so we wouldn't be doomed with overly bland food all winter, though salt was already missed.

Even with all the food in the cellar, we only had enough food to get us into the winter. We had to grow a hell of a lot of food if we wanted to survive. The fields weren't safe—too much open space, and we couldn't eat the corn or soybean seed as it had all been treated with pesticides and herbicides. So we planned to plant by hand seed corn and soybeans in rows closest to the farm since he had all the seed already on hand.

Clutch estimated that we'd converted the backyard into one and a half acres of garden. Within a year, living off the land would become our only source of food. It was terrifying yet empowering.

After the quick seven-step process—which had to be done in order—of getting into the house without setting off a trap, Clutch headed to the kitchen and I turned on the small battery-powered radio and began my routine during every break of slowly scanning both radio bands. Like every other day, FM was quiet. AM had a couple of transmissions, but they must've been too far away because static drowned out the voices. As I continued to scan stations, Clutch said, "Wait. Go back."

I tuned the knob, and turned up the volume. The man spoke in a slow monotone, which was why I'd gone right past the station the first time.

"...militia now controls the towns in southern Iowa and some in northern Missouri. I drove near Des Moines two days ago. Had to see it for myself. The rumors are true. It's scorched. The military dropped H6s on it at least a week ago since there were only a few fires left burning."

I suddenly found it hard to breathe, and I fell back on my butt. Des Moines...bombed? *Mom. Dad.* While I'd known their odds were hopeless, knowing with certainty...I pressed my hand to my heart.

Clutch handed me a glass of water. He placed a hand on my shoulder. "Maybe they got out."

His words were clumsy and rushed, and I knew he didn't believe them. "Yeah, maybe," I lied right back, breathless. The finality of the situation forced me to finally admit to myself that I'd been clinging to a strand of false hope for too long. Jaw clenched, I tried not to think about my parents, focusing instead on the stranger's words.

"...I heard all major cities have been bombed to contain the spread, and any intact military units have pulled back. Though, it's safe to assume there's not much government or military left. At least one National Guard base is taking in survivors in Iowa, and that's Camp Fox. Camp Dodge was destroyed along with Des Moines. I don't have status on any Iowa units at this time.

During the American Revolution, the active forces in the field against the tyranny never amounted to more than three percent of the colonists. We are the three percenters of today. We are the militia, and we will survive this war. We will defeat the zed scourge and rebuild. I'm wired into stations across the country and will broadcast every day at 0900. This is Hawkeye broadcasting on AM 1340. Be safe and know that you're not alone. Three percenters, unite!"

Silence came from the speakers, and I sat and stared at the radio.

"Any news?" Jase asked, walking into the living room, sweaty from his run.

"Des Moines was bombed," Clutch said in a low, rumbly voice.

Jase smiled. "Hopefully they cleared out all the zeds so they won't be heading this direction."

I tossed him a glare and then turned away.

"Oh," Jase said after a moment. "Damn, Cash. I'm sorry. I forgot—"

"It's time we head out," Clutch said.

I turned back to see him standing and motioning me to get up. My limbs felt like they'd been filled with lead, but I dragged myself to my feet.

"Where are we going?" Jase asked.

"To check out the Pierson farm and pick up those chickens Cash has been wanting," Clutch said.

"If they're even still alive," I mumbled.

Clutch ignored me. "But you're staying back and guarding the house. We'll be back within three hours."

Jase looked relieved that he didn't have to go. "You got it, boss."

"Whenever we're away from my farm, we're at risk of being overtaken," Clutch said to me. "So we'll clear the house and buildings first. Then, if everything's clear, we'll grab the chickens, food, and supplies."

"Do you think it's safe?" I asked.

"I haven't seen any of the Dogs on this road yet. Maybe it's because they're giving me this road as long as I stay off the others."

I nodded, but I also knew any time he used the word "maybe", he didn't mean it. Besides, the men we'd come across at the greenhouse seemed too greedy to give up a few miles along one quiet gravel road.

I grabbed my helmet and gear before rustling around for a couple duffels Clutch had gotten from his surplus run. This time, I packed a bottle of water and a protein bar in my jacket, a lesson I learned after finding myself empty-handed at the elementary school. Clutch was already downstairs, geared up and eating a protein bar. We needed the chickens. Having fresh food would be a much-needed morale boost for all three of us.

In the truck, I asked, "How many lived there?" Up until now, we'd only grabbed anything off farms that didn't require entering buildings, waiting for numbers to thin out. That was before we realized that zeds just kept on going.

We all knew we should've started cleaning out the nearby houses earlier, knowing that it was just a matter of time before the Dogs raided the area. But by the same token, they could've been watching us already, waiting for the time we left the safety of the farm to come after us or the supplies on the farm.

We had to be careful. We didn't yet know which farmhouses hid infected inside. The only way to tell was to check them out. Chances were, occupants—infected or otherwise—would likely be hostile. I gripped the machete.

"Two. The Piersons were a young couple. Just starting out," he replied, as we reversed the seven steps to get out of the house and headed for the truck.

Clutch drove slowly enough to not kick up any dust on the gravel road while I scanned for zeds and looters.

A creek meandered down the end of Clutch's property line. With all the rains, the Fox River had flooded, filling its tributaries, this creek being one. The ground had given way not far from the road, and I saw why we hadn't seen more than a few zeds for a couple days. "It's better than a mousetrap," I said, watching the zeds trapped in the mud.

They moved in dull, slow motions that only served to have the mud pull them in deeper. One zed was naked, with mud smeared over his bloated body. All the zeds were bloated, looking as though they'd ingested twice their body weight with polluted water. A pair had been pulled so deep that they'd become stuck under the dirty water, their mouths opening and closing like fish.

"Stop," I said.

Clutch pulled to a stop and watched me.

"Once everything dries up, they could break free," I said.

He looked outside, thought for a moment, and then nodded.

I opened the door, lifted my rifle, and took aim. The naked zed went down. I fired again. Fourteen shots. Twelve dead zeds. I needed to work on my aim.

"Happy now?" he asked when I settled back in.

I smiled. Twelve fewer zeds to trespass onto the farm. "Very."

The Pierson farm was only another mile down the road, just past a farmhouse much in need of a new paint job. "Since it's so close, we can check out this one next," I mentioned as we drove past.

"Earl's," he replied. "A bit of a hermit, so he may have ridden out the outbreak. If he's not around, we may be able to pick up an extra gun or two."

A new green combine sat next to a machine shed. I thought back to the zed I'd decapitated a couple weeks back. "Was Earl a tall, skinny guy? Wore a John Deere hat?"

Clutch narrowed an eye at me. "Yeah, why?"

"We don't have to worry about him anymore."

He was quiet for a moment. "I guess we'll check out his place next, then."

He stopped before turning into the Pierson's driveway, while we scanned their farm, but it looked quiet and untouched. But we knew that wasn't the case.

We knew at least Tom Pierson was home. The house was close enough to the road that on two different drive-bys we clearly saw a man staring blankly out the window. Close enough for the man inside to see us and start thumping bloody fists against the glass. I suspected the only reason he hadn't broken the glass yet was because zeds seemed to have a limited ability to retain focus.

Even though he wasn't standing in the window now, we knew better than to believe the house was safe. We had at least one zed waiting inside. The question was, where was Tom's wife? She could be in the house, or she could be lurking around the chicken shed. Or, if she was lucky, she got away.

I'd already learned that very few people tended to get lucky in this world.

Thunder boomed in the distance, startling me.

"You okay?" Clutch asked.

I nodded. "Sounds like another storm's coming."

Clutch parked the truck behind the Pierson's Ford truck and cut the engine. The garage door had been left open, and the driver's door was left ajar.

"We'll clear out the house first since we know Tom's in there. Then the yard," Clutch rumbled in his rough voice. "Be ready."

We moved with slow, silent steps into the attached garage. Putting my back to Clutch's, we scanned the two stalls. He checked out both vehicles. I bent down to check under the vehicles. When I came to my feet, I gave him the sign for *okay*.

We stopped at the door leading from the garage to the house. Streaks of dried blood marred the paint. Clutch reached for the handle and turned it slowly. The hinges protested with a small creak. He looked inside and then took a step in. I immediately followed, checking behind the door and then taking the side of the door opposite from Clutch.

Even wearing a Kevlar helmet with the face shield down, the stench of decay and excrement was overpowering, and I forced myself to breathe through my mouth. No zed had emerged yet, which meant that maybe it hadn't heard the door open.

Or maybe it just moved slowly.

A zed that I assumed had once been Tom Pierson ambled around the corner right when Clutch took a step forward. It saw us and gave a guttural hiss. I was closer.

I swung, cleaving the top section of its head clean off. Some brown goo hemorrhaged from the wound, but not nearly as much as had come from Alan's head in the back of Clutch's rig. It seemed like the longer they'd been infected, the less "wet" they were…and a hell of a lot more smelly. I gagged and tried to block the stench that made me think of what moldy cottage cheese, rotten eggs, and putrid ground beef blended together would smell like.

Clutch kneeled by the body, and lifted its shirt. "Looks like someone unloaded a small caliber into him. If I had to guess, I'd say it was done after he turned." Then Clutch stood, stepped over the body, and moved into the next room.

I followed, hoping the smell would improve. It didn't. The living room was a mess. Broken glass and suitcases littered the floor. On the coffee table sat a purse with several hundred dollars scattered about. It looked like the guy's wife was planning an escape. Too bad money couldn't have helped her. I noticed the pistol then. It was a .22, similar to my first pistol. I picked it up and checked the cartridge. *Empty.* I frowned and slid the .22 into the back of my belt. "I don't think she got out."

Clutch's lips thinned and he nodded before moving through the room and into the hallway. He took the stairs with silent steps, and I had to concentrate to be as quiet. Upstairs, there were no signs of struggle, though there were clear signs that someone had been in a hurry to pack. Drawers were open, clothes draped the bed.

But no dark stains or bodies.

I checked under the bed while Clutch checked the closet. We repeated the process with the next three rooms. "Clear," I said, though fear nagged at me. Where had she gone? Had she managed to flee the house before she turned?

We headed back down the stairs and finished off the rest of the ground floor. When we came to the last closed door, I groaned when I saw the blood on the handle. "It had to be the basement, didn't it."

I reached over and pulled out the flashlight from Clutch's belt, and clicked it on. He motioned *three-two-one* before opening the door. Pitch black and vile stench greeted us. Beneath the smell of decay that haunted the entire house, the basement also smelled of wet earth and mildew.

With no windows to let in light, I realized that this must be a cellar like the one at Clutch's house. I shone the light down the stairs to reveal dried blood stains on the steps but no movement. I glanced at Clutch. With a shrug, he called out, "Any zed-fucks down there?"

Something clanked, and then something grunted. The sounds of moaning, shuffling, and banging continued.

"Come out, come out, wherever you are," I sang, shining the light across the floor to draw it out. There'd been plenty of blood, and I suspected this was where Tom's wife escaped after being attacked. Dark water covered at least a third of the floor, and I realized that without power, sump pumps couldn't do their jobs.

At the edge of the water, the light fell on a horribly damaged carcass of something small that had tufts of yellow fur still attached. I cringed. "Ah, geez. She ate the cat."

A shape fell forward, and I jumped.

"And there's the missus," Clutch said drily.

Mrs. Pierson must've been brutally attacked by the man she'd trusted most in the world. Bites spanned the zed's neck, hands, and arms. Scratches covered its face, but I suspected those were from the cat fighting for its life. The zed stumbled forward, reaching for the light with each step. Clutch pulled out his Glock but didn't fire.

The zed kicked the first stair step. Bumped into it again. The third time, it fell forward.

"How about that," I said. "They can't climb stairs."

As it dragged itself up, it started the process over again.

"But they never get tired," Clutch replied. "I bet if it kept at it long enough, it'd get lucky and fall *up* the stairs." He fired the gun, and the zed fell backward, its hand making a small splash in the standing water.

"Let's make this quick," he muttered, taking the first step.

I kept the light in front of us, moving it to scan the sides. It was an unsettling feeling, entering the literal bowels of the house, not knowing what else could be down here. At the foot of the stairs, Clutch motioned for the flashlight. He took it and shone it across the basement. I held the machete in front of me.

Fortunately, the basement was wide open, with no doors or rooms, let alone shelves or boxes. In fact, the only things down there were two corpses, one zed and one tabby housecat. "There's nothing down here. Maybe they've always had flooding issues with it," I said, thinking aloud.

"Good," he muttered. "Let's get out of here."

He wasted no time hustling back up the stairs.

"Don't like dark basements?" I asked when he shut the basement door behind us.

"Not one bit."

I chortled.

"What?"

"I never would've guessed you to be afraid of anything."

After a moment, he shrugged. "I'm only human."

The thought of Clutch getting hurt—or worse—quickly sobered me. "Yeah. Guess so."

With the house clear, we moved quickly through to inventory food and supplies to load later. The Piersons weren't very good planners. They had little to offer, so we went ahead and loaded everything we found into one suitcase. I was about to open the refrigerator when Clutch pressed his hand over mine. "Before you do that, I'd hold my breath if I were you."

I bit my lip. "Oh. Good call."

Clutch stepped back as I sucked in a breath and opened the refrigerator. And I was glad I did. Milk, leftovers, and raw meat filled the shelves. I moved quickly, grabbing only the items I was hoping to find. Aluminum cans.

I pulled out the twelve-pack of light beer and the four cans of soda and slammed the door shut. I lifted the beer and smiled. I made the mistake of inhaling to brag about my find, and gagged from the lingering stench from the refrigerator.

Clutch smirked and opened the door to the garage.

I pushed past him and sucked in fresh air. He came out behind me and dropped the suitcase into the back of the truck. He pulled out an old wire carrier he'd found somewhere along the way. "Let's wrap this up."

I put the twelve-pack and soda in the back and followed. We'd only burned a half hour clearing the house, leaving us plenty of time for the only other building on the farm. It looked like an old hog house that had been converted to store machinery. A large caged-in chicken area had been built onto the side with a door leading into the old shed. The door was closed, likely blown shut in the storms. Four chickens and one rooster pecked at the grass. Their feathers were matted, and they were scrawny. They had to be near starving, with nothing to eat but what they could find in the twenty-by-twenty area of grass fenced in for their home.

They seemed agitated, ruffling their feathers and chattering away. I realized why when I saw the furred shape nearly hidden in the shadow of the tractor. It was big, maybe a wolf, and I nudged Clutch and pointed.

"Looks like we're not the only ones eying these chickens."

He took several steps toward the beast and waved his hands. "Shoo. Get out of here."

It growled, showing its teeth.

Clutch stomped closer. "Sorry, bud. But we need these chickens as bad as you."

It kept growling even as it backed up with every step Clutch took forward, until it turned and ran off. It was actually a mutt, big but skinny. Probably some farm dog in the area. I felt a bit bad that he'd probably suffered as badly as any of us had since the outbreak, going from an easy diet of dog food to having to fend for himself. But I didn't feel bad enough to toss him a chicken. Clutch was right. We needed them.

Other than the dog, there was nothing to scare up around the building. Only a tractor and lawn mower sat in the shed, making it easy enough to check for zeds.

Inside the building stood a chicken coop made out of plywood, probably used to protect the chickens at night and during cold weather. I knocked on the door and listened for any movement. When I heard none, I opened the door, with Clutch at my back. Inside was hay and wooden roosts. Eight white-feathered bodies lay dead across the floor, likely from starvation or thirst, if the empty water and food bowls were any sign. A few eggs rested undisturbed in the nest boxes, but I left those, unwilling to test their level of rottenness.

There was another door across from us, and I opened

this one without worry, having already seen where it led from the outside. "Hey, chickies," I said, taking a step onto the grass.

They came running to me, clucking happy little welcomes, and I grinned. "They're tame."

"Get them loaded up," Clutch said from the doorway. "I'm going to check out the fuel situation, and see if the vehicles have anything worthwhile."

"I'll take it from here." I didn't even look up. I was too busy enjoying being the center of chicken attention.

"And be careful," he warned.

I was sweating by the time I got three of the five chickens loaded into the carrier. Just because they were friendly creatures that couldn't fly didn't make them easy to catch.

Taking a break, I grabbed the three large bags of chicken feed from inside the building and tossed them in the truck next to the portable fuel tank, which Clutch was finishing siphoning gas into from the Piersons' two cars.

Finished, he disconnected the portable pump's cables from his truck battery, and slid the pump handle behind the tank. He'd used the portable tank for his tractors in the fields, but it hadn't taken him long to dump the diesel from the tank so we could use it for gasoline.

Clutch eyed the two chickens still milling in their fenced area and raised an eyebrow.

I shrugged. "They needed a break."

He smirked, leaning on the truck.

I went back to work getting the last two chickens into the carrier. I must've worn them out because I caught both in less than five minutes, only falling on my ass once. The scraggly chickens didn't look pleased to be cramped in a little cage, but I figured I'd earn their forgiveness by giving them a dry home with plenty of food and water.

I turned to find Clutch with his head in his hands. "What's wrong?"

He looked up, laughing. "I've never seen anyone work so hard to catch chickens before."

I lifted the cage. "Want me to release them and you take a shot?"

He cleared his throat. "You know, they're starving. You could've put a bit of feed in the kennel, and they would've practically run into it."

I wanted to snap back some smart remark, but he was right so I flipped him the bird instead.

A boom sounded in the distance, and Clutch's face fell.

Confused, I looked around. "That didn't sound like thunder."

His brow furrowed. He stepped back and snapped his head in the direction of the farm. "That was an explosion."

Shock blasted through me.

"The gate," he said before taking off at a run toward the truck. I walked as quickly as I could, without risking injuring the caged fowl. He had the engine going by the time I set the carrier in the back. I hopped in the front, and he tore out the driveway and sped out of the driveway and onto the road. I grabbed my rifle and Clutch pulled out his Blaser—a heavy, impressive rifle with an even more impressive scope.

I opened my window and leveled my rifle on the frame as he slowed. As we approached the farm, we found the gate collapsed and a Jeep on the other side with a blown axle. The bloodied driver slumped over the steering wheel must've taken shrapnel. Two other men with shaved heads were outside the Jeep, walking down the lane toward the house. One was clutching his bloody arm. The other held his rifle in front of him. He must've heard our approach, because he snapped around. His eyes widened, and he nudged the guy next to him and aimed his rifle at the truck.

"Follow my lead," Clutch said. He drove over the fallen gate and pulled off to the right of the lane where no booby traps had been set and stopped. "This is private property!" he yelled out. "Stop where you are and lower your weapons, or you will be shot."

They didn't lower their weapons. "This area is in the jurisdiction of the Fox Hills militia!" the injured man yelled back. "You have to pay tribute to stay on these lands."

Clutch fired, and I startled. The injured man fell to the ground and didn't move.

The other raider's eyes widened. "You killed him, you fucking bastard!"

"This is your one and only chance," Clutch said. "Drop your weapon. Leave in the next ten seconds and live. If you or any of your buddies comes near my place again, you will be shot on sight."

"But you can't. I'm with the militia!" He glanced from his dead buddy and back to Clutch.

"Seven," Clutch said.

"But, but my Jeep is busted!" He pointed to the sky. "It's going to be dark soon. There's zeds out there."

"Five."

The guy paused, then dropped his rifle like it was on fire and ran toward the road. Once he passed the truck, he yelled, "Doyle will kill you for this!"

Clutch got out of the truck and aimed. I froze.

The guy went down with one echoing shot.

In shock, I stepped out of the truck as Jase came running from the woods. "I was watching them the whole time. I wasn't going to let them get to the house, I swear," he said, breathless.

"I know," I said, squeezing Jase's shoulder.

He grimaced and took a step back. "Dang, you stink like a zed that took a shit bath."

Another shot fired, and we yanked around to see Clutch standing beside the Jeep, the driver now sporting a gunshot to the head. Clutch looked up. "Let's get this mess cleaned up."

"Do you think Doyle will know?" Jase asked.

"Oh, he'll know all right." Clutch looked outward. "Doyle started the war today."

WRATH

THE FIFTH CIRCLE OF HELL

CHAPTER VIII

Two weeks later

Jase slammed his machete through the forehead of the first zed, while I split the skull of the second one right down the middle. I stood back and let Jase take down the third, wielding his machete like a broadsword.

"I'm getting sick of Doyle's Dogs throwing zeds at us," he muttered as he wiped his blade on the grass.

For the past three days, a garbage truck had driven down this road and dumped hungry zeds over the gate. On the first day, they dropped one. The next day it was two. Today, they were up to three. Tomorrow, it'd be four.

Eventually, it'd be a truckload.

They were toying with us. With every assault, they were saying, surrender or we'll kill you.

"C'mon. They're giving us practice," I said, tugging a dead zed to the ditch. "What else is there to do on a Friday night besides killing zeds?"

Jase paused while dragging another zed and cocked his head. "Is it Friday?"

I shrugged. "No idea. Doesn't matter, I guess. We should be heading in for the night."

"Yeah. The fabulous dinner I made is getting cold," he said with a sly grin.

I looked down the road where the green garbage truck disappeared in the distance. After today's dump, the truck sported several new bullet holes, courtesy of Clutch, who was just coming down from his sniper's nest in the tree. But the bullet holes weren't enough. We needed to disable that damn truck. And soon.

Clutch checked his Blaser. "I should've taken care of those Dogs back at the greenhouse. Then they wouldn't have known about this place."

I didn't need to voice my agreement. Clutch was right. If we'd killed Sean and his buddies—without getting ourselves killed in the process—we could go about our business and no one would be the wiser. For the past few days, Clutch had been beating himself up about letting Sean get away and outing our location.

But it wasn't his fault any more than it was mine. They'd caught us off guard and now we were dealing with the repercussions.

We headed back to the Jeep. It had taken the guys two full days, but they had the Dogs' Rubicon running again. Jase had even added his own brand of style by painting "Zom-B-Gone" across the back.

The Jeep could get through anything the truck could, but it was smaller and faster to get in and out of, unlike the efficient Prius, which the guys bitched about every time they climbed in. And so the Jeep had joined Jase's motorcycle as a scouting vehicle around the farm.

Jase claimed driving rights and I snagged the passenger seat, leaving Clutch to hop in the back. When Jase gunned the engine, I grabbed onto the windshield. "Do you even have a driver's license?"

"Of course," Jase replied indignantly, and then shrugged. "Well, basically. I've got a school permit. But I've been driving tractors for most my life."

I would've snapped back a witty remark, but my stomach growled. "What's for dinner tonight, Jase? I hope it's take-out from Pizza Hut. I could really go for a Cheese Lover's with extra cheese."

"I'd take Red Lobster," Clutch added. "All-you-can-eat shrimp."

"It's better," Jase said. "Tonight you get my specialty: Spam and rice."

I let out a dramatic sigh with a hand fluttering to my chest. "My favorite."

"Stop the Jeep," Clutch ordered, and Jase slammed the brakes.

"What's up?" I asked.

Clutch held up a finger. "Sh."

I heard it then. The hearty growl of a big engine

heading down the road.

"Son of a bitch," I muttered. "They're coming back already?"

"Sounds different." Clutch said. "Get back to the gate, but be careful. Don't get made into a target."

"Did I mention that I'm getting sick of this shit?" Jase muttered as he whipped the Jeep around.

I picked my M24 off the floor and checked the cartridge. Jase parked at our usual spot just before the last curve in the lane leading to the gate, and Clutch took off running for his sniper's nest. Now that we were out of sight, I hopped out and flattened against a large tree, Jase took a tree on the opposite side of the lane.

A deep-throated engine purred nearby, and I poked my head around the tree to see a desert-tan Humvee parked at the gate. A single soldier climbed out of the passenger side. Another soldier stood behind a .30 cal mounted on the vehicle, leaving who knew how many more men with rifles hidden inside.

The soldier standing outside the Humvee held his rifle in the air before putting it back on the seat and then closing the door. He said something to the gunner, who took a step back from the .30 cal.

The soldier walked up to the gate. "This is Captain Masden with the United States National Guard," he called out. "I'm unarmed and have come here to talk."

This was one of those times I wished we had ear pieces so I could check in with Clutch. I wanted to ask him what to do, but I couldn't risk him leaving his spot in the tree. He was our best and last defense.

Masden checked out the pile of zeds in the ditch before looking up and scanning the tree line. "I know you're out there. I give you my word that my men will not fire unless you shoot first."

I glanced over at Jase and held up my hand. *Stay put.* He didn't look happy, but he readjusted his rifle to get a better view of the gate.

I propped my matching M24 against the tree so I could get to it easily in case things went to hell. "Don't cross the gate. I'm coming out." I waited a second before taking that first step around the tree. Knowing Clutch had me covered gave me the confidence I needed to walk up to the gate and into the view of the soldiers, even though I had no doubt each and every one of them had me in their sights.

Masden was attractive and well built, with tan skin and blond hair. Fatigues fit him nicely. The last time I'd seen him, it had been in Fox Hills, and he'd been behind the Humvee's .30 cal.

When he saw me, his eyes widened slightly in surprise.

I walked warily up to the gate and stopped just on the other side from the soldier.

He held out his hand. "I'm Captain Tyler Masden. But you can call me Tyler."

I shook his hand. "I'm Cash."

His lips twitched. "Cash?"

I took a breath. "What brings you here, Tyler?"

He smiled. His grin was warm, inviting, and hinted at a flirtatious personality. "I represent Camp Fox. We try to locate all survivors, and either bring them to the Camp for safety or see how we can help. Someone mentioned that there was a small camp of survivors out here." His smile fell. "It's also my responsibility to make sure some level of law is still obeyed."

I narrowed my eyes. "Meaning?"

He sighed. "I received a report of insurgents in this vicinity. My source said there were folks stealing from other survivors."

"You're looking in the wrong place for thieves," I said. "We've had supplies stolen from us, but we've never taken anything from a survivor."

His brows lifted. "Did you see who did it?"

"Of course," I said. "They held us at gunpoint. It was Doyle's Dogs. The so-called militia. And they've hit us more than once."

Tyler shook his head. "We send them out with supplies to help survivors, not to steal from them."

I cocked my head. "And you believe that?"

He lowered his head and rubbed his temples. "Honestly, I don't know what to believe anymore when it comes to the militia."

I felt sorry for him. His intentions seemed genuine, but we still had a problem to deal with. "If the Dogs are working with you, then you clearly have a communication problem or you're lying to me."

He sighed. His eyes narrowed and he smiled. "I've

seen you before."

"In Chow Town," I said. "It looked like you were picking up survivors."

"Chow Town." He gave a tight chuckle. "That's a good name for it. Yeah, I've been through there quite a few times." Then he slowly shook his head. "Dang, I wish you would've stopped."

"I'd had a long day," I said.

"Too bad. I wanted to meet you. And, I could've offered you Camp Fox's hospitality."

My breath hardened. "The Dogs wanted to lock me up with the other women for my own 'safety'," I said with air quotes. "If you're offering the same kind of hospitality as the militia, I'm not interested."

Tyler's jaw tightened. "The reserve militia was formed to kill zeds and rescue survivors. They have clear orders to send over any survivors to Camp Fox. They don't have the authority to house any survivors except for the minutemen and their families."

Even Tyler didn't sound like he believed his own words.

When I didn't speak, he continued. "Listen, I know they may be a bit unorthodox, but they're keeping the zeds clear of the Camp. And they've brought in eighty-seven survivors already. Maybe you misunderstood them."

"Maybe not," I said.

He glanced at the pile of zeds in the ditch, and then took a step closer and leaned on the gate. "It looks like you're having your own share of problems with zeds. If you're not ready to relocate to the Camp, I could have Doyle send over a squad every day or so to help clear the area."

I belted out a laugh, and Tyler frowned. "What's so funny?"

I pointed to the pile. "Those zeds are courtesy of Doyle."

He stepped back. "What are you talking about?"

I leaned on the gate. "Dogs come by in a garbage truck every day and dump zeds over our gate because we refused to pay tribute to the militia. We had no problem keeping zeds out of this area until the Dogs started importing them."

Tyler cursed. Then he reached up and his thumb brushed against my cheek, startling me. "Come to the Camp. Doyle has no authority there. You'll be safe from him and the militia." He motioned toward the tree line. "All of your friends here can come, too. Out here, alone, it's too dangerous. I've heard about entire herds of zeds moving through Missouri right now. At the Camp we're rebuilding the way things used to be."

I stood and watched him for a moment. "How long do you think Camp Fox is safe from Doyle?"

"Doyle reports into Lieutenant Colonel Lendt, and we've treated the militia fairly. I might not agree with Doyle's methods, let alone like the guy, but he's been effective in eliminating zeds. Even if he did try something incredibly stupid," he replied. "He has only eighteen men, most of them farmers or desk jockeys. We have over fifty trained troops holding down a base with a fortified perimeter. No one would be dumb enough to go up against Camp Fox."

From what I'd seen of the Dogs so far, I figured they'd be exactly that kind of dumb once they got enough numbers. The Camp would be Eden for the militia.

"Well," Tyler drawled. "I'm going to have a talk with Doyle. I'll make sure these attacks stop. Still, I'm glad I found out about your camp."

I cocked my head.

He grinned. "Because I got to meet you."

I couldn't help but smile in return.

He leaned on the fence, closer to me. "How about I come back in three days, just to check in?"

"Yeah," I said. "Sure."

"How many of you are here?"

I narrowed my eyes and tensed. "Why does that matter?"

He held up his hands. "Relax. I'm not scoping out the place. I'm only asking so that I can bring back some MREs when I return. That's all."

"There are several of us here," I replied simply. "Any food would be appreciated, and we could really use some 9mm rounds if you've got extra."

"I'll see what I can scrounge up." He paused and glanced back at the Humvee before looking back to me. "The offer stands. If you or anyone here wants to relocate to the Camp, you just let me know. You'd like it there."

I nodded. "Thanks. I'll mention it to the others." I didn't mention that the others had been listening the entire time.

He reached into his pocket, smiled, and handed me a candy bar. "See you three days from now."

Three days later

Clutch was crankier than usual while we scouted the woods. "I don't trust them to not take control of us or our resources."

"I don't either," I said. "But Tyler offered to bring us supplies."

"Feels like bribery." He shook his head. "We can't count on them for help. We take care of ourselves."

"But we can't turn down any food or supplies," I said.

"He's working with the Dogs."

"But he doesn't trust them." I shrugged. "Not completely, anyway."

"He was flirting with you."

I stopped and looked at Clutch. After a moment, I put a hand dramatically over my heart. "My, oh my. Is big bad Clutch jealous?"

He scowled.

I laughed. "Tyler's too pretty and not nearly grumpy enough to hold my attention."

Clutch narrowed his eyes. "What—"

A pained howl sounded beyond the trees, yanking our attention back to the woods.

"That sounds close," I said.

Clutch took the lead and jogged us through the trees, keeping our weapons ready for any zeds that could be skulking around.

More cries followed, and we closed in on the pitiful sounds.

At the edge of the woods, three zeds tore at a fallen tree trunk. A fourth zed, several feet away, chewed on something with golden fur.

A tiny shriek shot out from inside the log, and I gave Clutch a quick glance. He gave a nod, and we moved in. One of the zeds saw us right away. It came to its feet with a moan, bringing the attention of the other two at the log.

Clutch swung first. He took the zed's head clean off. My swing went wide and landed in the shoulder of the second. I stepped back and swung again, this time my machete lodged into the skull. I kicked up, planting my boot against its chest, and yanked the blade free. I pulled my weapon up just as the third zed reached for me, but Clutch decapitated it, just like he'd done the first, before slamming his machete through both heads on the ground.

The fourth zed looked up and snarled, its mouth covered in fresh blood. Bites and scratches covered its face, chest, and arms, enough that would have caused serious injuries in a human. It went after Clutch, and I stepped around it and took off half its head from behind. It fell, dropping the carcass it'd been feeding on.

I edged closer to the hollow tree trunk and got down on my knees. I rested my weapon against the trunk, and Clutch stood guard.

I leaned down to find the source of the whimpering inside.

Pups.

They were much smaller than the animal the zeds had been feeding on. She'd likely been their mother and had sacrificed herself defending her den. Two pups were already dead, one struggled to breathe. Without obvious injuries, I suspected they'd been crushed when the zeds dug at them in a frenzy. The fourth pup in the far back corner continued to whimper. I reached in. It cried louder and nipped at my gloved fingers.

I gently blanketed the pup with my hand. It was cornered and began to wiggle fervently. Wrapping my fingers around it, I picked it up as gently as possible and pulled it free. She screeched in my hand as I examined her, and then I pulled her against my chest. "Shh. It's going to be okay, sweetie," I murmured.

She couldn't have weighed more than a couple pounds. After a moment, the pup's shrieks turned into whimpers before it quieted but continued to shake.

Clutch came up behind me.

"There's another one in there, but he's hurt pretty bad," I said, while stroking the pup's fur with my thumb.

He took a deep breath, bent down, and reached in with both his hands. When he stood, his hands were empty. "It's taken care of."

I gave him a tight smile and held up the pup. "She's definitely a mutt, but she's cute in a mutty sort of way."

He chuckled. "It's not a mutt. It's a mangy coyote."

A coyote? "Oh. Well, it's a she."

He shook his head. "Coyote are wild. They're not domesticated like dogs."

"But she'll die if we leave her behind."

"That's nature, Cash."

"There's been enough death already," I said quietly.

After a moment, he scowled. "Let me see it."

I reluctantly held her out.

He picked her up by the scruff of her neck, looked her over, and then handed her back. "It doesn't look injured or sick. But it's young, not even weaned yet. It'll probably die, no matter what we do. I don't know much about coyotes except that they're a nuisance."

The pup snuggled into my arm and I scratched her oversized ears. "I'll take care of her."

"I can't believe you're bringing a coyote home," Clutch said.

I shot him a smile. "We're all leftovers in this world. She's no different." I carried her in one hand, grabbed my machete in my other hand, and started heading back into the woods. "I think she'll fit in nicely."

Clutch caught up and we walked in silence through the woods. Once we reached the yard, I lifted the pup. "What should we call her?"

"Ugly."

"Har, har." I smiled. "Jase is going to love her."

By the time we crossed the yard and reached the house, the pup had nearly chewed a hole through my glove. Jase rode up on his bike and pointed, his head cocked. "What kind of dog is that?"

"Coyote," Clutch replied.

Jase raised a brow. "A coyote? For real?"

"She's yours if you want her," I offered.

His eyes widened. "Really?"

"Yeah, really."

He held out his hands, and I handed the pup over. "Hey, little Mutt," he murmured, scratching her back.

I smiled. As soon as I held the pup, I'd hoped she could help fill the void for Jase. "Hopefully, she'll take to the powdered milk," I said. "And you'll need to make up a little bed or kennel for her."

"Yeah, yeah," he said and headed off into the house.

"Make sure it doesn't have fleas before you bring it inside," Clutch called out, but Jase was already gone.

Clutch tried to give me one of his hard looks but failed. When his lips curled upward, I knew he'd also seen the light in Jase's eyes.

There were too few moments like that to ignore.

"Let's check the gate," he growled. "The kid's going to be worthless the rest of the day."

I tried not to grin as I jumped in the Jeep, and Clutch shrugged off the backpack of extra gear he always carried now and drove us down the lane. About midway there, we heard the now-familiar sound of the garbage truck.

"Those sonsabitches just won't quit," he muttered before gunning the engine. "Get ready."

I lifted my rifle.

He stopped at the bend in the lane, and we got out and took cover behind the trees.

The garbage truck had stopped and was in progress of backing up. Either someone different was driving today or Sean was drunk off his ass, because the truck nearly backed straight into the ditch.

It would've been a lot easier for us if it had. But the driver overcorrected at the last moment and nearly went into the ditch on the other side. The back of the truck smashed into the gate, and the dump box opened. The box needed a couple more feet of space behind the truck to rotate. Terrible metal-on-metal screeching sounds ensued as the box tangled in the gate, lifting it, until something broke, and both the box and gate slammed to the ground, taking several feet of the barbed wire fence with it.

One zed caught between the box and gate was cut in half. The remaining five zeds began to crawl over it and onto the ground.

"You got to be kidding me," Clutch cursed. "You got the zeds?"

My first shot went through a zed's eye. "Yeah," I said.

"Good." Clutch walked straight toward the truck that was now trying to pull away, but it was locked onto the gate. It wasn't an ordinary garbage truck. They'd welded metal over the wheels so we couldn't shoot the tires. Same with the windshield and windows. With the exception of a few peepholes, everything had been covered by sheets of metal. Otherwise we would've shot them the first time they'd invaded our territory.

Its tires spun, trying to break free, and the collapsed gate protested.

I took down the next four zeds with easy back-to-back shots as they tried to drag themselves to their feet. One final shot took down the half of zed still caught between the gate and truck.

Clutch came to a stop less than a dozen feet from the truck. Its engine and wheels suddenly calmed. A barrel poked through the slot in the driver's side window, but Clutch fired first. His shot was close enough to hit or scare the driver because the barrel disappeared back inside the cab, and the truck engine roared. The gate moved several feet with the truck.

Clutch jogged up to the window, stuck the barrel of his rifle through and started firing.

I sprinted toward Clutch, holding my rifle ready. He quit firing by the time I reached the truck. Everything had stilled, with only the sound of the truck's engine going.

I reached for the door handle and looked up to Clutch. He took a step back, aimed, then nodded. I flung the door open and jumped back, pulling up my rifle. But the two men inside didn't move. Blood had splattered the interior. The driver was slumped over the wheel, and the passenger was lying back, sprawled across the vinyl seat. Neither was Sean.

Clutch took a step closer and fired two shots, one into each man.

A couple months ago, I would've found that action heartless. Now, I would've done it myself if he hadn't shot first. These Dogs had attacked my home and the only people left in the world that I cared about. There wasn't much I wouldn't do. The only thing that scared me was how quickly and easily I'd slid into a ruthless way of thinking.

Jase came tearing down the lane on his bike. He jumped off and jogged toward us, holding his rifle. "What the heck happened here?"

"We won this round," I said since Clutch was busy examining the mangled gate.

The pouch attached to Jase's belt wiggled and whimpered. I cocked my head. A furry head with big ears poked out and looked around before disappearing back inside the pouch.

"It's okay, Mutt," Jase said, patting the pouch. "Just taking care of bad guys."

"The gate's fucked," Clutch said, walking up to us. He sighed and then kicked the gravel. "Godammit. I've had enough of this shit."

"Without their truck and two men down, it should take them some time to regroup," I said.

"Doesn't matter," Clutch said. "The game's changed. This is the second time I've killed Doyle's men. He'll up the ante next. I need to see what we're up against."

My brows furrowed. "What do you mean?"

"I mean," he turned to me, "that I need to see what kind of numbers and firepower Doyle's got at his disposal."

My jaw dropped. "Going to see Doyle is suicide."

Of all the shitty timing, the Humvee pulled up outside the gate. When Tyler stepped out, I kept an eye on Clutch to make sure he wasn't going to gun down the newcomers. He didn't shoot. Instead, he stomped forward to meet Tyler at the gate. I followed, not trusting the situation.

"What happened here?" Tyler asked as we approached.

While I knew Clutch had been in the military, it surprised me when he saluted Tyler.

Tyler's brows lifted, and he saluted back.

"Captain," Clutch said. "You can't control your own goddamn militia."

"They attacked again?"

"Every fucking day." Clutch pointed at the truck. "Take a look. It's pretty clear who the aggressor was here. We're being forced to defend our home against the militia."

Tyler walked alongside the truck, pausing at the open cab and again at the zeds, before returning to the gate by us. He leaned toward me. "Are you okay?"

I nodded. "No thanks to the Dogs."

Tyler looked at Clutch. "You have my word. I'll do my best so that this won't happen again."

"That's what you said last time," Clutch said. "No. I'll make sure they won't bother us again."

Tyler ran a hand through his hair. "Those two minutemen lying dead in that truck were sworn in. Attacking the militia is the same as attacking Camp Fox. Even though this was a clear case of self-defense, I can't let you go after Doyle on your own. We have to go through the proper channels."

My hands flung to my hips. "So the Dogs have get-out-of-jail cards to kill, steal, and rape?"

"I'm not saying that," Tyler replied quickly. "You have to understand. It's a tricky situation."

Clutch paced, stopped, and paced some more. "If you want to help, take us to Doyle."

"I don't think that's a good idea," Tyler cautioned.

Clutch spun on his heel and pointed at Tyler. "I'm going to see Doyle with or without your help, Captain. You can either take me to him or stay out of my way. Doesn't matter."

Tyler frowned and stared at the truck for several agonizing moments. Finally, he spoke. "I was going to see Doyle today, anyway. You can ride along." He held up a finger. "But I have to take the lead. Doyle can be a bit…difficult."

"Difficult?" I asked. "You said he reported to this Lendt guy."

"He does, but Lendt's offered him some leniency as long as the militia delivers results," Tyler said before motioning toward the Humvee. A soldier stepped out from the back, followed by a teenager in jeans and a T-shirt carrying a cardboard box.

"Eddy!" Jase called out, coming out from where he'd taken cover behind a shrub.

The new kid nearly dropped the box in his rush. Tyler grabbed the box, and Eddy hurdled a collapsed part of the fence. "Jase!"

While the two teenagers slapped each other's shoulders and bantered, Tyler set the box on the gate. "MREs. Enough to feed six for one week."

Clutch took the box, set it on the ground next to him, and rummaged through it. "How about ammo?"

Tyler shook his head. "I can't authorize the transfer of ammo. Even if I could, Camp Fox is an armory, not a munitions site. We barely have enough for ourselves."

Clutch's lips tightened. He headed back to the Jeep and grabbed his backpack. "Let's go meet Doyle."

Tyler didn't look pleased, but he motioned to the young, clean-cut man behind him, who walked up to us. "I'll leave Corporal Smith behind to help bury the minutemen and guard the place."

"How do I know I can trust your man?" Clutch countered.

I put a hand on Clutch's forearm and looked at Tyler. "If he stays, he's not allowed in the house, and he does what Jase says. Aside from the MREs, you haven't exactly proven that we can trust Camp Fox."

Clutch's jaw was clenched, but he nodded. He turned to Jase. "You get all that?"

Jase looked up from where he and Eddy were playing with Mutt. "Yeah. Want me to start working on the gate?"

"No," Clutch said. "That truck isn't going anywhere. It's a better barricade than the gate was right now. We'll get it fixed tomorrow. Just keep an eye out."

"Can I stay, Captain?" Eddy asked.

"Eddy and I were in the same class. We played football together," Jase added, and then stuck out his chest. "Of course, I could outrun Eddy any day of the week."

Eddy razzed Jase right back while Tyler smiled. "You both stay out of trouble. We'll be back in a couple hours. Smitty has a radio, so have him call me if you need anything." The corporal jumped the fence and Clutch gave him a once-over as he walked over to the two boys.

"Let my mom know I'm all right, okay, Captain?" Eddy asked.

Tyler gave him a thumbs up before turning back to us, and he looked at my M24. "You won't need your rifles on this trip."

I clutched it harder as I climbed over the gate. "I always need my rifle."

He opened his mouth to speak but shut it. He waved at the Humvee. "Nick, Griz, Tack, you're with me."

Clutch hopped the fence, his Blaser in tow. He brushed past Tyler, and opened the back door of the Humvee. I climbed in, followed by Clutch who sidled next to me.

Tyler took the front passenger seat, and I noticed another soldier behind the steering wheel. In the rear of the vehicle, I found two more soldiers: a black man at the .30 cal and a younger, lanky white man who, after seeing us, closed his eyes and leaned his back against the side. Even though neither looked aggressive, I was glad Clutch had sat next to me.

"Meet some of my team," Tyler motioned to the other men. "Tack and Griz are handling the .30, and Nick's our fine driver. Guys, meet Cash and…" Tyler turned in his seat to face Clutch. "I didn't get your name and rank."

"Seibert, Joseph. Sergeant First Class," Clutch replied.

"With what unit, Sarge?" Tyler countered quickly.

"75th Ranger Regiment."

"Hoorah," the soldier manning the .30 cal called out.

Tyler nodded to the man who spoke. "Griz back there is a Ranger, too."

"Hoorah," Clutch replied, lifting a fist in the air.

"Being with the Rangers, I'm guessing you saw some

action, then," Tyler said.

Clutch gave a tight nod. "OEF-A. Two tours."

Tyler whistled. "Two tours in Afghanistan? Yeah, that counts as action. Have you thought about joining up at Camp Fox? We could use a soldier with your experience."

"How long do you think the Camp will be safe, Captain?" Clutch asked. "All those people confined in one place are going to attract zeds. And, all that heavy equipment is going to attract no-gooders. I'll support your efforts, but I've got my own people to protect. I can't relocate my people to Camp Fox until I know you can maintain a defensible position."

"I could order you to relocate to the Camp, Sarge," Tyler said. "All troops, including retired and inactive, were recalled to service when the outbreak started. And all remaining able-bodied men were called in for the reserve militia."

Clutch jutted out his chin. "Too bad I didn't get the memo."

Tyler pursed his lips. "I'll let that slide for now. I don't want to force you, but we need you. There may come a time when I'll have to order you back to duty, and that time could come soon."

Clutch's lips thinned and the tension thickened the air. "Yes, sir."

"If the militia is tied to Camp Fox, why do you let them do whatever they want?" I asked.

"What they did wasn't right," Tyler replied. "I'll

make sure we get to the bottom of it, though it won't matter much longer. The militia is just a temporary structure until order can be restored." Then he gave me one of those warm smiles. "Have you thought more about moving to the Camp? As you saw, one of your folks has a classmate there."

"Jase can make his own decisions. But I go where Clutch goes." Feeling a hard gaze on me, I turned and found Clutch scrutinizing me. Did he want me with him? Did he want me to go to the Camp? It drove me nuts that I couldn't make out his expression.

"Well, there's a lot of folks counting on our help at the Camp, and Sarge could make a big difference helping us rebuild," Tyler said.

"I'm a patriot, Captain, but I'm not suicidal," Clutch said. "Any notion at rebuilding is delusional until you put an end to the militia and fold them under your command. Do it before it's too late."

"Zeds!" Griz yelled behind me, and gunfire blasted from the Humvee.

The noise was deafening, and I gripped my rifle tighter. I snapped my eyes from one window to the next. Then I saw through the windshield several zeds collapse on the road.

"Are we clear?" Tyler called out after the shooting stopped.

"All clear," the gunner yelled, and the Humvee sped up.

I leaned back and caught my breath. I looked at my

window, contemplated rolling it down so I could shoot if needed, but decided to leave it up—the glass would provide some protection against zeds. I glanced to my right at Clutch. He gave me a questioning look. I forced a half-smile, and he turned his gaze back outside.

Tyler made a couple calls on his radio. Every few minutes, the gunner fired, and a zed fell. When we crossed Fox River, zeds floated in the water. Some lay on the mud banks. All dead. In a muddy field not far from the river, sat a tractor riddled with bullet holes. Inside, a body lay slumped over the steering wheel. "You've cleared out this entire area?" I asked.

Tyler nodded. "As much as we can. But more show up every day. Most are coming down from Chow Town. There's simply too many there for us to clean out without risking lives and burning through too much ammo. So we wait and hit the ones that migrate in our direction."

"How about the survivors still in town?" I asked.

"We used to make drive-throughs every day. At first, we'd fill our trucks with survivors. But after a couple weeks, we were lucky to find one or two, if any. Then a mob of zeds took down one of our Humvees. So Lendt cancelled the drive-throughs. The risk wasn't worth the payout." He pointed outside. "We're almost there."

In the middle of a flat marshland stood an old farmers' cooperative. Three large grain silos reached for the sky, with smoke billowing from the top of one. Tall chain fences reinforced with plywood and two-by-fours buffered the buildings from the road. What hung outside those walls made me grimace. Surrounding the militia camp, every fifty feet or so, a dead zed hung from a pole like a scarecrow.

"Do you think the zeds get the hint?"

"Doubt it," Clutch muttered.

On an ancient-looking billboard was written faded letters. I had to squint to read the words:

Doyle's Iowa Surplus

& Paintball Supplies:

Open Seven Days a Week.

The paint had long since faded, leaving only the bold capital letters D-I-S on the first line easily legible from a distance. Still, I shivered when I read Doyle's name. This made what we were about to do feel all the more real.

"It seems odd to have a surplus warehouse in the middle of farm country," I said while Clutch rolled down his window.

"Camp Fox is only five miles straight east of here," Tyler said. "This place is owned by a retired farmer, Dale Doyle. He had a connection with some brass at Fox a while back, and he worked out a deal to buy surplus at a hefty discount. It was right about the time they built the new farmer's co-op on the other side of town, so he bought this place at a rock bottom price."

"And it looks like the deal has already been sweetened," Clutch muttered, nodding toward the two armored vehicles sitting at the gate. "How many

M1117's did you guys hand over to Doyle?"

"They needed lead-in trucks for survivor runs," Tyler replied quietly.

"Christ, Captain," Clutch said. "You're handing Doyle everything he needs to take over the Camp."

"Watch your tone, sergeant. The militia has been instrumental in clearing zeds from the area and locating survivors. Doyle may have one hell of a temper and a superiority complex, but he's turned farmers and kids into a militia that gets results."

The Humvee slowed to a stop at the gate.

Guard towers stood behind the fence, one on each side of the gate. A man in each tower had his rifle aimed at us. Two more men—one of them Sean—with automatic rifles stepped through a small door next to the gate.

Sean saw Clutch and visibly tensed. After a moment's hesitation, he warily walked up to Tyler's window, while the other man stood back several feet with his rifle leveled on the Humvee.

Sean nodded toward us in the backseat. "What are they doing here, Captain?"

Tyler rested his arm on his door. "Open the gate, Sean. I'm here to see Doyle."

Sean pursed his lips, clutching an AR-15 that matched the rifles Tyler's team carried. "I'm afraid I can't, sir." He nodded in Clutch's direction. "I can't let in any unauthorized people. Not until I clear it with Doyle."

"It's not the reserve militia's place to turn back any citizen," Tyler gritted out.

"Doyle's orders," Sean replied.

"I have the authority here, Private," Tyler snapped. "Open the damn gate!"

The man behind Sean lifted his rifle. "You assholes from Camp Fox don't tell us what to do. That bastard killed our friends!" His wild-eyes homed in on Clutch at the same time he aimed his rifle.

I sucked in a breath. Pulled up my rifle. Clutch was in the way. I couldn't get a clear shot.

"Fuck this," Clutch muttered as he lifted his rifle and pulled the trigger.

ARROGANCE

THE SIXTH CIRCLE OF HELL

CHAPTER IX

The Dog yelped, dropped his rifle, and cradled his hand to his chest.

"Cease fire! Cease fire!" Tyler yelled, jumping out from the front seat.

I waited for the Dogs to gun us down, but they never did. Clutch sat, unmoving, next to me, with his Blaser leveled on the whimpering Dog.

"Beware the man with only one gun, because he knows how to use it. Ain't that right, Clutch," an older man with a voice that sounded like he'd smoked a pack a day for forty years straight said as he emerged from the door at the gate.

"Doyle," Clutch muttered under his breath.

I frowned. *This* was Doyle?

This man could have been anyone's grandfather. He was tall and slim, with a casual swagger in his step. His cap and sunglasses hid many features, though weathered skin and tufts of white hair curling out from his cap hinted at an advanced age.

Nevertheless, I held my breath as he picked the rifle off the ground and handed it back to the whimpering man who now sported a bullet hole through his hand. Tyler stood between the Humvee and Doyle, as though protecting us.

"At ease, men," Doyle said. "We don't turn folks away. Especially one of our own."

"But, Doyle," Sean said with a frown, not lowering his rifle from Clutch and me. "You said—"

"But, nuthin'," Doyle interrupted. He motioned to one of the guard boxes above the fence. "Open up."

Metal clanged and two Dogs pushed open the creaky gate.

Wary, I kept an eye on Doyle as he stopped in front of Tyler. The older man looked harmless enough, though I knew to trust my gut. And my gut was screaming at me to shoot him already, grab Clutch, and get the hell out of there.

I'd seen enough. We needed to get as far from these guys as we could and fast.

"Sorry about the confusion, Captain," Doyle said. "My boys simply tend to get a bit energetic in protecting their families."

"Bullshit, Sergeant Doyle," Tyler snapped. "You need to get your minutemen in line."

Doyle smirked, and then shrugged. "Guess you're

just going to have to eat that bullshit, Masden. I report to Lendt, not you. You can't touch me, not as long as my little militia is handling your zed problem. You know it, and I know it."

I watched Tyler tense as he seethed with anger. "Lendt's given you leniency, true, and I trust his judgment. But he also trusts my judgment. And after the stories I've been hearing from several survivors—including the ones with me today—I'm not convinced your militia should remain separate from Camp Fox, let alone continue to receive supplies."

Doyle narrowed his eyes at Tyler but said nothing before moving around Tyler to lean on Clutch's door.

Clutch was clearly tense but he pulled his rifle back inside the window and rested it on his lap. I readjusted mine so that I could take out Doyle in a split second if I had to.

The older man looked me over. His gaze narrowed and his lips turned downward. When Tyler slammed the front door shut, Doyle returned his focus to Clutch. I knew he'd already made his mind up about me: he didn't like me, plain and simple.

My lip curled in return. *Feeling's mutual, bud.*

"We need to talk," Clutch stated.

"We'll talk," Doyle said, giving Clutch a wide smile. "But first, let's get you folks inside where it's safe. Damn zeds are starting to come out of the woodwork." He swaggered back through the now-open gate.

An ominous feeling grew heavy in my gut as our

Humvee passed through the high gate and several Dogs closed in around us. "Well, we're in," I said, my voice barely a whisper. "And I'm ready to leave."

Clutch watched me for a moment and then gave a nearly imperceptible nod.

I cradled my rifle as I kept an eye on the Dogs. The man Clutch had shot held his injured hand to his chest as he disappeared inside the first building. Except for one, the remaining men warily watched Clutch like he'd do the same to them. The only guard who didn't seem concerned was the one too busy leering at me.

I'd seen him once before, when he'd called dibs on me at the greenhouse. I had wanted to shoot him then, too.

When we made eye contact, the weasel wagged his tongue and blew me a kiss. I would've flipped him the bird if I wasn't holding my rifle so tightly. Instead, I turned away to find Clutch watching me, his jaw tight. "Don't leave my side," he said gruffly.

I swallowed a nervous chuckle. Like I'd even want to. "I just want to get back to the farm as fast as possible."

Tyler turned in his seat. "No matter what happens, there's not to be one more shot fired here, understood? This situation is a tinderbox that's been getting hotter for some time."

"Unless we're forced to protect ourselves, you mean," I corrected. "Where'd Doyle get these guys? Prison?"

Tyler's lips pursed. "Stick with me, and everything

will be okay. Doyle knows better than to mess with Camp Fox. Still, I'm surprised none of them got trigger-happy when Clutch shot one of their friends. We're damned lucky to be alive," Tyler replied.

"That shit-for-brains was less than a second away from opening fire on us," Clutch grated out.

"How do you know that for sure, Sarge?" Tyler asked.

Clutch inhaled and then narrowed his gaze on Tyler. "I've seen that look before, plenty of times. I know."

Clutch's words evidently sunk in because Tyler seemed to accept them and turned away.

Inside the fence wasn't any more pleasant than outside. I counted twenty armed men in the camp. No telling how many more were either hidden behind doors or out looting the countryside. I looked at Tyler. "How many Dogs did you say there were?"

"Eighteen," he replied quietly.

Which would've made sixteen after their latest garbage drop-off today. "Looks like Doyle's been adding to his ranks."

"Yeah," Tyler replied, sounding none too pleased.

Doyle stepped in front of the Humvee, and Nick brought us to a stop. The gate behind us closed with a loud clank, locking us inside the camp, which appropriately, felt like a prison.

"They've got quite the setup here," I noted, and Clutch nodded, not looking any happier than I felt.

Second-guessing Clutch's idea to gain intel on the

militia, I stole a glance at him when he reached for the door. He had on his "hard" look, making it impossible to see any emotion except badassness. "Stay with me," he repeated his words from earlier as he opened the door, grabbed his pack, and climbed out.

Rather than opening the door next to me—and closest to the leering Weasel—I slid across the seat and followed Clutch.

"Seen enough yet?" I whispered.

"I don't know what Doyle's endgame is yet," he replied just as softly.

Nick remained with the vehicle, while Griz and Tack got out to stand next to Tyler.

"Leave your gear in the Humvee," Doyle said as he walked toward us. "You're safe within these walls. You won't need guns here."

"No," Clutch said simply, adamantly.

Doyle looked at me.

I gripped my rifle harder.

"As long as there are zeds, they can keep their weapons," Tyler said. "That's an order."

After a guffaw, Doyle relented with a brush of his hand. "Have it your way. Keep them, but you won't need them. You're under my protection here."

I didn't exactly feel safe under Doyle's "protection," and from the look on both Clutch and Tyler's faces, they felt the same.

"While we're here, you can also brief me," Tyler said. "I've told you this before: I've got concerns about how many rations you've been going through lately. And you have no authority to grow your numbers, not without Lendt's approval."

Doyle grunted and turned, leading our group through the militia camp. Three rundown grain silos towered into the sky. A line of smoke trailed out from the dome of one. A faded Iowa Hawkeye logo was painted across one silo. A large white cross was painted on the side of a long tin building with writing and graffiti all along its side. Overgrown grass and dandelions cropped up everywhere not covered by gravel. People milled about, including even a few children.

Woodsy smoke corrupted the fresh spring breeze. As we passed a small fire with a turkey fryer filled with boiling water, I asked, "What are all the camp fires for?"

"Cooking. Purifying water," Doyle replied. "Our generators aren't big enough to power the entire camp, so anything we can do the old fashioned way, we do. Besides, the smoke also helps keep the smell down."

"Not worried about smoke or the smell of smoke attracting zeds?" I countered, knowing that we only cooked at night to mask the visibility of smoke.

Doyle smiled. "I say, let 'em come."

As we moved into the shadows of the silos, I noticed two young women stirring a pot on a fire. The scraping of metal against metal overpowered the crackling wood. As we walked past, one of the women jerked up, revealing a black eye. Utter despair radiated through her swollen, red eyes. She quickly looked away, focusing all too intently on the pot.

My jaw tightened. "Tell me, Doyle. How many folks are here by their own free will?"

"Everyone is given a choice when they arrive," he replied without turning. "They can choose to abide by my rules and stay here or go it alone outside the walls."

"But only the minutemen and their families stay here," Tyler added, while watching the young woman. "The militia has strict orders to bring all other survivors to Camp Fox."

"Of course," Doyle replied. "And others have chosen to stay to support the militia."

Glancing back at the young woman, I doubted Doyle's words. If Clutch hadn't been with me that day at the greenhouse, I suspected I'd be in her situation now: trapped. I found both Tyler and Clutch stopped, still eying the woman, before glancing at one another. Whatever passed between them, I couldn't see, but they both started to follow Doyle again.

The gravel crunched under my feet as Doyle led us alongside a long warehouse. The words "Gone but not forgotten" were painted on the faded wood siding under the white cross, with dozens of names painted around it.

Many names were separated into smaller groupings, each under a different last name. *Lynn, Wahl, Hogan ...* the names went on and on, and I realized that while I didn't trust the Dogs, many of them had suffered as much, if not more, than I had.

At the end of the building, Doyle opened a door and gestured, "Welcome to my office and my home."

Tyler stepped inside, followed by his men. Clutch waited for me, his hard expression impossible to read. Just as I was about to step through the door, I heard a wretched cry. Pausing, I turned to the smallest of the silos. Then another cry, louder, almost forlorn, and I could make out a single syllable in its whimper. *Please.*

I shot a glance at Clutch before looking to Doyle. "I didn't realize zeds cried."

His lips curled upward. "Didn't you, now."

He turned and disappeared inside, and I stared at Clutch, frozen.

Because we both knew that zeds didn't cry.

CHAPTER X

Clutch stepped through the doorway. "What the fuck is going on inside that silo?"

"It's our smokehouse," Doyle replied calmly.

"Not that one," Tyler said. "I heard it, too. It sounded like a person in the middle silo."

Doyle lifted his hands. "It's not what you think, gentlemen. Any survivor who wants to join the militia must go through survival training. I need to know that every man on my team will obey me, no matter what the order. No man becomes a minuteman until every man on my team knows he can count on him with his life. What's going on within that silo is nothing more than a hazing ritual every man undergoes when he's ready to take on the title of 'minuteman'."

"Then show us," Clutch demanded.

Doyle smiled smugly. "I'd be happy to, but first, let's

eat. I'm starving."

No one moved.

"You have my word," Doyle added. "Now, come and have a seat. I've asked for some leftovers to be brought in for us." Doyle motioned us to a table. The room, with one large bay window, offered a generous view of much of the camp. In the corner sat a large wood desk covered in stacks of papers and books.

We moved cautiously inside.

Doyle laughed silently, as though he found something funny. "You know, Clutch, most folks wouldn't have the balls to rob me like you did."

"I figured your store was fair game," Clutch replied. "How was I to know you survived the outbreak?"

Doyle held up a hand. "Fair enough. But you killed five of my men. You're lucky I didn't repay kind with kind."

"Seven. The two men you sent today are dead," Tyler said, and Doyle's face tightened. Tyler continued. "While their deaths are tragic, I'm not arresting anyone. Attacking civilians stops now, Doyle. If anything like this happens again, I'm putting you in the brig and having your militia reassigned to Camp Fox."

Doyle's lips tightened. "Most of my men are simple farmers. The stress of the outbreak may have proved too much for some to handle. But I don't have anyone with military training here to help. If Clutch joined my team, I'd ensure there'd be no more...misunderstandings."

Clutch and Tyler chortled in stereo. I frowned. Where

the hell had Doyle gotten the idea that Clutch would join the Dogs? Hell, he'd been attacking us for the past week, and now he thought Clutch would sign up with a smile. He should hate Clutch for killing his men. It was almost as if he'd wanted Clutch to come to him all along. But why?

"You don't have the authority," Tyler said. "This man is Army and has been reactivated. He goes to Camp Fox under Lendt's command."

I could feel the tension roiling off Clutch, yet he sat there, saying nothing.

"Bah!" Doyle waved a hand through the air. "It'd be a waste for Clutch to join Fox, and he doesn't want to, anyway."

Tyler narrowed his eyes. "How would you know?"

Doyle blew him off. "Besides, the National Guard has never been anything but wet nurses. The militia is the people's real protector. I've seen the future, and it ain't pretty. The only way to protect people is to be hard. That Clutch took out two of my men today proves it all the more. Clutch would be a good fit here."

"Excuse me? You don't have the authority." Tyler came to his feet, and the two soldiers with him stepped closer.

Doyle ignored him. "Really, Clutch, tell me. Do you think you can hold down your farm against the zeds that will be pouring out from every major city with only a kid and a wetback?"

My jaw dropped, and I stood. "Wetback?"

Clutch grabbed my arm, whether to protect me or keep me from going for Doyle's throat, I didn't know. He glared. "Watch it, Doyle."

I put a hand on my hip. "My mother was Puerto Rican, and my dad was Irish. I was born here, just like my parents, and my parents' parents before them. That makes me as American as anyone in this room, so back off."

Doyle smirked. "No wonder you're keeping this one for yourself. She's feisty. She'd make good bait."

I went to raise my rifle, but Clutch latched onto my forearm. I tried to rein back my temper, failing miserably.

"Fucking racist," Griz gritted out from behind me.

I nodded.

"Enough!" Tyler slammed a fist on the table. "This ends now, Doyle. You hear me? No more games. We're all in this shithole together and need to be working together."

A door off to our side opened, and I swung my rifle around.

The three women carrying platters entered the room and froze, eyes wide.

Doyle motioned to the women. "Come in, come in." He sat down as though everything was dandy. "Have a seat. Oh, and Captain, I've already sent a plate out to your driver."

"Thank you." Tyler eyed the room cautiously as he and the soldiers with him pulled out wood chairs. He waited until Clutch and I took our seats before taking his own chair. I propped my rifle against the table next to Clutch's, keeping it in easy reach.

As Doyle poured the wine, I realized that all we were missing was Jesus because it sure as hell felt like we'd been brought in for the Last Supper.

Even with the heavy atmosphere, my mouth watered and my stomach growled as the aroma of roasted ham wafted through the air. Clutch hadn't yet let us butcher a hog or cow, not until we worked the kinks out of the smokehouse. When the older woman set down the tray full of meat, I made a mental note to finish the smokehouse tomorrow.

"It looks delicious. Thank you, my dear," Doyle said, briefly holding the woman's hand.

She smiled and kissed his forehead before leaving the room.

On the second platter lay a round loaf of bread and spring greens. "Mm, I missed bread," I murmured and craved to dig in, but I didn't trust Doyle. I watched him, and he smirked like he enjoyed having that kind of power over me. He took his time tearing off a chunk of bread and popped it into his mouth. After he swallowed, I pulled off a piece. As I took my first bite, I found Clutch watching me with a hint of a smile.

I savored the first taste of bread in two months. It had a heavy, whole-grain taste, making it easy to eat without any butter. I tore off a piece for him. "I like carbs."

Before leaving, two of the women bowed to Doyle as

though he was a god. There seemed to be a lot of that going on around here. I watched the two Dogs standing behind their leader, not eating. After swallowing, I turned to Doyle. "Why do you make your guys shave their heads?"

"It started as a matter of hygiene," Doyle said while carving the ham. "It took me less than a week to start up the militia, but within two weeks, three men already had lice. Now, it's become a badge of honor, and all new minutemen have their heads shaved before their training even begins."

"But you didn't shave your hair," I said.

"No, I didn't." He took another bite.

As I chewed, I suspected their shaved heads had little to do with hygiene and everything to do with Doyle's need for control. Not that I would ever say those words to his face, and I started to believe that Doyle had wanted Clutch to come to him all along.

Doyle handed plates to Tyler, who then passed them along to Griz and Tack.

"You keep this much extra food around?" Tyler asked.

"My men need to keep their strength up," Doyle replied.

"No wonder why you're going through rations at over twice the per capita rate at Camp Fox," Tyler said. "Last week I let it slide because of the survivors you brought in. But, your ration list is even longer this week. Yet, you've brought no more survivors to the Camp in four days."

"Just because we haven't found any more survivors, doesn't mean my men aren't working hard." Doyle handed a plate to Clutch, who then handed it to me.

I waited impatiently for Doyle to eat first. Could I trust the man enough to not poison us?

Hell, no.

"You need to start rationing better," Tyler said. "Camp Fox doesn't have enough supplies to keep this up. Our munitions are already under forty percent. With how many more zeds are projected to show up over the next few months, you need to conserve."

Doyle handed a final plate to Clutch before taking one for himself. "Without supplies, we can't clear out Fox Hills and make it habitable again."

Tyler didn't look happy. "I have three times as many men as you, yet you're going through more supplies. You're forcing my hand. I'm going to talk with Lendt about cutting your rations."

Doyle gritted his teeth. "You don't have the authority, Masden. Lendt runs the show, not you. And with Clutch joining up, we're going to need more supplies so we can hit the zeds even harder."

Clutch pounded a fist on the table "Godammit, Doyle. Get it through that thick skull of yours. I'm never hooking up with you and your crew of lowlifes."

"I bet with the right persuasion, you would," Doyle replied quietly.

Clutch looked at me. "Let's go." He came to his feet,

grabbed his rifle, and headed straight for the door.

The scrape of silverware on plates turned to silence.

Still chewing, I jumped up, grabbed my rifle, and followed Clutch.

"Hold up." Doyle shoved to his feet.

Clutch paused, his hand on the handle.

Doyle approached, his two Dogs alongside him. "Let me show you something."

Tyler stood, throwing a worrisome glance in my direction. Griz and Tack didn't look any happier.

Clutch stepped to the side, and Doyle walked outside, and we all followed him toward the northern edge of the camp. I kept eying Clutch, and I suspected that he knew, as I did, that Doyle's attempt at pretenses had just vanished.

As we walked, the sickly sour reek of decay became more and more prevalent.

Clutch was scowling. "What is this about, Doyle?"

"Patience. You'll see soon enough."

A Dog wearing a surgical mask stood at a chain-link door built into the plywood-covered fence. Doyle wrapped a bandana around his face and motioned to the guard, who hastily unbolted the lock and held the door open. He tilted his head as his leader walked through.

Cautiously, I followed Clutch through the door, with Tyler, Griz, Tack, and Doyle's two guards at my back.

I nearly threw up the food I'd just eaten. The stench was horrific. No wonder they'd had so many fires burning within the fences. They weren't for preparing food and water. They were to cover the stench of death.

With my hand covering my nose and mouth, I edged toward the rim of the deep pit piled high with bodies. Hundreds of zeds were piled onto one another. None moved. All showed severe head trauma. Many had been burned, but the bodies on top were fresh, not yet burned. Half-rotted corpses sprawled upon one another, as though they'd been dumped there, dozens or more at a time.

The zeds on top looked like they'd been killed within the last couple days. What had been an older woman in a floral apron lay contorted, with one leg bent behind its back, staring lifelessly at me through gray glassy eyes.

Not far from her lay a toddler with a Tonka truck in a death-grip to its chest. She'd been young when she died, smaller than the ones I'd seen at the school.

The school.

I swayed, and Clutch leaned closer, his solid mass grounding me.

"Zeds rely on their sense of smell more. The stink seems to serve as a natural deterrent," Doyle said. "And it helps mask the scents that humans live within the fence."

I shook my head, unconvinced. The risk of disease seemed too high to have this much death near the camp.

"Why are you showing us this?" Clutch asked from my side.

"Zeds are an inconvenient bunch." Doyle said. "My

men have taken out nearly five hundred deadheads since the outbreak. But we're seeing zeds passing through in greater numbers every week. My militia is the only thing standing between genocide and survival."

"*Your* militia?" Tyler asked. "Careful, Doyle. You're toeing the line."

Doyle brushed him off with a wave of his hand.

Tyler frowned. "I've given you leeway since your men have been doing a good job at taking down zeds. But that doesn't mean you're not replaceable."

Doyle's face reddened. "You have no concept of the type of leadership that's needed in times like these."

Tyler took a step closer. "I have a better idea than you think."

Clutch chortled. "I'm done with this bullshit. I'm taking Cash and we're heading back to my farm." He pointed at Doyle. "And from this moment on, your Dogs will leave us alone and stick with their job of killing zeds. Any act of aggression toward my people will result in more of your men being killed. Got it? I'm not fucking around, Doyle."

Doyle stiffened. "You need to remember one thing: You don't want to be my enemy."

CHAPTER XI

"Are you threatening me?" Clutch demanded, stepping between Doyle and me.

"If I was threatening you," Doyle said. "I'd have said how easy it would be to have you all shot and thrown into the pit to rot with these corpses and no one would be the wiser. I'm simply saying I'm someone you'd much rather have as a friend than as an enemy."

I glanced at Clutch who looked as tense as I felt. Without looking down, I checked my rifle to make sure the safety was off. I realized now it had been a mistake coming here today. Doyle was a power-monger. And he clearly wanted Clutch. That Doyle wanted Clutch alive or dead, I hadn't yet figured out.

"Watch it," Tyler said. "You're grossly overstepping your bounds."

Doyle pointed at the pit full of zeds. "My men are

protecting the Fox River valley. If we hadn't destroyed these monsters, how many more lives would be lost by now? We are not asking for gratitude. All I ask for is a little support and regular supplies. You need to talk to Lendt and get him to grant my men full access to Camp Fox's resources. Enough of this rationing bullshit."

"No," Tyler said. "From what I've seen lately, I'm going to advise Lendt that the militia should be reassigned under my command."

Doyle pulled down his bandana. "And exactly what do you think you've seen, Masden?"

Tyler jutted out his chin. "I know you're feeding me bullshit every week. For starters, do you think I wouldn't notice that you have a hell of a lot more people on this camp than just the militia and their families?"

"It takes a lot of support resources to run a successful militia."

"If you haven't been killing so many zeds and bringing in survivors, I would've shut you down a month ago," Tyler snapped back.

Doyle watched Tyler carefully. "You should tread carefully, Captain. Times have changed. Nature will take its course, just as it always has. The weak will die, leaving only the strong. If we waste our efforts protecting the weak..." Doyle shot a gaze at me before turning back to Tyler, "then we will all fall to the zed horde. You are incorrect, Captain. As the leader of the militia, I have the right to do whatever it takes to ensure my men are the strong."

"You're fighting each other when we should all be fighting the zeds together," Clutch growled out. "You two can work out your own shit. I'm out of here."

With that he turned, shot me a look, and headed back to the door, with me at his side. The guard from earlier blocked the door.

"Out of my way, boy," Clutch ordered.

The man looked nervously past our shoulders and didn't move.

"Think it through, Clutch," Doyle called out, sounded exasperated. "You're trained to analyze every situation. You know joining with me is the only logical decision."

Clutch's back straightened and he turned around. "And if I don't?"

"Then you'll realize your mistake when you find you're unable to protect your own people."

"Now *that* sounds an awful lot like a threat," Clutch said.

"Enough, Doyle!" Tyler yelled out. "Sarge isn't militia. He's retired military and has been recalled to active duty as of thirty seconds ago," Tyler said, his voice deeper and louder than before. "How he serves is Lendt's decision. We'll continue this discussion later at Lendt's office."

I heard it then. The hearty growl of a big engine. I searched until I found a green garbage truck barreling toward us. This truck was undamaged and didn't have all the armor plating, but it was from the same garbage company. When it approached, I tensed.

It stopped, then turned and backed up toward the pit, the sound of *beep-beep-beep* echoing around us. The back lifted and dumped two more bodies onto the pile. I covered my nose and scanned the pile to make sure none were moving.

"You see, Captain," Doyle said. "How many lives did we save today?"

Tyler didn't reply.

Smugly smiling, Doyle turned to the man getting out of the truck. "I trust everything went well, Keith?"

The driver bowed to Doyle before speaking. "No problems."

I gasped. "You."

The man looked. His eyes widened, and he froze.

We'd found the fourth rapist. The one who got away.

Clutch and I raised our rifles at the same time. Doyle's guards and Tyler and his men raised their rifles in response.

"Whoa." Tyler held up one hand above his rifle. "What's going on here?"

"Stand back," Clutch nodded to the newcomer Keith, "That rat bastard is responsible for the rape, torture, and death of a young woman."

"Do you have proof?" Tyler countered, though Tack and Griz both moved their rifles onto the Dogs.

"We both saw it," I said. "She tried to escape and he was one of the four chasing her."

"I didn't do nothing!" Keith shrieked.

I looked at Clutch. His hard gaze told me everything I needed to know. I aimed my rifle and fired. Keith fell back, into the pit, a bullet hole through his forehead.

I expected to be riddled with bullets, but surprisingly, no one else fired even though everyone except Doyle held a rifle.

Doyle's lips thinned. "You'll be sorry for doing that, girl."

Tyler leveled his rifle on Doyle. "We have laws, Doyle. I'm arresting her, and she's coming with me to stand trial."

"If you'd seen what he and his friends had done, Captain," Clutch growled, "you'd have done the same thing."

"Everyone, stand down," Tyler commanded.

None of the Dogs lowered their weapons, and so no one else did.

"Doyle, your men are ordered to stand down," Tyler said, reaching out to me, but Clutch grabbed me first and pulled me against him.

"That Dog got what he deserved," Clutch said.

He took us a step back, and then froze.

"No!" I cried out when I saw Doyle's pistol aimed point blank at Clutch's temple. I turned to Tyler. "Clutch is innocent."

"The only way anyone leaves here is if I allow it," Doyle countered.

"You are disobeying a direct order, Doyle," Tyler stated. "This camp is under the jurisdiction of Camp

Fox. If you do not have your men stand down now, you will be stripped of rank and deemed outlaws. This is your last warning."

Doyle snorted. "My camp, my rules. It's you who need to lower your weapons."

"If your men open fire," Tyler said, keeping his rifle aimed at Doyle. "You'll be the first one dead. Now, you are *ordered* to stand down!"

Clutch's eyes were completely focused on me. "Let them go, Doyle," he said, "and I'll join your crew."

I shook my head. *Don't do this.*

After a lengthy pause, Doyle pulled away his pistol and sneered. "You're lucky I'm in a good mood today, Masden. You have five minutes to clear out of my camp."

"Get her out of here, Captain," Clutch ground out.

"The militia is done, Doyle," Tyler said. "Effective immediately."

Doyle belted out a laugh. "Camp Fox needs me. I don't need you." He sobered. "And you're wasting your minutes."

Tyler reached for me. "You don't have to do this, Clutch," I begged.

Clutch's face hardened and he turned away, gritting his teeth while one of the Dogs disarmed him.

"Well, this worked out better than I expected," Doyle said to one of his men.

Tyler grabbed my wrist. He pulled me through the doorway and through the camp, flanked by Griz and

Tack.

Knots tightened in my gut with every step. Doyle had wanted Clutch. Defeated and under his control. And we'd let him do it. He'd expected Clutch to kill the rapist so he could imprison him. When I killed the man, Clutch had volunteered to stay, making Doyle's job easy. Doyle had got exactly what he'd wanted. Clutch was no longer a threat, leaving those he cared about easy game for the Dogs.

With a surge, I twisted free and grabbed Tyler's arms. "Clutch is a good man. He doesn't belong here. Promise me you'll try to get him out of here."

Tyler watched me for a moment. Maybe he understood, maybe he saw something in my eyes. He gave a thin smile. "I'll do what I can."

When his words registered as truth in my mind, I nodded and inhaled. "Good." I headed to the waiting Humvee, a thousand rescue scenarios running through my mind.

The only problem was, without Clutch, I couldn't do anything, let alone pull off a rescue.

Before I climbed into the Humvee, I looked back one last time to find Clutch, but only saw Doyle watching us smugly, promising retribution. Clutch had sacrificed himself for our freedom. And it was a waste, because Doyle wouldn't stop until we were all dead.

VIOLENCE

THE SEVENTH CIRCLE OF HELL

CHAPTER XII

I remembered the feeling of plastic restraints cutting into my wrists from my first night with Clutch. I understood why Tyler felt like he had to arrest me, and before the outbreak I would've agreed with him.

But the world had changed.

I felt even edgier without the weight of my gear and weapons. Being defenseless in the middle of zed country, with Clutch undergoing who knows what back at Doyle's camp, unnerved me.

I sighed. "You didn't need to tie me up. I'm not a danger to you."

Tyler turned from the window to me, looking none too pleased. "You killed an unarmed man today."

If he only knew the facts. "And I don't regret it."

Yes, I'd shot that criminal knowing that shit would hit the fan as a result. The man was dead, anyway. I'd simply fired before Clutch did. He was going to pull the trigger. I'd seen it in his eyes, just like he'd seen it in the eyes of the Dog he shot back at Doyle's gate. So, I killed the man to keep Clutch safe. I just hadn't figured that Clutch would be a victim in the ensuing cluster fuck. When I saw him again—and I promised myself I would—I was going to wring his freaking neck for playing hero.

Nick shot me a tender glance before returning his focus to driving, and I could feel eyes on my back from Griz and Tack behind me as well. None of them had seen what the Dogs had done to that poor girl. Still, being this close to the militia camp, they must've seen things or heard stories when it came to Doyle and his cronies.

"You know Doyle," I said. "He never would've let you take one of his Dogs into custody to stand trial. Face it, the only thing that kept that rapist from getting off free was my bullet."

Tyler narrowed his gaze. "How can you be so cavalier about taking a man's life?"

"You didn't see what they did," I replied quietly, remembering her broken body and hollow eyes.

He was quiet for a moment. "In case you haven't noticed, there aren't many of us left. We have to keep faith in justice. We'll never make it if we each take the law into our own hands."

I chortled. "We'll never make it if we *don't* take the law into our own hands." It was futile trying to convince Tyler that the world was no longer wrapped with a comforting blanket of rules and traditions. We could no longer afford the luxury of hiding accountability beneath layers of red tape. Doyle wouldn't follow the rules. Neither could we. In a matter of days, we'd toppled from thinking we were wolves to realizing that we were only rabbits.

I broke eye contact to look out the window. We were approaching tall chain-link fences, topped with razor wire, surrounding what looked to be at least ten acres of a National Guard base.

Camp Fox.

Too wide open for a solid defense. Too many areas for zeds to break through.

A white wind turbine rotated smoothly, towering above the base. My jaw dropped. "You have power?"

Tyler nodded. "Camp Fox has had its own wind energy for over five years now."

"Showers?"

His lips curved. "Yes, we even have hot water." I rested my head on the seat and fantasized about standing under a steamy shower as we approached the gate. Unfortunately, I couldn't allow myself the luxury of fantasies. Not with Clutch's—and my—current situation.

Several Humvees and armored vehicles rested on the other side of the tall fence. Camp Fox certainly wasn't lacking firepower, though Clutch and I had watched on television while cities like D.C. and L.A. fell, despite having massive military power on their streets.

Two soldiers stood while a third stepped inside a guard's box and opened the gate. They saluted Tyler as we passed through the gate, and he saluted in return. It was then I realized that I might never see the farm again.

"Will Smitty stay with Jase and Eddy tonight?" I asked, knowing that Jase had to be getting worried before long.

"I'm having the boys brought here tonight," Tyler replied. "I'll see that you connect with Jase tomorrow morning. I thought it would be safer than leaving him at the farm."

"I suppose so," I murmured, though I wasn't exactly confident in Camp Fox's strength, not after seeing the way Doyle had scoffed at Tyler.

Beyond the gate stood several small pens holding livestock. A lone bull with wide horns stood in a closed-off area across the road. No doubt this setup was to protect the animals from zeds, but to me, it was like setting out bait. Once zeds depleted the local population, they'd come in hordes to Camp Fox in search for food.

A single zed was easy to kill. They were dumb, slow things. Easy to outthink and outmaneuver. But a herd never tired. Tall fences and bullets couldn't protect these people. They were rounded up for an all-you-can-eat buffet. I felt a hundred times safer at the farm, where we were ready to bug out at the first sign of herds.

As the Humvee curved around the Camp's winding roads, people milled around, some worked the gardens while others carried loads. Two young children played with a ball. Several looked up as we passed. Many smiled and waved as though these men were their saviors, which I supposed was true.

Seeing so many people in one place, I couldn't help but feel a pang of hope. Maybe Jase would be safer here than alone at the farm, for at least now. Maybe Tyler was right. Maybe Camp Fox could recreate civilization. Maybe, just maybe, they could withstand zeds.

We continued past several barracks, all of which had people in regular clothes walking nearby. After another few blocks, Nick pulled to a stop outside a square brick building with a sign that read Camp Fox HQ outside.

Griz and Tack climbed out back before Tyler opened his door. Each man grabbed my arms and pulled me across the seat. With my wrists tied, I nearly stumbled climbing down from the Humvee.

As soon as Tack shut the door, the Humvee drove off, leaving the four of us standing alone in the small parking lot. The sun had already begun to set, casting a warm orange glow onto the red bricks. Clutch was in the direction of the falling sun. What would he be doing now? Would he be tied up like I was, or was he playing along with Doyle?

Tyler tugged me along and I had to hurry to keep up with his longer strides. Griz and Tack followed us up the steps and through the double doors.

Inside, the building seemed innocuous. With the exception of military insignias, the main area could've passed for any town hall. Tyler stopped us at the front desk, where a man and woman sat. He was in uniform, while she wore jeans. "Is the Colonel available?" Tyler asked.

The woman spoke first. "He is. Shall I let him know you're coming?"

"Yes, thank you," Tyler nodded and then turned to me. A pained look flashed across his face before he turned to the two soldiers with us. "Escort the prisoner to interrogation room one." He gave me a final, almost-pained glance before turning on his heel and hurrying down a hallway.

Tension grew in my muscles.

"This way, sugar," Griz said.

With one man on either side, they walked me down a hallway, stopping when we came to an opened door.

Tack flipped a switch, and light flooded the room. The room sat empty except for a table and two chairs.

Griz nudged me inside, and I winced at the sudden brightness. With his rifle, he motioned to a chair. "Take a seat."

I swallowed and obeyed and was somewhat surprised that they didn't restrain me to the chair, not that I was an expert on interrogations. The sum of my experience came from what I'd seen on TV. They left me alone, closing the door behind them. I suspected at least one of them remained just outside the door, but I could neither see nor hear them.

The room was small, maybe eight-by-eight, without any windows. No two-way mirror covered the wall, though I supposed video cameras had long since replaced two-way mirrors.

I closed my eyes. Focused on my breathing. Silently repeated my mantra to soothe my nerves until I realized there was no way to get the upper hand in this situation.

I was at their mercy, plain and simple.

Long after my butt had gone numb in the cold metal chair, the door opened, and I started.

A man I didn't recognize walked in first, followed by Tyler. The newcomer was tall, his face craggy, and looked to be in his late forties. He took the other chair, while Tyler stood off to the side.

"I'm Lieutenant Colonel John Lendt." The man sitting across from me looked every bit the leader Tyler had made him out to be. A piercing, sharp gaze, hard jaw, and strong shoulders hinted that this man was confident in both his intelligence and strength. He was downright intimidating without even trying.

"I'm Cash. I'd shake your hand, but my hands are preoccupied."

"Just Cash?" He raised a brow.

I shrugged. "I'm no longer who I was before."

One corner of his mouth rose. "I disagree. Who we were shapes us into who we are, and who we are shapes us into who we'll become." He leaned back. "But we're not here to talk philosophy, are we. Captain Masden witnessed you shooting an unarmed man without provocation today. What do you have to say to that charge?"

A thousand different responses shot through my brain. I settled on simple honesty. "Yes, I shot him, but I had provocation."

His brows tightened. "You realize that under military law the punishment for murder is death."

I looked down at the table and swallowed.

Lendt came to his feet. "Sergeant Nicholas Lee has volunteered to lead your defense. I'll have a tribunal scheduled for the day after tomorrow. No need to delay this messy business, but you have my word that you'll be treated fairly."

Tyler followed Lendt out of the room.

I frowned. This was an interrogation? No questions about why I'd done it?

"This way."

Griz stood in the doorway, motioning to me, and I rose and followed him, feeling as though my doom was already sealed. Numbness coated my thoughts as they escorted me out the other side of the building and across a wide sidewalk to a low one-story building. Inside, the short hallway was lined with several cell doors and more hallways, though I could hear no one else nearby. They put me into the first tiny, windowless cell with a narrow bed and a steel latrine and sink.

"Hold still for a moment," Griz said just before I felt a tug and the plastic restraint snapped free. I rubbed my wrists and faced the two soldiers as one shut the steel door.

Tack faced me through the bars in the door's window. "The bastard got what he deserved," he said before disappearing, leaving me alone in my cell.

I collapsed onto the bed and stared at the gray ceiling. How had everything gone to shit so quickly?

Silence boomed off the walls in response.

I thought of Jase. He knew people here. They could look out for him.

But Clutch…

For all I knew, he was lying dead in that zed pit right now.

The sound of boot steps echoing down the hallway brought me back, and I pulled myself up and walked toward the door in time to meet the driver from the Humvee.

He was looking to his left. "Open up."

"I can't, sir," an unfamiliar voice said. "Colonel's orders. He said the prisoner is a flight risk."

Nick rolled his eyes before turning to me. "Hi, Cash. I'm Sergeant Nick Lee."

"I remember," I replied. "Good to see you again."

"I'll represent you at your trial. Since you already admitted to the murder, I think our best defense is to prove that there was no premeditation, and, therefore, this wasn't first-degree murder. That way, you'll just get time in the brig, and the death sentence gets ruled out."

I watched him for a moment. "Why are you helping

me, Nick?"

He shrugged, and then lowered his voice. "I've seen some shit. Bad things that have happened to women *and* men. We've all heard rumors. If you said both you and your friend saw this guy hurt a girl, I believe it. Now, if we can get your friend to testify, it will help your cause. The fact that he's a veteran is even better." He paused for a moment. "But, honestly, I don't think we'll be able to get him here for the trial."

Not that I was surprised. Still, having my thoughts spoken aloud burned. "Can't Lendt order him to come to the Camp?"

"Sure, but I don't think it will do any good. Colonel Lendt ordered Doyle to come to the Camp after Masden filled him in, and Doyle hasn't shown up yet." Nick grinned. "And, Colonel Lendt doesn't take kindly to being screwed with. I think he's finally going to make Doyle come to heel and break up the militia."

"Watch out for Doyle," I said, a rock forming in my gut.

"What's he going to do? Attack Camp Fox?" He smirked. "Don't worry. We have many times the resources and firepower that Doyle's got. We're safe enough here. Let's start prepping for your trial. Start at the beginning, and tell me everything."

Several hours later, I woke, sweating and heart racing. I dreamed that Clutch was in the room with me. Except that he was a zed.

A siren pierced the night's silence, and I lunged to the door. "What's going on?" I called out, hoping someone was nearby.

"Echo Four reporting in, requesting status. Over."

The soldier's voice was to my right, but I couldn't see him around the corner.

"All units report immediately to assigned defense points. Camp Fox is under attack. Zed Alert. Code Five. This is not a drill. Over."

The voice on the radio repeated the message two more times before my guard stepped in front of my door, his eyes wide.

"What's going on?" I asked.

He stared at me for a moment, and then took off running. A door opened and closed. Then silence.

"Damn it," I muttered, kicking at my door. Without any visible doorknob or hinges, all I could do was shove at the door, but it was solid steel. Still I tried. Trying was better than accepting that I'd die in this tomb, either from starvation or when the zeds would finally find me. I turned and walked over to the bed. Pulled at the frame but it was screwed into the concrete floor. I returned to the door. After long minutes of kicking, a door opened somewhere. Buried under the piercing siren, I heard gunfire and screams.

Nick's helmeted visage filled the window in my

door, startling me. “It was Doyle,” he said, panting. “His men cut through the fence and laid down flares. Set off the sirens. They must’ve gone out and drawn all the zeds in the area here.”

He pulled off his helmet and wiped his forehead. “Doyle zed-bombed us.”

CHAPTER XIII

"There are zeds everywhere," Nick said, putting his helmet back on. "I can't believe it. Doyle attacked us. He really did it."

I pressed my hand over my heart as his words sunk in. While I didn't doubt Doyle's ruthlessness, the reality that he'd attack hundreds of innocent people made no sense. I pressed against the door. "Let me out. I can help."

Nick noisily fidgeted with keys. "This is your only shot. Lendt will make you stand trial, and you'll end up either in the brig or worse. And that's just not right. I've seen shit the Dogs have done. You've got to run."

More rattles, I heard a click, and the door swung open. I jumped out of my cell to find Nick already jogging away, his boot steps echoing through the empty hallway. When he opened the door, the gunfire sounded way too close, but there was no way zeds should have managed to cross acres of the outer camp to get to the center.

Before I stepped outside, I paused. "I have no weapon."

He patted a couple pockets with his hand not holding an AR-15 and pulled out a folding knife with a camo paint scheme. "It's not much, but it's all I can spare."

I opened the blade. "Better than nothing."

Nick gave my shoulder a quick pat. "Head east. That's the quickest way out of here. I got to get to my squad. As soon as all the civvies are in their barracks, we're going to start unloading the heavies on the zeds." Nick sprinted toward the tanks and Humvees rolling in, likely to congregate around the barracks in the distance, and I hoped that Jase was safe.

Movement in the darkness off to Nick's left kicked me into action. "Your nine o'clock!" I shouted, running toward him.

He twisted to his left where at least a dozen zeds tumbled out of the shadows. He held down the trigger, firing into the onslaught and taking down several zeds, but most bullets embedded harmlessly into their torsos and limbs.

I sprinted to close the distance between Nick and me.

A zed wearing a business suit emerged from the darkness behind Nick. I spun around it and embedded the knife up to its hilt into the back of the zed's skull. I hadn't been sure the blade was long enough until the zed collapsed.

Nick's rifle clicked on empty. He dropped it and pulled out a pistol that looked like a Beretta 9mm.

"Conserve your ammo," I said as I picked up the empty rifle. "Remember to go for head shots!"

Wild-eyed, he fired into the thinning group, and I pocketed the knife. I jogged over to the zeds on the fringe, ones too shot up to walk, and swung down the rifle butt, making sure to crush each skull before moving onto the next.

After Nick quit shooting, I slammed the rifle into the last moving zed.

Walking back, I held out the AR-15, now dripping with brown sludge. He finished reloading his pistol, holstered it, and looked up. He grimaced at the rifle, but took it and reloaded.

"Hasn't anyone trained you guys on the art of killing zeds?" I held a finger to my temple. "Always go for headshots. One shot, one kill. Anywhere else is a waste of ammo unless you're overwhelmed and have to slow them down."

"Lay off me, I'm just ROTC," Nick said, reloading the rifle. "It's just different when they're right *there*. They should never have gotten this far into the Camp."

Screams erupted in the distance, and we both jerked around.

Nick's eyes widened. "They breached the barracks!"

No. Jase!

We took off running toward the barracks, where

gunfire flashed like lightning bugs in the night.

Several zeds lumbered after us along the way, but we easily outran any Nick didn't take down with headshots.

By the time we reached the first barrack, cries seemed to be coming from everywhere. Zeds pounded at each of the doors and windows of the barrack. The people inside stood huddled together under the lights, making them look like fish in a fishbowl. Soldiers in full battle armor, unable to fire without risking casualties to friendly fire inside, used bayonet-knives, axes, and crowbars to take out the zeds and were making headway.

I came down on a knee by a soldier who'd lost his helmet and had been chewed to a pulpy mess. I relieved him of his rifle and knife before rummaging through his pockets to find two fresh magazines. His warm blood soaked my hands, making the mags slippery.

After reloading the rifle, I found a pale Nick nervously waiting for me instead of helping his comrades, his lack of experience all too obvious.

.30 cal machine guns belted out rounds into the darkness.

The first barrack had been nearly cleared by the troops. I tugged Nick's arm. "Let's check the other barracks."

We ran down the long building to the second barrack. Only a few zeds shuffled by its doors and windows. With no lights on inside, it was impossible to see if the barrack was inhabited, but I suspected these civilians had been smart enough to hide from the zeds.

The third barrack was a different story. Its doors were thrown wide open, and the soldiers were firing directly inside. The lights were on, and I couldn't make out who was zed and who wasn't.

I ran toward the building, searching for Jase. I wasn't used to the AR-15 so I got close to the crowd before I fired. My first shot went right through a zed's brainpan. The rifle had less recoil than I was used to, and I took down two more zeds before running to a more open spot and repeating the process.

The ground was covered with hundreds of zeds, some not moving, some dragging themselves toward prey. But, for every zed on the ground, there were four still on their feet. I didn't count my rounds, knew I couldn't have more than a dozen shots left if I was lucky.

When the rifle clicked on empty, I swung it at the zed nearest me. The rifle got tangled in the zed's clothing, so I let go and dodged to the side, narrowly missing a petite zed. I pulled out the longer bayonet knife I lifted off the dead soldier and planted it through the zed's eye, and it tumbled backward, collapsing to the ground.

I tried to get closer to the barrack, slashing at zeds, but it was impossible. More zeds were closing in every minute. I was forced to retreat and I ran toward the first Humvee. Manning the .30 cal was Tyler. A soldier leaned against Tyler's back, clutching a neck wound, but still managing to fire rifle shots at zeds coming at them from behind.

Something grabbed my foot, and I looked down to find a zed missing half its torso gnawing on my boot. I lifted my foot and brought it down on its head, breaking its nose. My next stomp was met with a pleasant-sounding crack of its skull fracturing.

I jumped onto the back of Tyler's Humvee. The other soldier had collapsed, either unconscious or dead. I relieved him of his rifle, checked him for ammo (found none), and shoved him off, knowing he could turn any moment.

I hadn't seen Jase yet, so I had to assume he was safely locked inside one of the other barracks. The alternative I couldn't deal with. As for Clutch, I hadn't seen any signs of militia yet, and I prayed that he hadn't been pulled into this mess.

Zeds, for all their viciousness, had a tough time climbing. Several relentlessly tried to get onto the Humvee but kept falling back. But, it wouldn't take long for enough zeds to surround us that they'd literally get pushed up onto the vehicle.

I searched around the bed of the Humvee for a mag, finding nothing for my rifle, but I did pull out a fresh belt of .30 cal rounds from under the pile of used shells and held it up for Tyler. He fed the belt into the gun, gave me a quick nod, and started firing again.

I noticed the Beretta in his holster and I tapped his arm as a heads up before freeing the pistol from his holster. At the back of the Humvee, I shot any zed that got too close. Then I stopped.

"Shit," I muttered when I watched the others use the bodies of the fallen to get higher. I swallowed, backed up a step closer to Tyler. We were surrounded on a small island that was about to get a whole lot smaller. I switched from killing zeds to my original plan of kicking them back.

An artillery blast nearby blinded me momentarily, and I remembered Nick's comment about bringing out the heavies. Through the windows of the long barrack, zeds were tearing into the people, ripping them apart like ravenous harpies. Many people had been dismembered, bodies covering the floors like gnarled stumps, while zed continued to feed. Dark blood covered everything.

Even with all the chaos, the noise and smells around the third barrack drew all the zeds to it. Civilians began to emerge from the other barracks, carrying weapons and joining the fray.

My heart lurched. The familiar saunter was unmistakable. *Jase.* I watched as he fought alongside Eddy, each teenager firing his own AR-15, and Mutt tucked into a pocket, seemingly fearless. "Be safe," I whispered before being forced to deal with my own issues.

I fired my last two bullets into a zed that made it onto the Humvee and resumed kicking the monsters back. My muscles burned and shook from exhaustion, but I kept pushing.

Finally, somehow, the tides began to shift. With the zeds centralized around the third barrack, Tyler shouted commands into his radio, and the troops formed a front against the mass. Soldiers with grenade launchers unleashed a fury of explosions onto the undead invaders.

Tyler's .30 cal clicked on empty. The sudden lack of vibration and noise washed despair over me. Tyler and I shared a knowing glance.

The soldier I'd shoved off the back had turned and now jumped at the truck. Freshly turned zeds were nearly as fast and agile as humans, and it worked its way through the lumbering rotted lot to climb onto the Humvee. It lunged at Tyler first, who was already pulling out his knife. I grabbed the zed's shirt to slow it down. It twisted around and lashed out at me. I jumped back, nearly tumbling off the edge and into the sea of waiting arms. As the zed came at me, Tyler shoved a blade through the skull of what used to be one of Camp Fox's loyal soldiers.

The zed collapsed, and Tyler fell to his knees, his shoulders slumped. "Jonesie was a good man."

I rested a hand on his back.

Tyler's head sagged. "He was the last of my original squad."

I stood there, staring out over the clawed hands reaching for us. Every now and then one fell. Confused, I scanned to find several troops shooting their way toward us. The heaviness from my chest lifted, and I was able to suck in a breath. "Look." I pulled Tyler up. "See? It's going to be okay."

By the time the soldiers reached us, no zeds were left standing. Single shots were fired sporadically as soldiers put down zeds still moving.

I jumped down, stumbling over bodies. The Camp was utter carnage. Blood mixed with brown goo. I searched for signs of Jase, and found him with Eddy, finishing off wounded zeds. I smiled. *You're going to be all right.*

My smile faded when I caught a glimpse of camouflage propped against the side of the barrack, and I burst toward him. But I wasn't fast enough. "Nick!" I cried out right as the badly injured soldier shoved his pistol in his own mouth and pulled the trigger.

I collapsed to my knees.

I never saw the zed until it fell upon me.

CHAPTER XIV

I rolled over, kicking away from the zed, and stabbed it through its eye before I realized that someone had already shot it from behind. Brown sludge seeped from the eye like half-set pudding, and I fell onto my butt, gagging at the stench.

"You okay?"

I looked up to see Griz standing before me.

"I am now," I said.

He held out a hand and pulled me up. "Hoorah," he grunted before heading after another zed that needed put down.

I stood near the third barrack—what remained of it, anyway—which was now a giant campfire, with flickers of embers and glints of soot showering us. Corpses covered the ground around me. Most lay unmoving. One zed had a blade through its mouth, pinning it to the ground. It chewed at the handle even while it convulsed and spasmed.

Someone had turned the sirens off, but the remaining sounds—cries of the dying—were heart-wrenching. A woman's weeping drew me to the shadows to my left. I edged closer, keeping the knife ready. She lay amid the corpses, her shoulder and leg badly chewed. She didn't have long before she turned, not with injuries that bad. She was clawing at the dirt with wretched, bloody hands, trying to pull herself toward something. "My baby," she cried over and over.

I frowned and looked to where she was trying to drag herself. A tiny body lay unmoving on the ground, its limbs twisted in unnatural ways.

I kept the knife ready in case the infant had turned, though I supposed it'd have no teeth to bite with. I rolled the baby over to find myself looking at the lifeless eyes of an infant, his fear frozen in his features at death. With such severe injuries, if he were going to turn, he would've by now. I'd seen a handful of people who'd died instead of turning. Maybe their bodies weren't strong enough to support the virus, maybe they had some kind of immunity, who knew. I figured those were the lucky ones.

I lifted the baby's broken body as gently as I could and carried him over to his mother. She reached out with her uninjured arm and pulled him to her. She buried her face in his hair and rocked him, murmuring loving words into his ears.

I left her alone while I went back to where Nick lay propped against the building and got what I needed.

I reloaded the Beretta as I walked toward the woman. Tears blurred my aim, but I was close enough it wouldn't matter. I fired twice at point blank.

Her suffering was over.

A hand touched my shoulder, and I snapped around to see Tyler.

He grabbed my free hand. "Come with me."

He led me down the block. He only let go to shoot a stray zed.

At the end of the block, he commandeered a Jeep. He drove in silence, taking me through the winding roads. As we approached the open square, I stared at the silhouette of the lone gallows under the moonlight.

"You were going to hang me?" I asked. "Is that part of your so-called justice system?"

"It wasn't for you," Tyler said quickly. "It was for a convict who killed one civilian and injured another when they caught him stealing food."

I rode numbly as Tyler drove us to an area of the camp where several large garages stood. In the fence was a gate that had been blasted open.

Tyler parked and looked me over. "Lendt's a stickler for rules, so even though you helped tonight, he'll still have you stand trial. I agree with him that you should stand trial, but the game's changed. But, I also think that, sometimes, the rules need to be broken. With all the chaos, it would've been easy for you to escape."

I cocked my head at Tyler's words.

"Though I wish it wasn't the case, we have to part ways. At least until I can get the charges against you reduced," Tyler said.

Before getting out, I paused. "Take care of Jase. He's a good kid."

Without waiting for a response, I jumped out and set a brisk pace into the darkness.

"Hold up," Tyler said, catching up.

I swallowed, then turned. He handed me another clip and then placed his hand behind my neck and kissed my forehead. "Be careful out there."

I gave a small smile and started walking again.

"Watch your six," Tyler called out behind me.

I paused for a moment, and then took off at a full run through the gate and into the night.

The east horizon was growing lighter than the west, meaning that dawn wasn't far behind. I jogged down the road to cover as much distance as possible before the sun would betray me to any Dogs and zeds in the area. I ran around a few zed stragglers on the roads, but didn't stop to kill them, instead, moving as quickly as I could before more showed.

My lungs burned. My body was drenched with sweat, and I'd run less than five miles because I could just make out the outline of Doyle's camp in my path.

I wanted to burst into the camp and save Clutch. Except stupid heroics would only get us both killed. Clutch had always told me to never go on an offensive without being prepared. He'd told me often, "Whatever you didn't plan for, that's what's going to happen." Worse, after the Camp attack (What the hell was Doyle thinking, to go after Camp Fox like that?), the Dogs would be on high alert, waiting for repercussions, and ready to gun me down the moment I stepped near their camp.

"I'm coming back for you," I promised Clutch and kept jogging.

As the first rays of sunlight ebbed over the horizon, I detoured through a field that had been freshly plowed in the spring but already showed signs of being retaken by prairie grasses. The ground was rough, and I slowed to a walk to not twist an ankle. Within minutes, I entered the woods that lined the field, where the trees could hide me from both zeds and Dogs.

But trees could hide zeds just as well.

When the sun lit up the world, I moved slowly but steadily toward the farm. I figured I had around thirty miles to go, which would take me a full day at the rate I was moving.

Spending a night in the woods with zeds wasn't my idea of fun, but any nearby houses could have Dogs. So I kept moving through the woods like a predator but feeling more like prey.

When I came to a road, I didn't cross. Still too close to Doyle's camp. I walked alongside the highway, weaving through trees until I came to small creek running under the road through a round culvert. Keeping my larger knife firmly in my grip, I crept closer, stepping into the water. Cold water climbed up my legs and trickled down into my boots, and I grimaced. Soggy feet would be hell in a few hours.

I moved slowly to prevent splashing water. Finally, I reached the metal culvert, and thankfully it was empty except for a few inches of water rippling through it.

My throat was parched. I wanted to drink from the stream so badly, but between farm runoff and the potential for zeds or dead bodies to be lying in it upstream, there was too great a risk of dysentery.

The culvert was small. I had to wade through it on my hands and knees, and with every move forward, I prayed that nothing hungry waited on the other side. God, I wished there was another way, but I had to cross. The road curved around to the east, and I needed to go west.

When I came out the other side, it was blissfully peaceful, with nothing but the sounds of the water burbling into the creek below. Feet forward, I pushed myself out but slipped on the wet metal.

I hissed at the sharp pain. "*Shit!*" I watched the blood as it grew from the deep slice across my palm. Red tinted the water as the blood dripped from my hand and washed downstream. Having no gear meant having no first aid kit. I leaned back and held my hand up to slow the bleeding. The cut was deep and wide and would likely get infected if I didn't take care of it properly soon.

The sun was high overhead. My tongue felt like it had doubled in size from dehydration and sat like a giant cotton ball in my mouth. My stomach growled, but hunger was an easier thing to ignore.

With my hand still bleeding, I continued moving through the woods, surprised at the absence of zeds, especially with their seemingly excellent sense of smell. Doyle's Dogs did a hell of a job, either by keeping their area cleaned out or by leading every zed in the area into Camp Fox. Regardless, it made my trip back to the farm easier.

But it wasn't faster. I still had to pause at every tree to scan for movement.

I came across my first zed in the woods sometime during late afternoon. It'd been a man about my age, wearing a sporty T-shirt with a big logo. I couldn't see any injuries. In fact, as the dull infected features went, its were almost gentle behind gold-rimmed sunglasses. That was, until it sniffed the air and snarled.

Taking a breath, I stepped out and it lunged. I jumped around the tree and came up behind the zed, shoved the knife through the base of its skull, and pushed upward.

Its body shuddered, and then collapsed.

Zeds were vicious monsters, but they had their

Achilles heels. One of those was that they couldn't corner worth a shit.

I bent down and lifted the zed's left wrist with a silver watch strapped around it. *Five-fifteen*.

Less than three hours until sunset. I was moving slower than I'd planned.

I couldn't make it much longer. I had to find clean water soon. Taking on the risk of creating noise, I moved faster through the woods, sloshing through two more creeks until I stopped at a mulberry bush laden with green and dark berries. Most weren't ripe, but I ate several handfuls, anyway.

With my energy somewhat renewed, I continued searching for a house to stay in for the night. When I finally saw the shape of a house in the distance, I sighed. "Thank God."

I set off into a jog toward the clearing. When I emerged from the woods, I slowed down, and then stopped. "Oh, fuck me."

Because standing before me wasn't just one house. It was Chow Town.

CHAPTER XV

I'd traveled too far north.

Clutch's farm was southwest of town. Camp Fox was southeast of town.

I never should've gotten close to Chow Town.

Without a GPS or compass, I'd let the woods guide me right to the backyard of a large two-story house in a row of cookie-cutter two-story houses in a newer sub-development for as far I could see.

"Sonofabitch."

I walked past the play set and up to the patio door. Certainly, not *all* of these houses had zeds inside. I crossed my fingers. After looking inside and seeing no signs of zeds or violence, I rapped on the glass. A clamor erupted from somewhere deep inside the house.

I sprinted over a short chain-link fence and into the next yard. That was the good thing about zeds. They clung to the *out of sight, out of mind* philosophy and lost focus on their prey quickly if they couldn't see, hear, or smell it. But once they'd homed in on a target, they could be damn near relentless.

I didn't even knock at the next house. I could see overturned chairs, something dead and furry and on the floor, and a shape hovering at the kitchen window. I crept away from the patio door.

Finally, at the fifth house—one with a nice rock garden in its backyard—I rapped on the glass and waited and rapped again.

Silence greeted me.

Even better, the patio door had been left unlocked, and it slid open silently and smoothly. I pulled out my larger knife and stepped inside, carefully closing and locking the door behind me.

The air was stale and hinted of rotten fruit but didn't contain the all-too-familiar stench of infection and decay.

I tiptoed across the open dining room and noticed drawers left ajar in the kitchen as though someone had left in a hurry. I bypassed the kitchen to the adjacent living room. No signs of struggle. Checked out the hallway, closets, a nicely finished basement, and upstairs. The master bed hadn't been made yet, and several shirts lay strewn across the mattress. "Thank God," I muttered and hustled downstairs. Whoever lived here must've left town as soon as the outbreak hit. If they got lucky, maybe they got to wherever it was they'd been headed.

Back in the kitchen, I turned on the faucet. Nothing, as expected. Before checking the refrigerator for liquids, I walked into the large walk-in pantry and smiled. Inside was bliss. It wasn't fully stocked by any means, but a dozen or so cans of food, several bottles of wine, and a case of flavored water waited on the shelves. I went straight for the water, tearing through the plastic, and grabbed two bottles. I chugged the first down without stopping.

I leaned back against a shelf, careful to avoid the fuzzy green bread. There was enough here to last me a week, maybe longer. Since this neighborhood hadn't been looted yet, the Dogs must've had the same idea as us when it came to Chow Town. The risk of drawing out a herd of zeds in this town was too high to take as long as we could still find food in solitary, secluded farmhouses with no more than a few zeds to deal with at one time.

It was a good reminder that I had to remain silent and unseen. I'd already stirred up zeds in at least three nearby houses. I could only hope they'd given up by now and gone back to lumbering around their homes. They could easily break out of the homes, especially through the all-glass patio doors. Clearly, they hadn't had a reason to…until possibly now.

No matter. I planned to be back to the farm by dark, which was only an hour or so away.

I closed the kitchen blinds and patio shades to hide

my movements.

I grabbed a can of fruit cocktail and looked around for a can opener. "Of course," I muttered when I noticed the power opener on the counter. Rather than wasting time hunting around for tools, I opted instead for a jar of peanuts while sipping a second bottle of water.

Finished, I grabbed my knife off the countertop, and headed back up to the master bedroom and adjacent bathroom. I peeled off my clothes caked with sludge, blood, sweat, and dirt.

Without water pressure, a shower was impossible. Instead, I grabbed a half-empty bottle of shampoo and soap from the shower. I dipped a washcloth in the tank behind the toilet and thoroughly scrubbed myself. After I'd used nearly all the water in the tank and made a mess of the floor, I grabbed a tube of Neosporin and Band-Aids for my palm that still oozed blood.

Leaving the wrappers on the counter, I headed into the walk-in closet and sifted through clothes until I found a pair of jeans and a long-sleeved T-shirt that fit. I hurriedly dressed, fastened my belt and weapons, and ventured to the garage. I tapped lightly on the door and heard nothing in response. This time, rather than going slowly, I threw open the door and scanned the three stalls.

I sighed with a smile and leaned back against the wall. Not only was the garage clear, but a Ford sat in one stall. After a quick sweep under the sedan, I opened the car door and a beeping tone reverberated throughout the garage, energetically telling me that both the keys were still in the ignition and the battery wasn't dead. I turned the battery on and found that the car still had over a half tank of gas. I turned off the battery and patted the dash. "You'll do just fine," I said as I hopped back into the house.

It took me several trips to carry all the food to the car. After another search of the house, I found a baseball bat. By then, the sun had long since set. Without knowing the roads—and roadblocks—in this area, I did one final sweep of the house before settling in for the night in an upstairs bedroom facing the street.

Even though there was no way zeds knew where I was, I didn't sleep well. After an especially violent nightmare of Clutch being attacked by zeds, I shot awake as dawn was just beginning to light up the street.

I went down on a knee to look out the window, and fell back on my butt. Now, at least twenty zeds milled around the street below me, sniffing the air, as though sensing prey in the area. Their sheer numbers could crush the car with me in it.

I cupped my head in my hands. *How the hell…*

After watching the herd for over an hour, I accepted the fact that they weren't going anywhere, and I changed my bandages and ate cereal out of the box.

And waited.

Their numbers never changed throughout the day. Some came, some went. Zeds shuffled in lazy circles as though waiting for food to come to them.

It wasn't until night returned that something snagged their attention and the street cleared except for a few stragglers. *Now.* I hustled to the garage. When I opened the car door, something thumped on the other side of the garage door.

I stood there, holding my breath.

Another thump.

I edged closer to the garage door and inched onto my toes to peer out the high windows. Under the moonlight, I could see a single zed on the other side, but as it banged at the door, it drew the attention of others. I came back down on my heels, my breath coming in short pants. Soon, a second pair of fists joined the first at the door.

"Shit!" I whispered.

If I waited any longer, the noise could draw out every zed in the area. It probably wouldn't take more than the weight of twenty or so to push in a garage door.

They had me exactly where they wanted me: in a gift box, ready to open.

I did a slow three-sixty, looking for anything to distract the zeds, trying to concentrate above the ruckus.

Then it hit me.

Get 'em where I want 'em.

I wanted them as far from the garage as possible.

I went back to the car, pulled out the bat and headed back into the house. I headed down the hallway and to the office near the front door. I took a swing and smashed the front windows. *Home run.*

I rushed back to the garage, looked out through the windows and found the thumping had stopped. I tossed the bat onto the front seat and grabbed the cord on the garage door.

One, two, three.

I yanked the cord, and the door opened with a clatter. I jumped into the car and slammed the door shut as I slid the key into the ignition. The car roared to life, and I had the tires squealing in reverse.

A zed slammed into the car before I was out of the garage. The car lurched over its body. More zeds shuffled from the darkness, filling the street with their relentless groans. As soon as I was on the street, I slammed on the brakes, shoved the car into drive, and rammed into zeds head-on.

The car snagged on bodies as I drove over them, and the right wheel ended up off the ground, leaving only the left front wheel with any traction, and it was burning rubber uselessly. I rocked the car between gears, using reverse and forward to try to nudge free like I was stuck in snow.

By now, the zeds that I'd drawn to the house had turned their attention to the car. The window behind me shattered. I pulled out my Beretta while keeping my foot on the gas. Zeds pushed against the car as they tried to get to me from all sides. The extra weight pushed the car forward, and the right tire caught traction. The car took off, pitching to a near stop when plowing through a wall of zeds trying to block me in.

Somehow, the car made it through and the strays slid off the hood. I took the first right, realizing too late that it was a cul-de-sac. "Shit!" Spinning around, I got back on the main street.

When the number of zeds dissipated, I chanced a glance in the rearview mirror. One reached out to me under the moonlight. It looked young—too much like Jase—though months in the sun had baked its skin into a jaundiced husk.

I sped away. Since I was on the edge of town, it took only three turns, some lawn driving around a roadblock, and a couple curb-checks before Chow Town disappeared behind me.

I drove west until I came to a familiar stretch of road. The car made a clacking sound and the steering wheel shuddered if I went over twenty, not that I could drive any faster without headlights, which would give away my location. According to the car's clock, it took me over an hour to make it to the gravel road the farm was on.

As I turned onto the gravel road, I slammed on the brakes. Taillights in the distance signaled a vehicle leaving the farm. After the taillights disappeared and no other lights appeared, I crept forward and parked the car by the garage of Jase's old house, making sure it was hidden from the road. After a wistful glance at the beat-up sedan with an arm caught in the bumper, I stepped into the night.

I didn't like the idea of walking at night, but I

couldn't risk driving into an ambush at the farm. The smell of smoke was strong in the air, and a bad feeling formed in my gut.

As I closed the distance between Jase's house and Clutch's farm, the smell of smoke grew stronger every minute. When I noticed the garbage truck had been shoved into the ditch, I avoided the lane and walked through a field that never got planted and into the trees enclosing the farm. I crept soundlessly through the woods, expecting a zed to pop out from behind every tree.

Not a single zed sniffed me out, likely thanks to the blanket of smoke over the area. Soon, I could see a glow through the trees and hear the crackle of a large campfire. I cautiously moved close enough to see the yard.

Or what was left of it. I gasped and covered my mouth. "*No.*"

The Dogs had burned everything to the ground.

CHAPTER XVI

I gripped the baseball bat as I fell to my knees. The house was nothing but a charred framework and a pile of burning ash and blackened debris with still-glowing embers.

This farm had become my home when the outbreak hit. It was a fortress. I was safe here. Months of hard work, the supplies, weapons, all the food we'd stored, *gone*.

It made no sense. Clutch had willingly joined the Dogs. Why would they destroy his farm? They wouldn't do something like this to one of their own. Which meant…

"No." I had to lean on the bat to keep from collapsing.

Clutch was dead.

I clenched my eyes closed. If only I'd gotten here

earlier. If I'd returned to the farm last night, I could've prevented this somehow.

I chortled. Who was I kidding?

Like I could've single-handedly held back the Dogs.

Furious, I pulled myself back to my feet. In the distance, I saw two men with shaved heads leaning against their truck parked in the lane several hundred feet away. Too far away for me to overhear their conversation. I looked for more Dogs but found none.

I heard a rustle to my right and saw three zeds encircle me, groaning through jaws that no longer worked. They were badly burned, their arms and faces charred.

I grabbed the baseball bat and swung, crushing the first zed's skull like it was a T-ball. The second zed was on me too quickly and I kicked its ankles together, knocking its feet out from under it. I left it floundering on the ground, while I swung at the third, nailing it in the chest. The force knocked it back, and my second swing crumpled its head.

After smashing the zed on the ground, I turned back to the house.

All the food, weapons…*gone.*

Everything Clutch, Jase, and I had built was destroyed. The Dogs had burned the fuel tanks, and it looked like the explosions took down two of the three sheds. Only the smallest shed still stood, though its door was open, and I suspected any valuable contents gone. They'd even slashed the tires on the poor Prius.

After giving the house a final brokenhearted look, I headed past the burnt gardens, careful to keep the still-burning house between the Dogs and me, and cautiously around the backside of the largest shed, held up only by Clutch's combine. Feathers littered the ground, though I couldn't find any sign of the chickens.

Coming down on a knee, I pulled at the tin and debris as quietly as possible. Blood dripped from my hand. When I finally pulled away the last bit of plywood, I sighed in relief.

The Dogs hadn't discovered Clutch's TEOTWAWKI bunker.

I opened the round door and climbed down a few steps. With one final look around, I noticed the Dogs were still lounging by their truck, and I tugged the plywood up so it'd cover the bunker door.

"Damn Dogs," I muttered before shutting the door and descending into the darkness.

Knowing I was secure, I curled up on the floor and slept.

That was, until the door overhead opened.

CHAPTER XVII

"Why the hell didn't you lock the door?" Clutch demanded in a gruff whisper, the moonlight casting him in an imposing silhouette.

"Clutch?" I asked, pointing the Beretta at him.

"Lower the gun, Cash. I'm coming down," he replied before closing—and locking—the door above him.

A lantern in Clutch's hand suddenly cast a gentle glow in the small space.

"I forgot the door locked," I said in a daze as I watched him climb down the ladder. Sweat glistened off his shaved head. Then I dropped the pistol and jumped him from behind. "You're alive!"

He was hot and sweaty and I didn't care. He turned around and pulled me into a full embrace.

"How?" I asked, holding on tight.

He rubbed my shoulder. "Doyle sent out most of his

Dogs that first night. He left me in the silo with only one guard." He paused. "I got out. That's all that matters."

I pulled back to look at him. Emotion laced his words. "Let me guess. You pissed off Doyle in the process."

"Yeah." He ran a hand over his now-shaved head and grimaced, like he didn't enjoy the feel. "Were you here when they..."

"No," I replied quickly. "I got here after."

"Good." He paused. "Jase?"

"He's at Camp Fox. He's safe."

Clutch sighed, and then looked around. "We can't stay here. Dogs will be sniffing around my farm until I'm caught or dead. There were two waiting outside tonight."

Probably the same two that I'd seen. "I'm glad you're here," I said softly. I felt safe with Clutch in this bunker, but I'd already realized it could all too easily become our tomb. Only one way in or out. Only one air vent that could be too easily blocked from the outside.

He slid to the floor. "The captain let you go?" he asked gruffly.

"Yeah."

"Good. I couldn't tell if he was playing to get you away from Doyle or if he was actually thinking of arresting you."

"He let me go," I said instead, sitting back down. Clutch didn't need to be burdened with the details. Not with his home lying in ruins above our heads. I wrinkled my nose. "You smell."

He grunted, resting his head against the wall. "Thirty-six hours in the woods will do that."

I grabbed a bottle of water and tapped it on his arm. "Here."

He took the bottle, and then grabbed my wrist. "What's this?"

I tugged back my injured hand. "Just a cut I picked up yesterday."

"Why weren't you wearing your gloves?" He narrowed his eyes and frowned. "Whose clothes are those?"

I shrugged.

"Hell." His jaw clenched. "Masden didn't let you go, did he?"

"He let me go," I replied. "I just had to find my own way back home."

Clutch pounded the floor. "Sonofabitch. When I find him, I'm going—"

"You're going to do nothing," I interrupted. "We've got enough shit to deal with right now than take on Camp Fox, don't you think?"

"And your gear?" he asked, hoarsely.

"Somewhere at Camp Fox."

Clutch glared for a moment before taking a long draw of water and leaning his head back again, eyes closed. When his eyes opened, he leveled a hard gaze on me. "You all right now?"

I smiled and moved to sidle up next to him. "Yeah,

I'm okay." I laid my uninjured hand on his knee. "You?"

He grunted again—his typical response of consent—and rolled up his sleeve. "I got lucky."

My eyes widened. "Holy shit."

There, on his forearm, was a dark bruise in the perfect semi-circle outline of human teeth.

"I was lucky I had long sleeves. But still, when they lock on, they bite hard. The bastards have got jaws like pit bulls."

I gingerly touched the marks and whistled. "I think you got *very* lucky."

"Your turn." He nodded to my hand.

"I cleaned it this morning," I said as I pulled back the first Band-Aid. Even in the dim light, the skin around the cut was red and swollen.

His brow furrowed. He grabbed a first aid kit off a shelf and motioned for my hand.

I held it out, and he gently peeled off each Band-Aid. He pulled out a small plastic bottle and poured it into my palm. I hissed as liquid fire shot through my arm. "Jesus, Clutch. Are you trying to kill me?"

"It's just alcohol. Don't be a baby."

I wasn't being a baby. It seriously *burned*. He dabbed a cotton swab at it until the sharp agonizing pain numbed into a constant throb. He covered my palm with a bandage and wrapped gauze around it.

"I'll clean your cut again in the morning," He said after putting the kit back.

Then he grabbed my uninjured hand and rested his forehead against it.

I rubbed his thumb. "It'll be okay." And I meant it. I knew that as long as Clutch was with me, everything would be fine.

He chuckled drily, the sound devoid of humor. "We've got no weapons, no food, no shelter. Doyle crippled us with one easy blow. Jase is at Camp Fox. And Masden made it clear that if we go after Doyle, we're attacking Camp Fox."

"Doyle's no longer with Camp Fox," I said. "He zed-bombed them a few hours after we were separated."

"Jesus." Clutch's muscles tensed under me. "So that's where the Dogs went."

"I guess Doyle saw a shot and took it."

"Were you there?" he asked quietly.

I nodded and laid my head on his shoulder. "They lost one of their barracks along with several troops in the attack." I thought of Nick. "They lost some good folks."

"The Camp will be better prepared against Doyle next time."

"You sure there will be a next time?"

"Yeah, I'm sure," he said, his voice low. "Doyle has a hard view on how to survive, and he assumes everyone will see that he's right." He chuckled. "He actually believed I'd willingly join his Dogs. Doesn't matter now. The only good thing is that Doyle will no longer get support from Camp Fox. I bet Lendt's guys are keeping the Dogs running as we speak. That should distract Doyle enough until we can secure a new location. We'll scout out places in the morning. How are we on weapons?"

"I've got a Beretta with nine rounds, a baseball bat, and two knives. And whatever else you have."

"It's not enough," he said.

"It'll be enough," I said, snuggling closer. I wasn't worried. I had Clutch back. I knew everything would be okay, and I found myself falling soundly asleep, safe in his arms.

I woke up with my entire body stiff from lying on hard, damp concrete. Being underground, I had no idea what time it was. I could've been asleep for only an hour or ten hours. I'd slept soundly, except for when Clutch's nightmares began, and I'd held onto him until he fell back into a more peaceful sleep.

Unfortunately, PTSD isn't curable. It's a way of life.

Clutch was already awake and heating something in a tin can. When he noticed I was awake, he tossed me a Gatorade. I caught it with my injured hand and winced. He then handed me a metal spork and a tin can wrapped with a towel.

I yawned. "What time is it?"

Clutch put another can on the tiny stove and glanced

at his watch. "Five-forty. It should still be dark enough to take out the Dogs that are topside before they see us."

After we ate our refried beans, Clutch rummaged through the shelves and pulled out a shotgun that had been vacuum-sealed in plastic. He loaded several shells into it. "I go first. If there's more than two, we'll wait them out. You stay by the shed and take out any Dogs who try to get away."

I checked the Beretta and grabbed the baseball bat. "Ready."

Clutch slung the shotgun over his shoulder and climbed the ladder. At the top, he slowly unlocked and opened the door a couple inches. No light came in. After a long moment, he held up a single finger and pointed to my right.

Only one Dog? Could we get that lucky?

I followed up the ladder and outside. The cool, damp morning breeze swept away any lingering sleepiness as I crawled behind a pile of tin while Clutch moved toward a four-by-four truck sitting in the drive. The Dog was sitting in his truck, facing away from us and watching the driveway.

It was too easy. Clutch snuck up behind the truck and had the shotgun leveled point blank through the open window before the Dog even noticed.

"Hands on your head," Clutch ordered.

The Dog obeyed instantly. Clutch opened the truck door and stepped to the side. "Out of the truck and on your knees."

"Don't shoot!" the scrawny teen cried as he fell from the truck and onto his knees. An AR-15 tumbled harmlessly off his lap.

"How many are with you?" Clutch asked, kicking the rifle away.

"I'm alone. I swear it," the guy answered, keeping his hands on his head. "Please don't kill me."

"I won't if you keep telling the truth," Clutch said.

"You…you won't?" The young man sounded genuinely surprised.

I could've asked Clutch the same thing. I scanned the area and saw a shape shambling around the edge of the woods. I pulled out the bat and stalked toward it while keeping an eye on the Dog kneeling before Clutch.

"I'm going to ask you some questions," Clutch said. "Take my advice. Don't lie."

The Dog nodded furiously.

"What are your orders?"

"Wa-watch for you. Call in if I see you."

"That's all?"

"Yes!"

"Why are you alone?"

The Dog didn't answer.

"Don't make me repeat myself," Clutch said.

"Camp Fox invaded our camp," the kid quickly replied. "A lot of guys are busy relocating their families."

The zed had noticed the two men and was making its way toward them. At first, I thought it was bloated, but then I realized it was pregnant, probably near-term when it'd been bitten. Bile rose in my throat as I readied the bat. A purse hung across the zed's body, and it hobbled in one sandal. It hissed and turned to me when I approached. I swung. Its head broke open like a beanbag.

"When's the next shift arrive?" Clutch asked, turning back to the Dog after watching me kill the zed.

"Eight o'clock," he replied, his voice cracking.

When I approached the Dog from behind, Clutch nodded, and I disarmed him, startling him. The Dog was young, not much older than Jase, and obviously scared shitless.

"Cripes, kid," Clutch said. "You're too young to be caught up with the likes of Doyle."

The Dog jutted out his chin. "Doyle saved my life. We're going to make Fox Hills safe again."

"Keep telling yourself that, kid," Clutch said.

I lifted a two-way radio I'd found on the Dog's belt.

Clutch narrowed his eyes. "How often do you report in?"

The Dog swallowed. "The bottom of every hour."

Clutch glanced at his watch. "Looks like you got seven minutes. What's the code for all-clear?"

He didn't answer.

"The code for all-clear?" Clutch asked more firmly, lifting his shotgun.

"The eagle soars," he replied quickly.

Clutch held out the two-way radio. "Report in. This

time, with the *right* code for all-clear, and I'll let your last fibs pass."

The Dog's jaw dropped before he snapped it shut. He nodded tightly. He took the radio, took a deep breath, and clicked the side. "Hamster reporting in. Over."

"Base. Report. Over."

"The swallow has flown, repeat, the swallow has flown. Over."

A slight pause.

"Affirmative. The swallow has flown. Over."

The Dog handed the radio back to Clutch.

"You aren't a bad kid. It's too bad you got hooked up with Doyle."

"I owe my life to Doyle," he replied.

"And he's made sure he gets exactly that from you," Clutch said. "Dammit, kid. You shouldn't have lied on the radio."

"Wha—what?" The Dog's wide eyes shot up. "No!" he cried out the instant before Clutch blew his brains out.

My mouth fell open.

Clutch slung his shotgun back over his shoulder. "The Dogs need to work on their codes. The Swallow Has Flown is an acronym for the Shit's Hit the Fan. Code 101." He kicked at the gravel. "Goddammit, kid, why'd you have to go and force my hand?"

"How much time do you think we have?" I asked, staring at the Dog's body.

"If he was telling the truth that Lendt hit Doyle's

Camp, then it may take them awhile. Then again, they could have a unit close by already."

"We better hurry, then."

We ran back to the bunker. Clutch disappeared inside and came back seconds later with a stuffed backpack. He fastened the door closed and set a combination lock that I hadn't noticed on top of the door before. We covered the door with tin and debris.

Clutch eyed his big rig, which looked like the Dogs had fun taking a bulldozer to it. "She was a good rig," he growled.

"We'll take the Dog's truck," I offered, not seeing Clutch's pickup truck or Jeep anywhere. "I left a car at Jase's house along with enough supplies to get us by for a few days."

We sprinted back to the truck and tore down the lane. Clutch turned onto the gravel road, and fortunately, there was no dust in either direction indicating that Dogs were on their way. "We got lucky this morning," Clutch said.

"I'll take every bit of luck I can get," I said.

Clutch nodded. "We can't risk stopping and grabbing the car right now. We'll come back for everything else in the bunker and the car after we've secured a new location."

I leaned back, a weight on my chest. I'd already been thinking through how soon I had to transplant the seeds from the garden before it was too late. Not to mention having to start all over with looting runs. It was hard the first time, when we had so much to work with. Now? We were screwed. I swallowed. "Any thoughts on where we can hide that's safe from Dogs?"

Clutch shrugged. "They avoid Chow Town."

"Oh, hell, no," I said in a rush. When he eyed me suspiciously, I tacked on, "Trust me."

"Any farm we move to won't be any safer than mine was," he said. "That leaves our only option to head out of the area. Or...wait a second." He snapped his fingers. "I got it."

He cranked a hard left on the next road and stepped on the gas.

"Where are we headed?"

"Fox National Park. It's as far from any town as we can get without venturing into unknown territory."

Thirty minutes later, we drove through the park's winding narrow roads. Clutch took us deep and high into the hilly park, and we saw no zeds, though I knew the monsters lurked in these woods just like they had everywhere else. Clutch stopped at the DNR office that seemed to be near the park's highest point. Only a park ranger's truck sat outside.

"This might be the best location for our camp," Clutch said, reloading his shotgun. "We'll check the cabins, too. They should keep keys to all the cabins somewhere inside."

I looked around. The A-line cabin sat on a ledge, leaving only three sides vulnerable to zeds. The narrow park roads would be easy enough to block. The place gave me a good vibe. I picked up the rifle I'd lifted from the Dog. "Let's do this."

Birds chirped in the distance, and a warm breeze blew scents of evergreens over me. Side-by-side, we moved to the two-story cabin.

Clutch checked the door. It opened.

He glanced at me, and I nodded, clutching the rifle. He rapped on the window. Nothing. He rapped again. Still nothing.

After a moment of waiting, Clutch took the lead inside. A familiar stench polluted the air. *Dammit.*

Clutch grimaced.

I sighed before calling out, "Hey, stinkface. Where are you?"

Something shuffled from above. My gaze shot upward to see a lone zed move around the open loft. It was wearing a brown DNR uniform and had wild, shaggy hair. It groaned and tried to walk toward us, but the railing stopped it. It continued to batter the railing, reaching out, until finally it toppled over and crashed to the ground floor.

The zed landed head-first, the impact sounding like a shattered light bulb. Its brittle skull collapsed into itself.

"That was easy," I said. Then the stench hit me. I pinched my nose. "God, that's awful."

Clutch held his forearm over his nose. "Let's hurry up and get Smelly outside."

Each grabbing a foot, we dragged the corpse outside and sent it off the deep slope that went off each side of the cabin. It tumbled down, disappearing into the trees below.

The rest of the office was thankfully clear, and the zed had made surprisingly little mess upstairs.

"He was here alone," I said.

"He must've gotten infected before he came into work."

We stood on the second floor, looking out through the two-story window over the wide expanse of the park. Trees went on for as far as the eye could see. No signs of violence.

"I like it here," I said.

"Yeah. Me, too," Clutch replied.

It was even more peaceful than the farm. Here, it was as though we were alone, free, and safe. As long as everyone thought we were dead, we had a chance.

But, we weren't safe.

Because as long as Doyle and the zeds were still out there, we'd never be safe.

MALICE

THE EIGHTH CIRCLE OF HELL

CHAPTER XVIII

Ten days later

The wet spring had turned into a humid summer. The park was lush and green, with only the sounds of nature as background music.

It was a pleasant mirage.

Clutch and I tried to make the best of the shitty situation. Despite having no fences, the park turned out to be a decent camp, its hills a natural deterrent to zeds. Another huge perk: the park's water supply was fed by a rural water tower, so water had suddenly become the least of our worries.

We were careful in our movements in case any Dogs passed through. After losing our stockpile, we had to start nearly from scratch. Fortunately, one of the rooms in the park's DNR office contained boxes of stuff either left at the park or confiscated by park rangers.

I used several hours of sunlight every day fishing and setting snares. But, living on protein alone was draining us, especially with the exercise regimen Clutch had us on. In just over a week, I noticed I had less stamina and energy. Even the cut on my hand was taking longer to heal.

I'd been sifting through the park's library to find out which plants and berries were edible in the area. The park no doubt had a wealth of food that could be eaten, but getting to it was the challenge. There was no telling what trees a zed could be lurking behind. And so I started to dig up soil around the edges of the office's parking lot for a new garden.

"Ready to hit the road?" Clutch said, coming down the stairs.

He looked set for battle in his camos while I'd been stuck in the same designer jeans for the past ten days, though we'd both been wearing T-shirts from the gift shop.

I grabbed the plastic water bottles I'd been refilling every day. "Ready."

Clutch gave a quick nod and headed for the door. Stubble covered his head now and would be as long as my thicker hair in no time.

"We need fuel," he said over his shoulder. "The truck has less than a half tank left."

"Seeds are critical, too," I added. "Ooh, and gardening tools. Maybe a net. Definitely food. Weapons would be nice."

Clutch raised a brow. "Anything else?"

I smirked. "I'll be sure to let you know." I followed him to the truck. "Do you know any farms in the area?"

He shook his head. "No, but there's a gas station not far from here. It was a hotspot for day-trippers loading up on ice and beer before heading into the park. They might also have some camping supplies."

I climbed in and rolled down the window. "Did you bring the hose?"

He held up a five-foot length of rubber water hose I'd found at the office and cut into sections. My life had become a state of improvising. Finding tools or weapons in everything.

He started the engine. "If we can get gas from the tanks, then we'll be able to head farther out for your wish list items. It's pretty rural around here and far enough away from where Doyle's camp was that it may still be good for looting without running into anyone."

As Clutch weaved through the maze he'd been making of the park roads, I kept an eye out for intruders. When I was working on food, he was busy blocking off the roads and marking safe routes on park maps. The roadblocks signaled that there were survivors in the park, but—more important—the roadblocks would slow down zeds and especially Dogs in getting to us.

Only three zeds had passed near the park office since we moved there, and they'd been on the roads. Since the roadblocks went up, no zeds had passed through. We figured the hills and trees caused too many problems for the decomposing shamblers, so they likely wouldn't show up at the office unless they were lost or had homed in on us. And we were far enough inside the camp, that zeds should have no way of hearing, seeing, or smelling us.

Still, without much for weapons, we'd been brainstorming ways to corral zed stragglers into traps. We had plenty of ideas, but so far no manpower or tools to make anything work.

We passed several of the park's cabins in the heart of the park. With over two dozen buildings, we could set up a small town of survivors here, though the park's rough and wooded landscape wasn't exactly ideal for growing food or scouting for zeds. When I mentioned the idea of bringing others onto the park, Clutch changed the subject. I suspected the loss of Jase to Camp Fox had hit him harder than he let on.

Ever since the run-in with Doyle, Clutch's PTSD had worsened. His nightmares lasted longer, and during the days, he often had a distant look. Whatever had happened had really hit Clutch hard. Since he refused to talk about it, all I could do was hope that time would help heal the wounds on his soul.

I pointed to a cabin nearly hidden by trees. "That's our bug-out cabin, right?"

"Yeah. You're starting to get the park figured out."

I smiled and leaned back. Clutch had covered more of the park than I had so far. He'd found us the most secluded rendezvous cabin should we get separated and couldn't get back to the office. He'd shown it to me a couple times already, but it was easy to get lost in hundreds of wooded acres with no straight roads.

I noticed the time on the truck's clock. "Oh, it's almost nine."

"Got it." He clicked on the radio to AM 1340. Every day, for a mid-morning break, we'd sit in the truck to listen to Hawkeye's broadcasts.

Like clockwork, the usual static silenced in favor of a voice. The broadcaster was either a hundred miles away or had poor equipment. We could barely hear his broadcast unless we turned the radio all the way up.

"This is Hawkeye broadcasting on AM 1340.

I have more news about zed-free zones for you. It sounds like Montana has built a city with high walls. But, if you are thinking of making the trip to Montana City, think again. Right now, they are only allowing Montana citizens into the city. Anyone else will be turned away. But, what's important is that there are zed-free zones out there. There is hope from the plague monsters wandering our lands.

For news closer to home, Lt. Col. Lendt's announcement last week that requires any Iowa militia to be commanded by a military officer has stirred backlash across the state. I've heard rumors that some militias are banding together against Camp Fox rather than submitting to Lendt's power play.

The militias are made up of good people, folks who've stepped up and volunteered to fight against the zed scourge. And now the government is trying to control them.

Here's my question for today: if all militias are forced to report into Camp Fox, what's to stop Lendt from misusing his power and becoming a despot over us survivors? I leave you with a warning: absolute power corrupts absolutely, my friends.

This is Hawkeye broadcasting on AM 1340. Be safe, stay strong, and know that you're not alone."

Hawkeye rarely had good news and showed no love for Lendt, but the final words he spoke every day grounded me.

You're not alone.

Even though we hadn't seen another living soul for ten days.

A large sign displaying gas prices that would never change again peeked out from the trees. As we neared the station, the stink hit me, and I wrinkled my nose. "Oh, that's horrible."

"Jesus," Clutch said, holding his forearm over his nose. "Smells like the sewer backed up."

"Lovely," I muttered. Add one more annoying trait of the apocalypse to an every-growing list.

Today, we at least had the benefit of dealing with fewer zeds at the gas station than we would have if the outbreak had hit during tourist season. Even so, there were still a half-dozen cars in the lot. Four zeds wandering nearby bee-lined for our truck the moment we approached. One was covered in dried mud, one was naked and chewed up, and all four were shriveled by months under the sun.

"How the hell do some of these guys end up naked?" I asked. Seeing a zed was bad enough. Seeing *all* of a zed was enough to make a stomach roil.

Clutch shrugged. "Caught on the shitter, maybe."

They stumbled in our direction as though coming to greet us, and Clutch stepped on the gas, taking down two with his first hit. He put the truck into reverse and rammed into the third. The naked zed moved too slowly and was too far away to be a problem.

Clutch stopped near the underground gas tank cover.

I swung open the door and clobbered the female zed struggling to get up with two newly broken legs. Clutch was out of the truck with a tire iron and taking down the least rotted of the bunch, and I walked up to the crusty mud-covered zed and gagged.

Shit. Not mud. My eyes watered, and I swung extra hard to make sure I finished it off quickly and moved away.

When I turned to Clutch, he was just finishing off the naked zed that had finally reached us.

"Keep an eye out." He got down on his knees and pulled out his knife.

I stood at his back, gripping the bat covered in layers of dark stains, and analyzed the wide one-story building. The gas station was covered in slate and had three glass doors, one to each section: the gas station in the middle, the liquor side to the left, and a small café to the right. The glass was shattered on the large door to the gas station. Two zeds lay dead in the shadow of the overhang.

"Damn," I muttered. "Looks like we aren't the first here."

With some muscle, he pried the cover open and peered inside. "At least there's plenty of gas."

"How do you know it's not diesel?" I asked.

"Smells like gas," he replied, going for the hose. He dropped one end into the underground tank, and held out the other with a smirk. "Want to do the honors?"

I handed him the bat and grabbed the hose. "Sure." I opened the gas cap, and then sucked hard at the hose.

I'd never siphoned gas before, but it looked to be a relatively easy thing to do.

Nothing happened.

I looked up.

He smirked. "Keep sucking."

I scowled but did what he said. At first there was nothing, then came the fumes, then the liquid.

"Ack!" I coughed out in between spitting out gasoline and shoving the hose into the truck's gas tank. Tears ran down my face. "That shit burns." More coughing.

Clutch chuckled while he pulled out a five-gallon red gas can from the back of the truck. "That's why I didn't want to do it."

I flipped him the bird before spitting again. At least I couldn't smell the sewage anymore. "Next time, you siphon," I muttered when I could speak again.

After we finished fueling and resealed the

underground tank, Clutch backed the truck up to the building. When he jumped out, he looked at me. "Ready to do this?"

I blew out a lungful of air. "Yup."

It was times like these when I especially missed the farm. We'd had enough weapons and ammunition to start a small war, over six months' supply of food stockpiled, and had it secure as any place could be without being a high-security prison. We'd reached the point where we didn't have to go into high-risk places like these to survive. I sighed. We had no choice now.

We either adapted or we'd die.

I held the baseball bat tight in my grip as Clutch rapped on the broken glass, sending several shards crashing onto the concrete. Every sound was razor blade to my nerves.

A distant thump greeted us. There was definitely something waiting inside. Clutch gave me one more look before stepping through the door. I quickly followed and pulled back the bat to swing, but no zeds attacked. Instead, a stack of pastel Easter bunnies smiled at us in front of long aisles shrouded in shadows.

The place gave me the creeps.

Whoever had come here before us couldn't have left with much. All of the shelves looked fully stocked. When I noticed the cash register open and a near-empty shelf of Marlboros, I rolled my eyes. Money and cigarettes. Whoever had that kind of shit for brains was likely shuffling around the countryside now.

Then again, their idiocy was a good sign. It meant more goodies for us.

"I look out, you fill?"

I turned to see that Clutch had grabbed all the plastic bags off the counter. I swiped a small item from a shelf behind the counter, pocketed it, gripped the bat, and did a three-sixty to scan for zeds. Hearing no signs of any predators—other than the constant thumping coming from the back of the store, I grabbed the bags.

"Let's do this."

With tension prickling my nerves, I started in the grocery aisle, filling up five bags with soup, canned meat, saltines, and anything else with a decent shelf life. The bags were flimsy and couldn't hold much weight, and I slid each bag onto my arm to start another. I skipped most of the candy bars, instead going for nuts and fruit chews. Then, out to the truck to drop off full bags and back inside for more.

While grabbing batteries, something thumped on the bathroom door behind us, startling me. Memories from a different bathroom on the day of the outbreak doused me with ice, and I dropped a bag.

"Don't worry. It can't get out," Clutch said, picking up the bag.

"I know." I hastily grabbed a few bottles of water, more for the reusable bottles than for the water and made another drop of supplies into the back of the truck.

After two more trips, one to the automotive aisle and

one for soap and cleaning supplies, I leaned against the truck. "What else?"

"The best part." He headed left, and I followed him into the liquor section. Most of the top shelves were empty, and several bottles were broken on the floor. Clutch slid the bat under an arm and grabbed a couple bottles of whiskey and I pointed at the Everclear. He dumped the bottles into bags, and I grunted at the weight.

I glanced out the front window to find the parking lot still wide open. "Still looking good. Knock on wood."

Clutch shot me a glare. "Cash, don't jinx us," he warned.

I shook my head. For being a badass, he sure was superstitious. Smirking, I followed him back through the gas station and toward the front door. Before stepping through, I had a feeling of being watched and I paused. I looked to my left toward the café.

"Clutch," I whispered, and he stepped back in.

"What is it?"

I glanced at him before looking again.

A glass door separated it from the rest of the station. When we'd first entered, it was empty. Now, on the other side, two jaundiced pairs of eyes stared at us. Two zeds—one who'd been a boy no more than twelve and one who'd been a slightly younger girl—stood. They were likely siblings, with the same hair color and similar features, but it was always hard to tell after bodies started to decompose.

Neither moved nor pounded on the glass. They simply watched. That was eerie enough. But what spooked me more was that they were holding hands.

Clutch tugged me outside. "Let's get out of here."

CHAPTER XIX

It had been a surprisingly low-key day. Zeds were blissfully few and far between, and we'd yet to see a Dog.

After the gas station, we hit two farms. The first was a quaint white house with an old couple inside who'd taken fate into their own hands by blowing out their brains. They were ripe, had likely killed themselves not long after the outbreak. Annoying flies buzzed around my head while I said a silent prayer for them.

"...Amen." I tugged the shotgun from the old man's stiff grip and went about my looting.

We'd gained some spices, home-canned foods, and much-needed canning supplies (even though neither Clutch nor I had any idea how to can), taking a load off our biggest stressor of not having any way to store food for the winter. The old couple had also been avid gardeners, but all the sprouts in the garage had long since wilted from lack of water. I'd found a few packets of squash and several gardening tools. It was a start.

At the next farm, the only sign of the outbreak were two graves with blades of grass just starting to break through the dirt. Hope pinged at my heart for the survivor who'd dug these graves. We'd spent several minutes calling out and searching, but no one answered.

Inside, we found the cabinets empty and little else in the house. Though, I discovered that the clothes in a teenager's room were a near perfect fit, even though they were boy's clothes. When I stripped out of my jeans, I paused in front of the mirror on the back of the door.

I had a solid farmer's tan from spending nearly every day in the sun without sunscreen. Messy dark spikes did nothing to soften my blunt features. My curves had disappeared, leaving behind straight, hard lines. No wonder I could wear a boy's clothes. Sure, Clutch had become leaner, too, but he'd been in good shape before so the change didn't seem so severe. Me? Even my parents wouldn't recognize me.

Mia Ryan truly was gone.

In a daze, I emptied the pockets of my old jeans, grabbed an armful of new clothes, and headed outside.

Frowning, I scanned the open area. "Clutch?"

He poked around the corner of a tin building, and he was grinning like a schoolboy. "There's a fuel farm here. They've got an entire tank of gasoline. You won't have to suck gas for a while."

I couldn't help but return his smile. Another backup plan to our backup plans. "I'll mark it on the map. But *you're* sucking gas next time."

By the time we had everything unpacked at the park, it was time to cook my morning catch: two trout, one bass, and a small rabbit. It was a typical meal. Most days we burned more calories than we took in.

Every day, I'd wait until twilight to start a fire, when the darkness smothered the smoke, though I couldn't do anything about the smell of fire attracting notice downwind. After a couple dismal failures in the first days at the park, I had finally gotten the hang of cooking meats so that they'd last through the next evening.

It was the first night in a long time we had seasonings for our meat. I closed my eyes. "Mm, I never knew salt could be so decadent."

Clutch leaned back, rubbed his shoulder, and took a long swig of amber whiskey.

"Oh. I almost forgot..." I reached in my pocket and threw the can at Clutch. "Happy birthday."

He frowned. "My birthday's in December."

I shrugged. "I had no idea when it was, so I took a guess."

He looked at the can of chewing tobacco and smiled. "My brand, even."

I smiled. "I know."

He tucked it into his pocket.

"You're not going to open it?" I asked.

"Nope," he replied with a smile. "I'm saving it."

After a moment, he came to his feet and stared out the window. The park office had no generator. The two-story A-line window of the cabin faced the west, so we had plenty of light up until sunset. After the sun went down, we either had to use precious batteries (we had even fewer candles) or get by in the dark. Fortunately, the days were getting longer, so sunset meant bedtime, or as Clutch called it, rack time.

Clutch turned. "I'm going to lock up."

I wiped off the tin dishes we used, and arranged our weapons near the two twin-sized mattresses Clutch had taken from one of the cabins. I made sure the shotguns were loaded and looked over our bleak inventory. An AR-15 with three clips, the two shotguns along with an extra shotgun we'd found in a locked cabinet in the office, a box of shotgun shells, a baseball bat, a camping axe I'd found in one of the lost-and-found boxes, and a few knives. We'd also found a tranq gun in the same cabinet as the shotgun, but we figured we'd have to be pretty desperate to try that on a zed.

Darkness had taken over the world by the time Clutch came upstairs. With only the two of us and few zeds in the park, we no longer did patrols like we had at the farm. Since the office sat on a ridge, it was the safest lodging in the park, but it didn't yet have a fraction of the security features we'd built around Clutch's house. If someone managed to break through the door or windows we'd yet to board up, we were fucked.

He lay down without a word, and I watched the stars wink peacefully back at me until I drifted off.

I awoke to the sounds of Clutch's nightmares, just like I did every night. He mumbled and tossed and turned. Like every night, I crawled over to him and wrapped an arm around him. He rarely woke, but when he did, he'd roll over and pull me to him like I was his anchor.

His muscles tensed and he shot awake.

"Shh," I murmured. "It's just a bad dream." I pressed him back down and placed a gentle kiss on his forehead.

He looked up at me. In the moonlight, his gaze moved to my lips.

I ran a hand over his short hair and gave him a soft smile.

He cupped my neck and pulled me to where his lips met mine. It was just a brush, but then I deepened it, pressing my lips against his. For a long second, he didn't move. Then he grabbed me and rolled, pinning me beneath him. He took over. He came crashing down to me, kissing me hard and deep, with take-no-prisoners intensity, and a moan escaped from my lips and into his mouth.

My thighs spread to cradle him, and he shifted, lodging him tight against me. I'd been careful never to cross the line into intimacy, but now that we had, I'd rather give up breathing than his kiss. After seconds—or minutes—of kissing me senseless, he pulled back, leaving me gasping for air.

He, too, was breathing heavily. His calloused hand brushed against me, and I shuddered in pleasure as he tugged off my underwear and shoved out of his boxer briefs. He cupped my ass and pulled me tight against him. I could feel his cock, hot and throbbing, press against my core.

"Clutch," I begged and grabbed his head, pulling him into a brutal, raw kiss.

He replied with a growl. He slid his arms under my back, grabbed my shoulders, and plunged into me. I raked at him, widening my thighs, pulling him to me with all my strength, but his weight held me in place. He clamped onto my hips to pull me even closer. He thrust hard and deep. Exactly what I wanted—what I *needed*.

His low growls combined with my shameless cries. The next instant I cried out, freefalling into a climax. Clutch's back arched and he bellowed as he pulled out, shooting a burst of seed onto the blanket.

I lay there, boneless, while he rolled onto his side, panting and sweaty. He lowered his head to the mattress next to mine, and pulled me tight against him.

Time was lost while I floated, the mattress unfeeling below me.

"I killed her."

The words were soft, barely audible. "What?" I asked, confused.

"At the Dogs' camp..." Clutch rolled onto his back.

"Doyle left me in the silo, with one guard outside. Only it wasn't a Dog. It was a woman."

I pulled myself up onto my elbows and watched Clutch.

"He'd threatened to go after you and Jase if I tried to escape. He assumed I wouldn't try it. He was wrong. He posted her outside my door. She had no training, no experience."

I laid a hand on his heart. His muscles tensed.

"I killed her. Broke her neck so I could get out. I had to make sure you were safe."

He jerked away, got up, and stood in front of the window.

I came to my feet. "It's not your fault. Doyle forced your hand."

"He didn't force me to kill her."

I walked over to him and watched him stare out over the dark valley below. "He did, in a way. He forced your hand. You did what you had to do. If you didn't, you wouldn't be alive today. *I* wouldn't be alive today."

He turned, looked into my eyes for a moment, then pulled away and grabbed his clothes and a bottle of whiskey. He paused at the top step. "She was Doyle's wife."

CHAPTER XX

Three days later

"There's one coming up your six," Clutch called out before diving behind a pew to reload. I twisted around and blasted buckshot into the head of an exceptionally overweight zed, pumped my shotgun, and then took out the aggressive one reaching for Clutch.

I continued shooting, taking out their legs if I couldn't get a good headshot. Clutch rejoined, and the church was like a Tarantino film, full of gunfire and gore. I used up my last two shells on a priest wearing a collar stained with dried blood.

"Reloading!" I yelled out and scrambled back several steps. I rushed to slide the shells into the shotgun while a zed in the form of a decrepit old woman stumbled toward me, its head askew with a broken neck. I'd only gotten five shells loaded when it closed in. I swung the gun up and shot it in the chest. The force sent it flying back, and my second shot was a direct hit to its face.

I looked around for what to shoot next but saw no zeds still standing. I frowned. "We're clear already?"

"All clear," Clutch said as he pulled out a knife.

I finished reloading my shotgun before slinging it over my shoulder and pulling out my knife. We went around to each zed, making sure it wouldn't come back. Shotguns packed a punch, but they didn't always get the job done.

Afterward, we stood at the baptismal fountain, washing up under the watchful gray gaze of a statue of the Virgin Mary. "Jesus," I said, and then glanced at the crucifix hanging at the front of the church. "Sorry," I mumbled. "Did everyone in a ten-mile radius come to church when the outbreak hit?"

"Plenty of folks get religious when things turn to shit."

My eyes fell on the priest. "Guess the priest would've had his hands full giving last rites."

"Too bad the dead didn't actually stay dead."

I dried my hands on my jeans and scanned the corpses and toppled pews. "We used up a lot of ammo."

"It'll all be worth it if this place hasn't been looted yet."

I grinned and clapped. "Let's check it out."

What we discovered quickly proved Clutch right. We'd struck gold at the Catholic church in the town nearest to the park, if you could call six houses and a church with an attached reception hall a town. According to the banner hanging outside, they'd been collecting donations for a local food pantry to help the needy at Easter.

And we definitely qualified as needy.

"See if you can't find a P-38," Clutch said as he rifled through cupboards in the kitchen.

"I have no idea what you're talking about," I called out in reply, stacking another box of canned food near the front door with the dozen other boxes. "You know, for a small town, these guys were really generous."

I headed back to the kitchen. "Everything's boxed up and ready to go."

"Aha, a P-38." Clutch held up a small metal can opener not much bigger than a razor blade. He pocketed it.

My brow furrowed. "It's a can opener?"

"It's a P-38."

With a sigh, I rolled my eyes. "Ready?"

"Ready."

We headed to the stack of boxes. "You carry, I watch," I said.

Clutch lifted two boxes and grunted. "Did you have

to pack them so full?"

I patted his shoulder. "Just doing my part to help you stay in shape." With the shotgun in one hand, I propped open the door with a brick. After a quick sweep of the area between us and the truck, I motioned Clutch forward. "Clear."

He carried the boxes outside, and I stayed close, constantly scanning a full three-sixty around us. Afternoon shadows of tall trees danced like taunting spirits across the tombstones in the quaint cemetery on the other side of the church.

I opened the back of the truck, Clutch slid the boxes onto the bed, and we headed back for more boxes. We were getting efficient at looting, but we both knew that there'd be nothing left to loot in another year. We'd deal with that problem a year from now.

On the third load, I came to a hard stop.

"Aw, hell." In one smooth move, Clutch set down the boxes and swung his shotgun around.

Parked next to our truck was a Humvee.

Don't let it be Dogs. Don't let it be Dogs. I treaded cautiously toward it, careful to keep the truck between us and them.

As I neared the vehicle, I let out a breath as Griz stepped out from the driver's seat and waved while still speaking into the handheld radio. Tack emerged from the other side of the Humvee. He casually gripped a rifle, looking none too bothered that we had two shotguns aimed at them.

When Griz put down the radio, I lowered my weapon. "What brings you boys all the way out here?"

"Standard recon," Griz replied. "Damn, I never expected to run across the pair of you. That teaches me for betting against Tack."

I lifted a brow.

Griz busted out a wide grin. "The odds were twenty to one that you two were zeds. Tack was the only one to bet on both of you."

Tack gave a nod.

"Thanks." I lifted a brow. "I think."

"So everyone thinks we're dead?" Clutch asked by my side.

"Everyone at Fox, anyway," Griz replied. "With the exception of Tack, me, and now Captain Masden."

Ah, so that was whom he'd been talking to on the radio.

Griz, joined by Tack, headed our way. Griz whistled at the church. "Gutsy move to clear out a church. We've learned to keep our distance from churches. They're right up there with grocery stores and police stations as being zed hubs."

"Beggars can't be choosy," I said.

Griz nodded to the boxes. "Here, we can help."

"We're good," Clutch said, grabbing the boxes.

Griz held out his hands. "We're not trying to take what you've rightfully stolen."

"Recon, you say? You guys still out looking for survivors?" I asked.

"Some, but our focus has shifted more to tracking down Doyle. His guys are still a pain in the ass."

My muscles tightened as I watched Clutch for any sign of emotion. I knew he'd never forgive himself for killing that woman. Not that Doyle would be any less forgiving if he found out Clutch was still alive.

"Lendt hasn't taken care of him yet?" Clutch asked.

Griz frowned and shook his head. "We busted into Doyle's camp and caught several of his men and freed some of his 'indentured servants'."

I cocked my head. "Indentured servants?"

"That's what Doyle told them," Griz said. "Doyle convinced them that Camp Fox wasn't safe. So, for food and shelter, they had to sign contracts to service the militia for seven years. Lendt figured his attack on Camp Fox was as much to convince people that with him was the only safe place."

My jaw dropped. "Holy. Shit."

"But he's surprisingly wily for his age," Griz added. "His guys have gone guerrilla on our patrols, but there have been no more attacks on the Camp, so we know we've got him on the run."

"I wouldn't be foolish enough to count on that assumption," Clutch said, pushing the box onto the truck bed and heading back for more.

"We're not," Griz said, keeping up. "But we'll get him one of these days. You can bet on it."

"It doesn't sound like you've made the smartest bets yet," I said with a smirk before stepping back to the reception hall. Tack and Griz followed.

Tack picked up a box, and Griz lifted the top. "Who would've guessed that cheap toilet paper would become a luxury item?"

"How's Camp Fox holding up? The civilians are all safe?" I asked, thinking of one in particular.

Griz sighed. "We're getting by, but Doyle's attack put a hurt on our supplies. Before long, we'll be out doing what you're doing."

Tack dropped the box into the back of the truck and faced me. "That friend of yours, Jasen Flannigan, he's all right. Fitting right in at the Camp."

I closed my eyes and breathed deeply. When I reopened my eyes, I smiled. "Thank you."

Griz and Clutch set down the last of the boxes.

"We'd better head back," Clutch said.

I checked the sun sitting just above the roof of a two-story house across the street. Zeds tended to disappear at night, especially on cloudy nights. I suspected it was some sort of instinctual need for self-preservation. They couldn't see any better than us, so they could walk right into a river or off a ledge in the dark. Not that they were bright enough to avoid doing that in the daylight.

Except last night was a full moon. Tonight wouldn't be much better, without a cloud in the sky. It would be a good night to be back at the park and locked in before the sun set.

"I saw what they did to your farm. That's a damn shame," Griz said. "Where you staying now?"

Clutch narrowed his eyes. "Why do you want to know?"

"I'm guessing it's out this way," Griz said, looking around. "We're tight on resources, but whenever we have a squad out this way, I can have them stop by to check in to see how things are going."

"Things are going fine," Clutch retorted.

"I read you loud and clear. But, the attack really cut into our numbers and decimated our ammo supply. We've started training civilians, but we could use all the help we can get."

"Help?" I asked with a hand on my hip. "Tell me something, do they still have the prison cell waiting for me?"

Griz's lips thinned and shook his head. "Lendt's wiped the slate clear on anyone charged with assaulting the militia. After the stunt Doyle pulled, Lendt realized that he had to revisit his approach to military law. Hell, you just might get a medal now."

I didn't share his confidence. "Clutch is right. We need to get going."

"Hold up." Griz jogged back to the Humvee and pulled out something. "This radio pack is fully charged, and it's got an adapter for a cig lighter. I already dialed in our frequency. Call if you need anything. Leave it on so we can reach you. If we see any herds or any of Doyle's guys sniffing around this area, we'll let you know."

Clutch nodded and took it.

"Thanks, Griz," I said and followed Clutch to the truck.

"Do you think they'll try to reach us?" I asked, closing the door.

"Yeah." Clutch paused. "The radio is Masden's way of saying I've been called back to duty."

CHAPTER XXI

"Why can't anyone just leave us the fuck alone?" Clutch growled as we drove back to the church two days later.

I reached out and intertwined my fingers with his. "That's because we're irresistible."

Neither of us laughed. I wasn't any more comfortable with the idea of tying ourselves to Camp Fox than Clutch. When Tyler had called in on the radio this morning and said he needed to meet with us, a rock had formed in my stomach and had been expanding ever since.

As we rolled up to the church, we found two Humvees waiting for us.

When Clutch turned off the ignition, the back door on the first Humvee flung open, a nearly full-grown coyote jumped down and a teenager with a wide grin stepped out.

My eyes widened. "Jase!"

He waved wildly and met me midway with a bear hug. Clutch came up from behind me and patted him on the shoulder. "Damn, it's good to see you, kid."

Jase took a step back. "Man, when Griz told me you guys were okay…well, it's just good to see you. Really, really good."

The golden coyote sat behind Jase, and I grinned. "I see Mutt's turned out all right."

He bent down and picked up the furry canine, and she licked his cheek. "Yeah, she's a regular zed hunter now. She comes with me scouting."

Clutch frowned. "You go on scouting missions?"

"Yeah." Jase nodded back at Tyler, Griz, and Tack, who were now walking our way. "They asked for folks to join up after the attack. Eddy and I are on Captain Masden's squad." He stepped to the side, making room for Tyler, while Griz and Tack stood back with their rifles ready, scanning the area.

Tyler smiled at me. "It's good to see you again." He held out his hand, and I shook it, having a hard time returning his smile.

Tyler didn't even try to shake Clutch's hand. Tyler never liked Clutch, and Clutch still held a grudge against Tyler for abandoning me in zed and Dog country. I wasn't angry. Not anymore. Tyler had simply been trying to do the right thing in a world where all the old rules had changed.

I still wanted to punch him.

"What do you want, Captain?" Clutch said.

Tyler gave a thin smile. "Always to the point, Sarge. I respect that. Griz said he filled you in on our current situation with Doyle and his minutemen."

"He said you guys were at war," Clutch said.

Tyler chortled. "It's been more like a hunt than a war. Though, Jase might have found a game changer."

"How's that?" I asked.

"Your boy here came across one of Doyle's outposts."

"When are you going in?" Clutch asked.

"Tonight."

Clutch narrowed his eyes. "But you're not here for a briefing."

"You're right, Sarge. To be honest, we're tight on resources. Before the outbreak, we didn't have many troops with real field experience. And Doyle's attack on the Camp put a hell of a hurtin' on us. You've served two tours, Sarge. I need you out there with my men tonight. It's not a request."

I watched Clutch turn and pace the sidewalk. When he returned, he ran a hand through his short hair. "What's the SITREP?"

"From what Jase and Southpaw reported, this isn't Doyle's primary camp, but we believe he's running out of multiple small camps instead of one larger camp now. Nevertheless, the camp Jase and Southpaw found would be a critical hit from a payback perspective. The payload is three fuel tankers, which we believe constitute all of Doyle's mobile fuel reserves. We could really use that fuel at Camp Fox, so we can't go in with guns blazing and risk blowing the trucks sky-high."

He motioned to Jase who handed Clutch his iPhone. After Clutch scrolled through the pictures, he handed the phone to me. Three fuel tankers sat side by side at a rest stop. Calling it an outpost was an exaggeration. There were no fences, hardly any people, and only the single building. If the trucks were lined up, I would've driven by without looking twice.

"As for tangos," Tyler continued. "We're looking at no more than five guys on duty at any time, but they're likely patched into Doyle through handheld radios we provided the militia awhile back. I think Doyle figured this place is far enough north that we wouldn't find it."

"Which rest stop is this?" Clutch asked.

"It's about twenty miles north of Chow Town, just south of the ethanol plant."

"I know the place," Clutch said.

"I'm leading the mission, and I'm taking my entire squad with me. That makes ten of us. With you, it'd be eleven."

Silence boomed, and I noticed Clutch watching Jase. "If I do this, both the kid and Cash are on my team."

Tyler nodded. "I was planning on that." He turned to me. "Since you're not ex-mil, I couldn't make you come along, but your assistance is appreciated."

I gave a tight nod.

Tyler faced Clutch and continued. "Griz has Alpha

team. You'll take Bravo team. That brings our total to twelve troops for the mission. It should be an easy in-and-out."

Clutch shot me a strained glance before turning back to Tyler. "Hoorah."

Tyler smiled. "We head out at zero-three. I'll make sure you both have clearance into Camp Fox. We meet inside the front gate. Got it?"

"Cash and I need weapons and gear," Clutch added.

"Roger that," Tyler said. "Those are two things we still have in good supply. Ammunition is another story."

"How low are you?" Clutch asked.

"If we're careful, we might have just enough to take Doyle down. But we're going to have to get creative with the zeds."

Clutch nodded and headed back to the truck. I shot Jase a quick smile before following.

We drove away, and neither Clutch nor I spoke until after we passed by the farms we'd looted a few days earlier. "I guess it's official. We're with Camp Fox," I said.

Clutch took in a deep breath. "Yeah, guess so."

My eyes widened. "Wait. Turn around."

He hit the brakes and did a one-eighty. He frowned. "What'd you see?"

I hurriedly pointed to a house with a couple rustic tin buildings. "Turn in here."

He pulled into the drive. "Is that—?"

"Yeah."

He stopped the truck next to the old tree, with dozens of red apples dangling from it. I shot him a wide grin before we both rushed out to the tree. The apples were high, and I had to jump to reach one. When I bit into it, tart juices splattered, and I groaned. *"Mm, so good."*

Clutch didn't reply. He was too busy chewing on his own apple.

It had been so long since we had fresh fruit. These tart apples were meant for pies, but they tasted like heaven. Clutch finished his before I finished mine and grabbed another apple. I tossed my core, and he held the apple out to me. I grinned, grabbed his wrist, and pulled him into a long, sugary kiss. *Bliss.*

I pulled away to find Clutch wearing one his rare smiles.

My smile fell at the same time the blood in my veins froze. "Watch out!"

He twisted around just as the zed tackled him.

I reached for my shotgun and realized I'd left it in the truck.

I pulled out my knife and ran at the zed snapping its teeth at Clutch, who was holding it back. I grabbed its legs and yanked it to the side, got to my knees and shoved the knife through its cheekbone. Clutch was next to me, stabbing it through its eye. Jumping to my feet I turned around to find at least a half dozen more heading our way, all looking less than friendly and more than hungry.

"We've got trouble," I murmured.

"Truck" was all Clutch said, and we both sprinted back to the still-running vehicle.

As Clutch tore out of there, I watched the zeds through the back window. They stood under the apple tree, watching us, as though daring us to come back.

I turned back around and sighed. For more apples, I just might.

CHAPTER XXII

"You'll stay at my side and do everything I say," Clutch said on our way to Camp Fox. "This situation could go FUBAR in a flash. I don't like you this close to the action, but I'd rather have you with me than alone at the park."

I yawned, then saluted. "Yes, Sergeant Bad Ass, *sir*."

He muttered something under his breath. I grinned and went back to scanning the dark landscape.

It took us two hours driving without headlights and around the ever-growing numbers of zeds to get to Camp Fox. By then, my nerves had amped up a million levels. I'd fought against zeds plenty. This was my first time playing the aggressor against other people, and I felt sorely unprepared.

At the Camp's front gate, we found a friendly reception and load of gear and weapons waiting for us.

Clutch helped me gear up before fastening on his own armor. As I checked out my new sniper rifle, Tyler drove up with a Humvee full of troops with faces painted black.

They stepped outside and we all formed a circle around Tyler.

He looked over everyone, and then threw me a plastic container. I unscrewed the lid to find what I guessed was dark face paint. Clutch dipped two fingers in and started wiping it across his face, and I did the same.

"Sarge, you've got Tack, Southpaw, Cash, Eddy, and Jase," Tyler said. "Everyone else is with Griz and me. Here's the plan."

Two hours later, Bravo team lay flat on the grassy hill behind the rest stop, waiting for Tyler's signal. To my right, Mutt, an honorary member of Bravo, was sprawled out next to Jase, seemingly unconcerned that shit was about to hit the proverbial fan. Eddy was on Jase's other side, one of his legs shaking. To my left, with Clutch between us, was Southpaw, the other sniper in Bravo. Tack was silent and unmoving next to Southpaw, and I couldn't tell if he was even awake.

Clutch looked like he was analyzing the situation, and I turned my attention back to my target. There were two guards on the backside of the rest stop, one on each corner. Southpaw and I each had our assigned target in our sights for the past ten minutes. Just waiting for the signal.

We each had a role in the straight-forward mission: *Go at them from both sides. Take down the guards. Smoke out any hiding in the rest stop and neutralize. Grab the fuel trucks and reclaim any weapons and ammunition.*

Clutch tensed, and I suspected he was getting the call from Tyler. Camp Fox had been ill-equipped for war, leaving only the three mission leaders with headsets.

"Bravo. Received." Clutch turned to Southpaw and then to me. "Green light." He paused for a three-count while we each readied to fire. "Green light, *go*."

I inhaled. As I exhaled, I pulled the trigger. My target fell to the ground, unmoving. My shot was echoed by Southpaw's rifle, and his target collapsed.

"Nice." Clutch held up two fingers and motioned back and forth.

Show time.

Clutch took the lead, with Tack, Jase, and Eddy lined up one by one in trail. Southpaw and I stayed behind to take out Dogs before they posed a risk to our guys, though I suspected Clutch's motive was to keep me out of danger, leaving Southpaw behind to cover me.

The rest stop, right off the interstate, was a smart location for moving large trucks. Instead of fences, every forty feet or so, there was a zed, buried up to its knees and chained to the ground. *Interesting defense.*

Lights erupted from an amped-up pickup truck and its horn blared.

"Shit!" I muttered.

"Guess the surprise is up," Southpaw said from my left, sounding none too happy.

Alpha team reached the rest stop as soon as the first Dog emerged. Clutch took him out with a clean chest shot.

Clutch slammed against the building, nearly dropping his gun. It was then I noticed the Dog he'd shot wasn't a man at all but a young woman. As Clutch leaned against the building, I wanted to shout, *she's a Dog, goddammit!* Instead, I fired off a shot at the next Dog coming through the door.

The shot snapped Clutch out of his stupor. He pulled up his rifle, shot a glance my way, and headed back into the fray. Jase fired off several shots, and I heard him yell. Mutt took off running and jumped onto an injured Dog trying to flee. The coyote tore at his throat and clawed at his skin until the Dog's screams found silence.

Clutch pressed his hand to his ear. He made a hand motion. Eddy and Jase ran toward one of the fuel trucks, with Mutt on their heels. Four of Alpha team met them at the trucks, and a pair climbed into each of the three trucks.

Heavy engines roared to life, and the lights on the fuel tankers came on one by one. As they started rolling, Southpaw and I continued to lay down fire whenever we saw a Dog.

Clutch held up a hand and shouted, "Pull back. Company's coming!"

When Clutch and Tack reached our position, Southpaw and I sprinted with them into the darkness. Bullets zinged past us and I wanted to dive for cover but kept running.

Southpaw stumbled, and I stopped to help him. He was trying to pull himself back up while holding his side.

"South's down!" I yelled, bending down to pull him up. Clutch moved me out of the way and he and Tack grabbed the fallen soldier.

I fired off cover fire as the guys ran past me.

"Haul ass, Cash!" Clutch yelled.

I fired off three more shots and reached the guys as they were loading Southpaw into the back of the Humvee. We climbed inside, and Clutch took the driver's seat. He was cussing at Tyler, but I couldn't make out the jargon.

But I did notice the onslaught of headlights in the distance, and they were coming right at us.

CHAPTER XXIII

Clutch sped dangerously fast without headlights. I had no idea how he managed to keep the Humvee on the road. He pressed two fingers against his headset. "We have one man down."

A pause.

"Affirm. Bravo team is still a go. Repeat, Bravo is still a go."

A pause.

"Wilco. Bravo, over and out." Clutch grimaced and turned on the headlights.

My eyes widened. "What are you doing?"

Clutch clenched his jaw. "Alpha is rendezvousing with the tankers to provide firepower support to the Camp. We're to lead as many Dogs as we can away from the convoy."

I swallowed, found it hard to breathe, and

immediately started reloading my rifle.

He glanced at me and then took a quick look in back where Tack was busy tending to Southpaw. "How's he doing?"

Tack didn't answer.

"Tack, report."

The soldier looked up slowly. "It was clean, through and through, no organs hit. But…I think he's gone."

Clutch hit the wheel. "Fuck!"

"I don't get it," Tack added on though in a daze. "It wasn't that bad of hit. He should be conscious and talking to us right now."

I looked around and noticed lights—a lot of them—closing in. "Do you know this area?" I asked.

"Not good enough." Clutch cranked a hard left, sending me against the door, and he barreled down the on-ramp and onto the interstate. "Let's hope for no roadblocks."

Something chinked the metal, sounding like a rock chip, except we were on pavement.

"Tack, take the .30," Clutch ordered. "Cash, feed him ammo."

I started crawling into the back.

"Shit!" Tack yelled and jumped back.

"What's wrong?" I asked.

"It's Southpaw. He's turning!"

"How's that possible?" I fumbled with my rifle.

Southpaw plowed into the much smaller Tack, but I was close enough I barely had to aim. I fired an ear-ringing shot, and Southpaw collapsed on top of Tack.

Tack sat up and shoved off his comrade.

I kept my rifle leveled. "Are you bit?"

He kicked away Southpaw's body. "No."

"What the hell was that?" Clutch asked.

"No idea," I said, making my way to Tack. We hadn't been close to any of the zeds in the area. So how in the world had Southpaw gotten infected? More pings against the metal reminded me that I didn't have the luxury to think right now.

Tack fired rounds at the headlights behind us. The first vehicle swerved but then straightened out, but at least we now had more space between us and them. Another pair of lights came up alongside the first, and flashes of gunfire from both trucks winked back at us.

"Can't you go faster?" I yelled toward Clutch.

"Humvee," he replied as if that explained everything.

I fed more ammo to Tack.

Clutch jerked the Humvee onto an exit ramp, knocking me across the floor and onto Southpaw's body. As I pulled myself back up, I saw the sign that read *Fox Hills 3 miles*, and by the look on Tack's face, he'd seen it, too, though he went back to firing.

"You're taking us to Chow Town?" I asked.

"We can't outrun the Dogs, and they'd be crazy to follow us into town."

We'd be crazy to go into town, I wanted to say. Instead, I warned, "It's almost dawn."

Clutch kept on driving. "I plan on only making a

quick drive-through."

As Clutch suspected, the Dogs backed off when we passed the sign that read *Welcome to Fox Hills, Midwest's hidden gem, pop. 5,613*. Clutch drove the Humvee off the shoulder and through the ditch, around the blocked road, and into the Wal-Mart's parking lot. Already, at least a dozen dark shadows lumbered toward us.

The truck behind us stopped but kept its machine gun leveled at us. The other trucks peeled out and headed in different directions. "Fuck!" Clutch stepped on the gas. "The shits are trying to block us in town."

Clutch turned left on the first street, running over a zed wearing a gaudy shirt, its sequins glittering in our headlights. "Come on, come on, come on," he muttered as he sped faster and faster.

When we reached the next road leading out of town, on the other side of the roadblock was one of the Dogs' trucks. They fired off several shots, and Clutch slammed on the brakes. He made a U-turn and headed for the next street. The gunfire had drawn zeds out from the darkness. Clutch dodged some and hit more on his way to one of the few roads leading out of town. Chow Town wasn't a large town. With a river running along two sides and all bridges blocked or destroyed during the outbreak, there weren't many roads leading out of town.

Clutch slowed, and I saw the Dogs on the other side of the roadblock.

The wheel creaked under Clutch's grip. "Shit."

"If we can't get out of town, we need to find a place to lie low until the Dogs clear out," I said, fear tightening my muscles as I remembered how well that worked the last time I was here. I looked from Tack to Clutch. "Any ideas?"

"My apartment is about three miles from here," Tack said.

I frowned. "Apartments sound too dangerous."

"When that sun comes up, anywhere is going to be too dangerous," Clutch said.

"How about the pharmacy we cleared out? It's not far," I said.

Clutch shook his head. "The glass windows will make it hard to hide."

"My girlfriend's house is across the street from First Baptist. She went to Des Moines with her parents shopping when...you know, so the house should be clear," Tack said.

Clutch sighed. "Let's give it a shot."

Tack gave directions, and Clutch weaved around cars and cut through yards. A lump formed in my gut when I saw the zeds building behind us.

As soon as we hit a side street, Clutch stepped on the gas to put some distance between us and them. "We're going to have to move fast. Run to the back door. Don't be noticed. If you are, take care of any that home in on us. Tack, you make sure you get us inside fast. Then we're going into silence so no zeds get a bead on us. Got it?"

"Got it," I said.

"Tack, grab any extra ammo off Southpaw. I have a feeling we're going to need every round," Clutch said before relaying our next coordinates to Tyler.

A moment later, Tack pointed. "There. That two-story brick one. That's the place."

"Let's do this." Clutch cut the engine of the Humvee while it was still rolling into the driveway, and I jumped out.

It was dark enough that the herd of zeds about a block away was only an ominous fog of shapes. Sweeping trees cast ominous dark shadows over the yard, hiding God only knows what. Clutch scanned the backyard alongside me.

Tack checked the back door. When it didn't open, he lifted a flower pot and grabbed a key. He opened the door and disappeared inside.

I went to follow but stopped cold. I pulled out my knife, walked down the steps, and stood on the patio. A zed emerged from the shadows. It groaned, and I lunged forward and stabbed it through the top of its head. I looked around for more. Clutch tugged my arm and motioned to the door.

I followed him inside. He locked the door, and I found us in a kitchen. Aside from the earliest glimmer of dawn coming through the windows, it was pitch black inside. I moved slowly to not make any noise and closed the blinds on the kitchen window. I turned, leaned on the sink, and inhaled.

Death.

I smelled death.

I stepped cautiously into the living room, where Tack was closing the curtains. The smell was stronger here. He noticed me, held up a hand, and whispered, "It's Daisy."

"Daisy?" I mouthed back.

"Golden Retriever."

Relief replaced my tension. Now all we had to do was wait it out.

Something thumped against the window.

Tack and I both stiffened. Clutch walked silently into the room. *Thump.*

I flattened against the wall and peered out of the crack at the end of the curtain. Several zeds grabbed at the Humvee. Even more zeds stood on the other side of the window, sniffing at the air.

Thump, thump.

I stepped back, mouth opened. Impossible. They couldn't possibly find us through brick and glass. Clutch exchanged places with me and he looked outside. Tack looked outside from the other edge of the curtain.

Both looked as surprised as I felt.

The pounding on the glass grew, and more zeds joined in.

"If I can get to the Humvee, I can unleash the .30 on them," Tack whispered.

"There's too many," Clutch said in a low voice.

"When that glass breaks, we're going to have to make a run for it."

All three of us checked our weapons one last time.

The glass shattered.

Clutch yelled, "Run!"

And we did.

CHAPTER XXIV

We bolted out the back door. Tack fired the first shots, clearing the patio. Clutch took the lead from there. I gripped my rifle as I sprinted behind him, with Tack at my side. It was still dark, but the coming dawn shed enough light to reveal outlines of zeds waiting in the shadows.

We ran in the opposite direction than we'd come. We ran through backyards, turning at fences and dodging zeds, shooting open escape routes. Once we broke from the herd near the house, Clutch set the pace at a quick jog, faster than any zed but slow enough that we could keep this pace for some time, if we had to.

And we had to. My clothes were soaked and my muscles burned by the time the sun reached into the sky. It was already easily eighty degrees and it was still morning. Body armor held the heat against my skin.

We could outrun any zed easily enough. But more just kept showing up. Around every corner, out of every alley. As soon as we got away from one herd, we'd find ourselves smack dab in the middle of another, and we'd have to zig and zag around houses and cars.

Tack ran out of ammo first. I was out eight rounds later. When Clutch's rifle clicked empty, I think we all sucked in a collective breath. With nothing but pistols and knives, we kept running. The sun baked my head under the helmet, and I had to drop my rifle and backpack to keep up with the guys' longer strides. My lungs couldn't suck enough air by the time the zeds' numbers dwindled and we reached an industrial park. Clutch slowed to a stop, bent over with his hands braced on his legs, and panted. I fell back against a wall, sucking air. Tack walked slowly, his hands on his hips, while he caught his breath.

Tack huffed, pointed to the north, his finger shaky. "There's an old bridge that leads out of town just beyond these buildings."

Clutch reported our status to Tyler, and then faced us. "They got the trucks back to Camp Fox okay."

"Thank God," I panted out.

Clutch did a slow three-sixty. Sweat dripped from his brow. "We have to keep moving. Too much open space. We're easy targets out here."

As though on cue, two zeds stumbled around the corner. The first, a farmer in jeans and cowboy boots, lumbered forward. At its side came a heavily tattooed biker zed with an intricate dragon climbing its sunbaked arm.

Two shots and the zeds fell. I turned to find Tack with his pistol still leveled where the zeds had been standing a second earlier.

Clutch sucked in another breath. "Let's move out. It won't take long for these guys' pals to catch up."

It took all my strength to push off from the wall and propel myself forward. Every boot step pounded the pavement. Every building seemed a mile long. We wheezed air. I stumbled over a curb.

At the end of an old warehouse, a bridge waited, its iron trusses reaching upward like welcoming arms. Several cars were smashed on it, preventing any vehicles from crossing.

Bodies rotted on the ground, but surprisingly, there were no zeds walking around.

I came to a stop at the same time Clutch and Tack must've seen it. A truck was parked not far from the bridge. The machine gun mounted on back was pointed right at us.

The Dogs were waiting for us.

CHAPTER XXV

"Shit!" I flattened myself against the wall, and Clutch and Tack did the same. "Think they saw us?" I asked.

"Maybe. Maybe not. But they had to hear Tack's shots," Clutch replied. "They're probably stationed there to hold us back until the herd gets here. They've got front row seats for watching us get shredded."

"There's no way we can cross that bridge without getting gunned down," Tack said.

"And there's bound to be zeds in the river," I added.

A zed came around the far corner of the building. It moaned and kept walking toward us, followed by at a least a hundred more, and more kept showing up. My heart lurched. "Looks like the party is about to start."

"Time's up," Clutch said. "We have to take our chances at the bridge."

"Wait," I said, and I examined the iron bridge. "What if we go under the bridge?"

Both men looked at me.

"The undersides of some of these bridges are just big I-beams. We might be able to shimmy across."

Clutch's brow furrowed. "It could work. If we stay low and behind the roadblock, the Dogs might not be able to hit us."

Moans and shuffling steps grew closer. The herd was halfway down the building now.

"Give it a shot?" Tack asked.

"Why not." Clutch took off in a hunched-over run.

I followed and Tack hung back to cover our flank. It was hard to run bent over, weighted down by what remained of my gear and exhausted from nearly four hours of running through half the alleys and backstreets of Chow Town. I stumbled and Tack helped me back to my feet. My legs were jelly, but from somewhere deep inside, fresh adrenaline numbed my body and senses, and I kept moving behind Clutch toward the bridge.

Two zeds emerged from the bridge and came at us, but they were easy enough to maneuver around. I dove to the edge of the embankment. Clutch already had a leg over the embankment. He held out a hand. "Grab on to me," he ordered. I reached out, and he snatched me against him and took a step down the embankment. He lost his footing and slid onto his back, pulling me against his chest. We slid several feet down before Clutch found traction again.

One of the zeds rolled past us and into the river below. The second followed a second later, grabbing Clutch's arm on its way down. We were dragged several feet before I was able to kick it loose, and it tumbled away.

Clutch held me tight. I lay against him, panting. I looked down, and swallowed. If we'd slid another fifteen feet, we would've landed right on top of a couple dozen hungry zeds hungrily trapped at the edge of the river. They couldn't climb the steep incline, and they couldn't enter the river without being swept away (which I suspected was what had happened to quite a few zeds already).

"Don't do that again," I muttered against Clutch's chest.

"Yeah," he replied breathlessly. Then he pressed a couple fingers to his headset. "Bravo needs pickup *now.* We've got half of Chow Town waiting for us on one side of the bridge, and Dogs set up to chase us down on the other."

Silence except for the growing hum of moans and shuffling feet.

Clutch scowled. "Copy that. Three hours. Over and out."

I pulled out a flask and took a quick drink. It was still half full, but no telling how long we'd be out here. There was no sound of engines, which meant the Dogs were still there but hopefully still oblivious to us. "Did you see how many Dogs were in that truck?"

Clutch shook his head.

I continued. "Once we get across we might be close enough to get clear shots."

"That's assuming they don't take us out while we're climbing across," Clutch replied.

"I guess we'll find out soon enough," I whispered and glanced back to find Tack climbing up onto an I-beam under the bridge.

I pulled away from Clutch but kept close by his side as I crawled toward Tack. The underside of the bridge was a zigzag of iron. After cracking my knuckles, I grabbed onto an I-beam. The beams were large, so there was plenty to grab on to, but I wasn't convinced I had the strength in my fingers and arms to get all the way across. I slid my legs around an I-beam and shimmied toward Tack.

He was already several feet ahead and putting more distance between us. I followed, with Clutch behind me. It wasn't a long bridge by bridge standards, but the arm strength it took for pulling myself across, it could've been the Golden Gate. Every time a gunshot rang out, I froze, waiting to feel horrible piercing pain. But none ever came. At only about a third of the way across, my arms shook, as much from my fear of heights as from my own body weight.

At the halfway point, two I-beams intersected and I was able to lean on one to catch my breath, though the humid air did nothing to help my breathing. Afraid if I stopped too long, I'd never get across, and so I continued. Minute by minute, putting one hand before the other, I made it to the three-quarters point, then only ten feet left. Eight, six, four.

By the time I reached the end, I had nothing left. I literally dropped off the bridge and collapsed onto the ground next to Tack. I rolled onto my back and grasped long grass with both hands.

Clutch dropped next to me, and we all lay there for several moments. When Tack moved, I stayed put, watching him Army crawl up the hill and scout the scene. This side wasn't quite as steep and—thankfully—zed-free. He backed himself down to us.

"SITREP?" Clutch asked.

"I see only two Dogs," Tack replied in a hoarse whisper. "One driver and one gunner. The driver looks like he's taking a lunch break. The gunner is busy watching the herd behind us. I think they've got him spooked. I count three zeds at the tree line. A few more dead on the ground."

Which explained the random gunshots.

"Can we get close enough to take them out without being seen?" Clutch asked.

"Maybe," Tack replied. "It looks like the gunner is still watching the other side of the bridge for us."

Clutch nodded and pulled out his pistol. "We head for the tree line. That way, if we're seen, we can still find cover. Cash, you take the driver. I'll take the gunny. Tack, make sure we're covered." He didn't wait for a response.

"There's no telling how many zeds are in those trees," Tack warned.

I shot him a quick glance, grabbed my pistol and crawled up the hill, and stopped next to Clutch while he scanned the area. The truck sat less than a hundred yards off. Easy shot with a rifle any day of the week, except I no longer had my rifle. The driver's side window was open, and he was taking a bite out of an MRE. The gunner in the back of the truck was leaning on the cab, still intently watching the bridge.

Clutch took off at a run toward the trees, and I dragged myself behind him. No shots fired from the truck. Clutch slid behind a wide tree, and I slammed into him, unable to stop my forward momentum. He caught me before I knocked us both down. Tack grabbed the tree next to us. A shadow moved several feet away, and Clutch took off, weaving around trees for the truck. A skinny zed emerged from a tree to our right, and Tack shoved a blade through its head.

When we reached the trees closest to the truck, we were no more than ten feet away from the zeds making their way to the truck.

"Ready?" Clutch asked.

"Ready," I whispered.

He motioned. "Now."

We ran out and started firing. Out of the corner of my eye, I could see the gunner spin the .30 cal toward us. Machine gun fire drowned out the pops of our pistols. My first shot planted harmlessly into the truck door, but as I closed the distance, my aim improved. The driver snapped back, and red splattered the passenger window. The .30 cal died soon after, leaving behind silence.

"Clear," I said.

"Clear," Clutch echoed before turning around. "How many zeds now?"

"Five," Tack replied, coming up from behind.

I sighed, and Clutch rubbed my shoulder. "Just a bit longer," he murmured.

The five zeds had broken from their way to the truck and reached out toward us. That zeds always seemed to prefer their prey living over the freshly deceased had never made any sense to me. I would've thought they'd go for the easy meal, but it seemed like they were predators at heart.

Tack took down the nearest zed. I fired a single shot at the zed on the left, and Clutch fired several shots to take out the cluster of three. No one bothered to make sure they were down for good. Seemed like we all had the same idea: get away from Chow Town as quickly as possible.

Tack jumped in the back of the four-by-four and threw the dead gunner off. I opened the door and found the driver still sputtering blood. Air hissed through the hole in his cheek. He wasn't moving, just in the final death throes. I grabbed his shirt and pulled him out the truck, let him collapse onto the ground at Clutch's feet.

Clutch rifled through the man's pockets. Movement

caught the corner of my eye, and I noticed another zed emerging from the tree line. "There are more headed our way," I said.

Clutch climbed behind the wheel, and pressed his headset. "Bravo is Oscar Mike in a Dog truck. Repeat, Bravo is Oscar Mike. ETA is one hour, over and out."

I sat down on the leather seat and sighed. Every muscle in my body was exhausted. After two long breaths with my eyes closed, I grabbed bottles of water and protein bars off the floor and tossed them to the guys. Between bites, I sifted through the glove box, finding a box of condoms, a flashlight, and a six-shooter. I grabbed everything.

I checked out the handheld radio on the seat. "I wonder when these guys were supposed to check in."

"Fingers crossed, they just did," Clutch said. "We could use extra time to put some distance between their last location and us."

If Clutch had said anything else, I missed it. I fell asleep somewhere between ten and twenty seconds into the drive.

I awoke with Clutch nudging me, and I grumbled. "*Lemme sleep.*"

"We're at Camp Fox."

I may have snarled at him, but I opened the door, climbed out, and grunted at my quickly stiffening muscles. I wasn't going to be able to move tomorrow.

"Damn, you're a sight for sore eyes," Tyler said walking toward us with a wide smile.

Jase ran out from behind his captain and pulled me into a hug. Mutt hopped around us. Jase stepped back and wrinkled his nose. "Jesus. You guys need showers."

"Happy to see you, too," I mumbled, and I really was. Seeing the kid alive and well made me feel like everything we'd gone through had been worth it.

"How many were lost?" Clutch asked.

"Three brave souls," Tyler replied. "But we gained fuel trucks and cut into Doyle's numbers." Then his jaw tightened. "How'd Southpaw bite it?"

"It was the darndest thing," Tack said. "He was shot. Then he turned."

Tyler frowned. "Same thing happened to two of Alpha team. The only thing we can figure out is that the Dogs dipped their ammo in zed blood."

I raised my brows. "Wow, that's low."

"But smart," Clutch said. "They don't have to be accurate, only good enough to nick one of us with a shot, and we're no longer an issue." Then he frowned. "I'd think the guns would jam from sticky bullets."

Tyler grimaced. "It's messed up, true enough. Let's head to my office and debrief."

"Later," Clutch said. "Bravo team needs rest first."

Tyler moved his gaze slowly over the three of us before nodding. "Understood. But we need to debrief as soon as you're up. We have extra racks in the troops' barracks if you want to stay. Tack can show you around."

Clutch looked to me, and I shrugged. "Okay, for now

at least."

Tyler smiled. "You'll find Camp Fox is more secure than ever. You're safe here."

"You haven't seen our camp yet," Clutch replied.

"No, I haven't," Tyler said. "Where are you at now?"

Clutch paused before speaking. "We're at Fox Park. Cash and I thought it could be made into a solid fallback location for the Camp. It needs a lot of work, but we should always prepare for the worst."

"Agreed. I'll mention the park to Colonel Lendt. A fallback location doesn't sound like a bad idea, though I doubt we'll need it. We've got Doyle on the run and the zeds will be gone come winter."

"What makes you so sure the zeds will die out when winter comes?" I asked.

"Their bodies are decaying, and they are running off the most basic of instincts," he replied. "They'll die from exposure because they're not smart enough to seek shelter. That is, if their bodies don't rot away by then."

After watching a zed continue to function completely under water for days, I had my doubts. "And if they don't die off or rot away?"

Tyler shrugged. "Then we keep killing them."

CHAPTER XXVI

Ten days later

"One vehicle coming in at our two o'clock," Jase said as he adjusted his night-vision binoculars. "I can't make out how many are inside yet, but Mutt doesn't like this situation."

I threw a quick glance at the fidgeting coyote at Jase's ankles before returning focus to my rifle's scope. "Does she like any situation?"

"Sure," he replied. "Dinnertime, bedtime, walks, any time there's a chance to steal someone's food."

I chuckled as I lay on my stomach, the approaching vehicle in my sights. I was here in case things went to shit.

Hmph.

I'd figured things had gone to shit the moment two Dogs called Tyler on the radio, asking for amnesty, especially with one of those Dogs being Sean. How many zeds had he personally dumped over the gate at the farm? I didn't trust him. Not one bit.

Clutch had agreed. That's why he took a second squad to come at the Dogs from behind in case this was an ambush. I wanted to be on his team, but unlike Clutch and even Jase, I wasn't particularly strong in the field, making Clutch pleased since he preferred me to be as far from the action as possible. At least I was a good shot, and so I was made one of Camp Fox's designated snipers.

The truck came to a stop at the prearranged intersection one hundred yards from our current position. Tyler might be an idealist but even he knew better than to allow Dogs to enter the Camp unescorted.

I adjusted my scope on the driver. *Sean, what are you up to?*

I moved a millimeter to the left to make out the passenger. *Weasel.* This situation just kept getting better and better.

"I only see two Dogs," Jase said.

"Same here," I added.

"Okay. Give them the signal," Tyler said while lying on the ground several feet from me.

Eddy came to his feet and clicked his flashlight on and off three times.

A light flashed three times in response from the Dogs' truck.

"That's our cue." Tyler looked at the three of us.

"These guys may be on the level, but play it safe. If anything smells funny, we cut and run."

"Yes, sir," the boys said, and I tacked on a "got it."

Jase and Eddy had become hardened soldiers seemingly overnight, though I guess that's what this world did to a person. They were young, and they clearly looked to Tyler as their hero, even though he couldn't have been more than ten years their elder. When not with Tyler, they were often with Eddy's mother, who had quickly adopted Jase as one of her own.

"Hold up. We've got incoming," Jase said.

"Dogs?" Tyler asked.

"No. Zeds. Ten o'clock."

"Cash, if you've got a shot, take it," Tyler ordered.

I adjusted my scope. It was dark, but the night scope lit up the zeds just fine. I focused first on the hunched-over zed. *Pop*. Then on the hunched over petite zed. *Pop.* Then on the large lumbering male. Fire engulfed it before I pulled the trigger.

I squinted at the sudden flames. "That wasn't me."

"It looks like someone from the truck threw a Molotov cocktail," Tyler said. "Jesus, just what we need. A flaming zed setting the countryside on fire" He pressed his headset. "Bravo, this is Alpha. Hold off. The Dogs are attacking the zeds only. Over."

"This is Bravo. Copy that," Clutch replied in my headset.

Tyler turned back to me. "Finish this before Sarge

gets trigger happy."

It was easy to find my target, since it was on fire and wobbling from side to side. "Swiggity swire, guess what's on fire," I murmured and pulled the trigger. Then smiled. "Swiggity swed, guess what's dead."

"All clear," Jase said.

"Then let's pick up our guests," Tyler said, coming to his feet. "Let's do this just like we planned. Jase, you're with me. Cash, you cover us and wait for pickup from Bravo. Eddy will have your six."

I gave Tyler a thumbs up.

"If these guys mess with us, try to avoid kill shots. We need the information they have."

I gave him another thumbs up.

I heard the Humvee start up and pull away, but I never took my eyes off the Dogs, waiting for them to make a wrong move. But the two men stood in front of their truck with its lights on. They stood without rifles and arms held out.

A gunshot behind me startled me, and I yanked around to see Eddy standing, facing away from me "Eddy?" I asked.

"Just one zed," he replied. "All clear."

I refocused. The Humvee headed down the gravel hill and stopped in front of them. Tyler and Jase got out and walked toward the Dogs.

Clutch's voice came through my headset. "*This is Bravo. Get your asses out of there, Alpha. You've got a world of hungry trouble heading your way.*"

I looked up from my scope but couldn't make out anything in the dark fields. I narrowed my eyes and realized that the darkness itself was moving. My eyes widened. There went the assumption that zeds moved less at night. I looked through my scope to target the nearest risks.

"Be ready, Eddy," I said. "Because a shitload of zeds are headed this way."

CHAPTER XXVII

I took my time targeting the zeds nearest to Tyler's Humvee. *Get 'em where I want 'em.*

Only when I knew I had kill shots, I fired. After four zeds fell, I clicked my headset. "This is Sweeper," I said, using the call sign Tyler had given me after seeing me take out a zed over a hundred meters out. "Clear out, and I'll lay cover as long as possible."

Eddy fired more shots behind me, and it took everything to not turn around.

"Talk to me, Eddy," I said.

"We need to get out of here soon. Very, very soon!"

I aimed and fired, accompanied by a symphony of gunfire to my right.

"This is Bravo. We'll pick up Sweeper as soon as you're clear."

I would've told Clutch to hurry up, but I didn't want

to take my hand off my rifle for even a second. I fired three more shots before a Molotov cocktail flew through the air. I noticed Tyler yanking a Dog to the Humvee. As soon as the Dogs were loaded into the vehicle, I switched my sights back to the herd, with the fire spreading.

Eddy was sending off long bursts behind me.

"Alpha is Oscar Mike. Clear out!"

I continued to fire until I had to reload. The gunfire to my distant right became sporadic.

"This is Bravo. Sweeper, we're on our way, so be ready."

I clicked the mag into place, and turned around to help Eddy. A couple dozen dark shapes were tripping over their fallen comrades on their way after us. I lifted my rifle and started firing.

When they closed in too tight, I backed up and fired at their legs to slow them down. Headlights came up the hill from behind me, shining light on the zeds. It was a sight that I knew would give me nightmares for years. Jaundiced eyes reflected light almost like cats. Zeds opened and closed their stained mouths like they were imagining what it would be like to chew on us. They reached out to us with clawed, gnarled fingers—those who still had fingers, anyway.

The .30 cal on Clutch's Humvee cut down the first line of zeds.

I grabbed Eddy and we sprinted toward the Humvee. The back door swung open and we tumbled inside.

Griz sped off. Tack stayed at the .30 cal.

"You okay?" Clutch demanded from his position in the front passenger seat.

"We're good. We're not bit," I replied before rolling off Eddy and leaning back.

"Zeds take the whole 'you are what you eat' thing way too seriously," Eddy chuckled then dropped his head back. "Jesus, that was close."

"Yeah." I sighed and eyed Clutch. "The information those two Dogs have better be worth it."

"...The militias are struggling, but they're still fighting the good fight. Keep them in your prayers.

In further news, I've yet to verify the rumors circulating that a centralized government is being organized and that new 'super' cities are being architected. I've asked Lt. Col. Lendt at Camp Fox for confirmation, but I've gotten no response. Same story, different day. But I'm going to keep asking. You hear me, Lendt? I'm going to keep asking until you give me an answer or send in your troops and shut me up.

Here's my thought for the day: The zeds are the enemy, so why is Lendt withholding information that could save lives? My advice? Trust no one, my friends, whether they have a pulse or not.

This is Hawkeye broadcasting on AM 1340. Be safe and know that you're not alone."

"That radio jockey is a splinter in my sphincter,"

Lendt said as he sat down at the table where Clutch, Jase, Eddy, and I were eating leftovers from dinner. Mutt was tearing into our scraps on the floor.

"Have you met with Hawkeye before?" I asked, twirling more spaghetti around my fork.

"He hasn't even tried to contact me," Lendt replied. "And I'm not exactly a hard person to find."

Hawkeye's transmission was a recorded broadcast, one that I'd heard earlier, but they replayed his daily transmissions every four hours at the request of the civilians on base. His voice had something familiar about it, yet I couldn't quite place him.

Not yet, anyway.

"Well, are you withholding information?" I asked.

"What goddamn information do I have to withhold?" Lendt countered, then cracked his neck. "Folks think that just because I'm a colonel that I have some super-secret handshake. I know as much as anyone else. NORAD hasn't made contact yet. Everything I hear is from other bases in the same boat as we are."

"Have you thought about tracking down Hawkeye to set the record straight? Maybe offer to have him interview you on the air?" I asked. "It sounds like he's trying to rile up the civvies against you." Then it hit me. Hawkeye disliked Lendt, just like Doyle had. Yet, Lendt had done all right by me so far.

Lendt chuckled. "He's definitely trying to rile folks up, but he's a conspiracy theorist, and that's what conspiracy theorists do. He's one of those people who's suspicious of anyone in authority. It doesn't matter what I say, he'd find a way to make me out to be the asshole."

Tyler set his tray on the table and saluted.

"At ease, Captain," Lendt said.

Tyler took a seat and started cutting his spaghetti. "The two men are being kept in the brig tonight for both their and our safety, per your orders, sir."

"They should be executed for treason," Clutch said.

"Agreed," I added quickly, especially when I discovered Weasel was the second Dog. I'd had the heebie-jeebies since.

"They will stand trial." Lendt smirked. "Then they'll be executed."

Tyler frowned and put down his fork. "They surrendered. They deserve a fair trial. Doyle put a militia together as quickly as Camp Fox moved into action at the outbreak. A lot of good men joined up to help, and a lot of the people here now owe their lives to the militia. Now, we're going to kill them for signing up to help and then going AWOL when they realized Doyle was no longer out for the greater good?"

"They'd had no problems obeying Doyle until now," I countered. "Why the sudden change?"

Tyler held up a hand. "I'm just playing devil's advocate, but maybe they did want out, but they couldn't get out until now. Have you thought of that?"

"Have you thought that they may be here under Doyle's direction?" Clutch asked, raising the same argument we'd been having ever since the Dogs contacted Lendt. "We should be thinking of what Doyle would want in this camp."

CHAPTER XXVIII

Three days later

My aim was off. The machete slit the zed's windpipe wide open instead of cleaving its skull. The near-severed head swayed, and my next swing scalped it, sending half of its brain and what had been long blonde hair to the ground.

Clutch had brought Jase and me back out to the apple orchard to win back the apple tree and for some much-needed close-up fighting. I didn't realize how badly I'd needed the exercise. I had become so dependent on my rifle that I'd let myself get rusty in hand-to-hand combat.

I swung the machete I'd grabbed from Jase's stash and took off the arm of the zed reaching for me. It hissed and reached out with the other. I swung again. This time, the machete snagged on bone and didn't go all the way through. I kicked the zed back and yanked my weapon free. When it came at me again, I quit playing with it and finished it with a slanted blow down its face. Half of its head and face slid off, and I looked to see how many zeds remained.

Five.

Clutch demolished one.

Four.

I went for the ugliest zed next. Its nose had rotted off and only one ear remained. I made my way around it, careful to keep plenty of space around me. It had been one of Clutch's first rules he'd taught me: *never back yourself into a corner.*

The zed followed my movements.

I let it come to me. *Get 'em where I want 'em.*

I raised the machete and brought it down in a straight line and shredded the zed from its chin down to its privates. "Oh, God." I stepped back, trying not to breathe, but the stench caused bile to rise in my throat.

The zed's organs tumbled out, jiggling with each step it took toward me. Clutch finished it off since I was too busy puking.

"Let's not do that again," Clutch advised, holding his arm over his nose.

"Yeah," I said, now dealing with the foul aftertaste in my mouth.

"Hey, guys. Check this one out," Jase said from behind us.

I wiped my mouth and turned to find Jase grinning.

In front of him was the last standing zed missing its hands and the lower part of its jaw.

"Finish it," Clutch said. "This isn't a game."

Jase shot an adolescent glare before taking his axe and bringing it down on the zed's skull. We double checked every zed before I grabbed an apple off the tree and took a bite.

Jase turned to the shed. "C'mon, Mutt. It's all clear."

Mutt peeked from the shadows, and then trotted over to brush against her master. He handed her an apple.

"She's quite the fighter," I said.

Jase shrugged. "She's more of a lover than a fighter."

The coyote preferred to keep her distance from zeds. I remembered that feeling. While I still hated zeds, I no longer froze in terror when I saw one. Maybe I was numb to the violence, but I could kill without feeling a single pang of guilt. Sometimes, when I spent too much time thinking, I wondered if we hadn't reached the end of the world but that we'd reached the end of humanity.

Something hit my head, and I jerked around to find Jase pulling back to throw another apple at me.

"Nice. Real nice," I muttered and picked up the apple and stepped out of the way as Clutch backed the truck up to the tree. I hopped onto the bed and started plucking ripe apples from the tree.

Jase joined me and we plucked several bushels of fresh apples while Clutch stood watch. Jase said Mutt was on guard duty, too, though with the way the coyote was sprawled out in the sunshine, I found that hard to believe.

On our way to the park, our work at the Camp done for now, we stopped at the gas station to grab more supplies. Several more zeds had meandered onto the lot, but they were easily dispatched. I'd forgotten how much easier looting was with three of us, rather than just two.

When Jase went to open the glass doors to the restaurant, I stopped. "Not there."

The two kid zeds were nowhere in sight, but it still didn't feel right. I'd never seen zeds retain any semblance of humanity, but this pair had seemed different. Maybe I'd let them get to me and my mind played tricks on me. They haunted my dreams. But that day, when we'd seen them, they'd showed no aggression. It had seriously freaked me out.

I didn't tell Jase about them, and Clutch had simply nodded in agreement as he walked into the store and started clearing shelves.

I looked across the shelves, and hopelessness wrenched my heart. This gas station was an easy place to loot yet many of the shelves were still full, aside from what we'd taken the last time. Were there really so few people left?

Listless, I helped Clutch fill the large bags we'd brought. The only other sound was the zed still thumping against the bathroom door. We'd cleared out much of the store before I realized there were only two of us. "Where's Jase?" I asked.

Clutch nodded toward the liquor section.

I rolled my eyes, and we headed into the section to find Jase with a nearly full cart.

"Not that," Clutch said, grabbing the wine coolers from Jase's hands. "If you're going to drink, do it right." He handed the kid a bottle of whiskey. I grabbed the remaining bottles of Everclear and vodka, but didn't have any intention to drink it. Alcohol worked great for disinfecting wounds, starting fires, and especially cleaning zed goo off things.

I grabbed an armful of wine bottles. "We should get going," I said. "I want to get unloaded before dark."

Jase hurriedly grabbed a couple more bottles before heading out with us. Mutt waited in the back of the truck, chewing on an apple.

"Save some for us," I called out.

The coyote raised her ears and then bit into another apple.

Clutch took a draw of whiskey before climbing in behind the wheel. Jase watched, grabbed a bottle, and took a drink. He coughed and bent over.

I patted his shoulder. "You're in the big leagues now." I hopped into the truck and Jase climbed in the back several seconds later.

Clutch smirked. "You look a little green around the gills."

"I'm. Fine," he choked out.

"Give it time," Clutch said. "It'll get easier."

And it did.

By sunset, Jase was drunk for the first time in his life, and we discovered he was a happy drunk, finding pretty much anything and everything funny. We sat in the park office, and the booze helped the MREs from Camp Fox taste better. And I had long since noticed that apples and wine paired beautifully together for dessert. Clutch was quiet, though he'd already put a hurting on his bottle of whiskey.

Still, it had been a nice night. The three of us together again and not running for our lives.

A couple hours later, we'd all passed out, though I awoke to the sounds of Clutch's nightmares. They were even worse when he drank, and he drank often.

"He still has them," Jase said quietly.

I found Jase propped up on an elbow.

"Yeah."

"He should get help," he said. "There's someone at Camp Fox he can talk to."

"Get some sleep," I replied.

Jase collapsed with a thud, and I figured he was asleep by the time his head hit the pillow.

I wrapped myself tighter around Clutch, and he quieted somewhat, but I could never break through his pain. Sometimes I wondered if he thought he deserved the nightmares and depression because of the things he'd done. He'd never said anything to that effect, because if he had, I would've firmly reminded him that everything he'd done was to save lives and that he was a hero. But, those kinds of words would fall on deaf ears. Clutch was the hardest on himself.

In the months that I'd known him, Clutch had opened only a tiniest sliver of himself to me. He kept things bottled up inside, acting impervious all day. But a mind was a pressure cooker. It could only take so much before it must let off steam or else explode. Clutch's nightmares and killing zeds were his steam.

I was afraid of what would happen if he ever exploded.

CHAPTER XXIX

"Wake up! Wake up!"

I bolted awake and then grabbed my throbbing head. "Shh," I ordered Jase as I reached for a bottle of water.

Clutch pulled himself to his feet, and I grimaced at him before taking a long swig. How could he drink three times as much as me yet wake up ready to take on the world?

"What happened?" Clutch asked, stretching his shoulders.

"Captain Masden just called on the radio. Colonel Lendt was killed, and both Dogs have gone missing."

I got to my feet and stood, in stunned paralysis, as his words cut through my cotton-filled brain. While we'd been drinking and enjoying ourselves, the Dogs had escaped, killed Lendt, and did God only knew what else at the Camp.

We should've been there.

Clutch scrambled into his clothes, and I kicked it into gear and hurried as fast I could in a hangover haze. We were loaded into the truck in less than five minutes. Clutch drove while I finished dressing and we all took turns with the Tylenol, food, and water. Twenty-two miles later, I started to feel semi-human again.

When we reached Camp Fox, the gate opened and the guards motioned us through. Clutch sped down the winding roads until we stopped at a familiar brick building. I grabbed my rifle.

We jogged up the steps and through the doors of HQ, which had now become town hall, to find at least half of the Camp's population milling around. Some looked like they were in shock, others looked downright pissed.

"Tell us what's going on!" someone shouted.

"We have a traitor!" someone else shouted back.

"String them up!"

The shouting and finger pointing continued. I gave Clutch the look, the one that insinuated we were mice about to step into a mousetrap.

Tack motioned to us from across the crowd, and we weaved toward where he was blocking people from entering the hallway. He looked like he was about to be overrun. "Captain Masden needs every hand on deck. He's in the Colonel's office," he said, moving aside to let us through.

Clutch nodded, and Jase and I followed him down

the hall. We stepped inside to find the walls riddled with bullets. Five body bags littered the floor, making dark heaps across the wood.

"Crap," Jase said breathlessly.

When Tyler saw us, he patted the injured man's shoulder and headed our way. "Glad you could make it. We've got a Charlie Foxtrot on our hands."

"The two Dogs," I said.

Tyler nodded tightly. "Likely, since they went missing late last night."

"How'd they escape?" Clutch asked, the tone inferring he knew they'd escaped all along.

"Someone killed the guard and let them out." Tyler rubbed his neck. "Damn it, I should've known better."

"Who carries the keys?" Clutch asked, ignoring Tyler's self-criticism.

"Doesn't matter," he replied, shaking his head. "The guard on duty always carries a set. They could've gotten the keys off the guard."

Clutch walked over to one of the five body bags and unzipped it, frowned, then rezipped it.

Tyler rubbed his temples. "Lendt had coffee every morning with the civilian leadership council. These guys knew exactly when and where to hit."

"What's the status on the Dogs, Captain?" Clutch asked, all business.

"Unaccounted for," Tyler replied. "I need every troop out there looking for who did this. I can't trust the civilians. They'd turn this hunt into a lynch mob."

"You can count on us," I said.

Tyler smiled weakly. "I know. Griz is on point. Go see him at the chow hall for your assigned sectors. You're relieved."

He turned and walked off, leaving the three of us standing alone.

"I guess Tyler's in charge now," I said quietly.

"C'mon," Clutch said and he led the way back down the hall and through the agitated crowd, several of whom threw us distrusting glares. When we reached the cafeteria, Griz was standing with Smitty. Both looked exhausted, though Smitty looked more tense than usual.

"Perfect timing," Griz said. "Jase, you're with Smitty. He'll fill you in."

"Yes, sir," Jase said and jogged to catch up with the slender, clean-cut soldier heading outside.

"Where do you need us?" Clutch asked before I could.

Griz turned and pointed at a spot on the map laid out across the table. "I've broken the Camp into sectors. We're too short-staffed, so every pair gets two sectors. You guys have sectors thirty-one and thirty-two, but stay together. Whatever you do, don't split up. Since everyone's been accounted for, the traitor is still walking around. If you find the Dogs, we need them alive to interrogate them."

"Understood," Clutch said. "That it?"

He handed Clutch a radio. "Let's find those

assholes."

Clutch and I headed out. Sectors thirty-one and thirty-two were on the far edge of the base so we drove there. We silently walked through buildings and examined every shadow, finding nothing. The Dogs should've been on their way back to Doyle by now. It made no sense for them to stick around after their job was done.

I smelled a familiar stench and stopped cold. I narrowed my eyes at the shadows near the outer fence. "What's that?"

Clutch took slow steps closer while I held my rifle at the ready.

I lingered until he got down on a knee and I came closer.

I kicked at the two zeds—one male, one female—tied together. They watched us, their mouths taped shut and their hands cut off. Each zed was cut wide open, with entrails oozing out. The stench was horrible, though they'd been open for long enough for some of the horrendous odor to dissipate. "What the hell is going on?" I asked.

"No fucking clue." Clutch stood, raised his rifle, and finished the two zeds.

These zeds were connected to Dogs, somehow. "Why would someone order a zed delivery here?" I thought aloud. "And why the hell would someone cut them open?"

Having zeds inside the Camp was dangerous

enough, especially if they got free and leaked their infectious goo all over the place.

I took a step back. "Oh, shit."

"What is it?" he asked.

"The Dogs aren't done yet. They're going to spread the infection."

CHAPTER XXX

Clutch and I looked at each other.

We left the stinking corpses and took off running back to the truck.

A blast detonated in the distance, and smoke rose from the direction of HQ.

My heart pounded. "No!"

We raced back to find soot-covered people pouring out of the building. Many were injured and wet with blood. Clutch slammed on the brakes just as Griz and several troops ran toward the building. I jumped out and yanked Griz back. "Anyone who got hit with shrapnel is infected!"

Griz's brows furrowed in confusion. "What are you talking about?"

I pointed at the building. "They used zed-soaked grenades!"

His eyes widened. "Are you sure? You've got to be fucking sure about this."

Clutch came up. "Yeah, Griz. They're using dirty bombs."

The soldier muttered out a string of curses before raising his handheld radio. "This is Griz. Anyone injured by the grenade blast is infected. You are ordered to eliminate anyone injured. Repeat. Kill anyone injured. Over."

Chatter erupted on the radio.

Repeat last.

Say again.

You're joking, right?

Griz sighed. "You heard me right! I'm not fucking with you! The Dogs used dirty bombs, goddammit. Kill the injured!"

"God help us all," Griz said and opened fire on survivors.

Screams erupted. People went berserk, running wildly away from us, seeking shelter.

I raised my rifle. My hands shook. My aim needed to be right. I took a deep breath and sought out the most injured. They would turn first.

I fired.

A woman holding her bloody stomach fell. From my side, Clutch fired into the crowd. The sounds of more gunfire from both sides filled the air.

I took down a man with a head wound. Then a kid getting trampled in the chaos that had overtaken the

Camp.

As if spooked by something, people switched directions and starting running toward us.

A zed with a massive chest wound sunk its teeth into the neck of a screaming man. I fired off two shots back to back, taking both down.

Clutch grabbed me. "Run!"

We sprinted toward the truck. The stampede was nearly upon us. Clutch grabbed my waist and threw me onto the bed. I grabbed his shirt to pull him up, but he was yanked from my grasp.

"Clutch!" I screamed, but I couldn't find him anywhere in the mass of running people.

People reached for me but were smashed against the truck by the sheer force of numbers. The four-by-four wobbled from side to side. A woman shrieked like a yippy dog as she was squeezed between the truck and people until she drowned under the stampede.

"Godammit! Clutch!"

In a panic, I continued firing as I crept to the edge, searching for him on the ground. A familiar man shoved a kid down on his way past.

"Sean," I growled out. He looked up right when I shot him. Weasel was only a few feet behind Sean, and I killed him with my last round.

The truck was rocking so much that I dropped the clip while reloading.

The stampede thinned out as the people spread out. Bringing up the rear were mostly zeds. When they first turned, zeds were nearly as fast as humans, and they were taking down people left and right, like they were at a wine tasting party.

I went through three more clips before I pulled out the machete. I jumped off the back of the truck and stumbled over bodies on the ground. I hacked at zeds and slashed anyone still living who bore shrapnel wounds. I shoved bodies aside.

"Clutch!" I screamed until my voice gave out. I kept going, pushing over bodies, searching, until my gaze fell on camo fatigues.

I dropped to my knees and pulled the lifeless man onto my lap and started sobbing.

I'd found Clutch.

BETRAYAL

THE NINTH CIRCLE OF HELL

CHAPTER XXXI

Three days later

Forty-two.

That's how many Camp Fox survivors made it to the park. After surviving the zed outbreak, only one out of every seventeen civilians survived the Dogs' attack. Of that number, over half the survivors were troops, as they'd been spread across the base hunting the Dogs when the attack started.

Forty-two was barely enough to protect the park from zeds, let alone protect it against the risk of Dogs. Same story, different day.

I snuggled against Clutch and held his hand, just like I had every day since the attack. On the first day, his fingers had trembled, but the doctor said not to think anything of it, that the spasms were due to the swelling on his brain. Even though Clutch no longer showed any response, I still held hope.

Jase clung to hope, too. He slept alone in a beanbag chair on the other side of Clutch's bed every night. He no longer had his faithful sidekick. The timid coyote had sacrificed herself to save her master when a zed tackled Jase. It seemed like he'd lost enough that he no longer had much to say.

He blamed himself for her death. But no more than I blamed myself for Clutch's situation.

Griz, Tack, Smitty, Eddy, even Tyler had come through without injuries. A selfish, dark shadow deep inside me was angry that they were okay while Clutch lay lifeless on the bed. It had all seemed so unfair. But as soon as the guys stopped by to offer respect, I'd been ashamed of my thoughts. Those men were heroes as much as Clutch. They'd just gotten lucky this time.

Clutch had been crushed under the stampede. His back was broken, along with three ribs, both legs, and his left wrist. He also had a dislocated shoulder and a fractured skull. If—*when*— he woke, the doc said he could have permanent brain damage. And he'd be paralyzed from the waist down.

Still, I prayed for him to wake.

I *needed* him to wake.

On the nightstand next to his bed—against doctor's orders—sat a fully loaded Glock and the can of chewing tobacco I'd given him. The doctor—a general practitioner—figured that if Clutch woke up, he'd be suicidal, and would put a bullet through his brain. I disagreed.

The Clutch I knew would never pull the trigger.

I only hoped that when Clutch woke, he'd still be the man I knew.

In the background, Hawkeye's latest transmission droned on over the beeps of Clutch's life support system.

"...The time is coming soon when we can all relocate to a zed-free zone. At the right time, I will give you all a date and time to meet, and we will head out together. A militia has volunteered to protect us on our journey. There is strength in numbers, my friends. Until tomorrow, this is Hawkeye broadcasting on AM 1340. Be safe and know that you're not alone."

Griz burst through the door and I nearly fell out of bed.

I got to my feet, gently, so as not to disturb Clutch's broken body. "What's wrong?"

"You better come quick."

I placed a kiss to Clutch's forehead and ran with Griz to his Jeep. "Where are we going?"

"Jase's cabin."

I sucked in a breath. *No!*

Fear stung my nerves. He'd been so quiet lately. He'd probably been planning on taking his own life since the attack, and I'd been so obsessed with Clutch that I ignored the signs.

I held on tightly as Griz squealed tires around winding roads through the dense morning fog. Three other vehicles were already parked at the cabin when we got there. I ran inside.

Expecting to find Jase's lifeless body, I was surprised to find Jase alive and well, and I let out a breath that I felt like I'd been holding since Griz grabbed me.

Then I noticed Jase had a rifle leveled at his best friend. Eddy kneeled on the floor, whimpering, with his wrists restrained behind his back. Tyler stood nearby, his arms folded over his chest.

I frowned. "What's going on?"

"Eddy couldn't take the guilt eating away at him anymore," Jase said with a cutting edge to his voice. "He'd figured his mom was exempt from getting chewed up by zeds. He figured wrong."

"None of that was supposed to happen. I swear it!" Eddy pleaded. "No one except Colonel Lendt was supposed to get hurt."

My jaw dropped. Eddy was the traitor? Of all people, a kid betrayed us?

Eddy sobbed. "I'm sorry, I'm sorry. I was trying to help everyone. I screwed up."

"What you did is *not* called screwing up. It's called treason," Tyler said coolly. "Your actions brought about the deaths of over three hundred innocent people, including your own mother."

Eddy lowered his head and sniffled, his body quivering.

"You can start making amends by giving us Doyle's location," Tyler said.

Eddy looked up, confused. He shook his head. "I had nothing to do with Doyle. Hawkeye arranged everything, even getting the two Dogs into Camp Fox."

Tyler frowned. "The AM jockey?"

The blood drained from my head as I finally placed Hawkeye's voice.

Eddy nodded. "Hawkeye had proof of zed-free zones that welcomed survivors. We could go there and be safe. But he'd said that Lendt didn't tell us about the zones because he didn't want to lose his power and control over everything and everyone at Camp Fox."

"And Hawkeye showed you this proof?"

"Hawkeye told me."

Tyler slowly shook his head. "Son, you were played for a fool. Hawkeye's the one interested in power and control. Not Lendt."

Eddy sniffled before looking across the faces in the room. His gaze stopped at one and morphed into a glare. "It's your fault. Mom would still be alive if it wasn't for you."

The room temp dropped twenty degrees when every pair of eyes turned to Smitty.

Smitty's gaze darted to Tyler. "I don't know what he's talking about."

Eddy's glare narrowed. "You said everything would be all right. That we were helping everyone."

Smitty fidgeted. "Stupid kid thinks to throw a scapegoat out to save his own ass. Don't try to pull me into this, Eddy. This is all on you."

Tyler took a step forward and shook his head. "You've always been a lousy poker player, Smitty." He nodded to Tack and Griz who I noticed both already had a pistol aimed at their fellow soldier. "Arrest him. Put him with Eddy."

Surprisingly, Smitty didn't rabbit. He stood, jaw clenched, while Tack disarmed and restrained him and Griz held the weapon level on him.

"I don't get it. Why, Corporal?" Tyler asked.

Smitty snorted. "When I joined up, I vowed to defend this country against all threats, domestic and foreign."

I rolled my eyes. How cliché. "And how does killing innocents fall under that?"

"None of that was supposed to happen. Hawkeye had said only the leadership had to go, so then everyone could relocate to the zed-free zone. The Dogs must've disobeyed orders. Maybe Doyle got wind of their plans and turned them."

"Hawkeye is Doyle, you idiot," I said and then walked out.

CHAPTER XXXII

Two days later

Tyler led a public tribunal for Eddy and Smitty where shouts for death had erupted within seconds. Tyler passed judgment two minutes later and condemned both to die—not by hanging but by zeds. Not a single person cried for leniency.

It'd taken only three months for society to return to Old Testament ways of thinking.

Tyler delayed the execution one day to make arrangements and assemble volunteers. Jase had been the first to step up. I had been the second, quickly followed by Griz and Tack.

After I checked on Clutch, we headed out from the park in Camp Fox's heaviest duty truck—a HEMTT—that was nearly impenetrable against zeds. It made Doyle's garbage trucks look like Tonkas.

Tyler sat up front in the cab with Griz, who drove us to Camp Fox. Tyler rode along because he felt like it was his responsibility to see his decisions through. He'd become a recluse since the trial. I imagined the hard decisions he'd been forced to make were tearing him up inside. Me? I thought Smitty and Eddy had it coming after the pain they'd caused. They'd been idiots to believe there were safe zed-free zones out there, let alone that we could move hundreds of people across states to such zones. Before the outbreak, I never would've thought I could become so ruthless. Now, I realized it was the only way to survive.

The rest of us sat in the HEMTT's open back with the prisoners. The numbers of zeds in fields and on the roads grew as we neared the camp, though we'd already figured most would still be within Camp Fox. Zeds weren't exactly adventurous unless in a herd. They were lemmings like that. Now if we could only find a giant cliff and lead them to it.

As we passed Doyle's abandoned camp, I was surprised to find relatively few zeds in the area. I was even more surprised to find the gate closed. "I thought Lendt's guys had blown open the gate," I said.

Jase shrugged, not taking his gaze off Eddy sitting across from him. "Guess not."

The thought nagged at me until we reached Camp Fox. The gate stood wide open from when the base was evacuated, and several zeds wandered around near the guard box. Griz ran over three on his way through.

The HEMTT drove slowly down the road, swerving around bodies, and came to a stop a couple hundred meters inside. We couldn't risk going too deep into the Camp where the risk of being overtaken by zeds was too high. Even here, I could make out over twenty stragglers wandering around the open grass area.

I stood. "This is it."

Both Eddy and Smitty looked scared shitless, though Smitty also looked pissed off as though he thought he should be exempt from punishment.

Jase grabbed Eddy's arm and forced him to stand while Tack and I dragged Smitty to his feet.

Eddy looked across our faces with wide eyes as though one of us could pardon him. He watched me and paled. Then I realized he was looking past me. "Mom?"

Eddy tried to lunge forward, but Jase held him back. "Mom!"

About thirty meters away, a female zed with the same hair color as Eddy cocked its head and sniffed the air. Then it started to shuffle toward the truck.

"Mom." His lips trembled and tears fell down his face. "I'm so sorry."

The breath hardened in my lungs. Of all the shitty, rotten luck.

Tyler climbed up. "It's time. Eddy, you're up."

Eddy bit back a sob. "But my mom's out there."

Compassion flashed in Tyler's eyes. He opened his mouth to speak but clamped it shut. After a moment he nodded to Jase.

With a clenched jaw, Jase nudged Eddy to the edge and cut his wrist restraints. I half expected Jase to shove his friend off the truck as payback for Mutt's death, but instead he lowered Eddy gently to the ground.

Eddy stood there for a moment before looking up. "I'm sorry. I didn't mean for any of this to happen."

"I know," Tyler said quietly.

Eddy's feet looked like they'd been tied to sandbags with the way he trudged away from the truck and straight toward his mother. "I'm sorry. I'm sorry. I'm sorry."

The zed held its arms out and pulled Eddy into an embrace that almost seemed motherly. Until it lowered its mouth, jaws wide open, and clamped onto his throat. Eddy screamed and fell back, taking the zed with him.

Smitty jerked, and I tightened my grip. "You did this. Watch," I ordered, though it was taking all my strength to watch the execution play out. If I was here alone, I would've put a bullet through Eddy's skull to end his pain, but Tyler had been adamant about setting an example of what happened to traitors. There simply weren't enough of us left. We had to be able to depend on each other with our lives, or else we were all doomed.

Tyler had declared that Eddy's death would be first so that Smitty would have to watch what was about to happen to him. Everyone knew that Smitty had coerced the weaker boy to help. Eddy had simply been an unfortunate lackey, and I even found myself feeling sorry for the kid.

Smitty was the real traitor.

Eddy's screams turned into a gurgle before quieting. He spasmed as a nearby zed joined in on his shoulder.

On the HEMTT, Jase reached under the seat and pulled out one of the long wooden spears the survivors had been making from the park's trees. Camp Fox hadn't had much ammunition before the outbreak. Now, their ammo supply was dangerously low and would likely run out by fall. We were forced to find new weapons. Jase walked to the side and skewered a zed that had been trying to climb onto the truck.

Eddy had quit moving, and I let out a breath. His suffering was thankfully over.

The zeds stepped back. They didn't like the taste of their own.

It wouldn't take long now.

The smell of urine snagged me, and I looked down to find that Smitty had pissed himself. Not that I could blame him. Death by zeds wasn't an easy way to go, but it was easier than he deserved.

The two zeds drenched in Eddy's blood sniffed at the air and turned toward the HEMTT. At least a dozen zeds were already on the way from every direction. Jase killed another that had reached the truck.

Eddy's foot jerked.

Smitty tensed. "Don't do this. Please."

The two zeds reached the truck. Jase impaled the

first, a male. He paused before killing what had been Eddy's mother. He inhaled. Then thrust.

What had been Eddy climbed to its feet. Blood was already congealing and browning around its throat and shoulder. It turned to the HEMTT and started jogging toward us.

Tyler turned. "Now."

We shoved Smitty off, and he collapsed, with his wrists still restrained, onto the ground ten feet below. He hopped up and started to run.

Tyler raised his pistol and shot the man in the leg.

Smitty grunted and fell onto his knee.

I reached down for a spear and killed an older zed bumping up against the back of the HEMTT.

Smitty tried to get back to his feet, but Eddy came up from behind and clamped onto his head. Smitty cried out and tried to shake Eddy off, but the zed held on, biting his scalp over and over. Smitty fell forward, screaming, twisting back and forth, but fresh zeds were strong, and Eddy hadn't been badly injured before he turned. The zed pinned the man and tore at his face. Smitty's high-pitched screams drew the attention of zeds that had been heading toward the truck.

Two more zeds joined in on Smitty's legs.

His screams abruptly stopped. A man could only take so much pain before the body shut down. Though his heart must've still kept beating since the zeds continued to chew for several minutes before backing away, leaving behind a mangled corpse.

Eddy was the first to reach the HEMTT. Jase thrust his spear through Eddy's eye, and the zed that had been Jase's friend fell.

Tack and I took out the next two zeds.

We waited. More zeds came, and we killed them.

Smitty's body quaked. It sat up. Its face and scalp were nearly gone, except for patches of skin and hair. For being a fresh zed, it took over a minute to climb to its feet with chewed up legs and restrained wrists. Once up, it hobbled right at the HEMTT.

Tack gave Smitty final rest.

"Let's go," Tyler said and thumped the roof of the cab. The HEMTT roared to life, and Griz drove, leaving nearly a hundred zeds slowly wandering toward us from the bowels of the camp.

Tyler sat next to me, leaned forward, and put his head in his hands. Jase stared off into the distance, and Tack pretended to sleep. When we approached Doyle's old camp, I stared at the gate. It didn't make sense that they'd lock up after they cleared the place. Light glinted off the silo with the faded Iowa Hawkeye logo, and I narrowed my eyes. The silos were old. Nothing should be *glinting* off rusted steel and dull aluminum. Then I saw another glint.

Binoculars.

I nudged Tyler. He looked up, his features worn by exhaustion.

"Doyle's camp isn't abandoned," I said.

He frowned. "I cleared it out myself. By the time I got

there, the place was a graveyard. Doyle had already moved all his supplies out. Only three injured Dogs were left behind."

I shook my head. "So why is there someone up on the silo watching us?"

When the truth hit, he leaned back and air whooshed from his lungs. "Jesus. Doyle's been under our noses the whole time."

CHAPTER XXXIII

Three days later

"I believe we should take him off the respirator," the doctor said. "We simply don't have the resources to use equipment and medicine on terminal patients when it could be used on others."

I didn't let go of Clutch's hand. "You said he could still wake up."

"He *could*, and I've seen much worse cases wake up in the past. But with these primitive medical facilities—"

"As long as there's a chance, he stays on." I came to my feet, kissed Clutch, and walked past the doctor. I paused at the door. "And if you take him off, I swear to God, I will crucify you in the middle of Chow Town for the zeds to tear you apart."

Without waiting for a response, I stepped outside the park office AKA town hall AKA makeshift hospital.

Wind cooled my cheeks, though anger still simmered just below the surface. It took several deep breaths before I could focus on what needed done.

My truck was parked just past the humming generators. I climbed in, gunned the engine, and put it into gear. With the window open, I rested an elbow on the door while I meandered through the park, savoring the fresh air, before finally heading into Tyler's cabin, where all troops not sleeping or on guard-duty sat.

It was the same as yesterday, and the day before that. Droning debates on how to attack Doyle with not nearly enough manpower and even less ammo. When it came down to it, there wasn't a single feasible plan that didn't run the risk of losing a life, and Tyler refused to sacrifice one more person for Doyle.

People rotated through as they rolled on and off shift. I listened, offering up a comment here and there, until my shift started at one of the park's four entrances.

The hours at the gate alongside Jase bled by.

"I heard what the doctor said," Jase said a couple hours into our shift.

I leaned against a tree. "Yeah?"

"I would've punched him for even suggesting pulling the plug."

"Believe me, I considered it." I watched a bald eagle fly over.

"Don't give up on him," Jase said.

"Never."

The following morning, I kissed Clutch good-bye.

"Be safe," I whispered and left him.

Numb, I returned to my cabin, shaved my head, loaded everything I needed into the truck, and drove away from the park. I had a plan to take out Doyle that involved the loss of only one life, though I had "borrowed" some of Tyler's ammunition stash during the night to make it work.

The Fox Hills Municipal Airport was only a couple miles northeast of town, not far from the river. I parked next to the only row of hangars, where seven old tin buildings of various faded colors stood side by side. I geared up with every weapon I owned and grabbed the crowbar.

A decrepit, lone zed meandered down by the last hangar. I rapped gently on the first hangar. Nothing. I checked the door. Locked. I pried it open and looked inside. An old Cessna 172. It would work but the nose wheel would make it more difficult to land in a field. I checked the next three hangars. One was empty, one held a Beech Bonanza, and I stopped at the fourth. *Perfect.* Inside awaited a yellow taildragger. On its tail, the Piper Cub logo matched the tattoo on my forearm.

The old hangar door pushed opened easily without power, and I pulled out the small plane. I returned to the truck and grabbed the duffel bag, admiring the way the airplane shone in the sunlight as I headed back toward it. Its owner had taken good care of the classic.

The badly decomposed zed had finally made it within twenty feet of the Cub. I met it halfway, and finished it off with my crowbar. I opened the duffel, kneeled, pulled out my knife, but paused before I cut the zed open. After a moment, I stood, sheathed my knife, and lifted my chin. "No," I said simply.

I checked the Cub over, made sure the gas tanks were full, and loaded everything up. It took only two hand props to start, and I climbed inside, leaving the door and window open. I skipped the warm-up because engine noise would quickly draw attention, and a plane this small would never survive a collision with a zed. The wheels broke free from the runway at under fifty MPH before the first zeds emerged from the tree line.

The wind made the flight bumpy. They'd hear me coming, but I didn't care. If Doyle hadn't fled his camp already, he would never abandon his camp.

The silos of Doyle's camp came into view eight minutes later. I descended as I approached. I flew right over the camp, looking down to see shaved heads looking up at me. They looked filthy and half-starved. Then I saw the only man without a shaved head. He waved his arms at his Dogs, and someone fired. Then a symphony of gunfire sounded around me.

Where the hell had they gotten their hands on all that firepower? Camp Fox had cut them off, yet these guys were shooting like they had an unlimited supply of ammo. Nevertheless, I couldn't turn back now. I started my one-eighty.

Get 'em where I want 'em.

I grabbed the duffel from the seat in front of me. I set the bag on my lap and opened it. As I neared the camp with nearly all of its occupants outside firing at me, I searched out Doyle. When I found him, I pulled the pin on the first grenade and dropped it. But the wind and velocity grabbed at the grenade, and it blew at least fifty feet away.

"Dammit," I muttered and quickly pulled the pins on two more, dropping them.

Dogs were running in different directions while continuing to send fully automatic gunfire my way. I tightly circled overhead, dropping grenades onto the camp.

Sudden agony pierced my calf, sending searing pain every time I touched the rudder pedal, but I remained focused on my mission.

The propane tanks in the camp exploded, and the blast rocked the small Cub.

I righted the plane and continued to drop grenades until the bag was empty. Then I broke away and cut the engine to land silently in a hay field just on the other side of a band of trees, hiding me from the camp. I went to climb out of the plane and winced, grabbing my left calf. My hand came away bloody.

I'd been shot.

If they were using tainted bullets, the virus was now

flowing in my veins.

Not much time now. I had to hurry.

I grimaced and tied a bandana around the wound and climbed out. I reached in for my rifle and started to limp my way into the trees and toward the camp.

I figured the Dogs would've assumed this was a hit-and-run attack. Since no trucks broke down their gates, they were now safe.

That's where they'd be wrong.

CHAPTER XXXIV

What came next had to be up close and personal.

I approached the camp from its backside. The zed pit was still there, full of rotting corpses. I held up my rifle, using the scope to scan the ground, then the silos. It still looked like an abandoned camp except for the smoke.

Even I hadn't given Doyle's camp a second thought when we'd evacuated Camp Fox. We'd all been fools to not double check.

As I limped closer, I could hear the voices. They sounded like an echo of the dying at Camp Fox. My heart clenched. I'd caused this. I knew not all these people were bad, some were simply misled. I inhaled deeply and moved forward. There was no other way.

Sometimes, only killing would stop further killing.

I'd planned to dip the grenades in zed goo and give

them a taste of their own medicine. I'd believed they deserved the karma after the hundreds of innocents they'd slaughtered. But, at the last moment I realized I couldn't go through with that. I refused to sink to their level. These men were getting off easy.

Not all would be so lucky. The noise would attract zeds from Camp Fox, which was part of my plan. I was counting on them to take care of anyone I missed.

No guard stood at the gate by the pit, and I cracked the gate open and peered inside. Through the dusty, smoky haze, I could see contorted bodies littering the ground. Some moved, many didn't. I limped across the camp, quickly glancing from body to body. One man covered in blood reached out to me for help but I continued on.

With my shaved head, no one seemed to notice me through the haze. They were all preoccupied. After I ran out of bodies to check, I gritted my teeth and headed toward Doyle's office.

I'd really hoped to finish him off the easy way.

I didn't even pause before throwing the steel door open.

Inside, I found Doyle alone, sitting with one leg up on a desk, wrapping his bloodied forearm. When he looked up, his eyes widened, and he reached for his rifle propped behind his desk.

"Don't," I ordered, pulling shut and dead bolting the door behind me.

He leaned back and watched me. His faded yellow

cap was stained and bloody cuts crisscrossed his soot-covered face. "Where's Clutch? I figured he'd come to finish the job himself."

"He's on his way," I lied.

Doyle seemed to relax. "So, you're here to keep me company until he gets here, is that it?"

"That's it." I kept my rifle leveled on Doyle. "I don't get you. You had a good thing going with Camp Fox. Then you had to go and screw things up by going after them. Twice."

"Hmph." Doyle leaned back. "It never would've lasted. Both Lendt and I were spreading my resources thin protecting the weak. Everyone would've all died if I didn't change the game. It's really quite simple. The weak had to die so that the strong can thrive."

I stared at him for a moment. "That's insane."

He narrowed his eyes. "Think about it. We have limited food, limited supplies. Yet, too many people to do anything efficiently. Thinning our numbers for the strongest to survive has been the way of every species throughout history."

"But that's so…heartless," I said, finding it hard to breathe.

He chuckled. "There's no room for that sort of thing in this world."

"You're wrong," I said coldly. "There's no room for *you* in this world."

He and I looked at one another for a split second. A wide grin crossed his face. "Your rifle's empty."

I dropped my weapon and pulled out my machete. The rifle had served its purpose as a prop. It had gotten me in front of Doyle.

He lunged, and I was too slow. We crashed to the floor, and the machete slid across the floor. He was strong for his age, stronger and bigger than me. I wasn't able to buck him off, so I rolled, squeezing out from under him. He caught me from behind and put a chokehold on me.

I couldn't breathe and knew I only had seconds before the lack of blood to my brain would render me unconscious. I threw my head back in an attempt to break his nose, but I hit his collarbone instead.

He grunted and then chuckled. "I'm going to have fun killing you. Clutch took Missy from me. I wonder how he'll like it when I kill his whore."

I pulled out my knife and stabbed him in the fleshy softness on his side.

He cursed and his grip weakened.

I shoved back onto him and rolled myself off, jumping to my feet. The room was spinning but my tunnel vision was slowly widening.

Doyle pulled himself up, holding his side. It looked like a shallow wound, just enough to piss him off.

"I'm going to keep you alive even longer for that," he snarled out.

Someone knocked, and Doyle turned toward the door, "Get in here now!"

Whoever was on the other side yelled something and

started kicking at the door.

I pulled out the last grenade from my pocket and pulled the pin. Doyle's eyes widened.

I smiled. "You had it backwards. I'm going to have fun killing you."

I tossed the grenade.

He rolled behind his desk. The grenade bounced off the wall behind him. He raised his rifle at me and sprayed bullets across the room.

I dove onto the table, knocking it on its side as I tumbled to the floor.

The room exploded.

I swam in a sea of vertigo and a high-pitched ringing. My body was numb and yet hurt everywhere at the same time. A faint pounding echoed somewhere in the distance. I dragged myself toward the overturned desk and clawed at the body lying there. I saw six glassy eyes staring back at me with my triple-vision, and I collapsed on my back. The floor felt less solid here. I rolled over and felt around the wood. I pried at a floorboard, and it lifted easily, revealing darkness below.

I pushed myself in and crashed onto the rough-hewn floor. Rifles tumbled down, nearly suffocating me. The floorboard snapped shut, leaving scanty light filtering through the cracks above.

I clawed out from under the rifles to an open space. My fingers wrapped around an ammo clip. There were more weapons down here than Doyle had ever received from Camp Fox. Clearly, Doyle either had other connections or had been preparing for war for a long time.

A door slammed open and boot steps pounded the floor above me.

"Doyle! No!" A man's voice yelled, and the shuffling of boot steps increased.

They'd find me. Within a few seconds, I'd be dead. I no longer cared. I'd done what I had to do. Doyle would never hurt Clutch or Jase or anyone else ever again. I closed my eyes and the noise above me faded into oblivion.

I woke up.

It was pure dark in the hole. Not even a splinter of sunlight fought through the cracks.

I sat up, and every cell in my body hated me for it. Pushing through the pain, I felt around the wall until I found a light switch. With a click, fluorescent lights lit up a basement that went the length of the building above it. It was filled with racks and racks of rifles, surplus gear, food, and wooden crates. Not far from where I sat was a desk with what I guessed to be radio equipment.

All the time Tyler had searched for Doyle, he'd been quite literally under our noses.

Shaking my head, I pulled myself to my feet. My leg

hurt worse.

I stood there for a moment.

I was still alive.

I wasn't a zed.

I'm alive!

Hope infused my muscles and I climbed the ladder behind me. I listened for long minutes for voices or movement of any kind. When silence greeted me, I pushed the floorboard up and pulled myself onto the floor.

The clear night sky blanketed the room with enough glow that I could see Doyle's mangled body still lying prone near the desk. I was surprised the Dogs hadn't moved him unless…

I crawled to the blown-out window and peered outside. Across the campground, zeds shambled, several with shaved heads. I ducked and glanced at the door standing wide open. It was only a matter of time before a zed discovered me.

The gates were too far away. I'd never reach them with a bum leg. I'd seen no vehicles. The silos were halfway across the camp.

A dark shape hovered near the door, and I pushed myself to my feet and pulled out my knife. As soon as the zed crossed the threshold, I shoved the blade through its temple. It collapsed, and I saw two more zeds turn toward me.

I stepped over the zed and outside into plain sight. Something moaned to my right, and I swung, hitting a zed's shaved head just as its arms reached for me. I twisted to my left, leapt onto the broken window ledge, and grabbed the edge of the roof. The knife tumbled from my grip and clinked as it bounced off the ground. With every ounce of strength, I pulled myself up. One of the fresher Dog zeds had nearly reached me by the time I pulled my feet up.

Panting, exhausted, I dragged myself onto the roof and rolled onto my back, staring into the night sky, the one place incorruptible by zeds.

I saw Clutch, wearing one of his rare smiles, reaching out to me for a dance. Standing not far from us were my parents, holding each other's hands and watching us with warm love in their eyes. Jase and Mutt were playing fetch. He looked up and laughed.

It was a good dream.

A soothing peace came over me, even while the zeds moaned and shuffled below.

I'd survived hell. Maybe there was such a thing as hope after all.

Taking a deep breath of fresh air, I smiled up at the night sky full of stars.

The saga continues in 2014

Deadland's Harvest

AFTERWORD

100 Days in Deadland is quite literally Cash's journey through hell, with Clutch as her guide. It follows the pair of survivors, caught up in the sudden rush of the zombie plague, which begins on Thursday, the day before Good Friday. Once thrown into Dante's "Inferno", Cash and Clutch come across the three types of sinful beasts: the self-indulgent (zombies), the violent (survivors), and the malicious (Doyle, who represents Satan).

As Cash progresses through each circle of hell, she is changed by her environment, her experiences similar to Dante's. Like Dante, Cash survives each circle by holding onto hope, having faith in her guide (Clutch, who represents the poet Virgil), and demonstrating unrelenting perseverance. At its heart, **100 Days in Deadland** is a study of the human condition, showing how our experiences change us.

Dante's "Inferno" lays out four key components of every apocalyptical (and even every zombie) story: the end of the world as we know it, cause and effect of the human condition, perseverance, and—as shown in the poem's last line—enduring hope:

"It was from there that we emerged, to see—once more—the stars."

Symbolism to the "Inferno" is lush on nearly every

page of **100 Days in Deadland**, from the obvious call-out, "Abandon all hope all ye who enter here" in chapter three to the subtlest hints, such as Cash shooting awake to the sound of a "thunderous" blast at the beginning of chapter four. The weather, such as the violent winds and storms starting in Lust (when Cash and Clutch come across the victim with pale lips at the corn bin, i.e. the "carnal tower"), echoes both the atmosphere of the "Inferno."

In chapter six, Cash ends up in a cafeteria full of hungry zeds, not much different from the sixth canto, which held tortured souls cursed with "insatiable hunger." In chapter seven, when Cash and Clutch arrive at the Pierson farm, they find money left on the table, a modest reminder of the Dante's message that money can't buy peace.

Doyle's camp represents Dis, the evil city in the Inferno that holds the darkest secrets and the most violent and treacherous sinners. Its true name is implied in chapter eight by the sign reading *Doyle's Iowa Surplus*, where only the capital letters are easily recognizable in the faded paint, foreshadowing that the camp will play a pivotal role in the final circle of Hell, where Cash must defeat Doyle.

In addition to Cash taking a journey parallel to that which Dante took, hundreds more echoes of Dante's "Inferno" can be found in **100 Days in Deadland**. But, the story you just read is not and never was meant to be a replacement for Dante's "Inferno." It is not designed to help you get an "A" in English if you read this novel instead of Dante Alighieri's epic poem. This story was meant to be an enjoyable read, which I hope is exactly how you found it.

CDC CASE DEFINITION

Zombiism (*Marburgvirus Zonbistis*)
2013 Case Definition

CSTE Position Statement
19-ID-52

Clinical Description
Zonbistis is transmitted to humans by direct exposure to infected tissues. The disease is characterized by clinical death, congealed blood, jaundice, stiff gait, insatiable hunger, and severe violent propensities. Infected hosts display minimal brain functioning. To promote transmission, *Zonbistis* enhances activity in the hypothalamus, thus increasing the host's appetite and likelihood of biting, although the infected have shown less interest in eating, and the underlying reason has yet to be determined. The virus has proven extremely resilient and virulent, continually replenishing itself within its host. Only severe trauma to the host's brain stem or destruction of the virus through fire is believed to eradicate the virus in the host.

If exposed to the virus, infection rate is 99.998%. There is no known cure. Upon initial infection, *Zonbistis* will take over its host anywhere from seven minutes to three hours, depending on severity of initial infection, level of injuries, and the host's physical condition. At the point of the host's clinical death, the virus is considered to have taken over.

When first contracted, initial symptoms include acute or insidious onset of fever and one or more of the following: headache, sweating, diplopia, blurred vision, bulbar weakness, hypoxia and/or dyspnea, nausea, vomiting, and shock.

Laboratory Criteria for Diagnosis

Detection of *Zonbistis* spp. in clinical specimen or isolation of *Zonbistis* spp. from wound or ingestion.

Case Classification

Suspected: Symptoms suggestive of *Zonbistis*.
Probable: A clinically compatible case with presumptive laboratory results.
Confirmed: A clinically compatible case with confirmatory laboratory results.

Comments

The virus is believed to have originated in a genetically modified pesticide undergoing testing in Brazil. When the pesticide was combined with an organic cleaning agent, the silica-coated cells of the pesticide were shown to have mutated into *Zonbistis*.

ACKNOWLEDGMENTS

With many thanks:

To my editor, Stephanie Riva, for making this story so much better.

To the Bards of Badassery—Elle J Rossi, Cynthia Valero, and Beth Ciotta—for the cheers.

To my husband for the hugs.

To Captain Dave for teaching me about things that shoot.

To Rampdog for coming to my aid in the 11th hour.

To Ann David for running to my aid after the 12th hour.

To Ashley of Support Indie Author for the support.

And especially to all those making sacrifices to keep our world safe.

ABOUT THE AUTHOR

Rachel Aukes is the bestselling author of the Deadland Saga. She lives in Iowa with her husband and an incredibly spoiled sixty-pound lap dog. When not writing, she can be found flying old airplanes and trying (not so successfully) to prepare for the zombie apocalypse.

Learn more at:
http://www.RachelAukes.com

CPSIA information can be obtained at www.ICGtesting.com
Printed in the USA
LVOW07s1738190515

439052LV00029B/59/P